stolen chances

CITRUS COVE
BOOK 2

CLIO EVANS

To finding love after a toxic relationship.
Broken hearts heal stronger.

content warning

- Money insecurities
- Healing from an abusive past relationship
- Discussions of suicide
- Discussions of homophobia
- Internet hate
- Discussions of mental health
- Feelings of unworthiness
- Stalking
- Gun violence
- Arson
- Car chase
- Body Insecurities
- *Detailed* sex scenes with: Fisting, DVP, cock piercings, sex toys, threesomes, breeding kink, spanking, bondage tape, anal sex, oral sex, Dom/sub dynamics, bratting, squirting, and biting.

If you have any questions regarding content warnings, please reach out to me via Instagram **@clioevansauthor** or via email clioevansauthor@gmail.com

sarah

Twelve Years Ago
Age 20

TODAY WAS the best day of my life.

We didn't have money. We didn't even really have a plan. None of that mattered, because I knew he was the one.

In less than an hour, a wedding band would shine on my ring finger. My wedding dress was thrifted and altered by my grandmother, Honey, to fit me. My shoes were a scuffed set of ivory flats I'd dug out of the bottom of the bin at Goodwill. None of it was fancy, but it was still perfect to me.

Boom! Thunder rattled the entire house, making me jump.

So much had gone wrong today, including the storm that had chased away the denim blue skies of this morning. Icing had already melted off the cake into a gloopy puddle, and my sister was running late.

But today was the best day of my life. I was getting married to David Connor and everything would be *perfect*.

The fan did lazy laps, squeaking as it attempted to move cool air around the room. I smoothed my hands down my dress and turned, sending up a silent prayer that the sweat pooling under my tits wouldn't show through the lacey fabric. For hours, my stomach had been twisted up in knots, my nerves a cloud of butterflies.

I was about to be Sarah Connor. Finally, I'd no longer be one of the *Bently Girls*.

A soft knock at the door made me twirl around. Honey poked her head in.

"Did Hal make it?" I asked immediately.

Honey's expression fell, and I swallowed hard. "No, darlin'. Her flight was canceled and then she got a call at work. I'm sorry."

Tears stung my eyes, but I would be damned if I was going to ruin my makeup. If my sister couldn't come to my wedding, so be it. Disappointment flashed through me, but I reminded myself she would be here if she could. It wasn't like Haley could control the weather, the canceled flight, or work.

"There's someone else here to see you." Honey crossed her arms, her lips pressing into a thin line. "Don't know if I should let him in."

"Him?"

I heard a muffled voice, and Honey rolled her eyes. "Best be quick. This storm has half a mind to blow the damn house away, and we got a grumpy groom waiting downstairs."

"David isn't grumpy." I couldn't understand why Honey always made comments like that about David. He just didn't like when plans went wrong.

She hummed in disapproval and stepped to the side,

revealing the last person I'd ever expected to see on my wedding day.

The blond god I'd gone to high school with, the first boy I ever fell for, and the man I'd barely spoken a word to in a year.

Colton Hayes.

My heart pounded louder than the rain rattling the windows. He stepped into the room and shut the door behind him.

"What the hell are you doing here?" I asked.

Goosebumps prickled on my arms as I stared at him. He looked possessed. This wasn't the Colt I knew. This was a man who looked like he'd been crying for hours, drinking for days, and on the verge of falling apart at the seams.

Colt marched across the room and grabbed ahold of my arms. "You can't marry him, Sarah."

"*What?*" I whispered, taken aback.

Was he joking? When was the last time we'd even had a full conversation? It had been a long, long time. He'd been the love of my life until I caught him kissing a boy from band class at a Harlow barn party.

I'd never cared about him kissing a boy. But I'd been devastated that I wasn't the one being kissed.

"You have no right to be here," I said firmly, crossing my arms. More thunder quaked the house. "I didn't invite you to this wedding."

"You can't marry him," Colt rasped. "He's not right for you. It was never supposed to be him."

"Yeah, well, you lost the chance to care when you kissed someone else."

"*What?*" he asked. The pain in his eyes tore open my already bleeding heart. "What are you talking about?"

I doubled down. "What do you mean? I saw you kissing Jackson years ago at a party. Meanwhile, I thought we were going to be dating. You told me I was the one, then you kissed someone else. I believed you, Colt, but I was clearly wrong."

"That ... that was ... you saw that? *That's* why you stopped talking to me? Because I kissed a boy?"

The crack in his voice killed me. I wasn't sure if anyone else knew about that kiss. I'd certainly never told anyone.

I pushed my palm against his chest as I stared up into those baby blues, unable to stop from wondering if he would have been the man waiting for me downstairs had it all not fallen apart.

A flash of lightning followed a bolt of anger. He couldn't do this to me now. It wasn't fair. It wasn't right. "I loved you. You knew that. And you kissed someone else. It had nothing to do with you kissing a boy, but everything to do with the fact that it wasn't *me*. And now, here you are, and *why*?"

I struggled to hold back the tears.

"You're ruining my makeup. My perfect day. How could you possibly show up like this?"

"Because I love you," he whispered. "I've loved you since the first day you came to Citrus Cove."

"Well, I love David now."

"He's not good enough for you."

"Neither were you," I whispered.

The heartbreak in his gaze stung more than whiskey on an open wound. *David is right for me. David is the one.* So many things had changed in my life and David was the man downstairs, not Colt.

"You should go," I said. "David doesn't like you. He wouldn't want you here."

"Sarah—"

"*Leave.* I never want to talk to you again. *Honey!*"

I shouted her name as I held his gaze.

My breath wavered as he leaned in, his lips nearly touching

mine. "This is the biggest mistake I've ever made. You will always be the one that got away. I'm sorry, Sarah."

I swallowed hard as I heard the door open. "Just go, Colt."

Honey cleared her throat. "Colton Hayes, I think it's best you get going before you cause more trouble."

He held my gaze a moment longer before releasing my arms. "I'm sorry. I'll still love you, even if you're marrying him. Goodbye, Sarah."

I loved him. He loved me back? I leaned against the wall and pressed my palm over my chest as he walked out.

I didn't want him to go.

"It's not too late to call it off." Honey gave me a pleading look.

I snapped back to the present. "Don't give me that. David is who I love now, Honey. I love him."

"Alright. If you say so, Sarah. Are you ready?"

Colt stayed on my mind for another moment. It had been a last ditch effort to stop me from marrying David, but I couldn't understand why he'd waited so damn long to try.

My future husband was waiting for me downstairs.

David was who I was meant to be with.

Right?

CHAPTER ONE

sarah

Present Day

STRAWBERRY POP-TARTS SPRUNG out of the
toaster and I tossed them on plastic plates. I poured two glasses
of milk, listening to the boys argue upstairs.

"*Boys!*" I shouted.

This was the fourth time I'd called for them. My patience
was wearing thin, but I took a breath, holding myself together.

One, two, three...

"Almost ready!" Jake yelled down.

I glanced at the clock on the stovetop. Dammit, I was going
to be late for my therapy appointment.

I didn't want to go. I always felt drained afterwards, but it
helped me get a grip. Slowly but surely, I was becoming myself
again.

Emma glided into the kitchen in pink silk pajamas and her
under-eye patches in place. Her dark curls were bound into a

topknot, adding a couple extra inches to her five-foot frame. Her golden skin glowed in the morning light, and her brows were perfect, even without makeup.

Nine months ago, I'd resented how effortlessly beautiful she was. But as I'd gotten to know her, I'd since let go of that. The first few weeks of living together had been a rough change for both of us, but it didn't take long for me to understand why Haley loved her so much. Emma quickly became a pillar in my life—in all of our lives—even if she regularly complained about Texas.

"Do you want me to run them to school?" Emma pulled a pitcher of cold brew coffee out of the fridge. "I don't mind. I don't have a call until eleven a.m."

"No, it's okay." I didn't want to burden her any more than I already had. "I've got it."

She glanced at the clock. "But it's Thursday. Let me take them, Sarah. Don't you have therapy?"

I swallowed hard, my ears ringing as I heard the boys fighting again. *Goddammit.*

"Davy! Jake!" My voice rang through the kitchen at full volume. "Come down and eat. Now!"

Emma raised a brow with a snort. "Damn, you've got that mom-tone down."

"Sorry." I sighed, rubbing my temples.

She was right, though. If I took the boys to school, I'd be late. And if I was too late, then I'd have to pay a fee and it would be another bill I didn't want to worry about.

Therapy was one of those things I couldn't skip, either. I'd made a promise to Honey, Haley, and myself that I'd go. I needed extra support, especially after what we'd gone through nine months ago.

My sister went through hell. After finding her neighbor

dead and being threatened by the killer, she'd come back home only for him to stalk her.

That killer ended up being my then husband's twin brother.

I was convinced David had been involved in all of it. I couldn't stop reflecting on the years we were married, remembering all the times where he hadn't quite seemed like himself.

Now, I wondered if it was truly David acting odd during those times. What if he hadn't been himself at all? What if Thomas Connor, his twin, posed as my husband? I wasn't sure I'd ever know the answer, and part of me didn't even want to.

The aftermath was life changing for us all. Several women were dead, and my sister had almost been one of them. That knowledge was a weight that sat on my chest. While I had no direct part in the pain and suffering caused, I felt like it was partially my fault. Shouldn't I have seen the signs? Shouldn't I have realized that David wasn't himself? That he was someone else entirely—even if they looked the same?

Given what I knew now, I couldn't help but wonder if I'd ever be able to trust another person again.

If I'd ever be able to trust myself again.

I was about to yell for the boys for a fifth time, but footsteps rumbled through the house. My shoulders relaxed a fraction as they flew down the stairs and emerged in the kitchen.

"Morning," Jake chirped as he beelined for the small table beneath the window.

"Thanks, Mom," Davy said. "Hi Emma."

"Hello, gremlins." She smiled at them as she took a sip of coffee. "I'm taking you to school."

"Does that mean I get to hold Donnie?" Jake asked excitedly.

"No, Donnie has his own car seat." Emma drummed her nails on her coffee cup. "You know this. Nice try, though."

Donnie was Emma's small, ancient, naked dog held together by pink sweaters, peanut butter, and some sort of spell. I glanced through the kitchen to the living room where he was curled up in a patch of sun, tongue out, eyes glazed in bliss.

Sunshine in January was a tease for spring. The weather couldn't make up its mind about the cold. Allergies were rampant. We all constantly had headaches or sniffles, and some days we needed coats while others we needed short sleeve shirts.

"Get your shoes on after you eat," Emma said to Jake and Davy. "I've got them, Sarah."

My shoulders relaxed a fraction. "Thank you. I owe you." I owed her a lot.

She rolled her eyes. "If you want to do me a favor, go out and get... go out and have *fun*," she said, taming her language with a side glance at Davy and Jake.

Heat crept up my spine. "I'm too busy for anything like *that*." Not that I didn't like the idea. "Thanks for taking them to school, Emma. I'll be home later tonight and Haley is picking them up."

I was ready for therapy and a double shift at the cafe. I gave my boys a kiss on the head and rushed upstairs to change quickly. I pulled on soft denim jeans and a clean T-shirt I rummaged from a pile of clothes that hadn't moved since I pulled them from the dryer four days ago.

Fun.

Emma meant I should go get laid, but the idea of being with someone after David scared the hell out of me. The two of us weren't sexually active the last few years of our marriage, and now I had to wonder if I'd slept with him or his psychotic twin. *Don't even think about that.*

The lump in my throat never went away. I ran a brush

through my auburn waves and raced back downstairs, snatching my purse and keys.

"Bye, babes!" I called.

"Bye Mom," Jake answered.

I lingered for a moment, waiting for Davy to say bye too. I ignored the sting of his silence and stepped out onto the front porch. Sometimes, being a mom was the best thing ever. Other times, it made me feel like I was doing it wrong all the time.

The porch spanned the front of the house with two rocking chairs and a swing, all courtesy of Hunter Harlow, my brother-in-law's older brother. I hadn't even asked how much they cost —outside furniture was expensive.

The house itself was bought for us by Haley. Another thing I didn't know how to repay. I was grateful, but it stressed me out knowing how generous she was. It was a spacious two-story home on a picturesque street where neighbors seemed to take a particular interest in watching the family of the infamous Citrus Cove killer go about their lives.

I breathed out and pushed my stress down. If I thought too much about it I'd cry, and I was so sick of crying.

My therapist, Brenda, had seen me break down more times than I cared to admit. She'd also hurt my feelings more times than I cared to admit with her very pointed questions and challenges, but ...

I was coming back.

The bits and pieces of the girl I'd been before David were still there—broken and covered in dust—but I was picking each one up and gluing them back together.

Brenda called our relationship abusive.

My ex-husband had controlled our finances, our whereabouts, our everything. In the midst of it all, though, all I'd ever been able to care about were my boys. Shielding them from his anger, his erratic drunken arguments, the threats. Walking on eggshells had become my default.

Brenda called me a victim.

It had been a slow decline. The flags were a different shade of red when wearing rose-colored glasses. I'd loved him once, with everything a starry-eyed girl, fresh out of high school, could. He'd used that. He'd twisted that.

Brenda said a lot, but she never called me weak. She never told me I was stupid. She never said I was a whore. And before going to therapy, I'd never realized how numb I'd become to that kind of language.

Looking back, my wedding day was the worst day of my life. But now, David was out of our lives. There were court proceedings still happening, but my part was mostly done. Last I heard, he'd never step another foot in Citrus Cove.

I hoped it stayed that way forever.

I had two boys who needed to be loved and cared for. On top of that, I was navigating a crash course in managing everything he'd taken control of. I went from having no control over finances, to having all the responsibility, and facing decisions I'd never had to make before.

Emma was the one who realized I didn't know how to pay an electric bill. Haley was the one who realized I didn't have a credit card or savings—all my checks had always gone to David. To say the last few months had been a learning curve would be an understatement.

On top of it all, there was a layer of tension between Honey and I so thick that we'd barely talked the last few months. I'd lied to her countless times over the years about how controlling David really was, and those lies had divided us. She was still there for the boys, but the two of us had yet to talk candidly about all that had happened. Every time I thought about finally talking to her, a wave of nausea hit my stomach.

I got in my beat up Honda and turned the key, sending up a silent prayer that today wouldn't be the day it gave out.

The engine light flashed orange. *Fuck.*

"I can't afford this," I whispered, holding in the tears.

I was already a burden on everyone around me. Haley had yet to charge me rent, even though I knew Emma paid her. Most of the furniture inside was bought by Emma or gifted by the Harlow family. When we'd rushed out of the house I shared with David last year, we'd only taken my clothes and the boys' things. Everything else had been left behind.

It was like they had all made a secret agreement that I needed help.

I hated it.

But I was so thankful for it too. Having Haley back in my life had been healing for both of us. I loved seeing how happy she was with Cam. He was a good influence on the boys.

My eyes shifted to the clock, and I muttered under my breath as I backed out of the driveway. The engine light would have to wait. The Honda had made it over fifteen years, I just needed it to hang on for a couple more.

All I needed was one day where everything didn't fall apart.

CHAPTER TWO

MY DAY STARTED with a two-mile run, and then slapping raw pizza dough like it was an ass cheek.

I pressed the red button on my phone, ending the video recording. I stood in my kitchen shirtless, a towel thrown over my shoulder, flour scattered over the counter. All of the lights were on, including the soft-boxes that made everything look professional.

My videos were recipe thirst traps, which put me in the crossroads of internet scorn and worship. But I loved doing what I did. I was proud of it too. The amount of money I made from online work snuffed out the worries that my brothers were embarrassed by me.

Out of the three Harlow boys, I was the odd one. Hunter had the farm, and Cam had the winery and bar (or would, once everything was rebuilt).

Both had steady, reasonable jobs.

Meanwhile, I created content online, played guitar, and sang at different venues in Austin, in addition to picking up odd jobs here and there around Citrus Cove.

It all certainly paid the bills, but there were moments where I still felt aimless. It was hard not to question my sanity when my first thought upon waking up this morning was whether the dough would make a good slapping noise for my video.

I pressed the record button again and reached for a bottle of olive oil. I squirted a generous amount on the dough, rubbing it over the surface and kneading.

One could never go wrong with sex pizza, right? Fondling boiled tomatoes, pulling off the skin after an ice bath—*how did this end up being my life?*—slicing fresh onions and basil to make a homemade sauce, sucking a bit of it off my fingers.

I washed my hands for the tenth time in the last hour. I rolled my shoulders and started the camera again.

"Dammit," I mumbled, turning up the stove heat for the pasta sauce.

Pause, restart, different angle. I reviewed it and frowned. How could I make it hotter?

Arm flex?

"My god, I've lost it," I sighed.

And now I was talking to myself.

An hour later, I had a fully baked pizza, all the footage I needed to edit for next week's video, and my kitchen was a mess. I washed my hands, humming to a melody I was working on as I cleaned up.

Just another Thursday, slapping dough. I cut the pizza into slices, snatched one as I made coffee, threw the rest in the fridge, and settled on my couch.

I pulled out my phone and sent my oldest brother a text.

Me: Got leftover pizza, do you want any?

Hunter: what kind?

Me: margherita

Hunter: no meat???

I snorted. Of course he'd say that. And dammit, he had a point. I could have cut up some sausage.

Oh well. Next pizza.

Me: brother you need to eat some veggies

Hunter: you're the one eating pizza for breakfast

Pizza was the breakfast of champions, and he wouldn't convince me otherwise.

Me: no pizza for you

I could text Haley. She was always happy to accept leftovers and liked to tease me about some of the comments I got on my videos.

I could also text Colt. He felt like a safer bet.

Me: Hey, I made a pizza for one of my videos but have too many leftovers. Do you want it?

Colt: Pizza before 9? Hell yeah. I'll stop by in a few

Me: perfect, see you soon

I should probably put on a shirt, but decided against it. I was certain Colt watched my videos sometimes, seeing as he occasionally commented.

Speaking of... I probably needed to check on those.

Most of the time, I didn't pay too much attention to what people said unless it was actually harmful, then it was a quick delete and block. Ninety-nine percent of the comments rolled off my back, but I'd occasionally see something shitty and get in my head about it.

Living in a small town helped, though. Having my family around me did too. There was the internet persona and there was the real me—the people I loved knew the real me.

I opened up the app as I sipped my latte. I sighed happily, thankful I'd invested in an espresso machine. I'd spoiled myself and was now disappointed if I didn't have a latte in the mornings.

The sheer amount of notifications made my stomach twist.

I took a deep breath, steeling myself to skim over them all. The video from a couple days ago had gone viral and was sitting at two million views.

God this guy needs to get a fucking life.
How did I get here???
Why is this on my FYP bro
Built this FYP brick by brick.
Oh my god you're so hot. I wish I was there to suck that sauce off your fingers
We love it Daddy, keep it up
Why the fuck can't you cook like a normal person???
I'd do anything he wanted
Are you married?
Are you single?
Does your mom know what you do?
I'd fuck him
You should K I L L yourself

That comment made me pause. I clicked on the profile, blocked them, deleted the comment, and continued to wade through it all to make sure there was nothing else like that. I'd set up filtered words, but they'd spaced out the letters on 'kill' so it'd slipped through.

When I first started doing videos like this, it was just for fun. I'd wanted to share recipes while also being myself. That had somehow progressed over the last couple of years to what it was now.

I sat my coffee down and leaned across the couch, grabbing my acoustic guitar from its stand. I'd had it since I was a teen, and it held all of my angst, happiness, horniness, and sadness. My muscles instantly relaxed as I cradled it, fingerpicking the bronze strings absentmindedly.

This was the guitar I wrote songs on. The one I played on stage hung on the wall above my desk—a cherry red Martin that was my prized possession. A vine with blooming flowers curled into a beautiful design on the pickguard, and the morning light that filtered through my sliding glass door highlighted the inlays along the fretboard.

I'd considered making a whole new account focused on my music, but that was far more vulnerable than licking a glob of icing up on video.

I needed to sit at my desk and work on video editing, but my mind felt too distracted. Restless. I continued to sip coffee, pick at my guitar, and stare at the wall.

A melody had been haunting me for months now, but something wasn't quite right with it. I'd written some words down, but it was... lacking.

A yellow notepad permanently lived on my coffee table. I leaned forward and grabbed the pencil next to it, tapping my chin with the eraser as I stared at the scrawled lyrics of the first verse.

"All of this is bad," I muttered.

With a grunt, I put my guitar aside. I raked my fingers through my hair and decided it was time to carry on with the rest of my workday. Which meant editing for six hours, following up on any emails from brand partners, and maybe seeing if anyone had plans tonight.

If they didn't, I'd pick up the book someone had recommended online. Yes, it was an alien romance. Yes, it was hidden on my bookshelf, even though I lived alone. And yes, I was envious I didn't have tentacles, because goddamn—*that* would be fun.

Ever since the old barn burned down, all of us had felt slightly off. Our routines had changed dramatically. I wasn't picking up bar shifts anymore, which had given me more time to work on my platform and music, but I missed seeing people a few times a week. It helped keep me sane.

Thomas Connor had fucked over everything. Aside from being a serial killer and ruining countless lives, the aftermath of finding out the truth had rocked all of us. Both Haley and Cam had almost died, and I'd never forget feeling so helpless.

The good news was that there'd been space for them to heal —space for Sarah, Haley's sister, and her boys to start healing too.

The way Colt looked at Sarah always made me feel a little envious. The history there was sticky. I didn't even know what had happened, but I knew Colt had never stopped loving Sarah, even while she was married to someone else.

Was that love?

I wanted to look at someone that way one day—and to be looked at like that in return.

The lyrics stared back at me, empty of the passion I longed for. Maybe because it was a love song? How was I supposed to write a love song if I'd never been in love?

Three brief knocks startled me from my thoughts. I got up and unlocked the door. Colt was on the other side, wearing a smirk, his eyes crinkling with mischief. A brow slowly raised as his gaze landed on me.

My heart beat a little faster. "Hey," I said.

"You gonna let me in or am I waiting out in the cold?" he asked.

"Sorry, yeah. Come in." I stepped aside, all too aware of the fact that I wasn't wearing a shirt now.

Colt slid past me, sliding his hands in his jacket pocket as he looked around my living room. "I don't think I've actually been inside your apartment before."

"It's not much," I said.

"I like it," he said with a shrug. "Coffee smells good."

"I can make you one if you'd like," I offered.

"Actually, yes, if you don't mind. I'll buy you lunch sometime."

I smiled as I entered the kitchen and pulled out containers. "A date, huh?"

Colt snorted as he followed me. "Do you want to go on a date, Sammy?"

I knew he was just teasing, but my stomach still twisted. "Do you like your lattes sweet?"

"A latte? Oh, you have one of those machines." He leaned against the counter, looping a thumb through his belt loop. As always, there was something effortlessly hot about him.

Don't even think about him that way.

Colt wrinkled his nose. "Make me what you like to drink. Can I help?"

"No," I said. "Just stand there and look pretty."

Silence settled over us as he waited and watched. Heat creeped up the back of my spine. What were these nerves? It was silly. I'd known him my entire life. But I still felt unsettled as I grabbed the handle of the portafilter, banged the coffee grounds into the trash, and reloaded it with fresh beans.

The machine roared to life at the press of a button. I grabbed a to-go cup and pulled two shots of espresso, the woodsy scent of coffee filling my lungs. "Whole milk okay?" I asked.

"Yep," he said. "You know how to do so many random things."

I smiled as I poured milk into a stainless steel pitcher. He watched as I steamed the milk with precision. Threads of tension glowed between us, making me wonder again if I was losing my mind. Why did I feel like my heart was going to give out? I poured milk into the cup and wiggled the spout like I'd taught myself, creating a heart shape.

He leaned in closer, his shoulder bumping mine. Colt grinned. "You make me wonder what we are."

"Friends, of course."

"Right." Colt picked up the cup and took a sip, foam clinging to his upper lips. He swiped it away with his tongue.

Heat crawled up my spine and then to my cheeks.

"Thanks for the coffee and pizza."

"You were helping me out," I said.

I handed him two containers of pizza. He tucked them under one arm. "I'll get out of your hair, but let me know when you want to grab lunch."

"Will do. I'll see you later."

He winked and headed for the door.

I blew out a steady breath as it closed behind him.

"Back to work, Romeo," I muttered to myself.

I had videos to edit and lyrics to torture myself over. It was just another Thursday, Colt was just a friend, and I was just a hopeless romantic.

CHAPTER THREE

sarah

WORKING at the cafe after an hour-long breakdown at therapy always left me especially drained. Today was no different.

By the time the dinner rush rolled around, every muscle in my body ached. My feet hurt. I needed new shoes, but the boys did too and they came first.

I carried a tray of empty plates to the back of the cafe, noting that Alice had been through here. Clean dishes were stacked and ready, and linen napkins folded. The walls had a fresh coat of robin's egg blue paint, lightening the atmosphere.

Alice was one of the few people I liked here. Thankfully, she was the manager, and had bent over backwards for me multiple times over the last six months.

Like my sister, she was determined to succeed. The cafe had thrived since she took over from her dad earlier last year. For years, we'd been known for having the best cherry pie in the county, but now we had other things that were also worthy of the title. It all ran on a tighter ship, but I liked that. It meant I could come in, do my job, and go home.

"Hey Sarah," Alice called. "Have you had a break?"

I put the plates in the sink and moved out of the way before I bothered Trey. The kitchen was his domain, and I certainly didn't want to overstep.

Alice waited for me to come back out of the kitchen before stepping in front of me, blocking my path before I could head toward the party of four that had entered the front door.

"Welcome in, pick a seat and we'll get you taken care of," I said, my voice carrying. One of the men nodded, and they chose a booth.

She pushed her silky black curls over her shoulder and looked me up and down. "Have you had a break?" she asked again.

"Let me help them first," I said.

"So I take that as a no." Alice arched her brow, pressing her lips together. Gold highlighter dusted her dark brown cheeks, catching a bit of light as she frowned at me. She always had the ability to cut straight through my bullshit, sometimes even better than Haley or Emma.

"I don't need one. We're in a dinner rush," I said. "I can keep working."

"I'll take over for you," she said. "You need to eat something. You've been working all day. I thought we talked about doubles and how you'd have an hour break between them? What happened to our agreement?"

"Today was busy," I protested.

Plus, I hadn't packed lunch. As if she read my mind, she held up a Ziplock bag with a cold cut sandwich and some chips.

"Go," she hissed. "I turned that extra room in the back into a break space for a reason."

"Did you really make me lunch?" I couldn't keep the waver from my voice.

She pressed her red lips together. "Sarah, go sit and eat. I can't be the only one taking care of you. Besides, you keep this cafe going. It's the least I can do."

She shoved the sandwich into my hands and darted around me for the table. I glanced up as more people came through the front door, but she was already grabbing menus to hand them. Between Alice and Debbie—a veteran server like myself—working the floor, we'd be okay for a few minutes.

Why do you feel guilty about people helping you?

Why do you feel unworthy of their care?

The questions at today's session were a knife to the heart. I bit my lower lip and stepped outside for my break. I exited through the back door and sighed, leaning against the blue brick wall as I opened the bag.

Citrus Cove Cafe sat on Main Street across from the Old Spur Museum and some other small businesses. It was painted bright blue and stood out amongst the dimming sky.

I devoured the sandwich and immediately felt better.

I checked my phone for messages and smiled. Emma had sent me a picture of the boys and Donnie on the couch watching a show. Haley was there too, her blond curls pulled back in a bun and eyes bright with happiness.

I'd forgotten it was their hang out night. Usually, the two of them watched a movie once a week, and often ended up with the boys. *Legally Blonde* had become Jake's favorite movie after Emma insisted it was fundamental for every kid to see.

I hearted the picture, and drew in a deep breath as the pressure on my chest eased. They looked happy, and I was hopeful that we were nearing the end of this storm.

The summer break had been long enough to let the Citrus Cove rumors die down, although they still lingered. Everyone knew what had happened, and the news had taken our little town over. *David Connor, local man, twin of the serial killer Thomas Conor.*

Had they met him before? Had they been in the same room with him? Everyone and their mother certainly believed so, and they loved to gossip about it. If one thing could bring a small town together, it was the horror of finding out their neighbor was a psychotic murderer.

The kids at school had treated Jake and Davy differently since then. Jake, in particular, had dealt with a lot of bullying. Davy stuck up for him, which led to fights, which led to kids calling him 'David' instead of Davy. It was so simple, but it always managed to hurt him. He was determined to be nothing like his father, and no matter how many times I told him he wasn't, it was hard to make him believe me.

All of that had brought me to parent-teacher meetings and countless arguments with the principal. There was also the cranky old hag, Agatha, who ran the front desk and was a constant source of headaches. She always gave me a hard time about getting the boys to school on time or wanted to yap about the woes of how being a single mother might impact them. I couldn't say she'd changed a bit in the decades she'd worked at this school.

Jake and Davy were in therapy too, which helped, but it wasn't a quick fix. Things couldn't simply stop.

So far, this school year had been a nightmare. The holidays had provided us with a reprieve of sorts and it had been a little easier.

I just wanted my boys to be happy.

Headlights flashed as a truck pulled into the parking lot. I stood up straight, my heart skipping a beat. All of my nerves lit up like fireworks, throat constricting.

That's his truck.

David wasn't supposed to be in Citrus Cove.

He wasn't supposed to be here.

But that looked like his truck.

I felt weak again. I felt broken *again*. I felt ...

The door opened and a man stepped out, but he wasn't David.

The amount of relief turned my knees to jelly. I collapsed against the wall, panting hard. My head spun as I counted to ten, reminding myself that David wasn't here. I was safe.

More headlights flashed, and another familiar truck pulled in and parked right next to the one that looked like David's. My heart fluttered, but not with dread.

Colton Hayes hopped out and immediately went to the other truck, hands on his hips as he checked the license plate. His gaze flickered over as he spotted me.

Dammit. I didn't want him to see me like this.

Cold panic laced with longing froze me in place.

The parking lot lighting didn't do him justice, but that didn't matter. Colt could be under grocery store fluorescents and still look like a rugged model. He'd cut his hair over the summer, taking it from almost to his shoulders back to curling at the top of his neck. He wore a steel gray shirt with a brown jacket and dark wash jeans, his belt buckle gleaming.

"I thought that was his truck," he said as he approached me, scowling.

"Me too." *Breathe. It's just Colt.*

His expression melted from anger to worry. It wasn't fair how good looking he was when he pinched his brows together and rubbed the back of his neck. "Are you okay, Sarah?"

Nope. "Yeah. I'm fine."

"Are you sure? I can give you a ride home, if you want."

"I still have three hours left on my shift. Thanks, though. I need to get back inside." If I didn't keep working, I'd break down, and I couldn't handle that again today.

His eyes swept over me. Every time he looked at me like that, I was torn between wanting to melt against him or run away.

There was too much regret. Too many *what ifs* between us.

I didn't like to entertain those thoughts. They led me down a path of wondering how different my life might have been if I'd listened to Colt on my wedding day.

What if I'd run away with him?

"Have you heard from him at all?" Colt asked softly.

He meant David. I shook my head. "No," I said. I swallowed hard, my heart finally settling in my chest. I couldn't help but glance at the truck again.

The idea of David coming back to Citrus Cove terrified me.

One of the first things I did after it all fell apart was file for divorce and take out a restraining order. I felt better knowing it had been granted and, in theory, I should never see him again. But, I also knew how he was. If he didn't end up in jail, a piece of paper wouldn't stop him from seeing me again if he wanted to.

"Last I heard, he was still dealing with the court and trial. I hope he goes to jail," I said.

"Me too. If you need anything, I'm always a call away," he said. "Always."

Always. His voice was soft and sweet. The man had slept on my couch for the first couple weeks after I left David. He'd been ready to do whatever it took to keep me and the boys safe. Then all hell had truly broken loose, and once the situation settled, Emma moved in.

Colt studied me a moment longer before clearing his throat. "Do you want me to see who owns the truck?"

"No," I said. "No, it's okay. I saw the man and it wasn't David. That's all that matters."

"The license plate is different too."

27

"Good. Thank you," I said, keeping my tone polite.

My heart thundered as I reached for the door.

"Have a good night, Sarah," he said.

"Goodnight, Colt."

I left him standing there with those sad eyes and an even sadder smile.

CHAPTER FOUR

I'D LOVED Sarah Bently since the day she showed up in Citrus Cove.

I'd never forget the day she stepped into our classroom. Back then, she'd been blonde with sun-kissed skin, freckles over her nose, and honey eyes full of so much sadness she hurt to look at.

Making her smile had become my number one mission in life.

Now, years later, it was still my mission. One I was failing miserably at.

The back door to the cafe slammed shut, and I stood there wondering how many times I'd watch her walk away from me in my lifetime.

I rubbed my chest. The ache never went away.

It didn't matter who I slept with. It didn't matter who I dated. When I saw Sarah, my world stopped.

My phone buzzed in my pocket, snapping me back to reality. I pulled it out and answered as I headed back to my truck, eyeing the one that looked like David's. He'd need balls of steel to show his face in Citrus Cove again, and part of me wished he would.

"What?" I asked.

Cam snorted on the line. "Okay. Hi to you as well. What's wrong?"

He knew me too damn well. "I saw a truck that looked like David's pull into the cafe. Sarah works Thursdays, so I stopped to check."

"Ah. I assume it wasn't him or else you'd be calling from the station."

"Correct," I said, memorizing the license plate. I got back into my Ford and started it up, the engine humming to life. Heat blasted, filling the cabin with warmth as I leaned my head back against the seat.

"Do you want to come over for dinner? Haley decided to have a night in with Emma and the boys. I'm rounding up Hunter and Sammy. I've got steaks and beer."

I couldn't help but perk up at the thought of seeing Sammy again today. Plus, it didn't take much to convince me. "Yeah, I'll head your way."

The drive to Cam's was one I knew by heart. It had been an adjustment now that I couldn't pop in whenever I felt like it. There were parts of my friendship I missed with Cam, but Haley was the best damn thing to happen to him. She was like a sister to me, and I loved her as much as I loved him.

I rolled down their driveway and wasn't surprised to see Sammy's car. He must have just pulled up, because he opened the door as I parked beside him.

The two of us were opposites, standing side by side. I was comfortable with my height at *almost* six feet, but Sammy was as tall as a goddamn basketball player. He had pitch-brown hair and stormy blue eyes and was the kind of guy I'd be drooling over *if* he wasn't my best friend's brother.

He was also five years younger than me—which didn't mean anything—but I liked to use that fact to tame my slutty imagination. Especially when I could have sworn I made him blush this morning at his apartment.

"Howdy," I called.

Sammy gave me a dry smile. "So you've been lured here with steak and beer too, huh?"

"Yup. Shocked to see you out and about this late."

He shrugged. "It's been weird without the winery."

I nodded, feeling the same way. The old barn had been in the Harlow family for generations, and it's been nine months since it burned down. Construction was starting up after we got through February. We'd been working on the blueprints and plans with a contractor who was a friend of Hunter's.

"Thanks for the pizza again," I said. "And coffee. They were delicious. I definitely ate the entire thing in one sitting."

Sammy smiled. "Thanks. It was fun to make. Hunter rejected it since it didn't have meat on it."

So he hadn't thought of me first. Which was totally reasonable, and definitely meant I was overthinking him blushing earlier.

Speaking of the devil, Hunter's truck pulled up next to mine and he hopped out. "I brought better beer and poker cards."

"And money to lose?" Sammy asked.

Hunter snorted as I opened the front door. The three of us piled in, and per Haley's house rule, we kicked off our boots and placed them on the shoe... whatever the fuck it was called. A shoe cabinet?

Sammy bumped into me and grabbed my shoulders to steady me.

"Tall motherfucker," Hunter muttered.

"You're just jealous," Sammy quipped.

He gave me a smirk, his hands still warm on my shoulders. Finally, he released me and I turned away. *Why the fuck did he have to end up so hot and why the fuck did his hands feel good and fuck—*

"Cam?" I called.

The silence made me anxious and all the other thoughts fell away. I wasn't the only one who didn't like the silence. Hunter immediately pushed past me and headed for the back door, his shoulders relaxing once he looked out.

"He's outside," he announced. "Looks like he's finishing the steaks."

Sammy and I both breathed out.

We were all still jumpy. David Connor had always been a son of a bitch, but finding out he had an evil twin had fucked with all of us. It was some next level bullshit.

I heard Cam and Hunter talking and stole a glance at Sammy. He was always so quiet. I'd known him my entire life and still didn't *know* him.

"There's a truck that looks like David's in town," I said. "Just so you know. I saw it pull into the cafe while Sarah was working."

He let out a quiet hum. "Wasn't him?"

"Nope."

Sammy pressed his lips together. His voice was quiet as he spoke. "I think he knows better than to come back here. We aren't the only one's gunning for him. All of the women his brother killed ... their families are angry. I read an article recently."

"An article?"

"Yeah, another one."

"You'd think the media would pick something else to talk about," I sighed. I worried about Sarah and the boys more when the news circled the story about Thomas again.

Sammy nodded. "I've been keeping an eye on it. People are furious. They want someone to blame. I think I'd worry more about Sarah and the boys, but Emma has a black belt in martial arts. Plus, Cam installed a security system. I don't think anyone will break in or bother them."

"What?" I snorted, thinking about the pint-sized Barbie. "Does Emma really have a black belt?"

"Yeah," he laughed. "I run into her sometimes at the store."

"Are the two of you going to stand at the door chatting like hens?" Cam called. "Or are you coming to the kitchen?"

The two of us scoffed. I left the foyer for the kitchen and Sammy followed behind. My skin prickled with an acute awareness of him as I grabbed a beer, using the counter top to pop the cap off.

Hunter pointed at me. "I want one."

"Already on it, hoss."

I opened each of us a beer as Cam brought in the steaks on a platter. They smelled great, looked great. He'd long since perfected the art of grilling, and I took full advantage of that, especially since I hated cooking.

Sammy scowled at his brother. "Surely we have something more than just steak," he said.

"Like what?" Cam asked. "We have meat and beer. What else do we need?"

"My god, how does Hal stay married to you?"

"Not sure you want to know." Cam smirked at the innuendo. "Also, I cook better for her than I do for you ugly bastards."

"I feel loved," Hunter said as he took a swig of his beer.

Sammy laughed. "You got any veggies? Potatoes? Something?"

"There are veggies in the fridge."

"I'll cook some up."

None of us protested. If Sammy cooked it, we typically ate it, even if it were veggies. He made a bet with Hunter that he'd get everyone to eat brussel sprouts over the holidays and damned if he hadn't won a hundred bucks off him.

"Done any real work lately?" Hunter teased.

"Oh fuck off," Sammy said. "You wish you could do what I do."

"Any viral videos?" Cam asked, leaning against the counter next to me.

Sammy shrugged as he pulled out an air fryer and dug in the fridge for vegetables. "A few. It's all going well."

He'd started a content channel a couple years ago. Every video I saw was expertly filmed and was of him doing sexy chef things. The comments were often filled with people either giving him shit or begging him to spit in their mouth in the most unashamed way possible. It was alarming sometimes to see what people said to him. I didn't try to creep on him but sometimes found myself scrolling his page while thinking a little too fondly of his forearms.

"Finger any more grapefruits?" I teased.

He shot me a dirty look. "Why don't you watch and find out? Better yet, how about you subscribe to my YouTube so it shows up for you every morning?"

I grinned. "Alright, chill out. For the record, I'm already subscribed. Your videos deeply concern me sometimes, but the recipes are good. Not that I cook any of them. But the pizza you made was fucking delicious."

He relaxed a fraction as he threw broccoli and carrots in the air fryer with some oil and seasonings. "Thanks. The veggies will take a few minutes."

"Paper plates?" I asked Cam.

"Nope," Cam said with a grin. "We have real plates in this house."

"My man is whipped," I teased. "A shoe cabinet. Real plates. What the hell happened?"

He grinned even brighter and got the plates together. "I love her so damn much."

"We know," we all echoed.

It was cute and romantic and we all envied him just a little. Well, I envied feeling that sort of love for someone. The only person I'd ever come close to that with was Sarah, but that was a long time ago and clearly unreturned. Everyone else I'd been with over the years had never reached that part of me. I'd come to accept that no one else ever would.

Hunter pulled out knives, forks, and napkins and carried them to the table. The dining room adjoined the kitchen and soon we were all seated at the table, plates full of steaks and veggies and cold beers cracked open. Cards were dealt and we played a slow round of poker, catching up about everything happening in our sleepy town. The Old Spur Museum was getting some new updates, Citrus Cove Park was being renovated, and the apartment complexes right outside of town were expanding. Our conversations looped in a circle, coming right back around to David Connor.

"You sure it wasn't David?" Cam asked me, referencing the truck I'd seen. He rubbed his beard with a frown.

"Yeah," I said. "But I saw Sarah out back."

"Was she okay?" Sammy asked.

"She said she was," I sighed.

"So, no then," Hunter said. He leaned back in his chair. His hair was a little long right now, a few stray silver strands sprouting around his temples. He looked like a more rugged version of his brothers, slightly older, and a little shorter. "I mean, how could she be? We made it through the holidays without any issues but they let David go."

"*What?*" I asked, shocked. Why the fuck would they do

that? That changed everything. "I thought he was being charged with accessory to murder? Wasn't he in jail?"

"He got a good lawyer," Hunter said with a grimace. No one could ever accuse Hunter of not caring—I swore he was always fully aware of everything happening in and out of Citrus Cove. Haley, Sarah, and the boys were now part of the family, which meant they got the full Harlow protection treatment. It was a good place to be.

I was certain he did the same for Emma even though he claimed she was the bane of his existence and despised him.

"They've been arguing that he didn't know. They managed to get him acquitted. Now the story is that David was completely unaware of what his brother was up to and he never concealed anything or helped him."

"That's bullshit," I growled. "How the fuck did he get a good lawyer? Isn't he supposed to be paying child support?"

Hunter held up his hands. "Don't shoot the messenger. Just what I've heard. I've been keeping up with it."

"Does Sarah know?" Sammy asked, looking at Cam.

I already knew the answer, but didn't interrupt Cam as he spoke.

"Considering I didn't know and to my knowledge Haley doesn't either, I doubt it. I don't think David has paid Sarah a dime. She's been taking care of those boys like she always has. She works her ass off and hates accepting help. I get it, but it's hard to watch as someone who's come to know and love her."

I had to remind myself to breathe. I looked away from the three of them as I took a sip of beer, trying to keep my emotions in check. But it was hard when my thoughts were on her.

"She's been through too damn much," I whispered.

Cam hummed in agreement. "She is doing better though. I think Emma has really been good for her."

Hunter grunted but didn't argue. He and Emma could

barely stand to be in the same room together, like oil and water. I liked Hunter, but I didn't understand why Emma pissed him off so much.

I could understand, however, why he pissed her off. Even though he cared, he was gruff and grumpy and an ass most of the time.

The rest of dinner was nice, but I still couldn't stop thinking about Sarah. Even as the night wound down and I switched from beer to water, she was on my mind.

I'd been trying to give her space. It wasn't right to push for a relationship after all that had happened, but...

I wanted to be in her life.

I just wasn't sure if she'd let me.

The day she got married was still etched in my mind, like it had happened yesterday. She'd been so sure of David, so certain he was the one. Meanwhile, it was clear I'd made the biggest mistake of my life not going after her. From the time we stopped talking to the day she got married, all I did was pine and torture myself over her.

Cam clapped me on the back and snapped me out of my thoughts as I washed dishes. "What's up with you?"

Hunter and Sammy were busy chatting at the table. I shook my head, keeping my voice low. "I worry about her."

"Have you thought about asking her out?"

My head snapped up. "*What?*"

Cam crossed his arms. "I'm just... it's not a fucking secret that you love her. I figured you would have made a move by now."

"Her husband's brother almost killed her sister, and... I don't want to push anything."

"But if you keep waiting, someone else will swoop in."

That was my biggest fear.

I couldn't let her go this time.

"She barely talks to me," I said. "Don't worry about me, Cam. I'm fine."

"Why did she stop talking to you in the first place?"

He'd never asked me so pointedly, and I didn't have to answer because Sammy came into the kitchen.

"I'm about to head out," he said. "I need to get ready for tomorrow."

"You mean you want to get in bed and read a book," Cam said.

"Well. Yeah, that too. Goodnight, thanks for dinner. See you Sunday."

"Love you," Cam said.

"Love you too."

I glanced over my shoulder as Sammy walked out, peeling my gaze off his ass.

He had no right to look that good in denim.

Cam and I finished up the dishes right as Hunter came back to the kitchen. He gave me a glance that meant he had something to say.

"Colt, have you talked to your dad recently?"

It took every ounce of control not to tell Hunter to fuck off. But, I knew he wasn't asking to upset me. "Why?"

"I saw him at the store the other day and he stopped me. Asked about you."

"Shocking," I said drily. "Didn't think he cared about me."

Cam winced, giving his brother a look that said '*shut up*'.

"I didn't tell him shit," Hunter said. "I'm not an idiot. He knew that too. He asked me to tell you he'd like to see you some time."

Not a chance in hell.

"Thanks, Hunter," I said.

Hunter nodded. "I'm headed out. Night."

"Night," Cam said.

I mumbled under my breath.

The front door opened and closed. Now it was just me and Cam. I could feel his eyes on me.

"Spit it out," I muttered.

"You have to see him at some point," Cam said. "This is a small town."

"I've managed to not see him for over a decade. He's the last thing on my mind right now."

Cam was quiet. He knew when to push and when not to, and right now was not the time. I was already worried about Sarah. Thinking about my homophobic, piece of shit dad wasn't exactly a high priority.

"I'm just saying, it might be healing to talk to him now that you're an adult."

"He kicked *me* out," I snapped. "Your parents took me in. He lost me the day he said he never wanted to see me again."

"Maybe he's changed."

Some people got to come out and still be loved. I had, for the most part, and was thankful for that. Cam's mom hadn't batted an eye when she'd found me crying on her porch. I'd never forget telling her everything, scared no one would love me, and her putting her arm around me with teary eyes, promising there was nothing wrong with me. I'd never forget Bob Harlow, Cam's dad, threatening to fist fight my father when he found out what had happened.

"I'm sorry," Cam said softly. "I can't imagine his thought process. It still infuriates me. He steers clear of me if we're in the same spot..."

I crossed my arms. "Spit it out. You got something else to say."

I'd known him my whole life.

Cam pressed his lips together. "I just think people can change, Colt."

Maybe they could. But not John Hayes.

He could tell I wasn't going to continue that conversation. I couldn't. There was a lot of shit I'd done my best to heal from, but the wound was still open and barely patched together with stitches.

"Hunter doesn't know what all went down," Cam said. "So don't be mad at him."

I dried my hands with the hands only towel, which was labeled as so on the oven handle. "I'm not mad at Hunter." I was mad at myself.

For several reasons.

"Well... Want to crash here tonight?"

It was tempting. They had a couple of extra bedrooms set aside for the occasion, since Cam had me as his best friend and Haley had Emma. It wasn't uncommon for one of us to crash at their place.

"I think I'll head home for the night," I said.

Cam nodded. It was clear he wanted to say more, but he wouldn't push.

He knew when to let me work through my feelings, and tonight was one of those times.

"I'll see you this weekend at some point," I said.

"Yep. And we have that meeting coming up soon with the contractor. I hope we can get shit rolling with the winery. I'm ready to get back to normal."

"Me too," I said. "It'll be worth the wait, though. The relaunch will be good. The whole town is ready."

Cam smiled. "Yeah they are. Alright, get some rest."

"You too."

I probably wouldn't sleep a wink.

CHAPTER FIVE

CITRUS COVE WAS a ghost town late at night. I eased straight through a red light after looking both ways and frowned as I passed the cafe.

"What's going on here?" I muttered.

I pulled into the parking lot next to Sarah's little Honda. The hood was open, blocking me from seeing whoever was there. I got out and walked around as Sarah jumped, wielding an oil dipstick like a knife.

"Whoa," I said, holding up my hands. "It's just me, Sarah."

"Fucking Christ," she said, her hand flying to her chest. "What the hell, Sammy? You scared me half to death. I was going to take your eye out with this."

"I'm sorry," I said, swallowing a laugh. "I saw your car and got worried."

She sighed, though it was clear her heart was still pounding. I eyed her weapon warily. That, along with the open hood, was a bad sign.

"What's going on?" I asked.

She wasn't wearing a jacket. Wasn't she cold? The temperature had dropped once the sun went down and she was in short sleeves. She looked really damn good too.

"My engine light was flashing this morning."

Damn. That wasn't good.

"And then I tried changing the oil. But it didn't help. It won't start."

I winced. "Mind if I take a look?"

"Have at it."

She chewed her bottom lip as I slid past her, pulling out my phone. I shined the flashlight on everything, checking all of the basics. "Can I have the dipstick?"

She stepped next to me, her hip brushing mine as she handed it to me.

Suddenly, I was painfully aware of her presence. Vanilla and labdanum hit me and I sucked in a breath, my mouth watering. My mind warned me she was off-limits, but every other part didn't get the message.

Maybe I was overly horny tonight. Some of the glances from Colt had made me want to jump in a cold bath. It was all sorts of fucked up to be drinking a beer and thinking about what it would be like to be with him while sitting at my brother's dinner table.

"See anything?" she asked.

"No," I said. I put the dipstick back in its spot and gave it all another once over, but I wasn't a car guy. "Can you take it in tomorrow?"

"I have to work," she whispered. "Fuck. And tomorrow is Friday. The boys have school, and I told them I'd take them somewhere on Saturday since I haven't had a weekend off in a while."

Don't do it. Don't do it. "I have to run into Austin on Saturday. I wouldn't mind the company and a detour."

"I don't want to burden you—"

42

"Seriously," I said, looking up at her.

I'd always thought she was gorgeous, but I'd never been this close to her before. Maybe around the holidays, but we'd always been surrounded by people. Now that we were alone, I drank her in. Soft skin, dark lashes that cast shadows over her cheeks, the curve of her plush lips. *Biteable lips.*

Fuck, what am I thinking? This was *Sarah.*

"I can't remember the last time I had some fun. I just need to go by a specialty market for some ingredients and sauces," I said, ignoring every single alarm bell ringing in my head.

I wasn't lying, either. I was chronically online and usually working, trying to keep up with social media trends and shit. Managing the horniness and hate in the comments, and reminding myself that none of it was representative of who I was as a person. Like the person who'd commented and told me to kill myself earlier, or the person that had asked if my mom knew about my channel.

Which she did. But I'd blocked her for my own sanity.

Sarah hesitated.

"Only if you want to," I added. The last thing I wanted to do was pressure her into spending time with me.

"I want to," she said. "Are you sure you're up for dealing with the boys? They're a handful."

"They can't beat growing up with Hunter and Cam." Or the fact that I was the youngest. It didn't matter that Hunter was seven years older than me, we'd had our fair share of scuffles.

Sarah chuckled. "Don't know how your mom managed. Two is enough."

"I don't know how she did either. I think Davy and Jake are better behaved."

The boys were wild but sweet, from what I'd seen and

heard. Davy was a little more quiet and stoic, but he always took the brunt from his dad—according to Cam, anyway.

"Oh god," she laughed.

As she smiled, everything slowed. *Thump, thump, thump.* My heart fluttered and I found myself smiling too.

"There's no way they are better behaved. But okay. If you're certain. If you change your mind, I won't hold it against you."

"I won't. They're good boys, Sarah. You've raised them right."

Her expression sobered and she sucked in a breath. "Yeah. Yeah, they are."

I'd struck a nerve of sorts. *Fuck.* "If you leave the car here, I'll have someone pick it up," I said. "I can drive you home."

Sarah crossed her arms and stared at her car for a moment, brows creasing. God, she was fucking gorgeous. Where the hell had I been? Living under a rock?

I thought about Colt again for a moment. I knew he wanted Sarah, but he would have made a move already if that was still on the table—right? It was one thing to pine over someone for more than a decade, and another to actually ask them out.

"I can call Haley," she said. "I don't want to bother you."

"You're no bother to me," I said. "Come on."

I closed the hood and her door. She leaned down and grabbed her purse from the sidewalk, giving me a wary smile.

"You sure you don't want me to call Haley?"

"Get in the car, Sarah," I chuckled. I opened the passenger side, holding it open for her.

She wrinkled her nose as she slid into the seat. "Your car is so clean," she muttered.

"Well, I'm a single guy with no pets or kids."

"Okay, but you're a single guy."

I grinned as I shut the door gently and rushed around to the driver's side. I slid in and started the car, turning up the heat for her. It bothered me that she didn't have a jacket on.

Mentally, I made a note to text Keith, our local mechanic and buddy from school, about Sarah's car before I went to bed.

I started down the street. Sarah folded her hands in her lap and looked out the window.

"Sorry if the heat takes a minute," I said.

"Oh this is good," she said. "I'm not used to it."

I scowled. Did her car not have heat? Or air conditioning? In *Texas*?

Was it too much to buy my brother's wife's sister a new car just because I could?

I mulled it over as I turned right down a quiet neighborhood street. A soft rumble echoed through the cabin and I frowned.

"Are you hungry?"

"Yeah, but I'll eat when I get home."

I'd already had dinner, but could always eat something. "You don't want a burger? I could eat."

"A burger from where?"

"There's Howdy Hank's... I'm sure the boys will survive without you for another few minutes." Howdy Hank's was a Texas burger chain with good fries and shakes.

"Not if I come home smelling like Hank's... Okay, fine. Yes."

Victory. I turned onto another street and headed toward the restaurant. It was a five-minute detour, but it would give me a little longer with her.

"What do you like to do?" she asked.

"Do you mean in general or...?"

"I'm not sure. I'm just curious, I guess. We've never really talked much."

"You're too pretty to talk to. Makes me nervous."

She laughed again. "Stop. You can't be serious."

I grinned. "I am. But to answer your question, I like cooking. Reading. I go for a run every morning and usually help out where I can if I'm not making content."

"Content? Like... porn?"

I barked out a laugh. "No. Not porn, although I wouldn't be against it. Have you ever seen my videos online?"

"No," she said. "Sorry. I don't really use social media much. David always said it was bad... which sounds so stupid now. Sorry."

"It's okay," I said softly. "No need to be sorry."

Fucking David. If I ever saw that son of a bitch, I was going to knock his ass out. His brother might have been the killer, but I didn't think he was innocent at all. My hatred for him was already more than justified for what he'd done to Haley, but the things I'd heard about Sarah...

My knuckles turned white as I gripped the steering wheel. I pushed him out of my head, focusing on the beautiful woman sitting next to me. "What do you like to do?" I asked.

"*Me?*"

"Yeah."

She was silent. "I don't know. I haven't thought about it in a long time."

I stole a glance at her as I slowed to a red light. I fought the urge to roll through it even as we sat.

"What did you used to like to do?" I asked. "Before David?"

"That was so long ago. Track? Weren't you like ten when I was in high school?"

The corner of my mouth tugged up. "You're only five years older than me."

I glanced at her, catching her smile.

"I like baking," she finally said. "When I have time. It's one of the only things David didn't mind me doing when we were together."

"I'm sorry," I said. I thought about what I'd heard about him at dinner, and decided I wasn't the right person to tell her he'd been acquitted. "The whole situation was really messed up. I'm glad you're safe."

"Me too."

"What do you like to bake?" I asked. "Any good recipes?"

"Do you like baking?"

"Yeah," I said. "That's the content I make. Well... sort of."

She raised a brow. "Light's green."

I eased down the road, passing a couple of cars.

"What the fuck?" I muttered.

Sarah burst out laughing as we slowed to turn into the parking lot of the Hank's—and joined the long ass line of cars.

"Everyone in Citrus Cove is here," she said. "I should see if anyone wants anything..."

"Call 'em up."

She pulled out her phone. I could hear Haley's voice as she answered.

"Hey, I'm stopping by for some food. Y'all want anything?" Sarah let out a hum. "Oh, good. Okay, I'll be home soon. Sammy is driving me home... Yeah, the car needs to be looked at. No, it's okay. I'll see you soon." She hung up and looked at me. "They showed the boys how to make macaroni and nuggets."

"A staple in every young man's diet," I said approvingly.

She laughed. "Yeah. Okay, so recipes. I have a few I can send you. There's one for an apple spice cake Honey used to make, but I made some adjustments to it."

"I'd love to try it. I like anything apple. That and pumpkin bread. It's my weakness."

"Pumpkin bread is your weakness? Really?"

I nodded. "Yeah, I go through like fifteen loaves every season. I'm shocked you didn't notice at Christmas. The stacks of pumpkin bread were from me."

Sarah shook her head. "I thought your mom made those."

"Nope." The line inched forward. "I made all the desserts."

"*What?* Oh my god, you really can bake."

It stroked my pride to hear her say that. It was the first year we'd managed to keep Mom from cooking a damn thing. Dad and Hunter had cooked up the ham and turkey, Cam and Haley had handled the sides, Colt had funded the alcohol, and I'd taken care of desserts. It had been a good get together with everyone, including Emma, Sarah, Honey, and the boys.

"I'll give you the apple spice cake recipe in exchange for whatever fucking magic you put in the pralines."

"I made the buttermilk from scratch. I think that helped." That video had made me a lot of money. Innuendo was a powerful tool. "But you've got a deal."

We finally made it to the ordering window. I told them what I wanted and then glanced at Sarah.

"Cheeseburger all the way, fries, and honey mustard."

"Drink?" I asked.

She bit her bottom lip. "Chocolate milkshake?"

"Yep. I'll have one of those too."

I rattled the rest off and pulled my card out before she could grab hers.

"Nope," I said.

"I can pay you back—"

"Nope."

"But—"

I leaned my head on the headrest and looked at her. "I've got it. You've been on your feet all day."

"I don't want you to feel like you have to."

"I don't," I said.

"I can pay for my own meal."

Now she sounded irritated. I raised a brow. "Yeah? I can also pay for your meal."

She pressed her lips together as I took my card back and pulled forward.

No one really knew how much I made from what I did, but it was a good amount. Enough for me not to worry, which was saying something in this economy.

"Can I be honest?" she asked.

"Of course."

"I don't like when people pay for me because lately it's become a default. And I work really hard to make money so I can take care of myself and the boys. I'm not a charity case."

"Understandable," I said. I reached out and took our bags and milkshakes. I rolled up the window. "Can I be honest?"

"Yes."

"I've never once looked at you and thought 'charity case.' I have looked at you and thought *damn*, that beautiful woman works really fucking hard. And maybe I could buy her a burger and a milkshake."

Her cheeks turned red. The bags of food balanced on her thighs and I reached over, plucking a fry from one of them as I pulled out of the drive-thru.

This was the most the two of us had ever spoken and I really didn't want it to end. Hell, I hadn't even talked to one of my brothers this much in a long time.

"Alright," she sighed. "I accept."

"Thank you," I chuckled.

Within a few minutes, I pulled to a stop in front of her house. The lights were on. Haley's new sports car was parked next to Emma's.

Sarah lingered for a moment. "Thanks for the ride. And dinner."

"Anytime."

She started to reach for the door, but I was quick. I leaned past her, reaching for the handle before she could touch it. I pushed it open for her and leaned back.

Sarah looked at me, her lips parting.

I thought about kissing her.

And then I thought about my brother sending me to an early grave. And Colt. Colt would not be happy.

"I'll see you Saturday," I said with a smile.

"See you then."

"Sleep well, angel."

CHAPTER SIX

CALLING HER "ANGEL" slipped out before I could stop it. Sarah's breath hitched and she was gone in a blink, taking her shake and food with her. She slammed the car door and high-tailed it for the house.

I waited until she went inside before I felt like I could breathe.

What the hell was that?

What the hell was I thinking?

Sarah was *off limits*.

Our plans this weekend weren't even a date. It was an outing with her kids. I needed to relax. It wasn't like I was breaking the law. *Just the unspoken code with Colt.*

I turned down the street, picking up speed toward my apartment. I'd ditch the alien romance book tonight in favor of a hot shower and some porn.

A few minutes later, I pulled into my regular spot in the apartment complex parking lot. With my food and shake in hand, I headed up the stone staircase to the second floor of the building.

The back of my neck prickled. I slowed and turned around, expecting to see someone there.

Nothing.

"Don't like that," I muttered.

I unlocked my door slowly, waiting for a sign of someone coming up the steps. When no one did, I went inside and locked the door behind me—both locks.

"Fucking weird." I sucked on the milkshake as I kicked off my shoes and took my food to the kitchen.

My apartment seemed empty compared to Cam's house. Every time I visited, it hit me again how little I'd decorated my space. I had everything I needed—my guitars, a couch, a coffee table, my TV, and a bunch of random equipment. There was a bookshelf in my bedroom, a closet full of kink equipment, and a big bed. But none of it felt permanent.

Really, this place was temporary. Eventually, I wanted a house close to Cam, Hunter, and my parents—but I also liked being on the other side of town. Newer developments were springing up, and it felt like a different place than the vineyard I'd grown up near.

I loved my family. I loved my brothers. But sometimes, they were too much. Coming off the holidays, part of me wanted to disappear somewhere for a couple of months, but I'd never hear the end of it from my parents. Plus, we'd be building the new winery soon and I needed to be home for that.

I put the fries and burgers in the fridge, but kept the shake, sucking on the straw.

Sarah and Colt were on my mind. Nerves fluttered in my chest. Something about the way Colt looked at me at dinner made me want him. And then Sarah? There'd been no confusion about the way my blood heated in her presence.

In both of their presence.

The bi panic was settling in. I couldn't help but wonder what it would be like to be with both of them. Between the tension this morning and at dinner with Colt, and what had just happened with Sarah, my imagination was being a little too *imaginative*.

I thought about a friend I had who lived outside of North Austin. Rosie. She was happily with three people in a polyamorous relationship. I hadn't known that was an option until I'd met her, but I'd done a fair amount of research since then and read a few books out of curiosity.

People certainly made it work. And they did so happily.

But, I lived in a small town.

Even though I liked the idea of being with them both, I wasn't sure Colt or Sarah would ever consider an arrangement like that with me.

Why am I even thinking about this?

It wasn't like Colt had hit on me. Hell, he'd probably fist fight me if he ever knew I was even thinking about Sarah like this. I was probably imagining the few moments at dinner where I felt like I was going to melt.

And then Sarah...

They were two people who should not be on my mind this way.

Off-limits.

Just a couple of little crushes that I needed to *crush* before I acted on them and ruined everything.

Or...

I stood still for a moment, thinking about the urge that had come over me. I wanted to visit home. It was the middle of the fucking night, and that meant my parents would be asleep. Which meant I could sneak through the vineyard to the Harlow tree without getting caught.

Maybe I was being a little unhinged. It was just a crush. It was just two crushes. Absolutely nothing was going to come from it, and it was delusional to even consider.

But I wanted to pick out a spot on the tree.

How far gone am I?

As far gone as I could possibly be.

I turned my headlights off as I pulled down the familiar driveway, rolling to a quiet stop behind my dad's truck. No lights were on in the house and the stars splashed across the sky above, twinkling in the crisp air.

I got out of the truck and walked to the gate, easily hopping over it. The fucker had squeaky hinges, so this was the only way to sneak by the house. Even in the dark, I knew the vineyard path like the back of my hand. The brambles eventually gave way to a hill with long grass that bowed beneath the occasional breeze.

The Harlow family tree sat at the very top, long branches twining up into the night. Sturdy boughs and roots tangling deep into the dirt supported years of history. Along the trunk were countless hearts and initials, all whittled into the bark.

Cam and Haley's were in the middle. I smiled as I shined my flashlight on theirs.

Really, I'd had my spot picked out since I was a kid. I'd always been hopeful that I'd meet someone, and now, maybe even two people... *I'm losing it.*

Whether anything happened with Sarah or Colt, I was still tired of being alone. Restlessness and yearning had taken root, growing through my heart with the same strength of the Harlow oak tree. And if, by some strange twist of fate, I could love two people and be loved in return...

I needed a bigger spot on the tree.

I circled the oak until I saw it. Right there in front of me, the place I envisioned carving initials into.

"Sammy, what in the seven hells are you doing out here in the middle of the night?"

My muscles jerked and I nearly jumped out of my skin. I spun to see Pops standing there in pajamas and boots, a gun in one hand and a flashlight in the other.

"Sorry, I should have texted," I said, wincing.

He snorted and shook his head, coming up next to me to look at the tree. My dad wasn't as insightful as my mom, but he still gave me a sideways glance.

"Don't think I've ever seen you come look at the tree before. Who is she?"

Not just she. My parents didn't know I was bisexual and they certainly didn't know I was polyamorous. While the second part was a newer revelation, I was still deciding what that could even mean for me. "No one," I said quickly.

"Son, you're standing outside in the cold, it's damn near midnight, and you're looking at the tree. It's someone, alright."

"Don't worry about it, old man."

He scoffed, giving me a playful jab. "Not that old. You spending the night? Mom will fuss if you don't."

"Yeah," I sighed. "I'll bunk in my old room."

"Alright. Did you pick out your spot then?"

"Yeah. You better not tell Mom."

He grinned. "No promises. That woman can smell secrets."

He had a point. "Okay, well at least wait until I'm out of here in the morning."

With a snort, he clapped my back. "Fine. Let's get going."

I gave the tree one final glance before following him back down the hill, my attention turning to his steps as he seemed a little off balance.

Realizing that my father wasn't invincible was one of the scariest parts about getting older.

We trudged through the vineyard. Most of the vines were leafless now, but that would change once late summer and fall rolled around next year. Then we'd all be out here picking grapes and apples from the orchard trees. The gate creaked as he pushed it open and I wasn't surprised to see Mom and their dog, Benny, sitting on the front porch. She narrowed her eyes on me.

"What on earth are you doing, Sammy?" she asked.

"I was just checking on the farm," I said smoothly, going up the porch steps and giving her a kiss on the cheek.

"At *midnight?*" she asked, exasperated. "Since when do you check on the farm?"

Pops shook his head. "Let's all go to bed. I told him he could sleep over."

"Well of course," she said, still hawk-eyed. "Want to tell me what's really going on?"

"Nope," I said. "It's nothing."

Just a couple of crushes on two people I have no business wanting.

CHAPTER SEVEN

sarah

THE PHONE ALARM BLARED, jarring me from sleep. I groaned, cracking my eyes open. I turned off the siren and squinted at the message.

Sammy: Keith will pick up the car this morning and let you know about it this afternoon. I think he needs the key though. I can pick you up for work and take it to him?

"Oh god," I whispered. He'd sent that at five a.m.

I sent a text back.

Me: What are you doing up so early? Also, thank you. I'll get the key to him. I'll find a ride.

He was a quick texter.

Sammy: I like to run in the mornings ;) I'm not doing much today so I'll pop by the cafe later

I rolled over in bed, staring at the ceiling. Butterflies fluttered eagerly in my stomach, the same ones that usually appeared around Colt.

I sent him back a thumbs up and fought a stupid grin.

In all the years I'd known Sammy, I'd never seen him the way I did last night. I swallowed hard and turned my head, eyeing the locked dresser drawer. I kept my vibrators in there and briefly thought about using one of them, but then the scent of coffee hit me.

Someone else was up super early.

I slid out of bed and made my way downstairs, discovering coffee already brewing and my sister perched at the breakfast table. I slid my arms around her shoulders in a hug.

"Hi," Haley said, leaning into me. "I spent the night. Slept in Emma's bed. I made coffee."

"Is Cam jealous you stayed over?"

She smirked. "Yeah. I'm sure we'll make up, though. A little space is good sometimes. Are you going over to Honey's any time soon?"

I sighed. She and I still needed to work things out. I didn't like having tension with her, but it was there anyway. "I planned to stop by tomorrow after we get back to town..."

"Oh?"

I'd walked right into that. I mulled over my thoughts as I went to the counter and poured us each a cup of coffee. It was early and the boys could sleep for another thirty minutes.

I slid her mug over and sat across from each other, wincing as my wrist landed in something sticky. "Dammit," I muttered.

"I got it." She hopped up before I could and grabbed a towel, running it under hot water. I took it and wiped down the table and then my wrist.

"I don't even want to know what that was," I sighed.

"Me neither. So tell me about last night."

I raised a brow. "It was nothing. Sammy happened to be driving by."

"Sammy is hot."

My mouth fell open. "*Haley.*"

She grinned and pulled her curls back into a messy bun.

"What? Even though I'm happily married, I'm not dead. And I'm just *saying*, he's cute."

He was. I rolled my eyes as I took a sip of coffee, fighting a smile. "He's headed into Austin tomorrow and invited the boys and me, since the car has to go to the shop."

Her brows shot up. "*Interesting.*"

"Don't you give me that look."

"Oh, I'm giving *that* look. Tell me more."

"This is ridiculous," I mumbled. "Sammy Harlow, of all people, is not interested in me like that."

Haley crossed her legs. "I'll be the judge of that. Tell me everything. Start from the beginning."

I'd missed this. I couldn't help but smile as I told her the full story from start to finish, including the texts. Since we had gotten close again, I'd made a point of telling her everything like we used to when we were younger. Her mouth fell open and I shook my head.

"It's nothing," I insisted.

"Okay, let me get this straight. And let me ignore the fact that he's my brother-in-law and this is Sammy. This man found you stranded at the cafe—which you should have called me about, but I'll let that go for now—asked you about what you like to do, you share an interest in baking, he asked you on a date tomorrow, took you to get some food—which he paid for—and arranged for the mechanic pick up your car so you don't have to worry about it. God, what did they put in these Harlow men?"

"I don't know, but I'm sure he just feels bad for me," I said.

"Mmhm. Okay. So tomorrow, Cam and I can take the boys."

"What? You don't need to do that," I said. "You're always watching them."

"I have years to make up for not seeing them," she argued. "Cam and I will come up with something fun."

"I haven't had a Saturday off in so long," I said. "I worry they miss me. Or I'm not around enough."

"You're around them all the time," she said. "You only work a half shift Sunday. You should go alone with Sammy. Go on a *date*."

"You and Emma are conspiring against me."

Haley gave me a guilty smile. "Maybe, but I had nothing to do with this development. Get out there, have some fun. Plus, we know he's safe."

"You mean, we know he's not a serial killer," I mumbled.

Haley's eyes softened. "Yeah. Sarah... I'm sorry to change subjects, but I heard something you should know. Cam texted me about it last night. Have you talked to the lawyer recently?"

My stomach twisted. I had a voicemail from Larry that I hadn't listened to. I'd forgotten about it until now. "What happened?"

"David is out."

I forgot how to breathe. Her words hit me like a punch to the gut, my ears ringing. "What?" I whispered.

She reached across the table and grabbed my hand, squeezing it. "He's not totally free. He just got a good lawyer. Things are still happening, he's still being charged. I thought you should know, in case he comes back to Citrus Cove."

My heart wasn't beating. I forced myself to take a breath, unable to stop the way my entire body started to tremble.

"It's okay to be scared," Haley said. "But you're not alone. You'll never be alone with him again. I'm here for you. We all are. You are safe, Sarah. The boys are safe. You won't ever be trapped by him again. I'm so sorry."

"I love you," I whispered, holding back tears. "I'm so sorry for everything that happened."

"I am too," she said.

She got up and came around the table. It was my turn to be hugged, and I leaned into her. I was still trembling. This was news I'd been dreading for months, but I was grateful to hear it from Haley. "Thank you for telling me."

"Of course," she murmured, kissing the top of my head. She paused, and then let out a hum. "Do you want me to dye your hair tonight?"

"You bitch," I hissed, swatting at her. A laugh bubbled up, breaking the tension.

"Or you could keep the random grays. They're pretty hot. It's giving single sexy mom."

"Stop," I laughed. "I'll take care of it after work. I'm only on for eight hours today."

She rubbed my shoulders as I sipped my coffee. The sun was starting to rise outside, and I needed to get the boys up.

"I have a nosy question. What about Colt?"

I damn near choked on my coffee. "What about him?"

"I mean... you know."

I sighed. "He's... Colt. I don't know what else to say." I wanted him, but didn't know what to do about it. I felt like an awkward teenager every time we talked.

Before we could continue, I heard Donnie's paws on the stairs, which meant Emma was up. Which meant she would be a zombie.

Sure enough, she was downstairs a second later. "I thought I smelled coffee," she sighed. "We need an espresso machine."

"Those are so loud though," Haley said.

I sipped my coffee as the two of them chatted, thinking about tomorrow.

I was going on a date—the first date I'd had with anyone other than David. I'd never dated anyone else officially, even in high school. My heart rate spiked as I took a sip of my coffee, stomach knotting with excitement.

The second alarm went off on my phone and I got up, heading upstairs to wake the boys. I pushed their bedroom door open, and peeked inside.

I loved them both so much.

I regretted a lot of things about the past, but never the two of them. Even on the hard days.

"Time to get up," I said softly, going to Jake's bed. I sat on the edge and ran my fingers through his sleep-mussed hair.

"I don't want to go," he sighed.

"I know, baby. But, it's Friday. Come on."

I got up and did the same with Davy. He was already awake. His internal clock had always been spot-on, whereas I always had to wake up Jake.

"Can I stay home?" Davy asked. "I don't feel good."

I frowned and pressed my hand to his forehead. He wasn't running a fever. "What's wrong, baby?"

"He had bad dreams," Jake said.

"No, I didn't," Davy snapped.

"Yeah you did. I heard you."

"Okay, Jake. How about you go take a shower? Aunt Haley is still over too, so if you're quick you might catch her before she leaves."

He was out of bed in a blink.

Between the two of them, Jake had always been the cheeriest. Davy sighed as his brother left, looking up at me. "I dreamed about *David*."

I swallowed hard. About six months ago, he'd stopped calling David 'dad'. It broke my heart.

"I'm sorry, baby. Was it bad?"

"Yeah," he whispered. "I don't want to talk about it. Does it cost a lot of money to change my name? Could I work at the cafe to save up?"

I held back tears. "I'll look into it. We all know you're Davy."

"But the kids at school still call me David. Even the teachers do."

Dammit. I'd been fighting with his teachers not to call him David.

"I just don't want to be like him, Mom."

My eyes burned as I pulled him into a hug, kissing the top of his head. "You never will be. What happened was awful, but it doesn't make any of us bad. Okay? You're nothing like him."

"Promise?"

"I promise. But you have to go to school, buddy."

"Okay," he sighed. "I guess."

"Tomorrow... how would you feel about hanging out with your aunt and uncle?"

He frowned. "I thought you were off tomorrow."

My heart skipped a beat. "I am, but I'm considering going to Austin with Cam's brother, Sammy, for a couple of hours."

"Oh. I guess that's okay."

"Okay," I said. "Come on. You need a shower too. You smell like rotten milk."

He laughed and got out of bed. I grabbed the hamper of dirty clothes, taking it downstairs. I could hear Davy and Jake chatting, then arguing, then yelling, then chatting again—always a constant cycle with those two. They were the best of friends, the worst of enemies, and I was proud they loved each other so damn much.

"Sarah—want breakfast?" Emma called.

"Yeah! Thanks!"

I got a load started in the washer and headed back up to take a shower myself and get ready for the day.

There was a little extra pep in my step. It was silly, but all I could think about was Sammy and Colt.

Thinking about getting back out there scared the shit out of me. I'd known them my entire life, but part of me worried they had skeletons in their closets that none of us knew about. It was absurd. Neither of them were killers.

But I hadn't known David had a twin who was, either.

Hell, I hadn't even known he had a brother.

I'd been married to that man for almost twelve years. What else didn't I know?

I cranked the hot water on and got in the shower. Heat permeated my body, leaving my skin angry but loosening the knots in my muscles. I got out and did my basic skin care routine—cleanser, toner, moisturizer, and sunscreen courtesy of Emma, who demanded I wear it every day.

Within the hour, we were all out the door. Haley dropped the boys off at school and headed toward the Citrus Cove Cafe.

"Thank you," I said as she pulled into the parking lot.

My car wasn't there.

"No problem. Want me to pick you up later?"

"If you can," I sighed. "Sorry."

"It's no problem. Hopefully the car doesn't have anything majorly wrong with it. If it does, we'll figure it out."

Neither of us was hopeful. But I nodded, and sat still for a moment. I needed to go inside and start my day.

Haley leaned over and rested her cheek on my shoulder. "Go talk to Honey soon. I think she's missing you."

"I will," I whispered. "We're just mad at each other."

"I don't think she's mad at you."

"Yeah, she is. She's mad that I let it get out of hand. She's mad I married David."

"You had no idea about him or his brother."

"But I should have." I fought back tears, swallowing hard. "There's a chance I had sex with a serial killer and don't even know about it. All those women, Hal..."

"I know." She was silent for a moment and then sighed. "It's all fucked up, Sarah. But it's been a few months. Things are clearing up. Have the boys had any more trouble?"

"I think some," I said. "The teachers won't stop calling Davy 'David.' It's really upsetting him."

"Want Emma and I to go have a chat?"

I laughed and felt myself relax. The thought of the two of them rolling up to their school to bitch out everyone was hilarious. "No. But thank you."

"I could bring Hunter. He knows everyone."

"Yeah, he does. But no. Alright, I love you. I have to go."

"I love you too."

I got out of the car and gently shut the door, heading to the back door to the cafe.

I'd worked here for over a decade. I knew every brick like the back of my hand. In some ways it was more of a home than anywhere else.

I wished I could quit.

There were a lot of days I wished I had my own place. Or that I could be like my sister and make my own choices. I'd open a bakery and sell all the things I loved making, if I could.

Dreams like that pulled me through long work days. Today would be no different.

CHAPTER EIGHT

I TICKED through my mental checklist for the day as I pulled into the cafe parking lot. I wanted breakfast and some hot coffee, and I needed to drive out with Cam to a lumber yard to meet a builder.

Our new location was going to be pristine. It was also going to cost a lot of fucking money, but I'd have everything I needed to start making the best wine and ciders in the damn state. Losing the old barn had set us back, but it had also given us all some time to rest and figure out what we wanted for the future.

Cam and I hatched a plan to not only reopen the winery, but expand bottling and distribution. It was a little ambitious, but it would open up new avenues for us. And I liked the idea of our little business being in local stores and ending up on dinner tables.

I pulled my truck into the parking lot and frowned. Sarah's car wasn't here, which was weird for a Friday morning. In the most non-stalker way possible, I knew her schedule better than my own.

Sunshine burned through the gray clouds that gathered in

the distance, the air crisp. We had a couple more possible cold fronts, and potentially a snow storm. Everyone was anxious this time of year, since the storm on Valentine's Day four years ago. All the cedar and oak trees had frozen and many snapped, damaging the power lines, roofs, and more. We'd all been stuck at home because not a single Texan motherfucker knew how to drive on ice, myself included.

I stepped through the cafe door and inhaled the savory scent of bacon and potatoes. My mouth watered and I spotted Alice waving at me.

"Pick a seat, Colt."

"Thanks, Alice," I said.

All the locals were here this morning and I nodded at a few people as I slid into a booth by the windows. I frowned as I looked out at the street, spotting Sammy's car backing into a parking spot.

He didn't usually come here. At least, not often.

"Hey, Colt."

I whipped my head around and my heart jumped in my chest as Sarah sat a mug of hot coffee down in front of me. She smiled, the sunlight haloing her dark hair and lashes.

Fuck, she was so pretty. I couldn't speak.

She raised a brow. "You okay?"

"Yeah," I said, clearing my throat. "You look good, is all."

Her gaze flickered, her cheeks flushing.

Then she looked up and smiled again.

But it wasn't for me, that was for damn sure.

I turned and watched Sammy Harlow wave through the window and came inside.

"I'll be back," she said quickly.

She left before I could say anything else. I found myself gripping my coffee mug, the heat stinging my palm through the ceramic. Sarah went to meet him, and the two of them stepped to the side. I shuffled in my seat and strained my neck so I could still see them.

I could see the way he leaned against the wall.

The way she smiled up at him.

The way he looked at her.

What the fuck is happening?

Sarah pulled keys out of her apron pocket and reluctantly gave the set to him. He grinned at her as he took them, her laugh ringing through the cafe.

My heart was going to burst out of my chest. Jealousy was greasier than the breakfast burritos being cooked up in the kitchen.

His gaze lifted, landing on me.

Maybe he was just being friendly with her. Maybe...

She said something and started to turn, but he caught her hand and landed a kiss on her knuckles. Sarah blushed, her eyes going wide as she stepped away and rushed toward the back of the cafe.

What.

The.

Fuck.

Sammy Harlow was hitting on my girl.

Sammy, the guy I'd grown up with. The brother of my best friend. Someone I trusted.

He looked up at me again and pressed his lips together, weaving through the tables. He slid into the booth across from me.

"What the fuck?" I whispered.

He sighed. "Listen, Colt. I planned to talk to you."

"You *know* I love her."

Sammy scowled, his dark brows drawing together. His eyes weren't bright blue, but dark and stormy. I saw an ember of anger there too. "I haven't done anything wrong. If you love her, why haven't you asked her out? Why haven't you done anything?"

"Because she's been recovering from an abusive relationship with an alcoholic who has a serial killer brother. Maybe that's why, *Sammy*."

His jaw ticked. A few people glanced at us and I sensed the gossip mill begin to turn. Fuck. I needed to keep my voice down.

"For the record, I'm here to get Sarah's keys because her car broke down. I helped her out on my drive home last night. And also, for the record, tomorrow was never supposed to be a date. I invited the boys too."

"What the fuck are you talking about?" I seethed.

Sammy leaned forward. "Sarah and I are going out tomorrow."

"You're a coward for telling me this in a room full of people and not in the parking lot where I can beat the shit out of you."

Sammy rolled his eyes. "Last time we fought, I put you on your knees. Don't you remember, Hayes?"

My mouth fell open, rage bubbling up. I was about to say something when a voice echoed nearby.

"That's her. That's the wife."

"Yeah, what a fucking whore. She should be in jail. It's all her fault, according to that article. She's the one who wanted all those women dead."

I immediately twisted in my seat and Sammy's attention shifted to follow. A man and woman were seated at a table, both of them eyeing Sarah with disdain as she put food out for another group. The woman had short copper hair, a fake tan, and about ten thousand rings on her fingers. The man was tall and well-built, balding, and had a face that annoyed me.

"She should be in jail too," the woman sneered. "I can't believe they let her walk free."

Whatever shit had come up between Sammy and I vanished as I stood up and he flanked beside me.

Sarah passed by the table, and the man grabbed a hold of her wrist and yanked her. She spun around and slapped him, her eyes widening.

"You bitch!" the woman shouted. "How dare you slap my husband? You psychotic whore!"

Sammy and I moved faster than two rattlesnakes. Sarah yelped as I pulled her to the side and out of the way. Sammy snatched the man's hand and twisted, pinning him down on the table. Coffee sloshed out of their mugs as the table rocked.

"You're fucking crazy," the woman snarled. "Let him go. He didn't do anything!"

"Apologize to her right now," Sammy said. "We both saw you grab her. We heard you talking."

"Everyone in this town is fucking crazy," the woman said.

The man Sammy had pinned down growled. "I'm not apologizing to that bitch. All those women are dead because of her. It's all her damn fault. Haven't you seen the news?"

Sarah grabbed onto my forearm. I could feel her shaking. I pulled her face against my chest. I slid my hand to the back of her head, keeping her safe.

The woman looked up at us, her eyes focusing on Sarah with a malice that scared the shit out of me.

"Get the fuck out." Alice pushed past us. "Get out of my cafe or I'll call the sheriff. No one harasses my waitress. Out. *Now.*"

Sammy yanked the guy to his feet and shoved him hard. He stumbled back and hit the floor with a sneer. The woman jumped up, scoffing.

"Why would you employ a murderer? She had to know what they were doing. She had to."

"Get the fuck out," Alice repeated.

"You heard her," Sammy said. "Leave."

Her eyes locked on Sarah again. "Stupid whore. She should be dead for what she did. Your boys should be locked up too. Whole family is cursed and goin' to hell."

Alice started to untie her apron. "I'm going to give you five seconds," she said calmly.

The two of them stalked out, casting dark glances our way. Everyone else in the cafe looked around, eyes wide. Quiet murmurs began, but Alice waved her hands to calm them.

"Go back to eating, folks. All is well." She spun around and lowered her voice. "Go get their license plate," she hissed.

Sammy nodded and went to the window, looking out at the small gray Toyota they climbed into. He rattled the numbers off and Alice nodded, writing them down. "We need a few minutes with Sarah," I said to Alice.

She pressed her lips in concern. "Are you okay, Sarah?"

"I will be," Sarah said.

Alice nodded. "I'm here for whatever you need. There's a break room in the back."

Sarah trembled against me as I held onto her, guiding her away from everyone. We made our way down a short hallway and into the break room. Sammy stormed in after us and shut the door behind him.

"I'm okay," she breathed out.

I held her tighter, looking up at Sammy over the top of her head. I'd never seen him like this before. His muscles were stiff, the vein in his forehead ticking. He rolled his shoulders and closed his eyes for a moment, visibly taking a deep breath.

"I'm sorry that happened," he said, looking at her.

"I don't know what article they were talking about," she whispered. "I didn't do anything. I didn't know. I only found out this morning about David being out."

"We know," I said softly. "We know that."

"They were assholes," Sammy said, stepping closer. "I'm sorry he grabbed you. I'm sorry she said those terrible things. Are you okay?"

"I just didn't expect it." She breathed out. "I slapped him."

"Yeah, and he deserved it," I said.

"He did," Sammy agreed.

Sarah nodded, letting out another deliberately slow breath. She tucked a stray wave behind her ear. "I'm okay. They really caught me off guard."

"Have you ever seen them before?" Sammy asked.

"No," she said. "They aren't locals. I haven't seen them in the cafe before, that's for sure. I think I'd recognize her again."

I nodded. I made a mental note of what they both looked like.

"I'm okay." Sarah was still shaking, but her voice sounded more steady now. Her eyes darted between us as she seemed to realize the same thing I did.

The room was small. Really small. Sammy and I were large, broad-shouldered guys. We were cramped close, her body pressed against mine and nearly against his too. She was still in my arms, with Sammy on the other side of her.

The tension between the three of us was hotter than a sweltering summer day.

"Colt, let me go," she whispered.

I immediately released her as if I'd been stung by a wasp. I took a step back, sliding my hands in my pockets as she hugged herself.

Fuck, I hated seeing her upset. I hated seeing her shut down.

Sammy blew out a breath, raking his fingers through his hair. "Alright. Can I be honest?"

Sarah frowned, looking up at him. "Yeah."

He looked at me.

"Yeah," I muttered.

"This isn't the right time to say this, but I'm going to anyway," Sammy said. "I want to be able to see Sarah without worrying about what's happening between the two of you. I care about you both. We haven't even gone on a date or even really talked about if that's what we're doing, but I'm not risking friendships."

Her mouth fell open and she turned to look at me. "Are you giving him trouble?"

I felt like the bad guy now. Every muscle tensed. "I..."

"Colt, you and I have been done for *years*. In fact, we were never even a thing."

Sammy winced. "Okay, I might have misread. Maybe forget what I just said?"

"No," she snapped, her eyes laser focused on me now. I felt like I could melt into the floor and never get back up. "I haven't done anything like this in so long and you are the last person I'm going to let stand in the way."

"I'm not trying to get in the way," I said. "Sarah, I've wanted you for years."

"Then ask me out!" she yelled, throwing her hands up. "Colton Hayes, you drive me fucking nuts. First, you show up on my wedding day and try to stop me. And now here you are again, getting in the way of something that might not even happen, and you're *embarrassing* me."

"I'm not trying to embarrass you," I breathed out. "I just—"

"Stop," she said. "Just stop. I need to get out of here. I feel like I can't breathe. I have to get back to work."

She pushed past Sammy and fled the office, slamming the door shut. I stood there like an idiot.

I'd watched her walk away.

Again.

I'd fucked it up with her.

Again.

"Colt," Sammy whispered. "I'm not trying to hurt you."

"I wish you would. It would hurt less than watching her run from me again."

"*Colt.*"

I took him in for a moment, his presence and the worry I saw on his pretty face. I wanted to punch him. I wanted to kiss him. I wanted to fight him or fuck him or *something.*

Without another word, I pushed past him and hurried out of the cafe. I didn't know what I needed or what I was supposed to do.

Everything always unraveled when I was around her.

CHAPTER NINE

sarah

I HAD to cancel the date with Sammy.

I wasn't sure it was the right move. It felt wrong, sending him the text. But after what happened at my shift this morning, I didn't know if I could ever look him in the eyes again.

My life was too complicated to date. Right? Whatever article that couple had talked about was a reminder of everything we'd been through. Maybe they weren't wrong. Maybe I deserved some sort of punishment.

I really hadn't known about Thomas. But the guilt from it all was still present. The idea of dragging someone else into my mess—I wasn't sure I could handle it.

I'd known Sammy for years. Even without the chemistry we'd recently found, he was someone I cared about.

I can't do this.

It didn't help that Colt made things more complicated.

I pressed send on the phone.

Me: I'm sorry, but let's cancel tomorrow. I wish you well.

Dammit. I slipped my phone in my purse, dreading what he might say back. He'd probably be angry.

I pulled my jacket tighter as I walked down the street. The car shop was a few blocks away, so I'd decided to see what was going on with the Honda after I got off work.

The wind picked up, numbing my cheeks.

I tried to keep my eyes ahead, but as I walked down the sidewalk, I noticed the truck that looked like David's. I couldn't help but stare, my heart jumping for the second time today.

I couldn't breathe as it rattled past me.

"Fuck," I rasped, clutching my chest.

There was too much happening. The hatred in the eyes of the woman and her husband today at the cafe, what they'd said to me... I couldn't get it out of my thoughts.

Maybe I needed to give Brenda a call for another appointment even though I'd see her in a couple of weeks.

I walked as fast as I could without running and finally made it to the mechanic shop on the corner. It was a three-car garage with a small office. I glimpsed my Honda through the window as I opened the front door, stepping inside. Warmth greeted me, and I was thankful for it.

Keith looked up from his desk, his eyes lighting up.

"Hey, Sarah," he said. "It's cold out there. Want some hot cocoa?"

"No thanks," I said. I kept my fingers crossed as I approached his desk and leaned against it, wincing. "How does it look?"

Keith grimaced, sweeping his rough fingers through his short hair. He was a short man with oil under his fingernails and a teddy-bear demeanor. "Well, do you have a few minutes? I just wanna show you a few things."

"With the car?" I asked.

"Yeah." He didn't sound hopeful. "Come on."

All of my other worries melted away as I focused on the car. Because goddammit, there wasn't a way for me to get around town without my car. I'd had it since high school and prayed that today would not be the day it gave out on me.

I followed him through the door leading to the back of the shop. A few other guys were working on cars. I recognized one as the parent of Jake's friend. I gave him a wave, and he returned it.

"Hey Sarah! How are the boys?" he called.

"They're good," I said. "A handful, as always."

"Oh, I'm sure." He gave me a genuine smile as he slid back under a car.

Not everyone in Citrus Cove hated me, at least there was that.

I followed Keith to the Honda in the middle bay of the garage. The hood was propped open, with tools laying around it.

"So, at first, I thought it was going to be simple. But then I noticed a couple of odd things. First of all, someone cut your hose."

"Someone *cut* it?"

"Yeah. There's no way for this to happen naturally. Someone did this to your car. Maybe it was a prank? A shitty one, though."

Blood rushed in my ears, heat creeping up my spine. No one would prank me like that. Not that I was aware of. We didn't have any kids in the neighborhood vandalizing property, and if they did, it was mischief like decorating lawns with toilet paper, not damaging a car. Hardly anyone in this town made enough money to do something like that to a neighbor's car without giving it a second thought.

David is out of jail. I swallowed hard. It could have been him.

"I just worry why someone would do this," he said. "I let

Sammy know, I hope that's okay. He asked me to keep him updated."

"Great." I bit my lip and crossed my arms.

Sammy was only trying to help. I thought about how he and Colt jumped in to help at the cafe. Being stuck between them in the break room nearly gave me a heart attack.

I'd liked being close to them way too much.

"Everything needs to go through me going forward, please," I said softly.

"Yes ma'am," Keith said. "Anyway, I already got the parts on order and I should have it back to you by Monday. The good news is it won't be a super expensive fix. For now. The bad news is your car's on the way out. A lot of things are wearing out, and they cost more money than I'd reckon it's worth. I think you've got a little time left with it, but I'm concerned it'll give out on you on the road. It's not the safest car to drive."

"But it's drivable," I said, relief flooding me.

"Well, like I said, it is for now. You've got kids, Sarah. God forbid something happened with you and them in the car. Have you thought about getting a new one?"

I couldn't afford a car payment right now. I was still working on paying down bills and debts we had owed that David hadn't paid. Not to mention, having two boys was expensive. Everything was fucking expensive.

"I haven't," I said.

"Well, let me know when you're looking. I can try to find you a deal."

"Thanks, Keith. I appreciate it. I guess... well, let me know if you hear of anything cheap."

"Yep, no worries. And don't worry about paying for this fix."

"What?" I asked.

"I owed Sammy one."

That son of a bitch. I pressed my lips together again, giving Keith a frosty nod. He offered me a smile and led me through to the office again.

I needed to call Emma for a ride home. Or I could walk home, though it was a little far. And with all that had happened, I didn't like the idea of walking down the street in the dark. Even in a small town like Citrus Cove.

"Have a good evening, Keith," I said. "Thanks for working on it so fast."

"You got it. Be safe."

I stepped outside and pulled out my phone to call Emma.

And waited to be rescued again.

I couldn't remember the last time I'd slept in on a Saturday. It had been months, at least. Once the sun was well in my eyes, I sat up and glanced at the clock. Realizing it was 9:30, I flopped back down onto my pillows, feeling miserable.

Everyone was on high alert again. I hated it. I'd filled Emma in on everything when she picked me up, which had led to us having a video call with Cam and Haley. The four of us had talked through the car situation and the fact that David was acquitted. Cam was going to look back at footage from the porch camera, but we were almost certain the driveway was out of range.

I still felt bad about canceling my date with Sammy. It'd been a week full of highs and lows.

A knock came at the door. "Mom?"

"Come in," I said.

Jake pushed open my bedroom door. He was already dressed and showered. I patted the blankets and he jumped in bed.

"Emma made us be quiet," Jake said.

"Sorry I slept in," I sighed.

"It's okay. I'm glad you did, Mom."

I smiled and pulled him close, kissing the top of his head. Eventually, Davy joined us and hopped into bed too. Jake giggled as the three of us wrestled the blankets until we were under them and cozy.

I had so much to do and figure out, but for the moment, these two were all that mattered in my world. I savored the small moments like this, logging them away in my memories to pull out on sad days.

"Are you going with Sammy today?" Davy asked.

"No," I said. "I'm yours all day."

He wrinkled his nose. "Okay."

"We should go to the movies!" Jake exclaimed.

"How about we watch a show?" Guilt rolled through me. I didn't want to spend money on the movies right now, with a new car on the horizon. I still needed to message Sammy about that, but I wasn't sure what to do after canceling on him.

"Yeah, that's fine," Davy said.

"But I want to see something new," Jake protested.

More guilt. Maybe movies wouldn't be too expensive.

"Jake, it's fine," Davy insisted. "Movie theaters are expensive."

"Hey," I said, reaching over to ruffle his dark hair. "It's okay. We'll go to the movies."

I could work extra hours next week.

"Let me get dressed and we'll check out the schedule," I said.

"Okay! Can we invite Aunt Emma?"

I smiled to myself. They'd been calling her their aunt more and more recently, and it made me happy. "Yes, go ask her."

Jake got out of bed and ran downstairs, with Davy right

behind him. I sighed and reached for my phone, checking it. There was a message I'd missed from last night.

Sammy: I'm sorry about today. I'll text you tomorrow, but no worries about the date. We'll find another time. Sleep well, Sarah.

My heart skipped a beat as I reread his message.

We'll find another time.

He still wanted to go out, even after what happened.

"Hey, Mom. *Someone* is here to see you," Davy said, poking his head back in the room.

"To see me?" I asked, frowning.

"Yeah."

"Who?"

He grinned and ran off.

I wasn't presentable. My hair was a rat's nest; I was in pajamas. I got out of bed and grabbed my robe, pulling it on.

Who would come see me?

I caught a glimpse of myself in the mirror and shook my head. I looked like a damn zombie. With a sigh, I went downstairs and froze as I hit the last step.

Sammy was in the living room.

Sammy was in my living room.

His back was turned. The boys were hunched over their video game system, showing him their favorites. His laugh echoed through the house.

Emma grabbed my arm, pulling me around the corner before he could see me.

"What the hell is this?" she whispered.

"I don't know," I said quickly.

"What happened to the date?"

"Ugh," I sighed. "That was supposed to be a secret."

She snorted and swatted my arm. "Bitch, you *knew* I would

find out. Go back upstairs and brush your hair, put on a bra, and then come back down."

"I canceled the date!" I said. "I don't know why he's here."

Emma raised a brow. "But he's *hot*."

"He's also my sister's husband's brother."

She scoffed. "And?"

"He's off-limits."

"Says who?"

Says Colt.

The sound of a throat clearing made my body tense. Emma gave me a knowing smirk as Sammy appeared. "I'll leave you two to chat."

CHAPTER TEN

sammy

SEEING her in pajamas made me want to cart her back upstairs, toss her on her bed, and worship every part of her. The thought of hauling her over my shoulder and taking her made me shift uncomfortably, all too aware of the fact I couldn't just do that because we weren't alone.

It took all my willpower to keep my cock at bay.

"Hey," I rasped.

"Hey," she whispered. Her eyes darted to the side and she grabbed my forearm, dragging me down the hall and out onto the screened back porch. She crossed her arms, hugging herself. "What are you doing here?"

"I'm sorry to intrude. I brought your keys and car," I said.

"Oh. I thought Keith said it would take all weekend."

"He pulled some strings." Basically, I'd driven out at the ass crack of dawn to a shop that had the parts, and brought them back for Keith. "I'm concerned that someone cut the hose, Sarah."

"Me too," she sighed. "You didn't have to do all that, you know? He said he owed you a favor."

"It's no big deal."

"It is," she said. "What... What are we doing? I have two kids. I'm divorced from a man who hurt people you love. You don't want to be around someone with so much baggage."

"Why not?" I asked.

I was so sure of this. In fact, I couldn't think of another time I'd been so sure of something.

Sarah was a shooting star through my dark skies. I couldn't just walk away from a wish granted, especially when it was one I never knew I'd made until now.

I *wanted* her.

"Do you want to date Colton?" I asked.

She winced. "It's... I don't know. Maybe?"

"And you're interested in me too?"

"Yeah," she whispered. "I'm interested in you, Sammy. I have no fucking clue why you're interested in me, though."

I took a step closer. I didn't touch her, even though every part of my body begged me to. "You're smart, beautiful, funny, and strong. You're so fucking strong. And brave."

Her brown eyes widened. I leaned in, our lips a breath apart.

"I don't know why I didn't see you before, but I see you now. You're so damn bright, it's blinding. I can't breathe when we're in the same room. I could sit and talk to you for hours. I could sit and never say a word."

Her lips formed a soft O.

I reached down and took her hand gently, closing her keys in her palm. I circled my fingers around her wrist, feeling the tremor of her heartbeat.

"Let me know when you're ready," I said. "And I will be here. Okay?"

She swallowed hard and nodded. "Okay. I will."

"But don't take too long," I whispered. "Please."

I released her and left the porch, heading back through the house. I'd left my car at the mechanic's, so I was going to walk back.

I paused to say goodbye to the boys. "I'm about to head out," I said. "What are y'all up to?"

"Seeing a movie," Davy said.

"Why don't you come to the movie with us?" Jake asked.

"He doesn't care about that," Davy snapped at Jake, crossing his arms. "Dad never did, remember? He said movies are stupid."

I shook my head. Mentally, it was just another reason to hate David. How could someone hate the movies? How could someone say that shit to their kid? "I love movies."

"How about you take my ticket?" Emma asked politely. She was perched on a chair, her gaze tracking me. Donnie sat on her lap wearing purple pajamas, tongue lolling as he eyed me with the same interest. There might have been a hint of coercion to get me to go, but I was an easy sell.

I thought about it for a moment. A movie sounded great, but I didn't want to make Sarah feel like she had to let me go, even if both boys wanted me to. "Only if your mom says yes," I said.

Jake beamed. "Mom! Can Sammy go with us?"

His voice echoed through the entire house. I fought a laugh as he took off to find her. Davy continued to study me quietly.

Both of them were growing so fast. I could have sworn at least an inch taller since I'd seen them a few weeks ago at Christmas.

"Do you really want to see a movie with us?" Davy asked me. He looked up at me, scrutinizing me. He wasn't impressed, but he seemed open to what I had to say.

"Yeah, bud," I said. "I really do."

He stared for a moment and then nodded. "Alright, I guess. I'll ask Mom too."

The moment he was out of the living room, I looked up at Emma. She drummed her pink nails on the chair's arm.

"You got any questions for me?" I asked.

"Plenty of them. But I'll save it for another time. If you were anyone else in this town, I'd make you work a lot harder to even step foot in our house." Emma got up and walked over to me, five feet of pure sass. I towered over her by a foot and a half, and it didn't matter. She held herself with the confidence of a star quarterback. "Sarah has been through hell. If you do a single thing to upset her, I don't care if you're Cam's brother. I will bury you. Understood?"

"I like knowing you're as protective of her as you are of Haley," I said. And I meant it. It made me happy to know that Sarah had people who cared for her.

"After my sister died, I didn't have anyone else until I met Haley. And now there's Sarah."

"I'm sorry," I whispered. I didn't know that about her. I'd always assumed Emma was an only child.

Her eyes darkened and she sighed. "It's okay. I have them both now. And the boys too. They've been through so much, Sammy."

"I know."

"Do you? Are you sure you know how much it's been?"

The implication behind her words, spoken slowly and clearly, hit me hard.

"I just want you to think about it," Emma continued. "You're the first person Sarah has been interested in like this after David. A man she was married to for years who didn't support her. Who smothered her. Who she had two children with, who are also hurt by his actions. Davy and Jake are constantly dealing with shit at school. They're also in therapy, which is expensive. Sarah works herself to death to provide for them. All of this is without the layer of shit from Thomas Connor."

I swallowed hard. "I care about her, Emma. I'm aware of what happened–"

"But you haven't been there to see her pick up the pieces the way I have. And I'm telling you here and now, you'd better be serious. This had better not be a fling. This had better not just be a crush you're chasing. Because Sarah deserves better than that."

"I'm not entirely sure what this is yet," I said honestly. "But I genuinely care about Sarah. I realize there is a lot I've missed or haven't seen, and I'll think about what you've said. But that doesn't change me wanting to take her on a date to get to know her more."

She pinned me with a heavy look for a long second, then nodded. "I believe you."

My shoulders relaxed a fraction. "Thank you."

Her expression softened into a faint smile. "Maybe think about if you're ready to be a dad as well."

Before I could say anything else, she turned on her heel. She left the room as I reeled in what she'd said, mind spinning. Donnie hobbled after her.

I was conflicted standing there, but I waited for the final verdict from Sarah. Despite Colt hating my guts and Emma's warning, I wanted to go out with Sarah and her boys.

Jake popped around the corner. "She said yes."

I grinned. "Excellent. I'll buy the good candy."

His eyes widened with excitement. I had a feeling Jake would be easy to win over.

I looked up, spotting Davy watching us with a frown.

He would be a lot harder.

Sarah reappeared breathlessly, ruffling his hair. He relaxed against her, still eyeing me. "Alright, I have to get ready. Give me twenty and I'll be back down. We don't want to be late. Sammy, are you sure you want to go?"

"He took my ticket," Emma called from somewhere in the house. "He's going."

I smiled. "I want to."

Sarah smiled back. "Okay. Wait here."

"I'm not going anywhere, angel."

CHAPTER ELEVEN

CITRUS COVE CINEMAS had one of the last drive-ins left in the state. I made a mental note to bring the three of them when it warmed up some. I could always borrow Cam's truck. A picnic under the stars while watching a movie sounded like fun.

The theater itself was a little old building that'd been here since well before I was born. It had low ceilings and permanent butter-scented air—just a whiff stirred up memories of high school dates.

I fulfilled my promise and bought all the candy Davy and Jake wanted, within reason. Sarah shot me worried looks, but I convinced her to pick out something too.

This made me happy.

In fact, for the first time in a long time, I felt alive.

Being a dad had never crossed my mind. Not really. But if there was a chance I might become important to these boys, I needed to step it up. I needed to earn their trust.

I popped a chocolate-covered cookie dough bite in my

mouth as we slid into our seats. Sarah ended up on one side of the boys, and I ended up on the other.

She glanced over at me and my heart skipped a beat. God, she was gorgeous. Even in the shadows, I was lost in her gaze.

Colt's words played back through my mind and I looked away, pretending to focus on the screen. The hurt in his eyes yesterday still hadn't left me.

Sarah mentioned her wedding day and him trying to stop her. I'd never heard about that.

What else didn't I know?

It didn't bother me that she was interested in him. Maybe I should have felt jealous, but all I could think was if he could make her happy, then he should be a part of her life in whatever way she wanted.

I couldn't deny that I wanted to know him more too.

I needed to talk to him again at some point. At the very least, to try to smooth things over. This was *Colt*. He'd been a staple in my life since I was born. Hell, some of my first memories were with him.

My stomach twisted as I tried to focus on the movie. It was some animated film about emotions, little characters running everything from happiness to anxiety.

A scene came on that made my eyes sting as the character dealt with an anxiety attack. I knew the feeling all too well. The helpless dread as ice spread through your chest, shattering in slow motion around you.

I glanced down at Davy and noticed his eyes were watering too. *It's okay to cry,* I wanted to say. How many times had I wished someone would have told me that growing up?

I heard a sniffle and looked up at Sarah. She wiped away a couple of tears.

"Are you crying, Mom?" Jake whispered.

"Yeah," she said.

"It's okay." He held out his hand and she took it.

Fuck, man. My heart.

I held my breath as the scene resolved, relaxing as we finally hit the happy ending. The movie ended and the other people got up to leave as the credits rolled.

I started to move, but Davy grabbed my arm. "Wait," he said. "Sometimes there are bonus scenes."

Like superhero movie style? I resettled and waited. He was right—there were two more scenes before the lights came up and I watched them with a stupid grin.

The four of us slowly made our way out of the theater. Jake chatted to Davy about the movie, and Sarah bumped me with her shoulder.

"Was that terrible?" she teased.

"It was great. I haven't seen a movie in so long," I said.

"Oh my god, are you that guy online?"

My head whipped around at the sound of the voice. A familiar woman stood a few feet away from us, her eyes widening as she approached me.

I recognized her as the woman who'd lost it at the cafe.

Fuck.

I immediately stepped in front of Sarah and the boys.

"Oh my god, it is you," she said, pretending like we were meeting for the first time. She gestured to my arm. "I recognized your tattoo. You're him, aren't you? The sexy chef." She smiled, her gaze flickering past me to Sarah.

Fuck. I'd never thought about that. I had a tattoo on my forearm of a swallowtail butterfly. Cam and Hunter had given me hell about it for years, but it was one of my favorites.

"Go to the car," I said lightly.

Sarah made a noise. I glanced back at her and could see she was torn between going and staying.

"Can I get a picture with you?" the woman asked. "Is *that* your wife and kids?"

"No, and no," I said. "I remember you. Get away from us."

She pulled out her phone anyway, and I glanced behind me. Sarah frowned and pulled the boys close to her.

"He said he doesn't want to take a picture," Davy said, narrowing her eyes on the woman.

"Just a quick one," she said quickly. "It'll be fast!"

Sarah grabbed my arm and pulled me out of the way as the phone was lifted. "Come on, let's go to the car."

I ushered them toward the Honda. I wished I'd gone back to get my car because I didn't like the idea of this psycho getting Sarah's license plate. My ears burned as I opened the door for the boys and they slid into the backseat.

Hell, I didn't like that she knew I lived in town either.

I glanced around the parking lot, looking for her husband. Was he creeping around somewhere?

Sarah got in the driver's seat as I rushed to the passenger door. I glanced up, and sure enough, the woman was taking pictures of us.

What the fuck?

As soon as I got in the car, Sarah backed up and peeled out of the parking lot. I stared at the side mirror, watching the woman disappear in the distance as Sarah sped to get away.

"I'm so sorry," she whispered.

"Not your fault," I said.

"She said she recognized you from online. Has that ever happened before?" Sarah asked.

"No. I mostly keep my face out of videos. It's really a focus on my hands and forearms while I... cook."

She glanced over at my hands, her cheeks turning red. We nearly swerved into the other lane.

"Eyes on the road, angel," I said so quietly, only she would hear.

"I don't like that lady," Jake announced.

"Me neither, bud," I said, twisting in my seat. "I'm sorry that happened. It was weird."

Jake nodded, but Davy frowned. "Did you know who she was?"

"She was no one," Sarah said.

Thoughts plagued my mind, even as I tried to force a smile for the kids. Was it just a weird coincidence, or were those people stalking us? Stalking Sarah? I glanced over at her, and her eyes met mine, a silent agreement passing between us to discuss it later.

I'd seen how angry the couple had been at the cafe.

"Will she do anything bad?" Davy asked.

"No," I reassured. "I doubt it. It's all good."

He stared at me with a haunted expression, making it clear he didn't believe me. I realized I had no way of knowing if everything would be fine at all.

"Okay, I take that back," I said. "I'm sure it'll be fine. I don't think she can do anything. But we don't know her and that was weird, and I'm sorry she was there."

He nodded, his shoulders relaxing a fraction. "It's okay."

Dammit. I was going to win this kid over one way or another.

I pulled my phone out to text Cam and Hunter. They both knew about the cafe run-in, and we needed to find out who these people were.

Within a few minutes, Sarah pulled into the driveway next to Emma's car. She glanced back in the rearview mirror. "Can you boys give us a minute? Maybe go get some hot chocolate started? I'm going to run Sammy to the mechanic for his car."

"Candy and hot cocoa?!" Jake asked. "This is the best day ever. Thanks Sammy."

He got out, followed by Davy.

Sarah watched them go inside and looked over at me. Her face softened. "You okay?"

"Yeah," I breathed out. "I'm so sorry that happened. I tried to shield the kids with my body. If she got any pictures, they shouldn't be in them."

"Me too. I don't understand why she would have come up to us. She acted like we were just meeting."

"Probably because of Jake and Davy. But she knew that we knew. It was a scare tactic."

One that really pissed me off. What would have happened if Sarah had been alone?

I took a deep breath and forced myself to relax. Her taking photos worried me. Partially because I didn't like the idea of being fully known on the internet, but more so because Sarah and the boys might be in the pictures.

"Thanks for coming," she whispered. "I know it wasn't like... a date. But I still enjoyed being with you."

"I enjoyed it too," I said. "I'm going to win your kids over."

She snorted. "You've already got Jake. Davy, I don't know. He has a hard time with men who are older than him. David has hurt him more than any of us in ways I never caught. I hate myself for it."

I slid my hand onto her thigh, giving her a gentle squeeze. "He's strong like you. He'll be okay."

"I hope so," she said. "Also... How dare you call me *angel* like that while I'm driving?!"

I gave her a smirk. "You were checking out my hands. Almost took us off the damn road."

"Oh, don't be dramatic," she laughed. She shook her head as she backed out of the driveway. "You've got good hands."

"Yeah? Want to take them for a ride?"

"Oh my god. What am I going to do with you, Sammy Harlow?"

I grinned. "I hope many, *many* things."

CHAPTER TWELVE

sarah

THE NEXT FEW days passed in a whirlwind. Work, school, dripping the faucets as cold weather settled over the Texas Hill Country, and repeat.

What was new, though, was Sammy.

He made me happy. For the first time in what felt like forever, I had butterflies for someone who was interested in me. I felt like a stupid teenager again—and that scared the hell out of me.

"You look happy," Brenda said as I sat down in the cushioned chair. "How's your week been?"

It was Thursday, which meant therapy and a double shift. It was always the most exhausting day of the week, but today... Well, today, I felt good.

"It's been different," I said. "Good different? I think? There was an incident at the cafe last week. A couple blamed me for Thomas' murders. The husband grabbed me."

"That doesn't sound good."

"That part wasn't. But then..." Fuck. I thought about the

way Colt and Sammy had intervened, and how good it had felt to be in Colt's arms, even though he made me so damn mad.

"Then?"

I swallowed hard. "Colton and Sammy came to my rescue. And he and I have started talking..." My cheeks were redder than a fire engine. "He's really good."

"Which one?"

Both of them. "Sammy," I said.

She raised a brow. Brenda knew me too damn well. Sometimes it was uncomfortable.

"Alright, so I like both of them. Well, sort of. Colt and I have history and I haven't talked to him yet. I've known Sammy most of my life and—yeah, he's always been cute—but I've never once thought about him as anything more until now. So I guess that's why this week has been good."

"I see." She clicked her pen. "Well, that's good."

"I think so," I mumbled, looking out the window.

As our conversation moved on, my mind kept returning to Sammy. And Colt. And how I needed to figure out what the hell Sammy meant when he'd asked me if I was interested in Colt too.

And how there was a part of me that really wanted them both.

That was selfish, though. Right?

The rest of the session flew by. I had my tools to help me navigate the stress of knowing David was out of jail and the paranoia and worry along with that. I probably needed to call my lawyer back, but that was a problem for tomorrow.

I pulled into the Citrus Cove Cafe parking lot and frowned. Colt was leaning against his truck, parked next to my normal spot. It was cloudy out, but a patch of sun had fought through just to land on him.

Some might say it was a wink from god, but I really wasn't sure when it came to him.

I parked beside him and got out. He looked up at me with a grim smile.

"What do you want?" I asked.

He winced. "I want to say I'm sorry."

I sighed. "Before work?"

"I didn't know when else to see you."

"Have you heard of this thing called a phone? With text messages? Or are we having this conversation by pigeon, Colton Hayes?"

He relaxed a fraction and flashed me a brilliant smile. "Alright, alright, you have a point. After work? Can we please talk? Or whenever you're free. I don't care how long I have to wait, I just need to clear the air with you."

I studied him for a moment. There was desperation in his voice, and it pained me. For years, the two of us had avoided each other because it hurt too damn much to wonder *what if*.

He was the first boy I ever loved.

He was also the first boy to ever break my heart.

Did I want to give him the chance?

Did I want to give *us* the chance?

"I work in the evening tomorrow," I whispered. "But I'm free in the morning."

"Can I take you to breakfast?"

"Yeah, so long as it's not here." I would rather eat anywhere else.

"Deal," he said softly. "I'll pick you up in the morning... Are you okay after what happened last week at the cafe?"

"Yeah. Well, I saw the woman again." Did I tell him Sammy was with me? "Sammy took me and the boys to the movies. And she was outside the theater afterwards."

"I heard about it," he said, dragging his fingers

through his blonde hair. "I've been keeping an eye out for their car, but haven't seen them again. I'm sorry that happened. I'm glad he was with you. Were the boys okay?"

"Yes," I said. "Concerned. But we didn't tell them about my run-in here. I'm trying to protect them as much as I can."

He nodded. "Let me know if there's anything I can do. I'll keep watching for them. Hunter had Bud run the license plate, but it was attached to a different car."

That didn't really bode well. "Great," I mumbled.

"It'll be okay. I'm keeping an eye out."

"Do you always watch out for me?" I asked. I meant to sound teasing, but he nodded so sincerely that my breath left me.

"Yeah, Sarah. I always do. I should have done a better job of it while you were with David."

Tears stung. I looked away from him, forcing myself to breathe. "Wasn't your responsibility."

"Maybe not. Doesn't change how I feel about you."

One breath, two... I crossed my arms and forced myself to look up at him. "It's been years. After all this time..."

I trailed off. I couldn't really do this right now.

He put his hands in his pockets, his boots digging into the gravel.

"I have to go. My shift is about to start."

"Okay. Sorry I caught you before work. I'll see you in the morning."

"See you then."

I practically ran for the back door. Once I got inside, I leaned against the wall and tried to hold back tears.

He couldn't possibly blame himself for how David treated me. That wasn't fair. It wasn't fair to him or me. I'd chosen to marry David. I'd believed he was the one, ignoring the voice inside my head that told me he wasn't. I was stupid and young and naive.

I wasn't any of those things anymore.

"Sarah? You okay?"

Alice spotted me from down the hall, her brows pinched together.

"I'm okay," I said, pulling on the mask I wore so well.

I pushed all my feelings down and grabbed my apron. I tied it around my waist and headed down the hall past her.

"You sure?" she asked.

"Yes," I said. "Really, I'm fine. I'll jump in."

Alice pressed her lips, the disapproval apparent. "Alright. Let me know if you need anything. And I want you to take lunch between shifts, Sarah. No more working so long without a break."

"Okay," I sighed, although I certainly wasn't going to make any promises.

"That couple hasn't shown up again, just so you know. Debbie, Trey, and the new hire all know to keep a lookout."

"Thank you," I said. "I'm sorry for the trouble."

She scoffed. "Not your fault. Don't forget to take breaks."

"I'll try."

Most days, I lost track of time while working. It was the same rhythm I'd been in for at least a decade—familiar, easy, and I could do it on autopilot.

And that's exactly what I did. I took orders, served tables, chatted with all the regulars about the boys, the weather, the holidays—small and easy topics so I could think about Colt and Sammy.

The thing was, even when I was still married to David, I dreamed about love. Real love. Being cared for and cherished. At the time, I'd been convinced that maybe I could make it work with David, even though I knew deep down that it would never happen.

After the boys were born, he stopped pretending to try. He'd tell me I was too ugly, too gross, or not the same as I was in high school. At the time, it devastated me.

Now it just pissed me off.

The idea of being with someone new who could fulfill my needs was exciting. But it also meant trusting again. It meant rebuilding a life. And why would someone want to date me?

Sammy and Colt had lost their damn minds.

I was a single mom with two rowdy boys. I'd been married to the brother of a serial killer, a man who had ruined the lives of countless families. As they'd uncovered more evidence from the house, it became apparent how far his violence had reached.

There was no way David hadn't been aware, even if his lawyer argued otherwise.

Then again, people said the same about me. The difference was that I hadn't ever known David had a brother to begin with.

Dating him had been a way to get back at Colt in high school. It was childish thinking about it now. If I'd just talked to Colt about what happened all those years ago, things would have been so different.

The moon shone high in the summer sky, my clothes sticking to my skin. I used my visor mirror to fix my makeup as I thought about kissing Colton.

I had to make it happen. Since the beginning of this past school year, the two of us had been dancing around each other for months.

I loved him. I'd never wanted someone as much as I wanted him. He was perfect in every way possible. He was hot and sweet and told me he wanted to talk alone tonight.

He hadn't dated anyone else either, so I was certain he felt the same.

Should I put on lipstick?

If he wanted to talk alone, I was certain that meant we'd kiss.

Nerves rolled through me. I decided against the lipstick and got out of the car, looking up at the Harlow family barn that rose in the distance. Other cars were parked in the grass, the sound of music and chatter drifting from within.

"*Deep breath,*" *I whispered to myself.*

I smoothed my hands down my dress and headed for the barn, looking for Colt. He was always easy to spot.

"*Hey Sarah!*" *one of the girls called.*

"*Hey!*" *I smiled at them, but didn't stop on my path to the barn, weaving between people.*

I spotted Cameron, which usually meant Colt was nearby. He was sitting on top of a hay bale drinking a beer.

"*Hey,*" *I called.* "*Where's Colt?*"

Cam snorted. "*I'm not his keeper.*"

I rolled my eyes. "*You guys are always attached at the hip.*"

"*Is your sister here?*"

"*No,*" *I snapped, crossing my arms. At the last party, he'd dumped his beer on her and upset her, and now I'd never hear the end of how Cameron Harlow was evil incarnate.* "*She hates you and has vowed to never come to a party again. So thanks for that.*"

He pressed his lips together and shrugged. "*Colt went outside, I think. Try around back?*"

Out back was where people usually went to make out...

"*Thanks,*" *I mumbled.*

I darted through the door that led back behind the barn. It was no surprise to see a few couples pressed against the walls kissing. Heat crept up the back of my neck as I felt a set of eyes on me. I glanced up, expecting to see Colt, but it wasn't him who was looking at me. It was a lanky boy whose name I didn't remember.

Laughter drew my attention. I looked out at the field that stretched for what felt like miles.

I spotted Colt in the distance.

What was he doing all the way out there? Was that where he wanted us to meet?

He ducked and disappeared into the tall grass.

I frowned and grabbed the hem of my dress, holding it close as I ventured into the grass. I was glad I'd worn boots. I'd taken them from Honey's closet, but she never minded. The three of us often borrowed shoes from each other because they were so expensive.

I headed in the direction I'd seen Colt. Maybe I could sneak up on him and surprise him.

A soft groan made me frown as I got closer. I slowed down, keeping my steps light as the grass parted.

Oh.

Tears sprang to my eyes. Colt was on top of someone, their lips sealed together as they rolled in the dirt. I recognized him as one of the boys from band class.

I stood still for a shocked second before taking a step back. Then another. Then another, until I took off running toward the barn, holding back tears.

Why would he kiss someone else? Wasn't he in love with me? I thought he wanted me.

I was such an idiot. I felt so foolish for ever thinking he would look at me that way. Maybe I'd been imagining things.

Over the heartbreak, a raw, burning fire consumed me. I was jealous.

Hot tears rolled down my cheeks as I stepped out of the field. I was done with the party, done with this night.

I wanted to get in bed and cry and cease to exist and never see Colton Hayes again.

"Hey, Sarah, are you okay?"

I looked up, spotting that boy from earlier again. He had shaggy hair and dark eyes and was cute enough.

Cute enough to maybe make Colt jealous.

Or to at least show him I didn't need him.

"I'm okay," I said, wiping away the tears. "I'm sorry, I'm trying to remember your name."

"David," he said with a smile. "David Connor."

CHAPTER THIRTEEN

I DIDN'T SLEEP a wink the entire night. I was too nervous about seeing Sarah.

After all these years, I was finally getting to take her on a date.

It was just breakfast, but I'd been waiting for this my entire life.

My alarm blared, startling me. I'd forgotten I'd even set it. I leapt up, nerves rattling as I rushed through the motions of getting ready. I took a hot shower, blow dried my hair, washed my face, and got dressed. I picked out dark-wash jeans, black boots, and a navy blue sweater that looked good. At least, I felt like it looked good.

What if Sarah didn't like blue?

That was the silliest thing I could have thought.

The rising sun turned the skies rose pink, filling the house with light. I picked up my phone and sat on the edge of the bed, rubbing my face as I checked messages.

I needed to look at a few emails from the contractor because Cam and I had to set up a meeting next week. I also needed to keep working on new cider flavors for our relaunch—maybe something soft and summery that would be easy to drink.

There were a million details to think about, but before all that, there was Sarah.

Me: Good morning. Still up for breakfast?

I knew exactly where I was going to take her. There was a diner in south Austin that wasn't too far of a drive, and if she had time for it, I wanted to take her there. If not, I'd take her to a closer one, even though I didn't like the food quite as much.

The One That Got Away: Yes! About to drop the boys off at school. I'll see you soon?

I smiled.

Me: Yes. I'll head your way in about twenty

Twenty minutes suddenly felt like eons. I grabbed my wallet and keys and headed for my car, warming up the engine and blasting the heat. I sat still until I couldn't stand it anymore, then decided I'd leave and just drive slowly.

Fuck, this was really happening.

A few minutes later, I pulled up to the house and parked in the driveway behind Emma's car. I'd beat Sarah here.

I sighed and glanced in the rearview, keeping an eye out for her.

And an eye out for David.

Knowing he was out on bail set my back straight. The idea of something happening or him showing up back in town terrified me, especially for Sarah and the boys.

It all looked normal. I took a deep breath, rubbing my palms on my thighs. I was anxious, excited, worried—all of the above.

I spotted Sarah's car in the rearview mirror. She slowed as she turned into the driveway. I got out quickly and approached her door.

I opened it for her and she flashed a smile brighter than the sun.

"Hey," she said.

My heart was going to stop. She'd stolen every ounce of oxygen from my lungs.

Sarah was drop dead gorgeous in a dark blue dress over some tights and knee-high boots. There was a scarf around her neck, her auburn waves drawn back into a bun. Silver flower studs glistened from her ears, glitter on her eyelids. Her cheeks were pink from the cold.

Slowly but surely, the light was returning to her eyes. Out of all the terrible things that had happened last year, seeing her come back to herself made me believe she would be more than okay.

"Emma got a hold of me," she laughed. "And we match."

"We do," I breathed out. "You're gorgeous."

"Thanks," she said. "You always look good."

I let out a soft hum. "Well, you haven't seen me when I wake up in the morning."

"Not yet. I'm sure you look just as good."

I smirked as her eyes widened.

"I mean, I'm just—"

"You can flirt with me, you know," I teased. "Are you ready or do you need to grab anything? My truck is warm and ready."

"Nope, I'm ready." She leaned over and snatched her purse from the backseat. Her dress hiked up slightly and I looked away, my cheeks burning.

I snorted as I realized Emma was surveying us from the window. She mouthed *'I'm watching you'* and pointed at me before disappearing behind the curtain.

I would have laughed, but I knew Emma was serious.

Sarah shut the car door. She followed me to my truck and I opened the passenger door for her.

"Your truck is huge," she said.

"Need help?" I asked.

She gave me a look that made me swallow a laugh. "I know how to get in a big truck. I'm a lady."

"Well, I'm a gentleman," I said.

I grabbed her waist and lifted her.

She squeaked as I placed her in the front seat. "Oh my god, Colt," she hissed. "I can't believe you did that."

I reached around her for the buckle, but she grabbed my chin.

"I don't think so, sir. Get in the truck."

Jesus Christ. "Yes, ma'am," I said.

I shut her door and walked around to the other side, ignoring the way my blood was already pumping. I started the truck up and turned down the heat, my entire body on fire though after touching her.

"Where are we going?"

"It depends," I said. "What time do you need to be home by?"

"Noon."

"Perfect."

I felt her gaze narrow on me as I backed out and started down the road. "Is this a date?"

"I'd like for it to be. But I think we need to talk first," I said. I glanced over at her. "Want me to go first?"

"Yes," she said.

"Okay. I'm sorry for hurting you all those years ago."

"The kiss," she said.

"Yeah. I..." I took a deep breath, steadying myself. I'd told myself I'd be completely honest with her. "I didn't realize I was bisexual until I kissed him. I was a little drunk. I was waiting on you and knew I had a crush on you. You were perfect. Are perfect."

"I'm far from perfect."

"Alright, well, perfect to me. But the two of us ended up walking off into the field and I don't know. We kissed. And I realized I liked guys too. And then my dad found out."

"What? From who?"

"I still don't know," I said. "For the longest time, I thought it was you. And I tortured myself over that. I'm not saying this to put anything on you, by the way. I ended up living at Cam's house for a while. And before I knew it, you were getting married to David Connor of all people. And I couldn't stand it. I was still in love with you."

She was quiet for a moment and then hummed. "I know I told you this on my wedding day, but I want to be really clear with you. I was never upset you kissed a boy. I never told anyone. Not a single soul. I was upset because it wasn't me. Because I really thought... I believed we had something special. And looking back, it was stupid. I overreacted. I was a starry-eyed girl with a broken heart. And to get back at you, I started dating David."

My grip tightened on the steering wheel. "You went to him because of me?"

She shook her head. "Do not take that on yourself. Okay? Yes. I was stupid and young and heartbroken. I thought being with David would make you fight for me. But you never did. I never should have expected you to. That was wrong of me."

I swallowed glass, my throat constricting. "I'm so fucking sorry."

"I'm sorry too," she whispered. "And it's just been easier over the years to ignore you. I've had a mental *off-limits* sign stamped over your name in my head. And with David... I really wasn't myself. I've been working on healing."

"That's why I've waited to try," I said. "I didn't want you to feel like I was ready to pounce. I don't know. I mean, I have been waiting to, sort of."

"I have children," she said. "His children. They're still hurting. Davy struggles the most, and I'm always fighting to make him feel safe and loved. Jake has a really bright outlook on everything, but he's internalized a lot. It'll take years to undo the damage David did. That *I* did."

"Both of them will be okay. They're loved by you and their family."

"But they're a lot, Colt. And they're part of my life. My entire world revolves around them and work. I'm fixing my finances slowly, but we struggle. There were a lot of bills that didn't get paid, so I'm working hard to try to pay them off. Some days, I still feel like a shell of myself. Other days, I'm full again. I just don't know if you want that. I'm not the girl you fell in love with in high school. I can't understand why you would ever be interested in me when you're *you*."

"Because you make the sun shine, the stars fall, and my world spin. You have since the day you showed up in Citrus Cove. For years, I've asked myself *what if*. What if I hadn't kissed that guy? What if I'd convinced you not to marry David?"

"I've asked myself if life would have been different if we would have just *talked*." She sighed. "What if we had said what we needed to say?"

I nodded. I'd asked myself that too. But sometimes that was the hardest part in a relationship or a friendship. Talking meant being vulnerable.

It was hard to be vulnerable when you were already hurting.

Regardless of what Sarah decided, I knew I had to put everything on the table now.

"If I have to wait for you to be ready for a relationship, I will wait. If you don't want me in your life as more than a friend, then I'll be the best damn friend you've ever had. If you want to be with Sammy because he makes you happy, then I'll stand aside. But I've never been able to walk away from you. I'll never be able to let you go."

She was silent as I pulled onto the highway. I didn't press her to speak, even as I felt my stomach knot in a variety of ways that would put the Boy Scouts to shame. Even if I could barely breathe.

"I like Sammy," she finally admitted. "But I like you too. I don't know what to do with that. There's so much history between us."

"There is," I whispered. "I... I don't know if I have a solution at the moment for everything, but if you see us both, I wouldn't mind."

"Both of you? You wouldn't feel jealous?"

Yes, but for different reasons. Because I was interested in Sammy too, even if it made me unsure about a lot of things.

"I'm just saying I won't mind," I said. "For now, anyway."

"Okay," she said.

The tension was finally gone. I stole a glance at her, and she surprised me by reaching over and placing her hand on my thigh. I grabbed her hand and brought it to my lips, kissing her knuckles.

"We're almost to the diner," I said.

"Good. Now we can talk about all sorts of things."

I grinned and kissed her hand again. Her scent lingered, and I inhaled before releasing her. "Like what?"

"Like what your favorite color is."

"The color of your eyes."

"Oh my god," she laughed. "*Stop.*"

"The color of your cheeks when you blush."

She snorted. "You've lost your mind."

"It's to be expected. I'm wild about you."

She shook her head, but she didn't stop smiling. I pulled into the diner parking lot and wasn't too surprised to see it packed. I parked and got out, hurrying to the passenger door. Sarah shook her head at me as I opened the door for her.

"My lady," I said, offering her my hand.

"You're so silly," she mumbled, but she slid her hand in mine.

I tugged her close, catching her waist and lifting her out of the truck. Her body was warm against mine as I put her down, the two of us toe to toe.

"You're gorgeous," I whispered.

"You keep saying that."

"I'll keep saying it until the day I die," I said.

She shivered as the wind picked up and I wrapped my arms around her. She returned the gesture, sliding her arms around my waist and laying her head on my chest.

"What am I going to do with you?" she mumbled.

"Eat breakfast and tell me all your secrets."

CHAPTER FOURTEEN

sarah

BREAKFAST WITH COLT WAS A DREAM. We talked about everything we'd missed over the years, and it felt like catching up with my best friend. The divide between us was closing, and it felt good.

It felt really, really good.

We also lost track of time, which meant I was almost late to work.

I wished I would have paid more attention because a few hours with him made me want a shower with my vibrator, but that would have to wait.

I walked through the back door of Citrus Cove Cafe and was immediately met by Alice. She raised a brow as I reached for my apron.

"How's it going?" she asked casually. "You're wearing makeup. And you smell like vanilla."

I knew what a fishing rod and bait looked like, and that question was suspiciously similar. "It's going good..."

"Well, I saw Colton talking to you yesterday morning.

Don't tell me he's harassing you. I'll tell your sister. I'm sure between us and Emma, he'll never see the sun again."

I laughed and shook my head. "I don't know where you've been my whole life, but I really appreciate you. No, he wasn't harassing me. We went to breakfast this morning."

Alice wiggled her brows. "And how did that go?"

My cheeks flamed. "It was good."

"Hmm, so talkative. I'm living vicariously through you and this development. How do you feel about taking time off today?"

"What? I can't," I said, straightening. "You know that. I need the money."

"I'll still pay you," she said.

"Alice, no," I sighed. "It's also Friday. Why would you send me home?"

"I have plenty of coverage and you never take a day. In fact, I think you're the only person I know who works more than me and I own this place. Which means I work twenty-four seven. I think you work twenty-five eight."

I frowned. I couldn't remember the last time I'd had a spontaneous day off. But after breakfast with Colt... a little self care sounded nice. "I don't know..."

"Seriously. The boys are at school, right? When was the last time you had some time to yourself?"

It was tempting. I chewed my bottom lip. "You'd still pay me?"

She rolled her eyes. "Yes. Of course."

I'd miss out on tips. But... I'd also never gotten those recipes to Sammy. The idea of baking today appealed to me too.

In fact, a day to decide what the hell I was going to do about both of them sounded like a good idea.

"Alice, are you sure?" I asked.

"I am," she said. "I know I've been giving you hell recently about resting, but I can't stand the thought of you not having some time here and there. Burnout is a bitch."

"I've been living on burnout for a decade," I said. "But, if you insist. I'll be here tomorrow."

"Yes. And maybe tomorrow you'll tell me about the date."

"It wasn't a date," I said, wrinkling my nose.

It was a date, sort of. I knew better than to confirm that. The whole town would be up our asses.

"Try telling that to Colt," she snickered. "Go. Enjoy your day. See you tomorrow."

Reluctantly, I stepped back outside. The wind whipped my hair, and I drew in a cold breath.

Now what?

I was supposed to see Honey last week, but had never gone by.

It was the day for clearing the air, wasn't it? I'd done it with Colt, and maybe it was time to finally do so with Honey. We'd let the tension between us go on for too long.

Maybe a visit to her, then home where I could take care of my needs and bake something, and maybe I'd drop it off at Sammy's...

That was a good plan.

I knocked on Honey's door and waited. The porch needed a good sweep. I craned my head, taking a peek at the oak tree in the front yard. None of the branches were threatening to drop on the house anymore, which was good considering we could still get a freeze before spring.

Honey opened the door and leaned against the frame with a raised brow. She wore a chunky pink knit cardigan Emma bought her for Christmas over a T-shirt and dark jeans. Her silver hair was braided to the side, reading glasses perched on her nose. She raised a brow. "Nice to see you know I'm still alive."

I crossed my arms. I'd been dreading this conversation, but it was time we worked things out. A weight had settled on my chest that demanded to be lifted. "We need to talk."

She looked me up and down. "What happened?"

My shoulders tensed. "Nothing. Alice gave me the day off, paid. And I'm here to try to sort out the strain between us."

It had been like this for a few months—we still talked and were occasionally in each other's presence, but there was a wall between us that I wasn't sure how to break down. I knew the lies I'd told over the years had hurt her, but I also knew I'd done what was needed to keep the peace with David. I would go back and change a lot if I could, but protecting Jake and Davy wasn't one of them.

"Alright. Come in," she said, stepping aside.

This house was still home to me, even after all this time. She'd redecorated since I'd come over last. The living room had new pillow covers and the color palette was different. Autumnal browns, oranges, burnt yellows—all warm and inviting. The scent of coffee was a warm hug, along with what I knew to be one of her casseroles in the oven. "Casserole?" I asked.

"Sure is. You should have some while you're here."

Well, that was a good sign if she was offering me food. The two of us made our way to the kitchen. Like the living room, she'd swapped out the decorations in here too. Instead of bright yellows and checkered patterns, she'd picked out a variety of cerulean blues and emerald greens.

I opened the cabinet and grabbed the mug I'd been using since I was a teenager. It was a cream color with butterflies painted above blades of grass. A wave of comfort soothed my nerves. *I can do this. I can have this conversation with her. The world won't end if I'm honest.*

I grabbed another mug down for Honey, poured coffee into each one, and took them to the table. The casserole still had twenty minutes on it. I settled into the chair across from her, my heart thumping faster. My palms began to sweat, my stomach twisted up like a pretzel.

I hated confrontation, especially when it came to someone I loved.

"Okay, Sarah Kate Bently," Honey said, using my full name. I was still getting used to hearing Bently instead of Connor, but found it refreshing. "What do you want to discuss?"

"Where should we start?" I asked. "Why are you upset with me?"

Honey's eyes narrowed on me. I felt like a child again. "It's not that I'm upset with you..."

"Oh, cut the bullshit," I snapped.

Her eyes widened.

"I'm serious," I said, shaking my head. "Honey, we have barely spoken for nine months. Ever since Thomas Connor was killed and Haley was almost hurt. You've checked on the boys, you've been there for Hal and Cam, but you've barely looked me in the eyes, except over the holidays when you were forced to. You taught me not to walk on eggshells, but here we are dancing on them."

I drew in a steady breath, feeling a weight lift. I remembered the things Brenda had helped me with, holding on to what I needed to say and doing it as calmly as I could.

"I've been going to therapy. I've been doing the best I can to make money and support my family and not be a burden to others." Now, I bit back tears. "What more can I do? What else do you need from me? I am not a superhero. I'm not perfect. But *fuck*, I am trying."

Honey shook her head, her eyes watering. She pulled off her reading glasses and set them on the table. "I knew David was bad. I knew it. And I should've told you not to marry that son of a bitch. For years, I bit my tongue and watched you suffer being married to a man who hurt you. And he may not have hit you, but I know he hurt you. Even if you told me he didn't."

"He did," I whispered, tears rolling down my cheeks. "And I don't even know if it was David. It could have been Thomas. They look exactly the same. Do you know how horrifying that is? Knowing I was married to a monster? And now, knowing that he's been let go? That he's still around?"

She sniffled and looked out the window. "I've been so angry. At first, I was angry at myself. I was mad I didn't do anything. I could have intervened more. I could have called Haley. But I just... I don't know. I didn't want to overstep. But I should have. And then when everything happened, I think all the anger shifted to you."

"I know I lied to you," I whispered.

Honey swallowed hard. "You did. Many times."

"I know," I said. "I was protecting the boys, myself, and in a way—you. I know it wasn't right, but I don't regret it. I did my best with what I had."

"I just wish I could have helped you more. I wish I would have known how bad things were. I could have pulled you out of that situation."

I couldn't help but laugh. "Honey, do you really think you could have convinced me to leave him?" That was the part of all of this that still stung. "It took the truth coming out for me to get away from him. I was trapped in it and I saw no way out. If you'd offered me the world, I would have still turned you down. This isn't your fault."

"It's not yours either, sweetheart."

"Some of it isn't," I sighed. "I didn't know about Thomas. I didn't know what was happening there. I did know that sometimes David just acted... different. And now I think maybe those times, I was talking to Thomas. I'll never know, but it's terrifying. It's terrifying to know I let a serial killer in my home. Around my children."

"It's terrifying for me to know that there was a killer around *my* child," she said. She wiped away tears. "All of those poor women. I've read the news over and over and I could have lost you and Haley... I can't even—"

"You didn't lose us," I said firmly. "I know how easy it is to get trapped in that thought cycle, because I've been in it. But we survived. She survived. Is this why you've been mad at me?"

Honey shook her head, more tears falling. "I was scared, Sarah. And it wasn't fair, but all of the fear and anger fell on you. The last few months, I've been so damn mad. I've felt like he took everything from us and then *I* failed you."

"But he didn't," I said. "And you didn't fail me. I didn't listen to you because I couldn't hear you. By the time I realized that David was bad, it was too late. He had all of our finances wrapped up. I didn't know how to stand on my own. He beat me down over the years, twisting my view of myself and others. I thought I was lucky to be with him. I thought he was generous for even letting me work." I scoffed. Shame, guilt, and rage mixed together into a painful tonic. "I hate myself for that. I hate myself so much. I'm trying to heal from it all and forgive myself, but it's hard. The only thing I did right was work and protect the boys. I was so weak."

"You were not *weak*," she said. "You were never weak, Sarah. Ever."

"I feel like I was." The tears came faster as a sob broke free. I looked away, clutching my coffee mug and trying to pull myself back together. I'd failed everyone around me, and that still sat on my shoulders. I closed my eyes for a moment, acknowledging the emotion like Brenda had taught me. One day, I'd forgive myself. "I failed everyone. Including you."

She took a deep breath and squeezed my hands. "You didn't fail me, Sarah. I'm sorry I haven't been there for you these last few months. I'm sorry I didn't talk to you about how I was feeling. I still make mistakes, even after all these years."

"Me too," I whispered, holding onto her. "I want a fresh start. I want to be happy. I want the boys to be happy. They've been through so much, Honey. I worry about them."

"They're going to be okay," she said. "Kids are resilient. They have a strong mama. They have a whole family looking out for them."

I nodded, feeling myself breathe clearly. The weight was starting to disappear. "They do."

We sat there for a few long seconds, soaking up all that we'd said. I sniffled and let out a groan, wiping my eyes. "I swear I've cried more this year than ever before."

"Tears are healing," she said, shaking her head. "Did I hear you say David was let go, or did I imagine that?"

"David is out. They didn't find him guilty of concealment. He got a good lawyer who convinced the jury he was just as innocent as me."

"That son of a bitch."

"Everyone is on the lookout for him. I don't think he'll come back here. I have the restraining order in place. But just in case, be careful."

"I have a shotgun with his name on it."

"*Honey*," I rasped, trying not to laugh.

She mumbled a curse and I raised a brow at her. The only

person who might hate David Connor more than me or Haley or even Cam was her.

She got up and came around the table, wrapping her arms around me in a hug. After my mom died, she'd raised me and Haley. She'd been there for us ever since I could remember, even through the grief of losing a child. She wasn't just our grandmother, she'd stepped in as our mother too. Back then, I didn't understand how much she'd done for us. As an adult, I certainly knew.

I hadn't realized how much I'd missed my Honey over the last few months.

The timer for the casserole rang and she kissed the top of my head. "I think we should have some lunch and you can tell me what else has been going on."

"What do you mean?" I asked.

"Sarah Bently. You really think after all this time I can't recognize that there's someone putting light in your eyes?"

My cheeks turned red. "It's a secret for now."

Honey snorted and wiped away my tears. "Fine. Better be a damn good one."

"It is." I smiled, thinking about Colt and Sammy. "It really is."

CHAPTER FIFTEEN

A KNOCK ECHOED from the front door and I cursed, pulling my hand off my cock. I was so hard and so fucking close —I was ready to fight whoever the hell had interrupted.

If it were Cam, he would have just walked in. So that meant it was someone else.

Which meant I didn't care.

I started to stroke myself again, grunting as I thought about Sarah.

Knock, knock, knock.

"Son of a bitch," I rasped.

I was so fucking close.

I groaned and cursed as I got out of bed and threw on my jeans, tucking my cock in my waistband. I was shirtless, but didn't care as I stalked down the hall to the front door and yanked it open.

Sammy's hand braced against the doorframe. He looked down at me, his eyes widening as he took me in.

Seeing that expression certainly didn't help my hard-on.

I cleared my throat. "Not the person I expected."

"Who were you expecting?" he asked.

"Not you."

Sammy sighed and rubbed the back of his neck. "We need to talk."

It was apparently the day for it. After I'd had breakfast with Sarah, I'd come home and stared at the ceiling, grinning like an idiot. It had gone perfectly. For the first time in years, I felt like I could shed the pain of the past.

Now, there was a new problem. My stomach did a slow flip as I stepped aside.

"Come on. You're letting the cold air in," I mumbled.

He stepped inside and I shut the door behind us. I snatched a sweater off the back of a barstool and pulled it over my head. His gaze pinned on me, heating my blood.

"Shoot," I told him.

"I want Sarah."

I blew out a breath and crossed my arms.

"I asked her if she was interested in you, and she said yes."

"I asked her the same," I said. "And I told her if you make her happy, then she should date you."

He raised a brow. "Really?"

"Yeah," I said. "And to date me too..."

"I see."

We studied each other, having some sort of silent dick measuring contest over Sarah.

"I want her, Colt, and I'm not backing down. So you're gonna have to be fine with me too."

"Or what?" I bit out.

I could have told him I'd assured her I was fine with this situation, but something about the heat in his gaze was riling me up. He closed the distance between us in one long stride. I stood my ground, looking up at him. Once again, I felt the tension, the heat, the desire creeping up my spine—unbidden and inappropriate given this was *Sammy*.

His cheeks turned red. Unlike the other day in his kitchen, I knew he was blushing for me now. Nerves rattled through me, twisted with curiosity and longing.

"I'm going to date her," I said. "I don't care what you have to say."

"What if I said I'm glad you are? That I'm fine with it?"

I put my hands on my hips. "What if I told her something similar?"

All of that tension boiled down into a hot simmering need. His shoulders relaxed slightly as he searched my gaze.

"I have a friend in Austin who's polyamorous," he said. "She has healthy relationships with three people. She's married to one of them, and they opened their relationship, and now have two other partners. Good boundaries. They're happy. Have been for years. They love each other."

"And?"

"Why can't we do something like that?"

I'd thought about it, hadn't I? In brief moments where I'd then decided it was too damn wild.

Why couldn't we?

I wasn't sure what Sarah would think about it. But given that I'd told her I was fine with her seeing Sammy too, and her reaction...maybe she would be.

I wasn't against it...

Everyone else would be.

"Everyone in Citrus Cove would judge us," I said softly. "Because..."

"I'm not saying you have to love me or want me. I'm just saying we don't have to fucking duel over Sarah like two lone cowboys having a standoff."

"Shouldn't she get a say in this?" I asked. "I mean, earlier when I told her it wouldn't bother me if she saw you too, she seemed happy. But I don't know... I don't know."

"Of course. But I wanted to talk to you."

"Why?"

"Because I want Sarah. But I want you too."

Fuck. My heart thundered in my chest. I grabbed his shirt, pushing him back until he tripped and landed on the sofa. He pinned me with his stormy gaze.

"You and I can't," I snapped.

I raked my fingers through my hair, trying to push away the thoughts of *why not?*

I couldn't do this. If things went south, then I'd lose my only family. Not to mention, I wasn't sure how Sarah would react if I was her boyfriend and he was too and I wanted him... fuck.

I wanted this so fucking much that it was hard to breathe, but acting on my desire put it all at risk.

"We're not doing this," I said firmly. "We can't. It's too much."

"Why?"

"Because you're my best friend's brother." I felt like I was trying to keep my footing on quicksand. "Because..."

I was at a loss for words as he sat up, his mouth level with my cock. Every single thought went up in smoke, vaporized by the way his lips tugged into a soft smile.

All my blood rushed *down.* I strained against my zipper.

"You're my brother's best friend," he said slowly, reaching for my belt. "But I don't see why that makes a difference."

"Because this could get messy," I rasped.

I bit my lip as he undid my buckle, the metal clinking. His fingers were long and nimble. My gaze raked up his forearms, to the butterfly tattoo I liked so much. I fought to find the voice of reason for us.

"Your parents are my family. Your brothers are my family. I have no one else."

"I'm not here to take them away." He scowled. "Let's make a deal with each other."

"Fuck, Sammy. What the fuck?" My question came out in a whisper as he pulled my belt free.

My cock strained harder. I was fighting every instinct from taking over as I breathed him in, drinking in his expression and the fire crackling in his gaze.

"I've never been with a guy before," he said. "But I saw the way you looked at me at dinner last week. And before that."

"Then why now?" I choked out. "Why are you doing this now?"

"Because of Sarah."

Something about that made me pause.

If we were going to be together, it had to be for us. Not for someone else.

I reached down and grabbed his wrist before he could undo the button. I held him firmly, my breaths shallow. Fuck, it was hard to think straight.

"No," I finally said. "No. If we're going to fuck, it'll be for us. Not for someone else, not even Sarah. If you want to be with me, then I'll break you in. I'll show you the ropes. But I'm not a toy."

The hurt was sharp and fast. I took a step back from him as if I'd been stung.

He rubbed the stubble along his jaw. "Fuck. Colt, that's not what I meant by any of this."

"Are you sure?" I asked. I looked away, my blood still pumping. This wasn't the first time I'd felt like this, but it was the first time it hurt this badly. "I'm bisexual. When I came out,

I was kicked out of the house. Your own parents were there for me and kept a roof over my head."

His eyes widened.

"That's why I lived with y'all when I was seventeen. Not only did I lose my family, I also lost Sarah. Something changed between us. For the longest time, I thought she knew somehow and hated me for it. That was wrong, though."

"Fuck," he whispered. "I didn't know. I didn't realize."

"No one but Cam and your parents knew. I might be open with my sexuality, but that's not an open invitation for sex. You're my friend, Sammy. We might not be close the way I am with Cam, but this isn't right. I want you, but not if it means I'm risking anything."

Sammy stood up and took a step toward me. He reached out, cupping my jaw gently and facing me to look at him. "I'm sorry," he said with conviction. "I am deeply sorry that came out the way it did. I don't think you are a toy or an experiment. I thought I would come over here and try to smooth things over about Sarah, but then I got in my head that maybe the three of us could try something different because I *am* attracted to you too. I've had a crush on you and I thought I was losing my mind, but I realized there could be a spark here."

He began to pull away, but I slid my hand over his, holding him in place. I closed my eyes, breathing in his scent. He relaxed and leaned down, his forehead pressing to mine.

"I might be a little nuts for even suggesting this," he whispered. "I'm sorry if I made you uncomfortable."

I kept my eyes closed for a moment, mulling it all over. It felt like a dream, the idea of being with him and Sarah. It turned me on. All of the jealousy that had been plaguing me for the last week rolled into raw desire.

Could we make it work?

Did I want to try?

127

He was my friend. I'd known him since he was learning to walk. We'd grown up together, seen each other through every awkward stage of life, had slept under the same roof countless times.

The sparks were flying, but my greatest fear was they'd burn down everything I had.

His lips were almost brushing mine, though.

His hands were hot.

His body was so close.

"Sammy," I whispered. "You better swear to me that if we fuck up, I won't lose everything."

"I swear," he said.

I sucked in a shaky breath and finally looked at him.

Good god, this man had beautiful fucking eyes.

"I promise."

"Okay. Fuck it. Kiss me, Sammy Harlow."

I wasn't sure who closed the gap. Maybe it was him, maybe it was me, but the moment our lips touched, I melted. Every concern, every fear—it all walked out the door as I curled my fingers in his shirt and yanked him close.

His stubble was rough against my face in a way that made me want to put him on his knees. He groaned against me as our tongues fought for dominance.

I really didn't know who would win.

I broke the kiss to catch my breath. He was panting and a little shaky. I drew him back into another kiss, this one slower. Deeper with the occasional lip bite.

The things I want to do with him.

The things I wanted to do with Sarah between us...

I ran my hand down his chest and over the bulge in his jeans. He grunted, thrusting into my palm.

"Fuck, you're hard," I whispered, kissing down his neck.

I walked him back to the sofa and shoved, sitting him down

again but this time with more force. His eyes lit up as he leaned back, his bottom lip a little swollen.

I straddled him. He grabbed the hem of my shirt and lifted it, tossing it to the floor.

Sammy let out a low whistle. "Someone hits the gym."

I unbuttoned the top of my jeans as he leaned forward, the two of us kissing as he grabbed my ass. *Fuck.* Need shot through me as he pushed my jeans down, gripping me hard. He grunted, rocking me over his erection.

"What the actual fuck?"

My blood turned cold and I practically flew off Sammy's lap. I hit the floor hard and looked up at Cam standing in the doorway to the house.

His expression was pure shock. He doubled over and planted his hands on his knees, squinting at the two of us as he breathed hard. "Am I seeing things? What the fuck did I just walk in on?!"

"Do you always walk in without knocking?!" Sammy yelled.

"Yeah, because that's my best friend!" he growled at Sammy, pointing at me.

"Cam," I said. I could barely speak. "I can explain."

He pointed at Sammy. "That's my fucking brother!"

"For fuck's sake. Can you go back outside and give us a minute?" Sammy growled.

Cam turned paler than a ghost and grabbed the front door, slamming it shut. The walls shook as silence settled over us.

I sighed and laid back on the cold floor, spreading out.

Fuck.

Sammy rubbed his face and then peeked at me through his fingers. "I'll go talk to him."

"Okay," I said. "I need a minute."

He got up and adjusted his clothes and leaned down. He

cupped the back of my neck and pulled me into a seated position, kissing me again.

"Dammit," I breathed.

"I don't regret a single thing," he said.

Sammy let out a soft hum and released me. He darted out the front door and shut it behind him, leaving me alone to pull myself together.

CHAPTER SIXTEEN

DAMN SMALL TOWNS. Damn having an older brother. And damn nobody knocking in this damn family.

My head was still spinning from what had happened between Colt and I. The possibility that I might have a chance to be with him and Sarah made me feel a lot of things, all of them good.

I shut the door to Colt's house behind me and crossed my arms. My older brother was sitting on the steps of the front porch. He turned slightly, looking up at me. He wore a brown jacket and jeans with boots, his eyes wide like he's seen a ghost.

I sat down next to him. "You weren't supposed to see that."

"Yeah, I agree," he said.

I took a deep breath, trying to process it all. I was still in a whirlwind of a headspace. One moment, I'd had Colt in my lap, hard and ready—the next, my *brother* was walking in on us.

Cam let out a soft scoff. "*Colt?* Out of all people. And I thought he wanted Sarah... God, I'm fucking confused as hell right now."

"This is new," I said. "Like as in—you just walked in on our first kiss. Why didn't you knock?"

"Because I saw your car in the drive and this was the last thing I thought I'd walk in and find. I'm sorry I did, for myself and for the two of you. And for the record, I'm not mad. Just shocked." He sighed and pressed his lips into a line. He threw his hands up, looking at me. "I didn't know you were into guys?"

"Yeah," I said. "I am."

He nodded slowly. I could see him recalling everything he knew about me and all the moments I'd definitely been checking out a guy instead of a girl.

"How come you never told me?"

I winced. This was one of those things the entire family would have expected to know about me, but sometimes I liked to keep my life private. I didn't know how to say that without hurting his feelings. "I don't know what to say, Cam," I said. "I don't go around telling you when I sleep with a woman. So I guess..."

"You don't go around telling any of us anything. Sometimes I learn things about you from your videos online first."

I didn't know what to say. I sighed and grit my teeth as a cold wind hit us.

"Whatever Colt and I decide to do, it has nothing to do with you," I said. "And I want to keep it that way. I don't want to do anything that might hurt your friendship."

"Sammy, I love you, but you'd have to pry my friendship with him out of my cold, dead hands. I thought he loved Sarah. And then Haley told me you took Sarah out on a date. So quite honestly, I am so fucking confused right now."

"He does love her," I said. "And I did take her on a date."

"Then I'm even more confused?"

I was quiet for a moment, not sure what to say. "We're still figuring it out," I said. "If we can just have some space to do so..."

"Okay. Alright. I hear you." He blew out a slow breath and clapped his hands on his thighs. "I'm going to go say bye to Colt and then get out of the way. I'll talk more to you both later."

I nodded as he stood and clapped my shoulder.

I looked up at him when he paused.

"So, I'm gonna say this once. But if you hurt my best friend, I'm gonna have to fist fight you. Understood?"

"Understood," I said.

"Now, I'm going to go give him the same threat. Then I'm going home to wash my eyes out, have a drink, and tell my wife everything."

I snorted as he went inside. I could hear the rumble of him and Colt talking, but couldn't make out their conversation. The sky was dark gray, clouds hanging low over the fields around the house. I focused on the scenery, wondering if we'd get ice soon. I hoped not.

Eventually, Cam came back outside down the porch steps. "I'll see you later," he said. "Love you."

"Don't tell anyone," I called as he unlocked his truck. "Love you too."

He mimicked a key locking his lips, even though we knew that lock didn't include Haley. I sat there as he backed out of the driveway, turned around in the grass, and sped off.

This was a disaster.

So much for secrets.

I should have known better than to think we could keep this from everyone else. It wasn't that I wanted to hide it, but I didn't know what was happening yet. Everything was so new.

In my wildest dreams, I hoped I could be with them both. It

was slowly but surely hitting me that I was polyamorous, which meant I needed to do some more reading. When I'd met Rosie years ago and we'd chatted about it, I'd always found it interesting.

But it made sense to me that someone could love more than one person. And it made sense that someone could be loved by more than one person too.

"Are you going to sit out here and freeze or are you coming in for some dinner?" Colt asked.

I twisted around to look at him. His eyes sparkled with mischief despite what had just happened. The back of my neck went hot as I thought about him straddling me again.

"Dinner," I said. "But let's go to my apartment. I have all the cookware."

"What—you think I don't have cookware?"

I raised a brow at him and he held up his hands.

"Fine. Does that mean you're cooking?"

"Yeah," I said, fighting a smile. "Wine and dine, and all that... I'll drive us."

"Should I meet you there? What about when I leave?"

My cheeks flushed. I'd thought about that and maybe hoped he'd stay.

Maybe I was rushing this.

"I can bring you back later," I said. "Or in the morning, before your date with Sarah..."

He nodded. "Alright, then. Give me a few to change and get my boots on."

"I'll warm up the car," I said.

I got in and turned it on, blasting the heat while I waited for him. I pulled out my phone and opened up my phone, scrolling the recent notifications from the pizza-making video. Most of the comments were positive this time. I scrolled through until one made me stop.

You got blood on your hands and I know it.

What the fuck? I scowled, my palms turning sweaty as I stared at the comment. What were they talking about? I started to click on their profile, but I heard the door slam and looked up.

Colt headed to the car. He wore a burgundy sweater that looked good against his tan skin and blonde hair, paired with dark wash jeans and boots. I tucked my phone away, making a note to delete the comment later.

He got in and gave me an easy smile. "You okay? You look pale."

"Just read a stupid comment," I said. I reached over and turned down the air.

Colt frowned. "Do you deal with a lot of shit?"

"Yeah. But it's fine. Comes with the job." Although someone saying I had blood on my hands was new.

"I guess I've never really thought about it. It seems like a lot to constantly have to read comments like that. Have you thought about having someone manage your socials?"

"It's not too bad," I said. "I mean, I've been told a lot of bad things, but no one on the internet knows the real me. I try not to let it affect me."

"Hmm. I can start fighting people in the comments if you want."

I chuckled. "That would just make it worse. But thank you."

We kept chatting as I drove to my apartment. My stomach danced with butterflies—a mix of nerves, lust, and excitement. This would be the second time Colt was in my apartment, and now it was for a reason that made my heart hammer.

No one else ever really came over. I always went to everyone else's home when we had get-togethers. What Cam had said about not knowing me stuck with me for a moment.

It wasn't intentional... well, maybe it was. I had a tendency to keep to myself unless I was working at the winery, but with that gone, I'd been focusing on making content and music. Hunter had been working the farm with Pops, keeping everything going smoothly despite his clear distaste for it all.

I couldn't blame him. Of the three of us, Cam had always been the one most interested in the Harlow family farm. The vineyard had sparked his passion, which eventually turned into him and Colt opening the winery that also focused on small-batch ciders.

"You think louder than Sarah does when she's stewing," Colt said.

"I'm thinking about something Cam said," I sighed. "He said no one knows me."

Colt was quiet. I glanced over at him with a frown.

"Is he right?" I asked.

"I mean, we all know you. But you kind of keep things to yourself. I know what you do, but don't know much else. Like who are your friends? You mentioned your polyamorous friend."

"Rosie, yeah. She's a lawyer I met through a cooking class. I don't know. I don't have a lot of friends outside of town or the family, to be honest. And I spend a lot of time online, probably more than I should. Maybe I'm just boring."

Colt snorted. "You're not boring. Far from it, really. I always thought you were the bookish type. I mean, Cam and I would always have to drag you outside."

I smiled, thinking back to a time when we were younger. He was right, he and Cam had always pulled me outside to play even though I was a few years younger than them.

"Even though I've known you my whole life, I feel like I'm just now meeting you," Colt said. "So I can see why Cam was shocked. For more than one reason."

"Did he give you a hard time?"

"He will later," Colt sighed. "And he should. But he wasn't mad, just shocked. He's as straight as they come. I remember when I came out to him."

"What was that like?"

I felt his gaze on me. "He thought someone in my family had died because I was crying so hard. I'd kissed a boy for the first time at a party, and Sarah had stopped talking to me. I found out years later that she saw us."

"Oh," I said, frowning. I pulled into the parking lot of the apartment complex. "Was she upset by that?"

"She was hurt he wasn't her."

"When did you tell her?" I asked.

"On her wedding day."

My brows shot up. I turned the car off. "Alright, I want to hear more about this once we get inside. I think I'll make us some chili and cornbread."

"Hell yeah."

"It'll have veggies in it."

He wrinkled his nose as we both got out. "If you insist."

I grinned and led him up the steps to my apartment. My grin broke as I saw my door standing ajar.

My heart skipped a beat. "What the fuck?"

Colt grabbed my forearm nervously. "We should call the police."

I shook my head and bumped the door with my foot, opening it completely.

My apartment was trashed. Blood drained from my face as I stepped past the threshold. All of my equipment was thrown across the floor—thousands of dollars worth of shit. My kitchen was wrecked. My guitar was busted.

"Fuck." I didn't know what else to say.

"I'm calling," Colt said quickly. "Don't touch anything."

I shook my head again. I couldn't speak.

"*Sammy,*" Colt said again, snapping my attention to him. "It's going to be okay."

This time, I nodded at him. Blood rushed in my ears as he made the call. All I could do was stand there, wondering who could have done this.

CHAPTER SEVENTEEN

sammy

I STEPPED INTO THE APARTMENT. Tears sprang to my eyes as I took in the damage. Both of my guitars were smashed over the hardwood. I rubbed the ache in my chest as I stared at the one I'd had since I was a teen.

"Fuck," I whispered.

"I'm so sorry, Sammy," Colt said. "We'll find who did this."

I nodded numbly. Footsteps echoed outside, and Colt and I looked up.

"Sarah," he said. "What are you doing here?"

Sarah. He stepped aside as she poked her head through the door, her eyes widening.

She shook her head and she surveyed the damage, as shocked as the two of us were. "What happened? I was just coming by to drop off some baked goods, but oh my god."

I drew in a shaky breath and wiped my eyes. "Someone broke in. I don't know why. Fuck, they smashed my guitars."

"Don't touch anything," Colt said quickly. "Police are on the way."

I stepped over some of the broken pieces to the doorway

and slumped against it. Sarah put down a bag she was holding and surprised me by pulling me into a hug. I wrapped my arms around her, meeting Colt's gaze.

It certainly wasn't jealousy shining there now.

Sarah turned to look at Colt as he hung up the phone, shoving it into his pocket.

"Not the time to ask," she said. "But I am a little curious what the two of you are doing together."

My cheeks warmed. Did she know about what we had done? Did she know we kissed? There was no way she would know unless Cam told Haley and Haley told her and... I could see the same questions in Colt's gaze, but he nodded.

"We'll talk later," he said. "Sammy, who could've done this?"

"That woman from the movie theater?" Sarah asked.

Colt raised a brow. "*What* woman?"

"There was someone taking pictures of Sammy after he asked her to stop. Like an online stalker?"

"I don't know," I sighed. "Maybe? I just know that it looks like everything I own is ruined."

The three of us waited for the police to show up. My life was being pulled into the middle of a hurricane, and there was no way out. Sarah slipped her arm around my waist, her brows pinched.

"You have glitter on your eyelids," I murmured.

She blushed and looked at Colt. He smiled at her. "She looks gorgeous," he said.

She sighed. "You always say that."

"He's right, though," I said.

"Okay, both of you, straight to jail."

I grinned. I was thankful they were here with me. In the face of all the destruction, I didn't feel alone. "What did you bake, angel?" I asked.

"I made pumpkin bread," she said.

God, was it too soon to propose?

"I also baked a couple other things and brought you recipe cards." She looked up at Colt. "I might be convinced to give you some too, if you're interested."

He leaned against the doorframe. "I'm always interested. We were going to have dinner together. You can join if you want."

"Oh," she said.

"We were gonna talk about you," I said.

Her cheeks turned pink. Before she could respond, an officer hit the top step, a little winded.

"Oh good, you made it," Colt said flatly to him.

"Yes. Whose apartment?"

"Mine," I sighed.

This certainly wasn't the way I expected to spend my evening. Far less fun than getting to know Colt more.

I spent the next hour talking with the officers as they went through my apartment, trying to figure out exactly what happened. It sounded like the door had been kicked in. So much for the locks.

The good news was that ever since Thomas Connor, security around the town had increased. They'd installed security cameras around the apartments.

The bad news was they'd been turned off when this happened. Without any footage, they started questioning neighbors, which meant everyone in Citrus Cove now knew that my apartment had been broken into.

I wasn't shocked to see my entire family waiting for me in the parking lot.

"We'll let you know if we find anything else, but right now we don't have much to go on," the officer said. "You mentioned you have an online platform. Could people have found you from there?"

I nodded, feeling numb. "Maybe."

I thought about the comment I saw earlier, about there being blood on my hands. Could that have been related to this? I got all sorts of comments though, and it was hard to keep up with ones that might have any merit. For the most part, I had keywords flagged so certain things wouldn't appear, but... maybe was time to look at those closer.

"It's a small town," he said. "We'll take a look at the motels and see if anyone fits the description of the woman you mentioned from last Saturday. If they've been here that long, they'll have been noticed."

He had a point. "Thanks," I said.

"Do you have insurance?"

"Yeah," I said, rubbing my temples. This was a nightmare. "I'll start sorting things out tomorrow."

I needed a beer, hot shower, food, and...

My gaze flickered to Sarah and Colt.

After finishing my conversation with one of the officers, I headed down stairs to where everyone waited. All eyes fell on me.

"I'm okay," I announced.

Mom gave me a hug first, squeezing me tight. "You scared me."

"I'm fine," I said. "Really. I wasn't home when this happened. Everything is okay."

"It's good you weren't," she said. "God, your brother scared the shit out of me with his call."

Hunter gave me a hug next and then glanced upstairs. "I'm going to go be nosy. We'll figure out who did this. You sure you're okay?"

"Yeah," I said. "I would tell you if I wasn't."

He seemed doubtful.

Pops clasped my shoulder and pulled me into a hug. He used to squeeze the life out of me, but as he got older, his hugs had become more gentle. I towered over him now.

Cam and Haley were standing with Sarah and Colt, speaking quietly. I wanted to join them, but I needed my parents to go home. I couldn't worry about them. Now that they knew I was safe, I doubted it would take much pushing.

"Y'all don't need to be here," I told my parents. "It'll take a while and I'm not hurt. I'll come over tomorrow morning."

"Surely you're not sleeping here," Mom protested. "You can't. It's not safe."

I felt the weight of everyone worrying about me and while I knew they meant well, I wanted to hide away and mourn the loss of my guitars, my equipment, and the safety of my home. "I'll stay with someone," I said. "I'd feel better if you were both at home."

Pops nodded and slid his arm around Mom. "We'll go. Keep us updated, okay?"

"I will," I promised. "I love you both."

Mom nodded and blinked back tears as the two of them headed for their car.

Hunter came back down the stairs with a grim expression and kept his voice out of earshot of everyone else.

"When were you going to tell me you were being stalked?" he asked.

Fucking hell. There was no such thing as a secret.

"I wasn't sure I was," I said.

Although the signs had certainly been there.

I'd told the officers about the incident outside the theater on Saturday. The neighbors hadn't noticed anything out of the ordinary, though one person claimed they heard a loud bang earlier, but assumed it was nothing.

Hunter scowled. "You didn't mention anything at all. Also, what the hell were you doing at the movies with Sarah and her kids? Since when do you babysit?"

"None of your business," I snapped.

He crossed his arms, taking on that older brother stance I knew all too well. "I'm trying to help. You're being a dick."

"You're being nosy. I already told the police everything," I said. "I was coming home to have dinner. Everyone keeps *interrupting*. It could have been a stranger, you know? It may not even be connected."

Before he could argue further, Haley intervened. I was grateful for my sister-in-law as she gave me a hug. With her gravitating to the two of us, Colt, Sarah, and Cam followed. The six of us made a small circle.

"I'm sorry this happened," Haley said. "Does everyone want to come over for dinner? We can grab whatever you need if you want to stay at our house."

"You can stay at mine instead if you would rather," Colt said casually.

Only Cam gave him a *look*. Then, he looked at me. Haley noticed it too and narrowed her gaze on her husband, and his ears turned red.

Sarah frowned at her sister.

"Yeah," I said quickly, trying to smooth over the moment. "You have a spare bedroom?"

"I do," he said.

"I'd offer you my house, but you'd be on the couch," Sarah said, glancing at Colt.

He smiled. "It's a pretty comfy couch, though."

She smiled back. Fuck, I loved when she smiled. Even if it wasn't at me.

Silence settled over us and Hunter threw his hands up. "Alright, then. Everyone is being fucking weird today."

"Maybe it's just you," I teased.

He rolled his eyes. "Right. I'm going to get more info. Where do we want to meet?"

"I just want some dinner and a movie tonight," I said. "I don't want this to be a big deal."

"It is a big deal. I want to make sure my baby brother isn't in danger from some psycho," he countered.

"We're not doing this right now," I said. "I need some time to breathe."

"I'm trying to—"

"I said no, Hunter," I snapped.

He walked off before I could say anything else and I cursed. Now I felt bad.

"Can I have a minute with Sammy?" Cam asked.

Haley frowned. "Yeah. We'll be over there."

He stole a kiss from her before she could walk off. Colt and Sarah followed, the three chatting about the cold.

"Are you okay?" Cam asked.

"Hunter is driving me insane," I sighed. "I know he's trying to help, but he's smothering me. I just had all of my shit broken and I'm mad and worried, but I don't need him to tell me what to do. I'll be fine."

"We're all worked up given what happened last year and the fact that David is out. I think he's probably concerned that it could be connected. I'm not going to lie, I'm frightened too, Sammy. We all love you."

I sighed, letting it sink in. Logically, I knew that, though I was still frustrated. "I know you love me. I love all of you too. I just need some space to sort through all of this."

He nodded. "You know you're always welcome in our house. Always."

"I know." I finally felt my shoulders relax a fraction. "All of this worries me. Because if it was that woman from the other day, she might have pictures of the kids, Sarah, and her car's license plate. Especially considering someone fucked up her car and that's why it wasn't working."

Cam's eyes bugged out. "*What?*"

Ah, fuck.

He turned around before I could stop him. "Sarah, someone fucked with your car?"

Haley and Colt both looked at her and she glared at me.

Sorry, I mouthed.

"That doesn't matter right now," Sarah said quickly. "Everything is fine."

Colt shook his head. "Alright. One problem at a time. Sammy, what can we grab from your apartment?"

"Let me see if my laptop still works," I sighed. "And if my clothes aren't shredded."

"Can I have dinner with you and Colt?" Sarah asked. "Haley, do you mind? I can text Emma—"

"We got them," Haley said. "Don't worry about them for the night."

"The *night*?"

"Yeah, you heard me. Whatever is going on here, I want to hear about it later."

Colt and I turned scarlet. Sarah's mouth fell open.

Haley pointed at Cam. "Yep. You and me, cowboy, let's go."

"Alright, sunshine," he said. "Sammy, we love you, I'm sorry this happened. If anything else happens, call us. We'll get out of your hair."

I watched the two of them head for his truck and shook my head.

"Back to my house we go," Colt said.

I nodded. It was the only place I wanted to be right now.

CHAPTER EIGHTEEN

sarah

WHAT WAS I DOING?

The question rattled through me as I parked between Sammy's car and Colt's truck. Colt had a stupid smirk on his face as he opened the door for me, the same dopey one that always made me fall in love with him for a second.

So much had happened today and I was doing my best to process my feelings. Being with the two of them together made me nervous as hell. "Can I help grab anything?" I asked.

Sammy and Colt shook their heads as they got a few totes from Sammy's apartment out of the back of the truck. I couldn't help but narrow my eyes on them, watching how they carefully avoided each other like two opposing magnets.

There was tension between the two of them, and it had nothing to do with the apartment break in.

I had half a mind to text Haley to ask her *why* she'd told me I could be gone for the whole night. I wasn't sure I'd ever had a night away from the boys since they were born.

The three of us climbed the steps to the porch. Colt opened the door and we stepped inside, kicking off boots and tennis shoes. Colt eyed my worn shoes with a hum and I winced internally. They were looking rough.

What am I doing? I asked myself again.

Sammy carried the tote down the hall to a spare bedroom, followed by Colt. I stood there, wondering if I should stay or follow or *god* I didn't know how to do this.

"I got things we can cook," Colt called from the room. He emerged like a lanky golden god, his eyes softening on me.

All I could do was nod.

He surprised me by prowling down the hall straight toward me, only stopping once I craned my head back to look at him.

"I promise we won't bite," he whispered. "Unless you want us to, of course."

"Okay, vampire," Sammy teased as he came up behind him. "I'll cook."

"You can use whatever you want," Colt said. "Just don't judge me for anything with mold on it."

Sammy and I both snorted.

"I will judge you," I said.

Colt scrunched his face playfully. "Where's the goods?"

"Here," I said, holding up the bag I'd brought from home.

He snatched it from me and skipped playfully to the kitchen.

"Excuse me. Those were for me, if I recall correctly," Sammy protested.

"Mmhm." Colt dug into the bag and pulled out the loaf of pumpkin bread first. I leaned on the edge of the bar and watched the two of them playfully fight over it.

Sammy reached around him, but Colt kept moving the bread out of his grip. I felt like I was imposing on something private, yet I couldn't pull my gaze away. I couldn't stop the way every thought short circuited with the desire to be right there between them.

Sammy pinned Colt to the counter. "Give me the loaf."

"No," he quipped playfully. "It's mine now."

Sammy pressed his body to Colt's, his gaze flickering up to mine.

Fuck. I swallowed hard, heat flooding me as I watched him press his mouth to Colt's ear, saying something low that I couldn't hear but had him blushing hard.

"Bastard," he mumbled, giving up the loaf.

Sammy lingered for a moment, his gaze still on me. "You look pretty when you blush. Do you like watching us?"

My mouth fell open.

Sammy unwrapped the foil around the bread and opened up a drawer, pulling out a knife. He reached around Colt again and cut it into slices.

"Enjoy," Sammy said.

Colt's face was red. "You know, for someone who's typically a quiet mystery, you sure are dominant."

"Yeah," he said, stealing a slice of the bread. He bit into it and groaned. "I am. Now, get out of the kitchen while I cook."

"Yes, sir," Colt said. He grabbed two slices, a napkin, and winked at me as he headed for the couch. "Come sit with me."

"Are you sure you don't need help?" I asked.

Sammy nodded. "Absolutely. Go relax."

I hesitated. I wasn't used to being cooked for. My hands felt itchy, like they needed to stay busy and be useful. With a deep inhale, I joined Colt on the couch instead.

"Have you thought about baking things to sell?" he asked with a mouthful.

"Sort of," I laughed, shaking my head at him. "My god, you're a mess sometimes."

He winked. My heart skipped a beat.

"You should do it," Sammy called.

"I'd have to think about when," I said. "I'm not confident I have time to bake everything I'd like to. Or if people would even be interested."

"When we get the winery back up, you could have a food truck," he said. "It's something Cam and I are working into the plans. We were always missing more food options for folks, so we want a space for food trucks. We can support local businesses that way. What about Bently...hmmm..."

"Bently Bakery?" A tingle spread through me and I smiled. It felt right. "There's no way I could start a business right now."

"I bet we could help," Colt said, wiggling his brows. "I'll be the taste tester."

"Ah, I see." I laughed.

It would be a dream, though part of me was scared to say it aloud. The idea of having my own little shop excited me—but I wasn't sure I could make it happen. It was one of those things that I let myself imagine before falling asleep at night, or when I wanted to think about anything except real life.

"So," I said, clearing my throat. "Want to tell me what's going on with the two of you?"

Sammy looked up at Colt. He pressed his lips together. "I think we should wait to talk until we're eating."

I raised a brow, but didn't argue. Mostly because now I was very intrigued. I wondered if the two of them had decided they didn't want to be with me, or if—

No, that was absurd.

Colt placed his hand on my knee and gave me a gentle squeeze. I liked the feel of his hand and wanted more. I wanted a lot more.

"Too much?" he murmured.

"No," I whispered.

"Do you want to know what I did when I came home after this morning?"

"Yes."

"I thought about finally kissing you. Finally touching you..."

I squeezed my thighs and whispered, "What else?"

He raised a brow and leaned in to whisper in my ear. "Then I imagined you riding my cock. I stroked myself and would have come, but then Sammy knocked on my door."

Oh.

"Then what?" I asked.

He was quiet. I kept my voice low as I studied him. "Did you kiss him?"

"Yeah. Does that bother you?"

Even after all these years, he was still so shitty about having a poker face. He tried, but I could hear the vulnerability in his question. But the truth was, it did not bother me.

"No," I said. "It doesn't bother me at all. In fact..."

"Tell me," he whispered.

He was patient. Which was good, because I'd never said anything before about what I was thinking. That I wanted the two of them to be together, that I wanted them to be with me.

For the last few days, I saw them in my imagination every time I thought about reaching for my vibrator.

I'd known them for years. Even though Colton and I hadn't been close, he'd still been a constant in my life. I'd never forget him sleeping on the couch for days to make sure we felt safe after what happened to Haley. Even with Thomas dead and David in jail at the time, I'd barely been able to sleep.

I felt safe with them.

"I haven't been with someone in a long time," I said softly. "David didn't touch me very often after the boys because he thought my body was ruined."

"*What?*" Colt snarled.

Sammy dropped something in the kitchen, startling us. We both looked up. His brows were pulled together, his muscles rigid, mouth twisted into a fuming frown.

"He said that to you, Sarah?" Sammy asked.

"Yeah," I said, shrinking into the couch. "Sorry, I didn't mean to bring that up, I was just going to say it's been a long time for me. This is all new again."

"He was wrong," Colt said gently, giving Sammy a *look*.

Sammy blew out a breath and shook his head, leaving the kitchen. He leaned over the back of the couch, and planted a gentle kiss on the top of my head. "He was very wrong."

I closed my eyes, the ghost of his kiss lingering. Between these two, I was a goner.

How long had it been since someone desired me?

Could I even say anyone ever had? I didn't know if David had ever cared for me. I was used as a way for his brother to get to Haley.

"We'll take everything slow," Colt said.

I pressed my lips together. I wasn't sure I wanted to take it slow. I had needs and wants and I'd been putting it all on the back burner for so long.

"I have a night away from responsibilities," I said. "That hasn't happened in a long time. I don't want to go slow."

His nostrils flared and he hummed. His hand was still on my knee, his thumb tracing circles slowly over the thin denim. A shiver ran through me, causing my breath to catch.

"Dinner is ready."

I started to get up, but Colt shook his head. "I've got it, sugar."

I sighed in defeat and stayed put. I watched the two of them in the kitchen, feeling a bubbly sense of nerves and excitement. Colt brought our plates back and Sammy followed. He'd cooked up a stir fry with chicken and veggies and it smelled delicious.

"Not chili and cornbread, but it'll do."

"It smells great," Colt said.

"It does," I agreed. "Thanks for cooking."

"I'm sad to say that I don't have a dining table," Colt said as he handed me a plate. "I usually eat standing in the kitchen or on the couch."

Sammy wrinkled his nose. "I'd judge, but I do the same."

"We can sit on the floor, picnic-style?" I suggested.

I slid off the cushion and leaned my back against the sofa. Sammy sat on one side of me and Colt sat on the other, the three of us creating a circle.

"I'm interested in both of you," Sammy said bluntly.

Colt nearly choked. "Fuck, I guess we're getting right to it."

"Do you mean like the three of us dating each other?" I asked.

I'd read romance books like that. I used to sneak romance books at the grocery store and hide them in my glove compartment from David. Looking back, I was embarrassed I'd stayed with him as long as I did. But it was hard to see the end of the tunnel when you were in it.

"Yes," Sammy said. "I like Colt. I liked him before things started changing between us, but never acted on it because he's Cam's best friend."

"Well, that makes sense," I said.

Colt crossed his legs and balanced his plate on his thigh. "I have always wanted Sarah, as we all know. I think the whole town knows."

I offered him a soft smile.

"But I'm also interested in Sammy. Cam caught us kissing earlier before we went to his apartment."

"Oh god," I laughed. "No wonder he was being so weird earlier. Haley picked up on it too."

"I gathered." Colt shook his head. "Thankfully Emma wasn't there because she would have figured it out."

"Oh for sure. Emma knows all." I wiggled a brow. "What were you going to do after the kiss, if Cam hadn't interrupted?"

Sammy smirked. "Wouldn't you like to know?"

I laughed and nudged him. "In great detail."

"What if we talk about what we want to do with you?" Sammy countered.

Now it was my turn to feel flustered again. "Like what?"

"Is there anything in particular you like?" Colt asked.

I raised my brow. "Like...?"

"Spanking, flogging, things along those lines..."

Oh.

Oh.

"I've never done anything like that before..." I whispered.

"We don't have to go that far," Colt said quickly.

"No, I'm interested," I said. "I'm just new to this. It's exciting."

"Have you had any fantasies?" Sammy asked. "About trying anything? I'm dominant in the bedroom and like rope, blind folds, choking..."

Colt's eyes widened. "Really?"

Sammy winked at him and then focused his gaze on me. I was going to combust. How was this really my life? Two hot men who I'd known forever wanted to be with me in ways I'd never experienced.

"Alright, well since we're putting it all out there, I'm a kinky motherfucker," Colt said. "And I'm a slut. A huge slut."

My mouth fell open, for what I was sure wouldn't be the last time tonight.

"And I'm a switch, so that works out," he said, winking at Sammy. "Who would have known Sammy Harlow, the most mysterious and broody guy in Citrus Cove, was a Dom? Although, it makes sense. Unless you mean you're just bossy and don't know what being a Dom really entails."

Sammy's gaze darkened and he lifted a brow. "Taunting me, huh? No, I'll put you on your fucking knees and make you beg for my cock while our girl watches."

I squeaked. "Oh my *god*."

Colt smirked. "Eat your fucking dinner, Sammy Harlow. We'll see about everything else after."

CHAPTER NINETEEN

WATCHING Sarah get flustered by my interactions with Sammy made me grin. I liked seeing the rosy red blush creep over her soft cheeks.

My heart thumped louder. I was drunk on nerves and horniness from being in the same room with the two of them. The bi panic had gripped me and refused to let go.

I grabbed our empty plates and piled them in the sink. Sarah reached past me, but I grabbed her wrist before she touched any of the dishes, raising a brow.

"I don't think so."

"I'll wash them," she protested. "It's the least I can do."

"Nope. I don't want you lifting a finger, sugar."

She shook her head at me, but caved, her lips slowly pulling into a dry smile. "Fine, I guess. But when you come over to my house, I expect you to not help out."

I snorted. That wasn't going to happen. Doing tasks for her, no matter how small, satisfied me deeply. I didn't want her to do more work when she already did so much, especially on top of being a great mom to her boys.

I released her wrist and slid my fingers into her dark waves, intertwining them with the silky strands at the base of her head. I gave her a gentle tug. God, the way her eyes lit up. She was so damn beautiful. Her lips parted on a gasp as I pulled her close, her warmth melting me.

I could feel the weight of Sammy's gaze on us from the living room, almost urging me to kiss her. *Does he want us to? I want to.*

I'd been waiting to kiss her since I was seventeen.

Sarah's lashes fluttered, gaze lowering to my lips.

"I want to kiss you," I whispered.

A subtle nod. Without a word, she leaned up on her tiptoes and slid her mouth against mine. It was a gentle, tentative kiss— like being brushed by a butterfly. A soft moan escaped me and I kissed her again, harder this time. Deeper. She curled her fingers in my shirt and pulled me close, folding into me with an ease that felt so damn right after all this time.

Fuck. I was really kissing her.

I could drown myself in her. Her moan caught in my mouth as her arms wound around my neck. I backed her up against the counter, still gripping her hair as I devoured her. Blood rushed in my ears, my pulse skyrocketing as she arched against me. I *needed* more. Craved more.

Sammy's presence emerged behind me. I broke our kiss and turned my head. Our gazes locked for a moment and I nodded.

"Yes," I rasped.

His throat bobbed, his eyes darting to Sarah as I grabbed hold of Sarah's hips and turned, pulling her between us.

It was natural. It felt right.

Shadows danced over Sammy's face, his blue eyes bright with desire. "Is this alright?" he asked.

Her breath hitched. "Yes."

She leaned back against him, lashes fluttering as she tipped her head back, exposing her neck. I dipped down and slowly kissed the base of her throat, breathing in her scent like some wild animal. I couldn't get enough of her.

Sammy was tall enough to bend down and kiss her from that angle. Knowing it was their first kiss made my cock throb against my zipper. Every touch of his was tender, but I knew beneath it all was a raging current of lust.

"That feels good," she moaned.

I kissed down her throat and cupped her breast through her shirt. She rolled her hips between us. Sammy reached around and curled his fingers in my hair, pulling me into a deep kiss.

Fuck. I could kiss the two of them for the rest of my life. He nipped the bottom of my lip, the sting going straight to my cock. I groaned as Sarah slid her hand to my belt, and then to my zipper.

She stiffened between us. "You're both so hard."

Sammy released me, both of us breathless.

I swallowed hard, trying to catch my breath. I knew what I wanted, but didn't want to take this too fast. "Do you want to keep going?" I asked her. "Should we slow down?"

"No," she said immediately. "I want this. I want both of you."

"If you need us to stop, say red," he instructed. "Green means yes, yellow means slow down, red means stop. Okay?"

"Okay," she agreed.

He looked at me and I nodded. "Yes." I was all too familiar with the stop light system and I appreciated him using it here. Sarah hadn't been with anyone in so long, and neither one of us wanted to do something that might do more harm than good.

I wanted to give her all of the orgasms she'd been deprived of for the past decade.

Sammy clearly wanted the same. Between us, it was clear we'd make a damn good team.

"Come to the bedroom," I said, slipping my hand into hers.

Sammy took her other hand, the two of them kissing as I led us out of the kitchen, and down the hall to my bedroom. Once again, I was glad I'd invested in one of those massive king-sized beds because we'd have plenty of room. I also mentally patted myself on the back for having a big-ass mirror in the corner of the room. Seeing our reflections turned me on.

I flipped a switch and sconces on the wall splashed golden ambient light over us. I was surprised as Sammy pulled me to the middle—and I found myself kissing Sarah as he kissed my neck with an occasional bite. A shiver of need worked up my spine.

"Fuck," I groaned. "Bite me again."

He did as I asked, biting my neck harder. Sarah rubbed her palm over my hard on, her eyes widening. "Just how big are you?" She sounded concerned.

"I've got all the lube we need to make it work," I grunted.

Sammy rocked his hips against my ass as he bit hard enough to make me wince, the pain shooting straight to my cock. I needed more.

I'd lost count of how many people I'd been with over the years, but now they all paled in comparison to how it felt to be between Sarah and Sammy.

Sammy reached around and grabbed my belt buckle, undoing it quickly and pulling it off. It dropped to the floor with a thud as Sarah unbuttoned my jeans, her fingers nimble.

"If I knew any better, I'd say you both want me naked," I huffed.

Sarah gave me a determined smile and shocked the hell out of me as she started to drop to her knees.

Fuck.

"Wait," I said, cupping her face and stopping her. "Your

pleasure comes first. It's been too damn long since someone else worshiped you. Let us show you how we feel."

She went still and then nodded. "Okay," she whispered.

"Why don't you strip her for us?" Sammy murmured in my ear.

"Yes, sir."

I grabbed the hem of Sarah's blouse and pulled it up over her head. Her movements stiffened.

"What is it, angel?" Sammy asked gently, noting her body language too.

"I just... I have stretch marks and scars and..." Her voice hitched and my heart was ripped out of my chest by her words.

I'd hated David Connor for a long fucking time, but this was too much. I fell to my knees in front of her and ran my palms over her stomach. "Sugar, stretch marks are fucking sexy."

Sammy moved around to her other side and very gently pulled her blouse off entirely. "Look in the mirror," he murmured. "Watch us show you how much we want you. How much you mean to us."

I pressed my lips against one of the silvery marks over her stomach, kissing it. "You carried two children," I whispered. "At one time. I don't know how you fucking did it. But every one of these is a mark of love and strength. They're beautiful, Sarah."

I looked up as I kissed her stomach. How could I show her just how gorgeous she was? How everything in my life had revolved around her for so long, and being in her presence was a blessing?

I unbuttoned her jeans and pushed them over her hips. She started to tense, but Sammy carefully cupped his hand around her throat, murmuring in her ear as I pulled her jeans to the floor. She relaxed, her breath hitching as I dragged my tongue over her skin.

"Fuck," I breathed. Her panties were shell pink. I wanted to rip them off.

"I didn't shave or wax, I didn't—"

"Sarah, there's nothing that could make me not want to make you come right now," I rasped. "You're a fucking goddess."

"Spread your legs for him, angel," Sammy commanded.

She did as he said and I looped my finger through the band and pulled her underwear down. Fuck, I was in heaven. I'd died and gone to heaven.

"Make her come, Colt," Sammy said.

His soft command sent a wave of pleasure through me. It had been a long time since I'd allowed someone to take control, but I trusted him.

I caressed the back of her thigh and lifted her leg, draping it over my shoulder as I spread her pussy. Sarah gasped as I ran my fingers over her slit.

"You're so fucking wet," I whispered, in complete awe of her. "Ah, sugar. Fuck. Let me help you out."

I buried my face against her cunt, circling her clit with my tongue. Her throaty cry rang through the room. Sammy held her in place as I lapped at her like a starved man, *needing* her. I teased her entrance with a finger and then two, easing them inside of her.

"Fuck," she rasped. "*Please.*"

"Good girl," Sammy praised. "I sure like hearing you say 'please' like that."

I groaned against her, reveling in the taste of her pussy on my tongue. My cock throbbed against my zipper as I thrust my fingers into her. Her whimpers and mewls echoed through my bedroom, her body tensing as I kept going. I could stay down here for hours eating her out. Hell, I could stay on my knees in front of her forever.

I pulled my fingers out and looked up at Sammy, holding his gaze as I sucked our girl off my fingertips.

"Good boy," he whispered.

Fuck me. I made a sound somewhere between a growl and moan. I pressed my tongue against her clit again, circling her. She gasped and grabbed my head, completely giving in to the pleasure. I loved the possessiveness, the way her grip on me tightened. She wanted to come, and I wanted to make her come more than anything else.

Fuck, baby. Keep riding my face. She held me in place as she rocked against me, moving until another cry shot from her lips.

Making her come was enough to send me over the edge. *Fuck, fuck, fuck*—I gasped as I came in my jeans, hot pleasure shooting through me as I tasted her orgasm.

Sarah melted against Sammy, her chest rising and falling with heavy pants. I sat back on my haunches and licked my lips, looking down at myself. A wet spot spread over the denim.

No one had ever made me come like that before.

"That was a first," I said.

All Sarah could do was nod. She collapsed against Sammy as he reached around to tweak her nipples. Her eyes flew open, but he was fast. I grinned as he swept her off her feet and carried her to the bed.

"Oh my god," she hissed. "You just—you just lifted me like nothing—"

Sammy deposited her in the middle of the blankets and planted a kiss on her.

I licked my lips, still tasting her. My gaze pulled from them back down to my jeans. Damn. I'd really come in my pants for her.

And I'd do it again.

I got to my feet and unbuttoned my jeans, shucking them and my boxer briefs into a pile. My cock glistened with my cum.

"I'll clean you up," Sammy said. "If you want."

"We both can," Sarah offered.

"Then I'll have my turn at making Sarah come."

Well. How was I supposed to say no to that?

"We have the whole night," she said, bending her finger to beckon me to the bed.

"Okay, okay," I said.

Sarah moved over and I reluctantly crawled to the middle of the bed. Even though I'd just come, seeing the two of them sent a rush of new lust through me. Fucking hell. My heart spiked, my body craving their touch.

"Hey. Lose your clothes," I said to Sammy.

He sighed dramatically and rolled out of bed, stripping quickly. We watched with interest and *fuck*, he was big.

And he was fucking pierced.

"When the fuck did you do that?" I stammered.

A cocky grin appeared. "Couple years ago."

"Is that going to hurt?" Sarah asked, her eyes glued to the Prince Albert ring through the head of his cock.

"No," he said. "It should feel good. If it doesn't, please tell me."

"Okay," she said. "Fuck, Sammy. What the hell?"

I felt the same way. Mr. Mysterious was a dirty-talking Dom with a pierced cock. I studied the dark hair that covered his chest, his lanky muscles, his sharp jaw, and broody gaze. All the years I'd secretly lusted after him still hadn't prepared me for how fucking hot Sammy Harlow was. "What am I supposed to do with the fucking god of sexy poets, huh?" I asked.

"Fuck me?"

I laughed and patted the bed next to me.

"Y'all are going to destroy me," Sarah squeaked.

Sammy snorted. "We might, but I promise we'll take it slow." His gaze shifted down to my growing cock and he hummed. "Better get you cleaned up before you come from watching me fuck our girl."

"Fuck," I muttered. "You sure have a way with words."

He joined us in bed. I softly cursed as Sarah traced her fingertips over my stomach and down to my cock. She slowly wrapped her hand around my shaft, her eyes widening.

"You're hard again."

"Yeah," I grunted, my eyes fluttering as Sammy kissed down my side. "Being in bed with two sexy people does that to a man."

Fuck. This was a dream come true. My body was on fire, desperate to be drowned in their touch. Sarah inched her body closer to my cock and Sammy joined her.

I watched in pleasure and agony as the two of them kissed, their tongues intertwining. I thrust my cock into her palm, horny and losing my mind.

Both of them started to work on my cock. I propped myself up on my elbows and gasped the moment Sammy touched me with his tongue. He started at the base and licked up the underside to the tip, his tongue meeting Sarah's as she gave me a tentative lick.

"Holy fuck," I groaned. "This feels too good."

My eyes closed as Sarah's hot mouth closed over my cock and she started to suck. I groaned, gripping the blankets as I fought for control. Sammy took one of my balls into his mouth and I nearly lost it.

She took me deeper before drawing back, licking her lips. "I think I got it all."

The deviousness in her voice made me narrow my gaze. "I think you missed a spot, sugar."

"Oh yeah?"

I thrust my hips up and she giggled as Sammy drew back. His calluses from playing guitar were rough against my cock as he gripped me, and they felt damn good when they touched me.

"I'll get it," he said.

I watched as he slowly took the head of my cock between his lips and sucked, swirling his tongue. He grunted as he took me deeper, his head bobbing up and down as he found a rhythm that drove me wild.

"Come here," I said to Sarah. "Straddle me."

I twisted and pulled her over me, her soft thighs straddling my waist. Her hands planted on my chest, pushing her breasts together. I stared for a moment, tracing every curve, freckle, and mark on her body and committing them to memory.

"She's stunning," I whispered.

Sammy moaned in agreement around my cock. I leaned up, taking one of her nipples. Her expression morphed with pleasure, a whimper escaping as Sammy kept sucking me.

I was already on the edge again. Between the two of them, I didn't know how much longer I'd last.

"I don't want to come again yet," I groaned.

I felt Sammy's chuckle as he pulled off. "Are you sure?"

"Yes. I thought you wanted me to watch the two of you."

"That is true. I do want that." Sammy rose behind her, wrapping his arms around her. He cupped one of her breasts, teasing her nipple as I flicked my tongue over the other.

"Who do you want to fuck you first?" Sammy asked.

"Either, both," she moaned, rocking her wet cunt against me. "I'm not on birth control, though."

"There are condoms and lube in the nightstand," I said, gesturing to the left side of the bed.

Sammy leaned over and pulled open the drawer, plucking out a bottle of lube and two condoms.

At some point we needed to talk about sexual health and testing, but right now, I needed to fuck or watch them fuck. I made a mental note to circle back around to that before all thoughts went up in smoke.

He tore open one of the wrappers and pulled the condom over his hard cock, rolling it all the way down. He opened the second one and worked it over my cock next, stroking me.

"Fuck, Sammy," I grunted.

"Sit back on his cock," Sammy said, holding my cock in place as she adjusted her body. "Slow, angel. You're in control."

Her gaze locked with mine as she slowly sat back. I reached up and cupped her cheek, stroking her gently as he guided my cock to her entrance.

"You're in control," I reminded her.

She nodded. We gasped together as she slowly sank down, taking the first couple of inches.

"Oh god," she whimpered. "Fuck. It's been so long and you feel so good, Colt."

That stroked my ego.

"Good girl," Sammy praised. He let out a low hiss. "Watching his cock spread you like this is so fucking hot. Goddamn, angel, you're taking him so well."

I grunted and ran my hands up her thighs, holding her hips as she took more of me. Her lips parted, her face twisting with pleasure as she stopped for a moment, her pussy gripping me like a vice.

"Colt," she moaned.

"Yeah, sugar?" I whispered.

"I've never felt this good before."

Blood roared in my ears, my pulse racing. "We're going to make you feel even better," I huffed.

I lifted her hips, pulling out of her nearly all the way before bringing her back down. She yelped, taking me deeper.

"Too much?" Sammy asked.

"No," she rasped.

Her nails raked down my chest as her head tipped back. Auburn waves tumbled down her back, her skin dewy beneath the golden light.

"I want both of you inside me," she said. "Is that possible?"

"We can certainly try," I said. "If Sammy wants to."

"Yes," he said. "We can try."

CHAPTER TWENTY

SARAH STRADDLED COLT, his cock buried inside of her and spreading her apart. I leaned down to kiss her shoulder before shoving her forward gently against him.

Colt cursed, giving a slight thrust. My mind spun with all the things I wanted to do to them as I grabbed the bottle of lube. I poured a generous amount on my cock, applying some to both of them as well.

She moaned as I pushed a finger inside her alongside his cock, stretching her further. It was going to take some work if we were going to get my cock inside her too.

I worked her pussy as I thought about how damn lucky I was. Never in a million years had I thought I'd end up in bed with them together.

I leaned in, studying the way his cock spread her. I continued to tease her, stroking my own with my free hand.

Each of them made the most delicious sounds and I fought the urge to slap her ass. There was a lot I wouldn't do until the three of us negotiated more.

"Sammy," she huffed.

"Relax," I chuckled. "So impatient."

"Man, I'm so fucking close already," Colt said.

"I'm sure you can hold out longer."

He groaned as I continued until I felt like we might stand a chance of fitting me. I inched closer and pressed the head of my cock against her pussy, gliding against Colt as I carefully eased forward.

She gasped and tensed.

"You have to stay relaxed, angel," I grunted. "Otherwise there's not a chance in hell."

Sarah visibly relaxed. Colt held her hips as she kissed him, a soft moan following. I'd never been so fucking turned on in my entire life. I eased forward and pushed inside of her slowly, feeling her grip both of our cocks like a vice.

"Fuck," I huffed.

"Slow," Colt panted. "*Fuck.*"

He kept muttering fuck as I pushed further inside of her. Sarah groaned and sank back, taking more of me.

"More," she rasped.

I growled and thrust forward, grabbing a handful of her dark hair and pulling her head back. She gasped as Colt moved his hips, his cock grinding against mine.

I could hardly think straight. I closed my eyes, savoring the moment before finally giving into the frenzied need. I pulled back and then thrust forward. Sarah gasped, her nails leaving angry marks on Colt's chest as he pumped up and down.

The two of us found a rhythm that was just right, taking her together. I kissed up her back, sliding my hand over Colt's as we held onto her.

I tightened my grip on her hair and leaned down. "How do we feel?"

"Good," she groaned.

I tugged her hair and she whimpered. "Too much?" I asked.

"No," she rasped. "Don't stop. Please don't stop. I'm so close."

Hearing that made me fuck her harder. She moaned as we slid in and out, Colt's voice joining ours in chorus. Pleasure rocketed through me as she gasped, clenching around us as she came.

Feeling her orgasm nearly sent me over the edge, but I clung to control, not quite ready to give up the high. I groaned as I thrust harder, holding her in place. I met Colt's gaze over her shoulder and he huffed, his eyes glazed with lust.

"Fuck," he grunted, leaning up.

I met him halfway, kissing him hard. Sarah relaxed against his chest, watching the two of us as we continued to fuck her. His tongue swept over my bottom lip before he nipped me, the pain making me grunt. I bit him back, enjoying the sound he made.

"Pull out," he rasped.

I nodded and pulled back, both of us there. His cock came free and I grabbed hold of him, stroking us together to the end. I shuddered as I came, filling my condom in hot spurts. Colt did the same before melting against the bed, panting.

It took a couple minutes before I could even think again. "Where should I throw the condoms?"

He pointed to the side of the bed. "Trash can," he rasped.

I nodded and pulled both of our condoms off carefully before leaning over, discarding them. I collapsed on the bed next to them and Sarah rolled between us, fully relaxed.

"I haven't orgasmed like that in... I can't even remember," she said.

"Me neither," I said, kissing the top of her head. "You smell good," I mumbled.

She chuckled as Colt held up his thumb.

"You alright, baby?" I asked him.

He raised his head, narrowing his eyes on me. "Baby?"

"Yeah," I said, fighting a smirk.

He mumbled under his breath.

"What was that?" I asked, raising a brow.

"He said he's never been called 'baby' before," Sarah said with a soft giggle. She slid her hand into his. "I can call you baby too if you want."

Colt hummed as he turned onto his side, looking at both of us. "Fine. I'll take it."

I chuckled, still studying him. There was an air of vulnerability I'd never seen from him until right now. I wondered if I'd done too much.

"Do you both feel okay?" I asked.

"Yeah," Sarah said, frowning. "Do you?"

"Of course," I said.

"I'm more than okay," Colt said.

I breathed out and relaxed.

It felt right lying in bed with the two of them. Sarah turned over toward me and laid her head on my chest. Colt spooned her, his arm laying over her waist and settling on me. I curled my fingers with his and closed my eyes.

There'd been a lot of big changes for us in a short amount of time. I was grateful to be with them. Thinking about the apartment and how everything was wrecked scared the shit out of me, but I wasn't alone.

"I want to do this again," Sarah whispered.

"Me too," Colt said.

"Again and again," I teased. "We can plan another date night."

"Maybe one on a day where there's not so much chaos," Sarah said.

I nodded. "I'd like that. Just let me know when, and I'll make it work."

"Same," Colt said, kissing her shoulder.

She let out a soft hum. "I worry that..."

We waited for her to finish her words patiently.

"I worry I'm too much, with everything going on. Are you sure you both want this?"

"Do you want us, Sarah?" Colt asked softly. "Both of us?"

"Yes," she whispered. "I really do. I can't choose between you. I don't want to choose."

"I don't want to choose either," I said. "I care about you both. I want you both."

"Then we'll make it work," Colt said. "We all have lives. We all have things that are happening or have happened. But we can share those burdens and wins with each other."

Sarah breathed out. "Okay. I'm going to trust that both of you know what you want."

"I do," Colt said. "I've wanted you for years. And Sammy... I don't know. I've never let myself even think about you until recently."

"I've thought about you," I mumbled sleepily. I closed my eyes as we continued to talk. "Sometimes things shift, you know? Sometimes you meet someone you've known your whole life and think 'wow, this person is amazing.' You wonder how you've never seen them as more than just a friend. I feel like that about you."

He squeezed my hand.

"Sarah just knocked me flat on my ass. Colt, you snuck up on me."

Sarah snickered. "You are a poet, aren't you?"

I smiled. "I mean, I do write songs sometimes."

"You're really good at it," she said. "I've only heard you play a couple times."

"Sammy used to sit outside and sulk under the stars," Colt said. "I remember when you got your first guitar for Christmas. And then your fingertips bleeding because you practiced so damn much."

I laughed, opening one eye to peek at him. He was smiling too. "Yeah, I played for hours and hours. It was school, homework, and playing guitar. I'm pretty sure my parents regretted getting it."

He shook his head. "Nah. They were proud of you. We all were."

My heart squeezed. "Thank you," I murmured. "I'm going to get us some water. We all need it."

I slid out of bed before they could protest and left his room for the kitchen. I double checked the locks on the front door before pouring us each a glass of cold water.

What I was feeling right now was hard to put a finger on. I stood at the counter for a few moments, trying to understand it. I hadn't ever been with anyone who knew me the way Sarah and Colt did.

The connection made me realize how much I'd been missing.

I carried our glasses back down the hall to bed and paused in the doorway, smiling.

Sarah and Colt were curled up, their fingers laced together. I wondered if they looked at me the way they looked at each other.

I felt like they did.

"Drink your water," I said, handing them each a glass.

"Yes, sir," Colt said, draining half of his in a gulp.

Sarah shook her head, eyes wide as she took a small sip. "I don't know how you did that."

"Easy," I teased, draining mine.

"So thirsty," she mumbled.

"Yes, ma'am." I winked at her.

"Water and a movie?" Colt suggested, reaching for a remote.

"How about a shower, more water, then a movie?" I asked. "I'll probably fall asleep once I get snuggled up."

"Well, my bed is big enough for the three of us," Colt said.

"I'll set an alarm," Sarah said. "I'll sneak out in the morning. But yes, a shower sounds nice..."

"Pretty sure my shower can fit the three of us too." Colt smirked.

"Let's find out."

CHAPTER TWENTY-ONE

sarah

I SNUCK through the front door of my house, praying that Donnie wouldn't hear me and start barking. I shut it quietly behind me, slipped my shoes off, hung my purse on the entryway hook, and listened for movement in the house. Everyone seemed to still be asleep.

The last twenty-four hours had been a whirlwind. From having a day off, to Sammy's apartment break-in, to last night's *activities*.

I'd never had sex like that before. They'd awakened something inside me—an unquenchable need for more touch, more kisses. For more snuggles too. They were both pretty damn good at cuddling.

On the way home, I'd decided to call the doctor's office to ask for a birth control prescription. My doctor was someone I'd known since I'd given birth to the boys, so I didn't think it would be an issue to get it quickly. And I'd been right. A perk of being in a small town meant that Dr. Garcia had texted me they'd be ready at the pharmacy on Monday.

I crept upstairs to the bathroom and started the shower, my

thoughts on Sammy and Colt as I undressed and stepped under the hot water. Steam shimmered in the air as I washed my hair.

I kept smiling. It was hard not to after the way they'd touched me, kissed me... It just felt right. All the years I'd been with David, and there had never been a moment where he'd made me come that many times. Hell, I wasn't sure he'd *ever* made me come.

I'd never felt so wanted before.

My pussy was sore after taking both of them at once, but it'd been worth it. I wanted to do that again and again. I tipped my head back as the hot water ran down my skin, thinking about Sammy's mouth on me. On the way Colt had gripped my hips...

Fuck.

I flipped the water to cold and bit my lower lip, fighting the scream that froze all my horny thoughts in place. It was necessary to clear my head for the rest of the day. Otherwise, I'd be an incoherent, cock-hungry mess until I saw them again.

I finished my shower quickly and wrapped myself in a towel before sneaking to my bedroom. I opened the door and flipped on the light, and then paused.

The boys were snuggled under the blankets, fast asleep in my bed. I sighed, quietly grabbing a pair of sweats. I changed in the bathroom before deciding that I was too awake to go back to sleep. I'd let the boys keep sleeping and go downstairs to make coffee.

I heard Emma's door as I started the coffee maker. I spun as she came into the kitchen holding Donnie. Today, he wore a bright orange sweater to keep him from freezing. She put him down and he ran to me, his butt wiggling with excitement.

"Hi," I crooned, leaning over to pet him. He sat obediently as I rubbed his head.

"Well, well, well," Emma teased. She'd thrown her hair up

into a messy bun and was wearing pajama pants with hearts and a tank top. She crossed her arms and leaned against the fridge. "Look who's here."

"Coffee?" I asked, trying not to immediately grin.

"Yes, please. Tell me everything."

"Don't tell me you got up at the crack of dawn just to find out how my night went." I gave Donnie a few more scratches before straightening. He sat patiently, waiting for Emma to pick him back up.

"I have some things going on early today," she said, her voice carrying a strain that I didn't hear often from Emma.

I frowned and she shrugged, her smile faltering. "What's wrong, Emma?" I asked.

"It's depressing, I don't want to talk about it. I much rather hear about your evening with Sammy and Colt."

I studied her and shook my head. "Okay, we'll circle back to that," I said.

"*Tell meeee*," she hissed playfully.

A grin cracked my face as I hit the start button on the coffee pot. I just couldn't stop smiling after last night.

"I fucking knew it," she hissed. "Both of them?"

I nodded and grinned wider. "I've never done anything like that. *Ever.*"

"I bet it was good too. They seem like they'd know how to find the clit."

I burst out laughing and stifled it with my hand. "Oh my god. Yeah, they do. It was really good, Emma. And they're both... into things." My cheeks flushed. "I'm glad I can talk to you about this."

Emma's face softened. "Me too. I don't know what I would do without you and Haley."

I noted the way her eyes teared up and shook my head. "Okay, what's going on? Talk to me. We can circle back to my suddenly-existent sex life later. For once, let me be there for you."

"So..." She blew out a breath and pressed her lips together, looking away. "My sister died fifteen years ago today. My dad wanted to do an online memorial of sorts to honor her and I don't even want to go."

"Oh my god, Emma," I whispered.

I reached for her hand and she took it, and then I gave her a hug. I squeezed her tight, holding onto her. I couldn't imagine how she felt right now.

"It was so long ago," she sighed. "It still seems like yesterday."

"I didn't know," I said, giving her another squeeze. "I can't imagine. I'm so sorry."

"Only Haley knows, and now you," Emma said. "I just tell people I'm an only child. Makes it easier than having to explain. I'm okay." She drew back and wiped her eyes. Donnie whined at her.

I couldn't imagine losing Haley. Well, I had imagined it after Thomas took her, but we'd been lucky that she'd been found. She was a fighter. Every day, I was thankful for that.

I rubbed Emma's arm. "Go sit. I'll pour coffee. Do you want any breakfast?"

"Not yet," she said. "Coffee will do just fine. Distract me? Tell me more about the kinky cowboys."

I couldn't help but chuckle, even though I still worried about her. I imagined Haley would be around today, especially since she knew about Emma's sister too.

I pulled out two mugs and poured us each a cup. I settled in across from her at the table, finding a comfortability in sitting with someone I loved over coffee to talk. For so long, I didn't have this. I didn't have friends I could simply sit with. I'd been isolated in my own world, just trying to get through day-to-day tasks and life. Most of the years felt like a heavy fog now, with the brightest stars being my boys and the moments with them.

But that Sarah was gone now. I wasn't alone and I had people who cared about me. I had people I cared about.

"Have you ever been with anyone that's... kinky?"

Emma snorted and patted her lap. Donnie jumped and curled up into a small ball, eyes squinting closed. "Hell yeah, I have. One time, I went to Cancun with this guy who was into shibari and he tied me to his bed and left a vibrator tied to me."

My mouth fell open. "*Oh my god.*"

She smirked over the rim of her mug as she took a sip of coffee. "Yeah. He was hot. Didn't work out though. He called his ex a slut and laughed about her, and that gave me the ick. I hate guys like that. Anyway, yes, I've dated plenty of guys who were into fun things."

"It's all so new to me," I said. "David... I really need to stop talking about him."

"It's natural for you to compare everything to your relationship with him," Emma said. "I mean, you were married for more than a decade, Sarah. That doesn't disappear overnight."

"You have a point. Well, I was just going to say that we didn't have much sex after the boys. Maybe a couple times when he came home drunk. But he was disgusted by me."

"Fuck him," she growled. "God, I wish I could kick that man in the nuts wearing my Louboutins. They have a nice sharp tip."

I couldn't lie, the thought made me laugh.

"I'm glad they were good. I hope they gave you all the O's because you deserve a whole decade's worth."

"I do," I said. "And they did."

"So... are the three of you *a thing* now?"

I winced. It was a lot to think about and I certainly wanted to take my time given that this was the first relationship I'd been in since David. I'd never called him my high school sweetheart, but in a way, he had been.

It should have been Colt all along. But then, we wouldn't be the people we were today, and maybe we wouldn't have Sammy too.

After last night, I felt more confident about exploring a relationship with both of them.

"I want us to be? The three of us are interested in each other. I think Colt has some worries because he's so close to Sammy's family. I'm a little worried about how people would react if they knew the three of us were dating."

Emma sighed and shifted in her seat, letting Donnie down. He reluctantly left us to go sit on a heating vent in the living room. "I would hope they'd mind their damn business."

I was doubtful. "People already say a lot about me. I just worry about the boys. We live in a small town."

"Well, they're wrong. I have to say, there are so many things I love about this little town, but the way you and the boys have been treated pisses me off. If someone says shit to you, you let me know."

I reached across the table and grabbed her hand, squeezing it. "Emma, I am so thankful for you. I don't say that enough. But you're the first friend I've had in years. You and Haley are too good to me."

She teared up. "Stop. I'm already a basket case today, you can't say sweet things to me."

"Okay, last one. Thank you for giving me a chance," I said. "I feel like I'm finally becoming myself and that's partially thanks to you."

She smiled through the tears. "Thank you."

I took a sip of coffee and thought about breakfast. "I made some pumpkin bread yesterday. Want a slice?"

"Well... Between the boys, Cam, Haley, and myself—we devoured the whole loaf yesterday. It was really good."

I laughed. It pleased me to hear that. "Sam and Colt said I should open my own bakery."

"You should," Emma said immediately. "I'd do all the marketing for you. There's no good bakery in Citrus Cove, just the cafe, and their stuff is good but it's not like... it's not like what you can bake."

I thought about it again. The idea of running my own business terrified me, but it also felt exciting. Something new and challenging that would give me a solid foundation. Something I could call my own.

"I don't know..." I trailed off. "I love baking. It's the only thing I'm good at."

"It's not the only thing you're good at. But you're really damn good at it," Emma said. "I think you should do it."

"I'd have to figure out when," I sighed. "And I still have to work at the cafe. I can't just take off."

"You should ask for a set schedule," Emma said. "If only for six months. I'm sure Alice would be down for it. Maybe she'd even be open to carrying your goods at the cafe."

I frowned, thinking it over. Maybe I was getting ahead of myself. "I'll think about it," I said.

"Isn't there a farmer's market at the end of the month?" Emma asked. "Maybe try there first? I'll help however I can."

"You already do so much," I said.

"So do you." Emma shrugged. "I don't have many hobbies here except for yoga, work, and taking Donnie on walks. I like projects, so when I help you, it helps me."

"Are you still liking Citrus Cove?" I asked.

"Yeah," she said. "I can't imagine being anywhere else now. There are things I don't like about it at all, but being with family makes up for it."

Knowing she meant me and Haley made my throat tighten. "I'm glad you're here. Is there anything I can do before I go to work? Honey will have the boys today, so I'll drop them off in a bit."

"No," she said. "You've already done it for me."

I nodded and watched as she got up, still concerned.

"I really think you should go after the bakery idea if it feels right for you," Emma said. "I know everyone would love anything you'd make. I think you'd love having the freedom of running your own business. It would be a lot of work, though."

"It *would* be a lot of work," I agreed. "But I already work a lot. And maybe this could help me make some more money. I need to start thinking about building up some savings but have no clue how to even get there."

"Talk to Alice," she encouraged. "Everyone has your back."

That was true. Now my mind was bouncing all over the place with ideas and recipes. There was a bakery in Austin I'd been to a few times over the years—what were their best sellers?

Emma left the kitchen and I was alone to think. I checked my phone and smiled. Colt had created a text chat between the three of us. I wondered if the two of them were still in bed.

Sammy: Get home safe?

Me: Yes! Thank you :)

Colt: Want to do dinner Wednesday night?

Me: I have the boys that night

Sammy: that's fine, I'll cook for all of us

I hesitated for a moment. It would probably be good for the boys to get to know them more though, right? Not that I needed the approval of two eleven-year-olds, but I kind of did.

Me: sure! That would be great

I couldn't believe this was my life.

Knock, knock, knock.

I lifted my head and got up, heading to the front door. This early in the morning, it was probably a package delivery. I unlocked it and opened the door, my heart dropping.

"Hi, Sarah."

My ex-husband stood on the porch.

"David." My breath whooshed out as if I'd been punched in the gut, my body completely deflating. My heart hammered as he took a step closer.

All of the therapy I'd gone through had prepared me for this moment, but every tool went out the window. I felt trapped again, just standing there. I needed to tell him to leave, but I couldn't find my voice. Why couldn't I speak? Why couldn't I slam the door? I couldn't even move a muscle.

"Been trying to find out where you live for a while," he said. "You took my children from me. Who bought this house, huh? Sure as fuck wasn't you, you stupid whore."

Donnie rushed down the stairs, barking like a maniac. He shot between my legs, nipping at David. He took a step back with a startled curse.

"Oh, what the fuck?!" Emma's shout came from behind me and I felt her hand on my arm, pulling me back. "Get the fuck off our porch, you son of a bitch! Sarah, call the cops."

I was still frozen. His eyes met mine, sending a bolt of fear through me. He didn't say anything, but I felt his hatred. I felt his disgust. I felt useless again.

Emma snapped her fingers and she grabbed Donnie, who was still barking non-stop. "Call the cops, Sarah. For the boys."

Her words cracked through the shock. I took a breath and pulled out my phone, calling 911. David gave Emma a dark glare before stepping off the porch, heading for his car. It was one I hadn't seen before.

"Yeah, that's right," Emma yelled. "If I ever see you again, I'm gonna crush your balls, motherfucker!"

The operator answered and my words rushed out finally,

although shaky. "We need police at 129 Hummingbird Lane. My ex-husband showed up and I have a restraining order on him."

"Are you in any danger?"

"No. He's leaving now," I said, watching as he sped off down the street. A few of our neighbors emerged onto their porches, watching everything unfold.

"We'll send someone over," they said.

"Mom?"

I whipped around, seeing Davy at the top of the steps.

Fuck. "Go back to bed," I told him. "Everything is okay."

"Everything is *not* okay," he snapped, taking off for his room. I heard the door slam and fought back the tears.

I got off the phone and put my hands on my head, trying to breathe. Emma shook her head, her gaze full of fire.

"That son of a bitch," she said. "Are you okay, Sarah? Come sit. The boys will be fine, okay? It's all okay. God, what a fucking psychopath."

"I just want one week without something happening," I whispered.

She gave me a sorry look. "I know."

"Don't call everyone," I said. "Not yet. I need to talk to the officers first and probably call my lawyer. I'm so sorry, Emma. I don't know how he got this address."

"People talk," Emma said. "I'm so sorry."

"I froze up," I whispered, tears springing now. "I failed. Again."

"You didn't fail," she said. She grabbed hold of my shoulders and shook me. "He hurt you. For years. You were trapped with him. For years. And today, you didn't break. You didn't crumple. You are strong, Sarah. It takes someone strong to make it out of a situation like that."

"I don't feel strong."

"You are," she said.

I swallowed hard and wiped my eyes as I spotted a police car pulling up.

Deep breath. Pull yourself together. I had to, for the sake of the boys, Emma, and even myself.

The message David had sent was pretty clear.

He was back.

And he hated me now more than ever before.

CHAPTER TWENTY-TWO

CLOUDS BLOTTED out the blue sky with potential rain as I pulled up behind Cam's truck in Sarah's driveway. Every light in the house was on.

Sammy jumped out as soon as I parked and I did the same. I was ready to hunt down David, but first I needed to know if Sarah was okay.

The two of us stalked to the door and it swung open. Jake stood there, his eyes wide. "Hi," he said.

"Howdy," I said, holding out my hand for high-five.

He grinned and gave it to me before looking at Sammy.

"Can we go to the movies again?" he asked.

"Yep," Sammy said. "We'll go again soon. Where's your mama?"

"She's in the kitchen with Aunt Haley and Uncle Cam and Emma."

"Thanks, bud," I said.

We stepped inside and Jake took off up the stairs. I looked up, seeing Davy sitting at the stop step with a scowl on his face. "Hey," I said to him.

He didn't say anything. Sammy hummed. "I'm gonna go talk to him."

"Okay," I said.

Sammy went up the steps and plopped down next to Davy. Jake leaned against the rail, watching them curiously. Davy went still for a moment, and then slowly leaned against Sammy. His body language softened and Sammy put an arm around him.

It infuriated me in so many ways, knowing the bastard had just shown up here. Seeing how her boys were handling it, it made me even angrier.

Sammy gave me a short nod as if to say he had them. I continued on to the kitchen and I froze in the doorway when I saw Sarah.

It was like he'd snatched the light right out of her.

Cam looked up at me and shook his head, his expression tight. Whatever anger I had for David, I pushed it to the side, focusing on everyone here.

"Are you okay?" I asked.

"No," Haley snapped, her arms around Sarah. Haley was pissed, her eyes dark with malice.

"Hal," Cam said, although he clearly was too.

Hell, we all were. This was the thing we'd all been worried about.

Haley took a deep breath, her nostrils flaring. She reluctantly released her sister, who wouldn't even look at me. A deep ache spread through my chest for her.

"Sarah," I said softly.

I went to her and she leaned into me. I hugged her tight and pulled her face against my chest, kissing the top of her head.

"Hunter is already out patrolling the town," Cam said. "The lawyer has been updated. The police are aware."

"Giving them a handful this week," I said lightly, thinking of Sammy too. "Sammy is upstairs with the boys."

Sarah drew in a shaky breath. "Davy is mad. I told him everything would be okay and he didn't believe me. What else am I supposed to tell him?"

I didn't have a good answer.

"Can you give us a minute?" I asked.

Emma, Haley, and Cam nodded and filed out of the kitchen. I heard Cam's voice as he greeted Sammy.

"I froze," Sarah whispered. "I'm so fucking mad at myself."

I tightened my hug and was about to speak, but she continued.

"Please don't tell me I'm strong. I'm so tired of hearing it. I'm so tired of this."

"I know," I said. "What did he want?"

"He just... he asked who paid for the house, called me a whore, and said I took his kids from him."

My jaw ticked. I heard footsteps and glanced up as Sammy came into the kitchen. "I might have made an error and told the boys I'd take them to the movies next weekend," Sammy said. "It seemed to make Davy brighten up some. I hope that's okay."

"Are you sure you want to?" Sarah asked.

"Of course," he said. He stepped closer and gave her a hug. "What happened?"

She told him what she told me and he shook his head, eyes blazing with anger.

"Why would he do that? He knows you have a restraining order," Sammy said. "This won't look good in the courts, which is good for you. Cam said you called the lawyer."

"I did," she said. "Everyone knows as much as I do now. I have to leave for work in an hour and all I can think about is him showing up there."

"I'll go sit at the cafe," I said.

"You can't go my entire shift," she scoffed.

"I sure as hell can," I snorted. "I have work on my laptop I can do. I'll camp out all damn day."

"He can stay with you, and I'll join Hunter and Cam to be on the lookout. I'll keep an eye on Honey's house."

"You don't have to," Sarah said.

"I know," Sammy said. "But I want to."

"You still have all of your stuff to sort out," Sarah said. "Hell, you're still probably being stalked. Don't worry about me."

"No can do, angel."

Between the two of us, I felt confident we'd be able to help. Although, she had a point. I worried about him too.

"Maybe you should camp at the cafe so you can make insurance calls and stuff," I said.

"It's the weekend," Sammy said. "I can't do shit until Monday. My apartment is locked and full of broken shit I can deal with next week. David is a bigger issue than anything else at the moment."

It was a much larger problem than he was making it out to be. His entire apartment had been destroyed. He'd lost all of his equipment, his guitars, and more. I wanted to do *something* for him, to show him that none of us had forgotten about what happened and he wasn't alone, but wasn't sure what that gesture was quite yet.

At the end of the day, I was a gift man. Whatever I did, I wanted it to be perfect for him.

I heard the front door open and close.

"Sarah?" Honey's voice called before she came into the kitchen, and the three of us all stepped apart.

Honey paused, raising a brow at me and then Sammy. "I have questions, but want to know if my granddaughter is safe first."

"I am," Sarah laughed nervously. "We were just talking..."

"Hmm." She shook her head and turned around, leaving the three of us alone.

"I thought that would go differently," Sarah admitted.

"Me too," I breathed out.

I thought back to the day I'd crashed Sarah's wedding to beg her not to marry David, and how Honey was there that day too. I'd never forget that rain storm or how stupid I realized I was.

"I have to get ready," Sarah sighed.

"Need any help?" I offered.

Her mouth fell open and she swatted my chest. "While the whole damn family is here?"

"I can be quiet." I wiggled my brows.

"Not sure our girl can be, though," Sammy chuckled.

"*Sammy*," she hissed.

I saw the spark come back into her eyes and felt myself relax. "Go get ready. We'll be here."

She nodded and slipped past us, heading upstairs. The moment she was out of sight, Haley came into the kitchen and crossed her arms.

"Hi," Sammy said.

"Don't you 'hi' me, Sammy Harlow," she said. "Sarah has been through a lot."

"We know that," I said.

I half expected Cam to join us in the kitchen and spotted him beyond the doorway, creeping on whatever talk we were about to get.

"She deserves someone who will love her and be the balance she needs. She's a mom, she works all the time."

"We know," Sammy said.

Haley lowered her voice. "Whatever is going on with the three of you—I'm happy if Sarah is happy—but if one of you steps a toe out of line, you'll never see the sunshine again. Got it? I don't care if you're my husband's brother and best friend."

"Both of us care about her," I said. "We're figuring out what that means for us."

"And Sarah can make decisions for herself," Sammy said.

That was braver than I'd planned to be, but Haley crossed her arms, her shoulders relaxing. "I just want to see her happy."

"Us too," I said.

She pressed her lips together. "Okay. Well, now that we've got that settled, if you want to win Sarah over, you need to win the boys over first. They had a hard time adjusting to Cam being around initially because of the bullshit their sperm donor has put them through. They don't trust older men easily, especially Davy."

I fought the urge to rub my chest where it ached. I knew all too well how hard it could be to have a dad like that. Growing up, I'd never gotten along with my own, and he'd said and done things that had left scars on my heart to this day.

All I could do was hope that, if I was lucky enough to be in their lives, I could be there for them in a way my dad never was.

"Did he ever hurt them?" Sammy whispered.

Haley's face softened and she crossed her arms. "I don't know, truthfully. Sarah says David was never physically abusive."

"There's more than one way to hurt someone," I said. "I think we all know that. Haley, your concerns are valid, and I know what has started to develop might be unconventional, but I'd like to ask that we're given the space to grow and explore what this might mean for us."

She raised a brow. "I can do that. I just needed you both to know I will fight for my sister, no matter who you are."

"I wouldn't expect anything less," Sammy chuckled. "Is my brother hiding while you talk to us?"

"Maybe," she snorted. "I'll go find him."

She left us. I crossed my arms, giving Sammy a wary glance. All of us were on red alert now. All I wanted to do was track down David and guarantee he never saw the sun again.

After everything this family had been through, it infuriated me that he dared to show up at their front door. It upset the boys, it upset Sarah, and it worried all of us that something could have happened if we weren't around.

Sammy nodded as if he felt the same way. "I'll help Hunter," he said. "We'll figure out what's going on. And you'll keep an eye on her at the café."

"I'll sit there all damn day," I said.

Neither one of us wanted to leave Sarah alone again.

CHAPTER TWENTY-THREE

sammy

A COUPLE of days had passed since David showed his ugly face. Since then, none of us had been able to rest. The thought of the bastard being out there made me sick, but there was nothing I could do about it at the moment.

In fact, I really needed to take care of my own shit so I could fully focus on Sarah's situation.

I pulled into my spot in the parking lot of my apartment complex, and stared up at my building. A knot twisted my stomach. I'd been avoiding this, but I had to start the cleaning process. I couldn't keep avoiding the destruction.

My guitars hurt the most. The camera equipment and everything else could be replaced. But the fact that my first guitar had been smashed—a part of me had broken with it. I'd always been an awkward kid, lacking the confidence that both Cam and Hunter had come by naturally. Learning to play guitar had given me a sense of purpose, and it had helped me through the angst of being a teen.

My phone buzzed in my pocket. I immediately fished it out, Colt's name flashing across the screen.

Colt: What are you up to today? Haley is staying with Sarah while she works

I swallowed hard. We'd decided to take shifts keeping an eye on her. She didn't like it, but none of us wanted her to be alone, even at work.

Me: I'm at the apartment

Colt: I'll come over to help. I wanted to take you somewhere if you have time

Me: Where??

Colt: it's a surprise. Be there in five

I snorted and smiled. The knot in my stomach loosened just enough for me to breathe easier. My eyes drifted back up to the apartment. As silly as it was, I didn't want to go up there alone. I'd wait until Colt got here.

My thumb hovered over the phone screen. I clicked on the Instagram app out of habit, sighing at the amount of notifications. They were giving me anxiety now. My stomach tightened again, but I needed to check on the profile that said there was blood on my hands.

"What the fuck?" I growled.

The account had gone through several of my videos and spam commented the same thing over and over. *You have blood on your hands*.

Could it be from the woman? Or someone else? I clicked on a video and scrolled until I found their comment again. Someone else had replied to them with a few question marks. I pressed their profile, and hissed through my teeth.

It was a private account. The photo was just a red circle, and the handle was a series of numbers. The only information I got was the bio—which said *Never Forget*.

That didn't help.

Tires crackled over gravel, drawing my attention to Colt as he pulled up next to me. I closed Instagram and got out of the car, offering him a weary smile as he hopped out and came around to meet me.

"Hey," he said, moving toward me.

"Hey—"

My words drowned against his mouth as he pushed me against my car and kissed me. All the tension melted out of my body, my breath hitching as he kissed me deeper until I was putty in his hands. I was used to being the dominant one in relationships, but right now I craved the comfort of his touch.

He drew back and studied me. The corner of his mouth tugged into a frown. "What's wrong?"

"So many things," I sighed. "Someone is commenting on my Instagram saying I have blood on my hands. Like spam commenting."

His brows drew together. "Could it be the stalker? David?"

"I have no idea," I said. "Their profile doesn't have anything notable except 'Never forget' in their bio."

"Weird. I can do some digging. Or better yet, I can ask Hunter to."

I didn't like the idea of Hunter digging around on my socials. Mostly because I didn't like the idea of being perceived by him.

Colt's hand rested over my heart. "Or I will. It's going to be okay, Sammy. Sarah is in good hands right now, so we can focus on what you have going on."

A shaky breath released. My shoulders sank and I nodded. "I hate this," I whispered. "I don't even want to go up there."

"I know. I hate it too. But, let's go start cleaning up. We'll get some good work done. Then we'll go somewhere nice."

I raised a brow. Mischief sparkled in his gaze, a look I'd seen a thousand times over the years. But it meant something different now that it was for me. My heart thumped faster as he grinned.

"What do you have planned?" I asked suspiciously.

He shook his head. "Not telling. Come on."

"Does Sarah know about it?"

"Not telling. Let's go."

Two hours later, we were both covered in a sheen of sweat. But, my apartment was cleaned up. A few bags of trash sat on the living room floor, each full of the shards of everything I owned. The couch and bed were still intact, so that was good. They'd also been kind enough to leave my sex toys alone.

I leaned against my bedroom wall and breathed out. Colt planted his hands on his hips as he looked around. He stooped down to pick up a book and held it up. "Aliens?"

Fuck. Heat immediately crept up my spine. I lunged for him, but he held the book away, dancing out of my grip.

"They've got tentacles, man," I said.

He laughed as he opened it up, flipping through the pages until he found a sex scene. His brows shot up. "This is gold."

"Colt," I growled.

"Don't worry, your secret is safe with me, tentacle man."

"I will spank your ass until you can't walk for days if you tell a single soul."

He grinned as he tossed the book onto my bed. "Maybe I'd like that. But also, there's nothing to be embarrassed about. It's just a book."

"Somehow I don't think Hunter or Cam would ever let me live down reading an alien romance book."

Colt shook his head. "You'd be surprised. Cam is into some freaky shit too."

"I don't want to know," I chuckled as he stepped closer.

The tension shifted. We'd been working side by side for a couple hours now, but we'd finished the job, and...

I slid my hand around the back of his neck and pulled him close. "Thank you for helping me."

"You're welcome," he said. He grunted as I started to massage the tendons. "I'm always happy to help. Fuck, that feels good, but we can't get distracted. Are you ready to go?"

"Are you not gonna tell me?"

"Nope," he said, groaning again as I deepened the massage. "But if you're ready, so am I."

I sighed dramatically and released him. "Fine. What does Colton Hayes have up his sleeve, huh?"

"Wouldn't you like to know?"

I let him lead me out the front door, only pausing to lock up before we went down the stairs to the parking lot. "Should I meet you somewhere?" I asked. "Or should we take your truck?"

He hesitated. "Are you okay leaving your car here for a bit? We'll swing back by for it. Or we can take it to my house."

I glanced around the parking lot, looking for anyone or anything out of the ordinary. Nothing caught my eye. "We'll come back for it."

Colt nodded and pulled his keys out, unlocking the truck. We got in and I leaned back in the seat, still looking around warily. He started the truck and backed out, hitting the road to take us out of town.

I frowned. "Are you kidnapping me?"

"Consensually and for fun, yes."

I stole a glance at him. He was relaxed except for his fingers, which continuously tapped on his steering wheel. He sped up as we hit the highway.

"Close your eyes," he said.

"What?" I laughed. "Colt. Be serious."

"I am being serious. Close your eyes."

I scoffed, but I did as he asked. "You're one of the only people I'd do this for."

"I know. It'll be worth it. Just keep 'em shut for a few minutes."

I sighed, but ultimately, decided to give into his plan. Whatever he had up his sleeve, it was a good distraction from the sadness I'd felt cleaning up the apartment.

"Thank you for helping me," I mumbled.

"You already thanked me, silly. And I already told you I was happy to help out."

I swallowed hard. "Do you think Sarah is having a good day? Should I text her?"

"We'll text her in a bit."

So bossy. I wrinkled my nose at him, earning another chuckle.

"You don't like being told what to do," he said.

"Oh? You noticed?" I teased.

"It'll be worth it."

I believed him. I focused inward, a comfortable silence settling between us as he drove us to our destination. It took about twenty minutes, but then he slowed and eased to a complete stop.

"Open them."

My eyes flew open and my heart dropped.

"Colt," I whispered, my throat constricting. "What..."

We were in the parking lot of a music store south of Austin that was known for carrying some of the best acoustic guitars in the world. The Moonshed had been around for thirty-five years, and was more of a boutique than a music mega-store.

I'd always wanted to buy a guitar here, but never had the chance to. Tears immediately sprang to my eyes, my words faltering.

"I know how much your guitars mean to you," Colt said quietly. "I'm sorry they were destroyed. I know there's a lot happening right now and we're worried about Sarah, but you had something big happen too. So, I talked to Cam and Hunter, and the three of us pooled together some money to buy you a new one."

I stared at the Moonshed sign until it blurred. "I can't—"

"This is a gift we all want to give you," he said. "It's the least we can do. Let's go pick one out."

"This is a huge gift," I whispered. "Guitars are really expensive."

"Oh, I know. I damn near fainted when I saw how much your Martin was. But, that doesn't matter. We're doing this, Sammy. You deserve this. I know it's not replacing all of your belongings, but it's a start."

No one had ever done anything like this before. I wiped the tears away and forced myself to shudder out a breath.

"This is too much. I'm too much." Where had that last part come from? A new weight settled on my chest as I realized a deep fear of mine. Had that been what held me back before? That I felt like I was too much?

Colt reached across the seat, his hand settling on my thigh. He gave me a gentle squeeze. "You're not too much to me, Sammy. I want to do this for you."

I wiped my eyes. "You are... I can't... I can't find the words."

I didn't know how to tell him how much this meant to me.

But I did know I'd now be able to write the song I'd been working on for months.

"Well... are we going in?"

The question lingered for a moment. To accept a gift like this was a huge deal, but mostly because I couldn't think of a time where someone had seen me so clearly.

"Are you sure?" I whispered, looking over at him. "It's a lot of money."

Colt's smile lit up the whole truck. "I'm sure."

I needed to dry my tears then. I let out a loud sigh and slowly grinned. "I'll text Cam and Hunter later to thank them."

"Even better, I'm going to send them a pic of us," Colt said, pulling out his phone.

I leaned in, our heads tilted against each other as he snapped a picture and sent it to my brothers. He turned and stole a kiss before opening his door, hopping out of the truck. I rubbed my chest for a moment, but the ache was a good ache, something I'd never felt before Sarah and Colt.

He waited on the sidewalk with a broad smile, spreading his arms. "You coming?" he called.

I wiped my cheeks again with my sleeve, and got out. The two of us went through the red door of the Moonshed, a bell jingling above. We entered a room lined wall-to-wall with beautiful acoustic guitars. In the center, an older man hunched over the neck of a guitar at a desk, a thick gray mustache disguising his lips.

"Howdy," he said. "Welcome in."

"Thank you," I said.

"Anything in particular you looking for?"

"An acoustic guitar," Colt said proudly, making me laugh. "He's the one shopping. I don't know anything about music. I can play a D chord."

"That's more than nothing," I said. "I'll take a look around."

The man nodded and returned to his work as we started to wander. My gaze swept over each instrument, but one across the room beckoned me like a siren. I hesitated, but couldn't resist the call, immediately gravitating toward it. It was a Gibson acoustic with a rich blue burst. The abalone inlays on the pickguard, fingerboard, and head depicted a hummingbird hovering over a flower vine and a couple of swallowtail butterflies.

It was also ten thousand dollars.

Colt crossed his arms. "Isn't that the same as your tattoo? The butterflies?"

"Yeah," I whispered.

"You should get it."

"Absolutely not," I said. "You can't buy me something this big. It's ten grand."

"We pooled together three, but—"

"Jesus," I sighed. "Colt—"

"Don't tell me I don't have to do this. Gifts are my love language, but aside from our relationship, I've known you my whole life, Sammy. You mean something to me, and I know music means something to you."

I swallowed hard, unable to pull my gaze off the guitar. "You're not paying that much for a gift. That's wild. It costs more than Hal and Cam's wedding."

"It's just a down payment on forever, Sammy."

My mouth fell open. "You're..." Ridiculous? Amazing? He'd rendered me speechless yet again.

I'd have it the rest of my life. I could put the three thousand down, pay a little more, and then finance the rest...

Have I lost my mind?

"You're an enabler," I mumbled.

"I for sure am."

I shook my head at him.

"You gonna play it?"

I damn near jumped out of my skin as the man appeared next to us. He reached up and pulled the Gibson down, nodding his head toward a bench. I followed him reluctantly, giving Colt a side eye.

If I held it, I'd never want to put it down.

"What's your name, son?" the man asked.

"Sammy Harlow," I said.

His eyes lit up. "Don't tell me you're Bob Harlow's son. Citrus Cove?"

I raised a brow. "I am. How do you know him?"

He handed me the guitar with a grin. "I play golf with him. Good man. Funny how small our world is. My name is Joey Grace."

"Nice to meet you, Joey. It is a small world," I said slowly, my attention already turning to the guitar.

I sat down on the bench and stared at it for a moment, absorbing the weight of its body against mine. Fuck. It felt really good. My fingertips brushed the strings and I started to play the piece that had been haunting me, forgetting about the man and even Colt. The *sound* of it. *God.* It sounded so good. The melody was meant to be played on a guitar like this.

When I played it, Colt and Sarah came to mind. The way they made me feel, the way I wanted forever with them.

My eyes closed as I continued, humming softly.

A throat cleared.

I looked up, startled by the presence of other people. Colt's eyes were wide, his smile faded.

"What's wrong?" I asked him.

He shook his head. "I don't know if I realized how good you are. That was beautiful."

It was for you and Sarah.

"It was," Joey agreed. "You got a gift. Tell you what, Sammy. I'll give you a deal on it if this is the one for you. I'll bring it down to seven."

"He'll take it," Colt said immediately.

"*Colt*," I hissed.

"*Sammy*."

Joey grinned and crossed the room to his desk. "I'll give you two a moment."

I stood up and set the guitar down on one of the available

stands. Colt took a step closer to me, craning his head back to look up at me.

"You know you want it," he said.

"I do," I admitted.

His brow raised. "Don't tell me you're still feeling bad about us pitching in?"

"It's not that," I chuckled. "Although, it's certainly a factor. It's a lot of money, but I know I'll have it the rest of my life."

"Then what's holding you back?"

"I know I'll always think of you when I look at it."

Colt smiled. "Then we can't fuck up, huh?"

No, we couldn't.

I held his gaze for a moment and then decided I didn't care if Joey saw us, I leaned down and kissed him hard enough to leave him breathless. "That song was for you and Sarah," I whispered in his ear.

His eyes widened as I snatched the guitar and walked over to Joey.

"I'll take you up on that offer, Joey. This guitar is meant to be mine."

CHAPTER TWENTY-FOUR

SAMMY and I took turns sitting at the cafe over the next three days. Alice had agreed after hearing what happened and the only reason she hadn't told Sarah to take off for a couple weeks was because we all knew Sarah would say no.

Today was my day at the cafe with her, and Sarah's shift rolled by fast. I managed to get some work done too, even though focusing was a struggle. Sammy regularly sent us text updates. We occasionally got a selfie of him with his new guitar, which was the type of joy we all needed right now.

Seeing his face had been a gift to myself. The guitar was perfect for him, and I had to admit—hearing him play it in my house really made it feel like a home.

Aside from occasional slivers of happiness, the rest of the news wasn't good.

David clearly wasn't driving his old truck. Emma said she thought he was driving a small, gray car, which helped, but not enough to completely narrow down our search. I ended up going through all of the security footage, but discovered that the front porch camera wasn't working.

Which meant we didn't have anything to give to the cops to prove he was on the doorstep.

It infuriated me. It scared the shit out of me too. The fact that he'd had the balls to show up like that put us all on high alert. The group chat we'd created with the seven of us—Haley, Cam, Emma, Hunter, Sammy, Sarah, and me—was constantly popping off as we all sent updates. Emma had changed the name of the chat to *'Operation Jail David,'* which we all approved of.

My eyes wandered across the cafe to Sarah. Her auburn hair was pulled back in a bun, but a few loose strands framed her face. She was so efficient in how she handled tables and talked to locals. Most of the people who had come through today were familiar Citrus Cove faces. Occasionally, one of them had come up to me to chat, but for the most part—I'd spent eight hours simply watching Sarah.

My phone buzzed on the table. I picked it up and smiled as I read Sammy's text.

Sammy: How's our girl doing?

Our girl. My smile widened. Everything was changing fast between us, but we'd known each other our entire lives so it was a natural jump. I didn't have to question who he was, even though there were certainly things about him I didn't know.

I could say the same for Sarah. I knew her. And that burning love, which had simmered to a quiet ember over the years, was reignited, burning hotter and brighter the more I found myself back in her orbit.

Me: Working hard, as always. Anything yet?

Sammy: Nope. Do you want me to cook dinner for us tonight?

For us. My stomach did a slow flip. How was it possible to feel so smitten with two people? All the butterflies I had with Sarah, I felt with Sammy too.

Me: Yes. I'll eat anything you cook.

He sent back a wink emoji and I chuckled.

"Whatcha smiling about, Colton Hayes?" Sarah asked.

She slid a glass of sweet tea with a lemon wedge in front of me and planted her hand on her hip.

"Our man is sweet," I said.

Her cheeks bloomed pink. "Yeah, he is. Tell him I said hi."

"I'll tell him you said you can't wait to roll around in bed with him again."

Sarah gasped and swatted my arm with a chuckle. "Sure, do that. It's quiet tonight, so I think I'll be here for only another hour. You sure you're okay?"

"Yeah, sugar," I said. "I'd rather be here with you."

She tucked one of those stray strands of hair behind her ear and nodded. My gaze roamed over her as she turned to check on one of the other booths, chatting with the few customers left as the Thursday evening rush wound down.

I glanced out the window and frowned as that truck drove by, the one that looked like David's. What if he'd sold it? Or maybe he'd swapped his truck for another car?

I made a mental note to follow up on that. Maybe it could lead us to where he was staying. Hunter, Sammy, and Cam had been driving around Citrus Cove for hours. Hell, I'd seen their cars drive by the cafe several times. This town was small so there was only so much area to cover.

Even Bob and Lynn, their Mom and Pops, were on the lookout. Honey and Lynn had mobilized every lady in the Citrus Cove Crafting Facebook group to keep an eye out.

All of us were pulling together around Sarah and the boys. That at least gave me some peace. And Emma and Haley were working on deep diving Sammy's social media to flag potential stalkers—so that situation was being addressed too.

At the end of the day, we were all there for each other.

Even with the rift between Emma and Hunter, we were a family.

Another hour went by quickly and I watched as the last of the customers left. Sarah locked the entrance as I got up, gathering plates and other dishes from tables.

"You don't have to help," Sarah said.

"I don't mind. Who else is closing up?"

"Just me and Trey," she said. "He's closing the kitchen. He's usually done fast. I'll clean up out here."

I nodded and made a stack, carrying them to the back. She was right about Trey, he had almost everything done already. He was an older guy with silver hair, glasses, and a gentle demeanor.

He glanced up and nodded. "Think it's good you're watching out for her," he said.

"Me too," I said. I didn't really know Trey. He moved here a few years ago with his wife and kids—who were now teens, if I remembered correctly. I never ran into him outside of Citrus Cove Cafe or occasionally the grocery store. "Have you seen anything weird?"

"Nope. I'd tell Alice if I saw anything, though. Just leave the dishes in the sink."

I nodded and did as he asked. I headed back to the front of the house and grabbed a broom.

Sarah shook her head at me. "Colt, just let me work."

"I am," I said. "Let me help. I've been sitting all day. Moving around is good for me."

She pressed her lips together but returned to wiping down tables. I glanced at her shoes.

Earlier this week, I'd noticed she needed new ones. So I'd done the natural thing and had asked Emma to investigate for me. I found out what size and brand it was and ordered her a new pair. They'd be arriving today.

I pulled out my phone and sent Emma a quick text.

Me: Operation Shoe is still a go. They should be arriving today.

Emma: Got it. I'll replace them when they arrive ;)

Emma was the best wingwoman around.

Me: Thanks, I owe you one.

Emma: If you can convince her to actually take some time off, then I'll owe you one back

Me: I'll do my best

Emma: Good. Haley approves too.

"You have that look on your face like you're conspiring against me," Sarah said.

I slipped my phone into my pocket with a shrug. "Maybe. Maybe not."

Her honey-brown eyes narrowed on me and rolled when I did jazz hands, being silly as I used the broom to dance my way toward her.

"My god, you are such a dork." She laughed as I spun and set the broom against one of the tables.

Once she was within arms reach, I tugged her close and dipped her low. She squeaked and held onto me, giggling as I kissed her.

"I'm working here, mister." But she kissed me back, her arms winding around my neck.

"Mmhmm." I cupped her face, stroking her cheek. "I wish I could spend the night with you."

Her eyes lit up. "Me too, but..."

"We don't need to rush," I said. "How are Davy and Jake doing?"

"They're okay," she sighed. "They're... This is a lot. It's hard on them. And I think they're slightly suspicious of you and Sammy, but I'm going to talk to them soon. Not that I need their approval."

"I do." I brought us back to standing, still holding her close to me. "I'll steal you away again sometime this week," I promised.

"Please do."

I lowered my voice to whisper in her ear. "If Trey wasn't here, I'd take you in the break room."

Her cheeks turned bright pink. "*Colton.*"

"I could fuck you against the wall and make you come over an over..."

Her breath hitched. Both of us stiffened as we heard footsteps and I stepped back right as Trey came around the corner.

"Just wrapped everything up. Are you good to lock up?" he asked.

"Yeah," Sarah said. "I have Colton with me. We'll be fine."

He nodded and put a ball cap on his head, tipping it as he headed out the back door. I heard it open and close before giving Sarah a wide grin.

"You fucker," she said, slapping my chest playfully.

"Okay, but now he's gone... Last I checked, the cafe doesn't have cameras..."

"I've been working all day and I'm sweaty..."

"And?"

I held her gaze as I took a step back, and then another, until I flipped the light switch for the dining area. Light filtered through the wide windows from the parking lot, dipping us in shadows.

"What if we get caught?" she whispered.

"We don't have to if you don't want to," I said. "I'm happy just being in your presence."

Her eyes lit up and she closed the space between us. I sucked in a breath as she pulled me close, wrapping her arms around my neck again and kissing me hard.

My brain short-circuited.

I kissed her back, drinking her in. My hands slid to her waist and I twirled the two of us, pushing her against the wall hard enough to rattle the paintings.

The heat between us was explosive. For the last few days, we hadn't caught a moment to have sex. And while I'd take whatever kiss or lingering touch I could get, I was starving for her.

"I want this," she breathed out. "I want you."

I leaned down, kissing her hungrily. I'd been watching her all day, wishing I could flip her over my shoulder and have my way with her, and now I was getting the chance to.

She yelped as I lifted her, pulling her legs around my waist. A nervous giggle escaped before melting into a softer sound as she felt my erection against her.

"I'm so fucking hard for you, sugar." I nipped her bottom lip. "I've been thinking about bending you over the diner table for hours and fucking you until you can't think of anything else."

"Oh," she rasped.

I put her down and spun her around, unbuttoning her jeans quickly. She squeaked as I pulled them and her panties down, exposing her. I slid my fingers against her pussy and groaned, finding her wet.

"Tell me," I growled in her ear. "How long have you been wanting me to fuck you, Sarah?"

"All day," she said. "I couldn't stop looking at you while I was working. You kept distracting me. You were all I could think about."

"Good. The only other man I want on your mind is Sammy."

"Oh."

I meant every possessive word said. I slid my fingers over

her clit, circling her. She gasped and bucked against me, but she wasn't going anywhere.

Right now, she was mine.

Right now, I wanted to make her cry out my name and forget her own.

I moved my other arm around her and gently grabbed the sides of her throat with my hand.

"Yes," she rasped.

My brows shot up. "Tap my wrist if you need me to stop," I said. "Understood?"

"Yes. *Oh god.*"

Her voice pitched high as I kept circling her clit. Her pleasure shot through me, edging me closer to coming myself. Pleasing her always pleased me. I squeezed her throat, holding her in place as her muscles contracted, her ass grinding against my cock.

The urge to fill her up with every fucking drop was so damn intense. Heat licked up my spine, desire pumping through me. I wanted to make her come and then bury myself deep inside her.

"That's right sugar," I huffed. "Fuck, you're so wet."

I circled her clit faster and she writhed against me. Sarah squeaked, arching back one last time as her voice rang through the cafe, her orgasm racking her entire body. I closed my eyes, inhaling her sweet scent.

Fuck, fuck, fuck.

I was so damn close. I jerked the button of my jeans and slid them down with my boxers, aiming my cock. She gasped as I shoved inside of her in one swift motion, her cunt slick and welcoming me with ease.

"Colt," she cried. "You feel so good."

I panted as I cupped her breasts, thrusting my hips eagerly. "Sarah," I groaned.

I'd imagined moments just like this countless times over the years. Having her against me, my cock throbbing inside her, the thrum of her pulse at the base of her throat— "Fuck," I grunted. "*I'm there*, sugar."

"Come inside me," she rasped.

"I can't," I growled, even though I so desperately wanted to. "You're not on birth control."

"I want you to," she rasped. "*Please.*"

Fuck it. I slid my hands down her body and gripped her hips hard, ramming into her right as I came. I grunted as I filled her, pinning her to the wall and holding her tight.

She melted against me. I kissed her shoulder and then the side of her neck, enjoying every soft sigh and shiver.

I could barely think straight, my mind in a soft after-orgasm haze.

"Sarah," I whispered, realizing what we'd done.

I slowly pulled out of her, cum dripping down her thighs. I hiked my pants back up, wishing now that we had more time to be together. But I'd still take these moments with her whenever I was lucky enough to have them.

I loved her so much. I pressed my face to her hair as she let out a soft hum.

"Fuck," I mumbled. "I want to spend days with you. Weeks. Forever."

"Me too," she said.

My fingers grazed over her skin. I took my time to touch her, to feel her, and slowly helped her redress. Once we were situated, I turned around, kissing her again gently.

"We should talk about sexual health though," I said, wincing.

It didn't really seem like the right moment to, but it was something we had yet to discuss. The three of us needed to talk about it.

"I wanted that," Sarah said, cupping my face. "I started taking the pill earlier this week. I should have told you and Sammy."

A wave of relief washed over me. "I think I might look into getting a vasectomy. As much as I want to be a father to your boys, I'm not sure if I want biological children."

"I can't even think about another kid," Sarah said. She smiled, relaxing against the wall. "I do like the process involved in making one, though."

"Me too," I said. "I like coming inside you."

Her cheeks were already pink, but they went three shades darker. I kissed her forehead with a smirk.

A flash of headlights had both of us looking up. She let out a soft curse. "We should get going."

I nodded. Luckily, the car that had pulled into the parking lot was just using it to turn around. They drove off, leaving my truck alone.

"Let me get you home," I said. "I'll talk to Sammy tonight. He's making us dinner."

"Jealous," she teased. "I'll talk to him too. I was sort of hoping to see him this week, but I don't know when," she said. "You taking him to the music store is one of the sweetest things I've ever heard. I'm really glad you did that."

I nodded. "I can't tell you how happy it made me."

She smiled. "I'm glad. Also, I just wanted to say—I don't want there to be any secrets between the three of us. I know we're still figuring out what all being together will look like, but I think communication is probably most important."

"It is," I agreed. "I'm an open book, sugar. My heart is on my sleeve for both of you."

Her lips tugged into a soft smile. "It sure is. Let me do a couple other things and then we can get out of here."

I helped her put up any last minute items before heading

out the back door into the cool night. She locked the deadbolt and skipped to my truck with a pep in her step.

I caught up to her and looped my hand in her long hair, tugging her back against me. She laughed as she turned, her hands sliding up my chest.

"Haven't you had enough of me?"

"Never," I breathed. "I could never get enough of you."

I opened the door for her and lifted her into the passenger seat before she could protest.

She shook her head at me. "What am I going to do if you keep spoiling me this way?"

"Fall in love with me?"

Her eyes softened as I reached around and buckled her in. I stole one final kiss before shutting the door and going around to the driver's side. I got in and started up the heat.

"Alright, sugar. Time to get you home."

CHAPTER TWENTY-FIVE

sammy

I SPREAD OUT ALL the containers and added a heap of cilantro rice to each one, followed by black beans, grilled fajita veggies, grilled chicken, corn, and a small container of sauce. I'd cooked enough to feed Colt and I tonight—and Sarah, the boys, and Emma for the next few days.

Colt's love language was giving gifts. My love language was meal prep. Cooking for everyone brought me an immense amount of joy. I hoped the boys would eat it too, but if not, I'd find out what they liked and cook that instead.

I heard the front door unlock. I poked my head around the corner as it opened and Colt stepped inside. He immediately lifted his nose to the air and groaned. "Smells good."

"Good," I said as he locked the door and kicked off his boots.

He came to the kitchen and raised a brow at the army of meal containers.

"I'm cooking for Sarah's house too," I said quickly.

"That makes sense. Fuck, that's really sweet. I think they'll all love it."

"I wasn't sure if the boys are picky eaters or not," I said. "But I kind of wanted to surprise them. Well, I didn't want Sarah to tell me no."

He smiled and surprised me by looping his finger in the top of my jeans and pulling me close. I grabbed his jaw and leaned in to kiss him, and then paused, raising a brow.

"You smell like sex," I said.

"We may have gotten carried away at the cafe..."

The thought went straight to my cock. I planted my hands on the counter to either side of him, caging him in. "Tell me everything."

His eyes fluttered. "Fuck. I can't think while you're this close to me and I wanted to be serious."

I cocked my head. "I believe in you."

I liked seeing him flustered. Especially because I knew how smooth he could be. But after he took me to the music store and made me forget how to use words, he deserved to be a little flustered.

"I came inside Sarah."

My eyes widened. "Oh. That's a big step."

"It is. She started the pill and forgot to tell us. I was relieved. Because I may or may not have a breeding kink, but I don't want to have biological kids."

"Relatable," I said, smiling. "Did you think that would upset me?"

"I wasn't really sure. This is still so new."

"It is," I whispered. "Colt, feel how fucking hard I am right now."

His mouth fell open as I guided his hand to the outline of my cock. He made a noise, somewhere between a groan and a whimper.

"Help me put all the lids on everything and clean up," I said. "Then we can keep talking *seriously*."

"Alright. You know how to motivate a man."

I chuckled as the two of us worked together to get lids on the containers. I separated ours from the others.

"I'll take these over in the morning," I said. "Probably before Sarah goes to work. Are you going to the cafe tomorrow with her? Or should I?"

"I think you should," he said. "I think she wants some time with you this week. Maybe the three of us can plan something on her day off."

I nodded. "I'd like that. I think trying to maintain some sort of normalcy is good."

"I think so too. I take it there hasn't been any progress with finding David?"

I sighed as I put the last of the containers in the fridge. Colt was already starting on dishes. "No. We looked everywhere. Cam and Hunt were tearing up the whole area. We even checked the house where..."

I trailed off because Colt nodded, already knowing what I meant. The house where we'd found Haley, where Thomas Connor had lived and killed and god knew what else. The horrific events of last year still haunted all of us, and we couldn't move past it because David was still around.

It was terrifying that someone so evil could live in Citrus Cove.

"This is back to the conversation earlier, but I think I'm going to get a vasectomy," Colt said. "I've been thinking about it for a while and well... Not that Sarah has complained, but I know birth control can fuck with hormones and stuff. And it's an easy process for me."

I'd considered it before, but this made me think about it even more. "Maybe we could go together."

Colt snorted. "Partners who get vasectomies together, stay together?"

"Yeah, something like that. Although no sex for a few weeks would be torture. But worth it in the long run."

He chuckled. "We could make up for it after. If you're serious, then I'll be serious too."

"I am," I said. "I'll talk to Sarah more tomorrow. I also plan to go by a clinic this week to get STD and STI tested just to be safe. I'd also like to have sex without a condom if that's something we're all comfortable with... breeding kink and all that..."

"I'm comfortable with it. Obviously, you and Sarah can set your own boundaries. And for the record, I'm comfortable with you and me having sex without a condom too."

"Once I get tested, we can revisit not using a condom," I said.

He nodded in agreement and I stepped up behind him, circling my arms around his waist and setting my chin on his shoulder as he did more dishes. I couldn't complain about him taking over on the clean up, and there was something about the mundane actions that warmed me.

He continued talking. "I'll tag along when you go. I mean, I was tested awhile back, but it doesn't hurt to do so again and it's quick and easy."

"Oh to be responsible sluts," I teased.

He chuckled as he set the final pan on the drying rack, washed his hands, and turned off the faucet. "Did you already eat?"

"No, I was waiting for you. I think I could wait a little longer..."

"Good. So can I."

He turned around, his body pressing against mine. I cupped my hand behind his neck and kissed him. His hands slid under my shirt and ran over my stomach and up to my nipples, teasing them.

"Fuck," I muttered.

"Tell me what to do," he whispered.

I moved my hand around his throat, holding him there as I growled in his ear. "How do you feel about getting rough?"

He nipped my bottom lip in response. Tension flared as I tightened my grip. "Pretty damn good, Sammy."

"You know our safeword?"

"Yes, sir."

"Is there anything you don't want?"

"No."

"What if I said I have a paddle?"

He smiled, dimples showing as he batted his lashes. "What if I said *is that all you've got?*"

"Fucker," I mumbled, licking my lip where he bit me. "Go strip and bend your ass over your bed. Understood?"

"Yes, sir."

I heard his smart ass tone and smiled, knowing he'd regret it when he couldn't sit straight in the truck tomorrow. I let him by and watched as he slinked down the hall to his bedroom. I heard the sound of his clothing hitting the floor as I stepped into my room, opening up one of the duffle bags.

I was still thankful that whoever destroyed my apartment had left my kink equipment alone. I dug out the wooden paddle made from an old wine barrel, sturdy and thick. It would *absolutely* leave marks.

The idea of doing that to Colt sent a bolt of desire through me. My cock throbbed against my pants as I stalked to his bedroom, pausing in the doorway.

Fuck. It was hot seeing him so damn obedient. I stood there for a moment, taking him in. His muscles were lean and toned, his ass damn near perfect.

He looked back over his shoulder at me and quirked a brow. "Just gonna stand there?"

"You're a brat," I said. "You're not going to be able to sit tomorrow."

"Is that a promise?"

My jaw stiffened as I fought a smile. I'd never been with someone so sassy. He was pushing my buttons perfectly and I liked it.

There was no way in hell I was going to admit that to him right now, though.

I prowled to the edge of the bed and tossed the paddle next to him. His eyes widened when he saw it. I remained silent as I slowly undid my belt. Even the sound of the metal clinking against metal had his muscles tensing.

I tossed it to his pile of clothes and added the rest of mine. I stood naked now, my cock piercing gleaming, every inch hard and ready to fuck him. It would be a while before we got there.

"I'm going to spank you and fuck your sassy mouth," I said. "Then we'll see about me breeding you."

"Fuck," he whispered.

His cock was clearly hard.

"Don't touch yourself, or we'll stop," I said. "Understood?"

"Yes, sir."

"Relax," I whispered.

He took a deep breath and attempted to. I ran my palm over his ass cheek and began to warm up the skin, patting each one to bring blood to the surface. With a paddle like this one, I wanted to get him ready before any sort of impact play.

"I can't believe we never knew this about each other," Colt whispered.

"Knew what?"

"That we're kinky."

"You're my brother's best friend. Wasn't exactly a topic of conversation before now."

"I'm not used to being on this end of things. It's vulnerable."

I paused and softened my touch some. "It is," I said. "It's sexy that you can do both."

"Thank you."

"You never told me about you and Sarah. Start talking."

His breath shuttered.

"I want to hear exactly what you did to our girl," I prompted.

Colt grunted, his fingertips digging into the blankets. He looked back over his shoulders at me as I continued to pat his ass, readying him to be spanked.

"I'd been sitting there all day thinking about her," he said. His voice was heavy with desire as he continued. "And once everyone left, she locked the front door. All I wanted to do was fuck her. I kept imagining bending her over one of the tables."

I gave his ass a few slaps, increasing the pressure.

"I kissed her and couldn't get enough. I pushed her against the wall and grabbed her throat."

I paused. "Did she like it?"

"Yes, she did," he moaned. "She liked it a lot."

I struck him harder this time, his skin blooming red. He sucked in a breath.

"She was so fucking wet. I played with her until she came and I couldn't take it anymore. I fucked her hard and fast and came inside her."

I reached for the paddle. He arched as the cool wood touched his hot skin. I brought it back to swing it, but paused.

His whole body tensed and then he shot me a glare. "You're so mean."

I smirked and brought it down, hitting one cheek fairly hard. Colt sucked in a breath and grunted.

"*Fuck.*"

I spanked the other cheek. His whimpering made my cock strain.

The paddle smacked against him over and over. I varied the intensity, teasing his mind too. That was what I enjoyed the most about kink and being a Dom. Playing with his mind was just as hot as playing with his body.

I reached down and worked my fingers through his hair, gripping him as I spanked him hard. He cried out, grunting as I held him in place.

"Don't you dare fucking move," I snarled.

He released a long, muffled moan into the blankets. Bruises started to form in long lines from the paddle. He yelped as I spanked him harder than before, his body lurching forward.

I didn't release his hair. He reached for my wrist, his nails clawing at me as I spanked him again.

"Fuck, Sammy," he barked. "You fucking bastard."

He shoved at me and I tossed the paddle to the side, grabbing hold of him and wrestling him to the center of the bed. He was strong and fast, but so was I, and I managed to pin him beneath me, forcing his arms above his head.

"I told you not to fucking move," I said.

"Fuck you," he snapped.

I bit down on the soft muscle of his shoulder and he cried out, bucking against me.

"You know your safeword if you need me to stop," I reminded him.

He threw his elbow back hard into my ribs, the pain distracting me long enough for him to roll out from under me. With my breath knocked out, he attempted to pin me down beneath *him.*

Ha. That was cute.

The two of us wrestled until he ended up right back where he started. I grabbed a fistful of his hair and yanked his head back, using my weight to hold him still.

"You really are a brat," I panted.

"If you weren't my boyfriend, I'd put you on your knees."

"Well, you *are* my boyfriend, and I'm going to put you on *your* knees."

His words were lost as I rolled him off the bed and took him to the floor. He grunted as he hit the wood and I put him on his knees, gripping his chin and forcing his lips apart. Before he could say anything else, I shoved my hard cock between them.

His eyes rolled back on a moan and he took me deeper, sucking me. I was so fucking hard, I was already close to coming.

I drew back right as I came to the edge, breathing hard. He stared up at me with such submissiveness that I melted. I leaned down, kissing him hard, his tongue swiping against mine.

"Fuck me," he whispered against my lips.

I nodded and reached for the drawer in the nightstand. I grabbed the bottle of lube and a couple of condoms as he got back onto the bed, rolling to the middle. His bed shifted as I knelt between his knees, putting on the condom quickly. I poured a generous amount of lube onto his hole and worked it in, and then even more over my cock.

Colt relaxed. Sweat glistened on his tan skin. I planted a hand above his head and looked down between us, lining up the head of my cock with him. I slowly pushed forward, easing inside of him. We groaned together and I took it as slowly as I could, giving him time to adjust to the size of me.

"You feel so fucking good," he said, lifting his head as he watched me fill him.

He milked my cock as I pushed further into him. Pleasure rushed through me, and I grabbed ahold of his chin, forcing him to kiss me. His legs wrapped around my waist, cock rubbing against me as we moved against each other.

"Bite me again," he rasped.

I thrust into him harder, a surge of need taking over. I dragged my tongue up his throat before biting his other shoulder hard. I wanted to mark him, to claim him like some feral monster.

"I'm so close," I rasped.

"Breed me, Sammy," he begged.

Fuck. I prided myself on lasting longer than this, but I couldn't take it. I gasped as I came. My muscles trembled as the waves stretched out, pleasure rolling through me.

I relaxed on top of Colt, the two of us breathing hard. He cupped my face, stroking my cheeks with his thumbs as he kissed me. Every touch was gentle and felt so damn right. I ran my hands over him gently, kissing the bite marks I'd left.

"One day I'll get used to making love to you," he whispered.

"I hope not," I mumbled. "Then you'll get bored of me."

He tipped my chin up, making me look at him. Brows drawn together, he shook his head. "Never, Sammy. I'll never get bored of you."

I swallowed hard. Something about this stung, and I finally realized what it was.

I'd fucked countless people and knew what I enjoyed when it came to sex and kink.

But I'd never let anyone get close. Not even family, not really.

Until now.

Intimacy like this scared the hell out of me.

I also worried I was both too much and too boring at the same time...

"What is it?" he whispered. "You can talk to me."

I shook my head and drew back, pulling out of him. I rolled to the side of the bed, sitting there.

He grabbed my forearm before I could stand up. "You're not running away so damn easily. Sit down."

In a rare moment of obedience, I remained seated. "I'm sorry, Colt. I don't know what's wrong with me."

"Lay down."

I sighed, tempted to run. I was a runner, after all. I could be out the door in the blink of an eye, out into the cold and far away from the warmth radiating from Colt.

That would be cruel to both of us.

"Sammy."

I leaned back and turned away on my side. I was being a bad Dom right now. I was being ridiculous, stupid, and—

Colt slipped his arms around me and rested his head next to mine. "You've always been quiet, but I'm no mind reader. I can't guess what's upsetting you."

"I don't know," I admitted softly. "I realized I've never been with someone I care about. This scares the fuck out of me."

"This scared you more than the guitar?"

A laugh bubbled up. He had a point.

"Truth be told, I'm scared too. But I think it's the good kind of scary."

I nodded slowly, trying to digest my feelings. The thing was, I didn't exactly know why this was coming up. I didn't know why I was like this. Anytime someone tried to get close, I ran the other way.

I had a family who loved me and did everything they could to help each other. We weren't perfect though, and some of the cracks in the foundation came from my relationship with my dad. My mom had always balanced out his harshness, and he'd mellowed out as he'd aged. Although he and Hunter still weren't on good terms.

"Maybe I need therapy," I sighed. "I'm sorry, Colt. Everything we just did was amazing, I didn't expect to feel this way."

"I think you're having some drop," he said gently.

He was right, I realized. I knew subs could have an emotional drop after an intense scene, and I knew Doms could too—but I'd never experienced it. Nothing could have prepared me for the ball in my chest and the way every nerve felt raw and exposed. Suddenly, all of the stress and fear and worries in my life couldn't be ignored. I worried that I'd hurt Colt. I feared I'd done something wrong or had gone too far—that I'd somehow ruined it all by pushing for a relationship with him and Sarah.

What if I didn't deserve them?

He'd already done so much for me. Sarah had too. I wanted to earn their love and trust. My throat burned as I swallowed and I turned over, finally looking at him. His eyes were full of so much kindness.

The comfort in the familiarity, the trust I had in him—tears threatened to fall.

"This is stupid," I muttered.

"It's really not. You can cry, Sammy. I'm not going to judge you."

"I really hate crying."

He pressed a gentle kiss to my forehead. "Doesn't make you weak to cry. It makes you stronger."

"That's my line," I whispered, sniffling.

I couldn't stop it. I couldn't remember the last time I'd cried like this. It'd been years.

I buried my face against his chest and cried. And everything hurt for a moment as I sobbed, and every time he held me tighter, my heart only ached more because I couldn't think of a time I'd let someone see me like this.

All he did was hug me and occasionally kiss the top of my head. That was all I needed.

"When I first realized I was bisexual, I wanted to kill myself," Colt whispered.

I drew back, looking up at him in shock. "What?"

"Yeah. My dad kicked me out and I thought something was wrong with me. But your parents were there for me. Cam was there for me. And then as I grew, I realized there was nothing wrong with me. I realized it was so normal, no different than anything else really. But goddamn—society really fucks with us. Especially living in a state like this. It is really difficult to make the decision to be authentic to yourself, but the amount of relief and happiness that comes after that decision is worth it."

I wiped my eyes, frowning. "I live authentically."

"Do you? Baby, I've learned so much about you in the last few weeks that the Sammy I know now and the one I knew before are two different people. And for the record, this Sammy is my favorite. This is the man I'm falling in love with. The man who played me a song the other day that stole my heart. Who is willing to meal prep for an entire family."

My heart skipped a beat. I considered his words, along with what my brother had said about not knowing me. Had I really been keeping everyone in my life at arm's length? What was I scared of? "I didn't realize how much space I'd put between myself and everyone in our lives. I think I've always worried I would be in the way or that everyone was too busy."

"Too busy for what? To know you?"

"Yeah." Fuck. I breathed out, wiping my eyes again. "I don't know. I think I've gotten used to keeping secrets and somehow keeping my family separate from my real life. After I graduated, I wanted that privacy because they were always in everyone's business. But eventually, it became more detrimental than not. I mean, Cam didn't even know I was bi."

He thumbed away a tear. "Have you ever come out to your family before?"

"No," I whispered.

"And do they even know how cool your content is?"

"No, they don't. I blocked my mom on Instagram. I mean, I know Cam and Hunter have seen my videos. I don't think they think it's cool."

"Yeah they do," Colt said. "You should hear about how they brag about you when you're not in the room. They're proud of you, Sammy."

"Maybe I should tell them more about my life. About me."

"I think you should," he said. "And not that it has to be a big ordeal or anything. But I think it might be worth having some conversations and letting the people who love you back into your life. I can't speak for you, but I can tell you that your family loves you. Your dad is a hard-ass, but he was there for me when I lost my own father. You know he threatened to fist fight mine?"

I laughed and relaxed, trying to take another breath. God, I was a fucking mess. "I think I got snot on your chest," I mumbled.

"You just fucked my ass, I think we're okay."

I snorted, feeling the dark clouds finally part. "Thank you," I murmured.

"Of course." He smiled and sat up, glancing at the doorway. "We should shower and eat. Then maybe you can play me a song."

"I'll play you anything you want."

Our stomachs rumbled.

He rolled out of bed with a wince. "I'll start the shower."

"Your ass is red." I grinned as he went to the door and planted his hands on his hips, wagging it at me.

"I feel the bruises already." He shot the paddle the bird before padding down the hall.

I stared at the ceiling for a moment.

Everything was going to be okay.

Like Colt said, it was scary to live authentically.

But it was about damn time I did anyway.

CHAPTER TWENTY-SIX

sarah

I STARTED a pot of coffee right as a knock echoed through the house. My heart leapt to my throat, but then my phone buzzed.

Sammy: It's me at the door

"Oh," I breathed out.

The stress over not knowing who was at the door would linger for a while. I winced and looked down at myself. Once again, he'd caught me looking like a raccoon that'd crawled out of a trash can. I wasn't even wearing a bra.

He's seen me naked. It's not like it matters now...

Those thoughts didn't help. I hesitated before unlocking the front door and opening it quietly.

Fuck, he was hot.

Sammy stood there with a big box in his hands and a tote bag slung over his shoulder. Dawn turned the sky pale purple behind him, while the quiet neighborhood was still tucked in bed. He was dressed in dark jeans and a henley shirt that showed off his forearms, and his lips tugged into a smile. *He's too hot for me.*

A cold wind lifted, hitting me right in the chest. His stormy blue eyes slid down to my breasts as my nipples hardened.

"Mm. Good morning, gorgeous," he said. "I come bearing gifts you cannot return."

"What?" I hissed. "Sammy..."

He slipped past me before I could protest further. I shut the door and followed him to the kitchen, crossing my arms. He sat the box and bag on the table and started to pull out containers.

I frowned. "What...?"

"So, I hope the boys like it too. But I prepared meals for you, them, and Emma for the next few days. Most of them are chicken fajita bowls, but I also made some sandwiches with chips that they can take to school. I thought it might give you some extra time back."

I was stunned. I stared in shock, not sure what to say.

"This is too much," I whispered. "Why did you do all this?"

He looked up at me. "Because I care about you. And you work so damn much. Cooking brings me joy, and for the first time ever, I've had people to cook for."

I stared at all of the containers, thinking about the amount of time he'd just saved me by not needing to cook or worry. It wasn't even about the time, but the fact he'd even thought that much about me.

And that he'd thought about Davy and Jake and Emma.

He took a step toward me, rubbing the sides of my arms gently. "Is this too much?"

"It is," I whispered. "But it's also one of the nicest things anyone has ever done for me. Thank you."

I slid my arms around him, all of my earlier insecurities melting away. He cupped my face and kissed me gently, humming as he drew back.

"I heard about your shift last night..."

His smirk made me scoff. "That rat bastard told you everything, huh?"

"Yeah, he did. All I'm saying is that I, too, will be at the cafe with you all day..."

I snickered. "I see. Noted. I'm glad I get to see you today."

"Me too."

He kissed me harder this time. I wrapped my arms around him, leaning into him.

"Mom?"

Sammy released me and I turned around, surprised to see Jake up so early. "Oh, good morning," I said, blushing. He wrinkled his nose at me and Sammy.

It was probably time I talked to him and Davy, right?

"You're up early," I said. "Are you feeling okay?"

"Yeah," he said. "I heard a man's voice and didn't know Sammy was here."

Fuck. I hadn't even thought about that.

"Sorry, bud," Sammy said. He left my side and held out his hand for a low-five. "I didn't mean to scare you."

"I'm not scared," Jake said defiantly, slapping his palm.

"Can I tell you a secret?" Sammy asked.

Jake's eyes lit up. "Yeah. What secret?"

"I'm really good at making pancakes. Do you and Davy like them?"

"I want pancakes! I'll tell Davy."

He took off running. "Quietly!" I hissed. "Emma is still sleeping."

Jake nodded and darted up the stairs. Sammy offered me an apologetic smile. "Hope that's okay."

"Yeah," I said. "I'm not going to complain about being cooked for. I'll talk to them this week about you and Colt."

"There's no rush," he said. "But of course, I think we'd both like that. Also, Colt and I were talking about vasectomies so you don't have to stay on birth control. Does it mess with your hormones a lot?"

"It can," I said. "It's been a long time since I've taken them though. Is that really something you both want?"

He closed the distance between us in one step and leaned down to whisper in my ear. "I want to fuck you and fill you over and over again, so yes. It's something I'm interested in. And I think our boyfriend wants that too."

My cheeks flamed. He peppered soft kisses on my forehead, then started to put the meals in the fridge. I stood there like an idiot for a few moments, trying to make my brain work.

"I'll pull out pancake stuff," I finally said.

"Okay. But then you should sit and enjoy your coffee while it's hot."

Maybe I was becoming spoiled, because I didn't argue. I pulled everything out for him, poured a cup of coffee, and took a seat to watch him cook.

I sipped my coffee. My shift didn't start until this afternoon, so I had some time to enjoy the morning. Sammy winked at me as he closed the fridge, with all of the meals organized within.

"Are they picky eaters?" he asked.

"Davy is sometimes, but they're both pretty easy," I said. "But no shellfish. Jake is allergic."

Sammy nodded. "Good to know. I'll make a note."

"Okay, chef," I teased.

I heard footsteps again. Jake practically dragged Davy down, both of them dressed and clearly ready for the promised pancakes.

"Morning, love bug," I said.

"Hi," Davy sighed. He eyed Sammy suspiciously and I could see his mind working. "Is Sammy your boyfriend?"

Welp. So much for waiting for this conversation.

"Okay. Family meeting time. Let's go talk in the living room," I said, getting up.

"I'll have pancakes ready in a few," Sammy said.

"Thanks."

I led my boys to the living room and pointed to the couch. They took a seat and I opted for the ottoman in front of them, gripping my mug.

Davy crossed his arms and scowled while Jake kicked his feet. It was clear he was anxious too, though.

"I have decided to start dating Sammy and Colt," I said.

"*Both* of them?" Davy asked.

"Yes," I said. "The three of us are dating each other. There are different kinds of romantic relationships, and what we're doing is called polyamory. It means that you love more than one person."

"Is that even possible?" Jake asked.

"It is," I chuckled. "I love both of you, don't I? I care about Colt and Sammy and I want them in our lives. I know they want to get to know you more too."

They looked at each other. I couldn't imagine what either of them were thinking. This was one of those moments that only the two of them could have.

"I want you both to know you can ask me anything," I said. "You boys are old enough to understand what polyamory means. I'm still learning about it myself."

Davy pressed his lips together. "I guess it's cool. I like Colt and Sammy."

"I do too," Jake said. "Do we have to call them dad?"

"No," I laughed, grinning. "We're still figuring this out, so I think it might be a little soon for that. Don't you think? Besides, you're still getting to know them too."

"Yeah," Davy said. "They make you smile. That makes me happy."

"Me too, baby," I said.

"Why isn't Colt here?" Jake asked.

"I think he's busy this morning." I leaned forward to pat his leg. "Maybe we can plan dinner with all five of us at some point."

"With pizza?" Jake asked. "And games? I showed Sammy our games and he liked them."

Davy shook his head. "He was probably just kidding."

"I don't think he was," I said. "But you should ask him. Give him and Colt a chance. They're not like... Well, they're nothing like David."

Jake and Davy both frowned. "Are we safe?" Jake asked.

"Yes," I said, my chest squeezing. "Uncle Cameron's brother, Hunter, is going to install more cameras around the house. And the two of you are super duper safe."

"Are *you* safe?" Davy asked.

"Yes. Sammy and Colt are helping keep me safe."

Davy nodded. "Okay. I'll give them a chance then."

I smiled as the two of them got up and headed back for the kitchen. I sat there for a few moments, trying to decide if I'd handled that well. Some parts of parenting were really just guessing. I'd never thought I'd be explaining why I'm dating two men to my kids, but here I was. And it seemed like it worked.

There were a lot of things to be worried about right now, but if Sammy and Colt could win me over, they could win Jake and Davy over too.

I leaned forward to see Sammy cooking and chatting with the boys. My heart leapt as he handed the spatula to Davy and showed him how to flip a pancake.

Seeing them together healed a part of me I'd never realized was broken until now.

I took another sip of coffee and smiled to myself, taking a

mental snapshot and tucking it away. I never wanted to forget this.

———

After pancakes and dropping the boys off at school, I took my time getting ready. Sammy sprawled out on my bed, his feet hanging off the edge, watching me as I got dressed in jeans and a t-shirt. I'd closed the bedroom door for some sort of privacy and to hide from the smirk Emma had when she saw Sammy cooking breakfast earlier. She'd left a few minutes ago to 'run errands'.

"What if I stole you from the cafe and made love to you all day?" he asked.

My eyes widened and I gave him a look that said 'hush.' "Sammy," I hissed.

He smiled as I pulled my hair up into a bun. I glanced at myself in the mirror and flopped on the bed next to him. He rolled over, snaking his arm around my waist and tugging me close.

"You're beautiful."

He ran his thumb over my bottom lip before kissing me. While his touch was soft, it was also electric. Tiny shocks scattered over my skin as I arched against him, so desperately wanting more.

"I have to get to work," I rasped.

"I know," he murmured. "Are you sure you can't be late? We have the house to ourselves..."

He was right. We were alone.

I glanced at the clock. "I only have twenty minutes. I don't think we have time, Sammy, I'm sorry."

"Don't be sorry, angel. We'll find time today or this week then," he said, kissing my forehead.

I nodded and slid my arms around him, hugging him tightly for a few seconds before peeling away. The bed creaked as we got up and he followed me downstairs.

I smiled as I opened our shoe cabinet, taking a seat on the bench right next to the front door. I reached for my tennis shoes, and froze.

They looked brand fucking new.

In fact, as I turned it over to study the bottom of the shoe, I realized there was no way that these were mine. I scouted around for my beat up pair, but they were nowhere to be found.

Where the hell were they? And where did these come from?

They were the same size too.

I stared at them and then shook my head. Was I imagining things?

Someone had bought me new shoes.

Sammy frowned. "What's wrong?"

I held up the shoe. "Did you do this?"

He raised a brow. "Did I do what?"

"Buy these?"

"Nope."

Dammit. Who had? Colt? I pulled my phone out and immediately texted him a picture.

Me: Did you do this??? Why would you buy me new shoes?

Colton: Sugar, that's just the first gift of many.

I scoffed. "I can't believe he did this."

A wide grin split Sammy's face. "I approve."

"How did he even pull this off?" I asked.

"I don't know. That man is full of surprises. Clearly."

I sighed and unlaced the shoes. The moment I slipped them on, I closed my eyes, holding back tears. I wasn't sure how long I'd kept the other pair, but the immediate relief in my feet was too much.

"I don't know what I'm supposed to do with the two of you," I whispered, looking down at the shoes. I wiggled my toes and bit back tears. "You're both too good to me."

Sammy knelt down in front of me and slid his hand over mine. "We want to take care of you."

"But why? What do I do in return?"

"What do you mean? You're a gift just by being you, Sarah. That's what you give in return. Your presence, your smile. That's all we need."

I pressed my lips together, but nodded.

Even with the hell-storm around us, I felt hope. I longed for the happy ending I'd dreamed about as a teenager.

With Colt and Sammy, maybe that could really happen.

sarah

I WAS ALREADY HALFWAY through my shift, but my feet didn't ache like they normally did. Even though I didn't like the thought of Colt spending money on me, I was incredibly thankful for the new shoes.

I carried a tray of food to a booth with two familiar faces. Katie Mays and Anna, her wife, smiled at me as I put their plates down in front of them. "How does it all look?" I asked cheerily.

"Good," Katie said. "How's everything going?"

"It's going as well as it can," I said honestly.

I'd gone to high school with Katie and while the two of us weren't close then, I considered her a friend now. I liked Anna too. Plus, they were friends of Colt and Sammy.

"I see Sammy is watching you like a hawk," Anna said with a smirk.

My cheeks heated and I glanced up at him, meeting his gaze across the cafe. Even this far away, the electric shock of him went all the way down to my toes.

"He is. It's all been a little chaotic…"

"Well, if you need anything, just let us know," Katie said. "We're on the lookout for David too, but haven't seen him around. It's like he's a damn ghost."

My stomach tugged. Not knowing where my ex-husband was made me uneasy. Since he'd shown up on my doorstep, it was like he'd disappeared in thin air.

"He's not that smart though," Anna said. "He'll turn up eventually."

"True," I agreed. "Just hopefully not on my doorstep again."

Katie cracked her knuckles. "Seriously, have the Harlows call us if some shit goes down."

Anna shook her head. "Okay, Wonder Woman. Relax. I think she's ready for a fight."

"Ready to save a beautiful woman from a stupid son of a bitch? Yep."

I laughed. "Thank you both. Holler if y'all need anything."

They nodded and started in on their food. It was a little early for the dinner rush, but the cafe was still bustling. I checked on a few more tables before darting to the back.

Alice glanced up at me from a stack of napkins and silverware she was prepping. Her curls were down today and haloed her head, her eyes glimmering gold.

She arched a brow. "I take it we're keeping Colt and Sammy as part of the staff every day?"

I winced. "Yeah. They want someone with me with everything going on."

Alice hummed in agreement. "Good. I like that. How are you feeling?"

"I'm doing okay, actually," I admitted. "Hopeful? Scared? A lot of things."

Her lips pulled into a soft smile. "Let me know if you need anything. Also, do you want Saturday off again?"

I hesitated. "Yes, I'd appreciate it." Did I shoot my shot? "Actually, Alice, I wanted to ask you something."

"Sure," she said. "Anything."

"Well... It's stupid, really. But I'm thinking about making baked goods to sell. Would that be something you're interested in carrying here? Like grab-and-go muffins. If not, it's fine. I don't want to step on toes—"

"Do it," she said, grinning. "Why not? We don't have anything like that. We can try it out."

"What? Really?" I was shocked. My stomach did a slow flip. "Are you sure?"

"Yes, ma'am," she said brightly. "So long as I get to taste them first."

"Okay," I said. "I'll make a batch soon and drop some off for you to try. How does that sound? If you hate them, there are no hard feelings."

"It's hard to hate a muffin, but I promise to be honest," she chuckled.

I smiled. "Thank you for giving me the chance. I'll bake them on my next day off." Which wouldn't be until next Saturday, but that was fine.

"Perfect."

I breathed out and fought the urge to squeal. It was just a small step, but it felt right. It felt good.

"Now, go take a quick break," Alice said. "Take a breather and then come back in. I'm trusting that Sammy is keeping you fed."

"He is," I promised. I reached into my pocket for my phone, and realized I must have left it in the car. I set the tray down on a table and checked my purse hanging by the back door, but it wasn't there. "I'm going to run out to my car real quick."

CLIO EVANS

"Take a real break," Alice called without looking back at me.

I opened the back door and stepped out into the cold. It was a bright blue sky today with not a single cloud in sight, a nice respite from the gray. Still, I held my arms as a brisk breeze blew straight through me.

I crossed the sidewalk to my Honda and frowned. Someone had left something on my windshield. I leaned over and flattened the paper down, every muscle freezing me in place.

Tucked beneath the wiper was a newspaper article with Thomas Connor's face printed on it. **YOU'RE NEXT** was written over the headline, circled in blood red ink.

Arms circled me. I screamed, driving my elbow back into a hard stomach.

"*Angel*, it's me," Sammy grunted quickly, releasing me. "Fuck. Christ. I'm so sorry. I shouldn't have done that. I wasn't thinking."

"God," I gasped, my entire body trembling. "What the hell?!"

He'd scared the fuck out of me.

"I'm so sorry," he said again. "Come here."

Sammy held out his arms. I immediately buried my face against his chest. I tried to breathe, holding onto him as my heart slowed.

"I am so sorry. I won't sneak up like that again." Sammy pressed his face against the top of my head, squeezing me tight. "Are you okay? I saw you out the window and decided to come outside."

"There's an article on my car," I said.

He didn't let go of me as he leaned forward, muttering a curse. I looked over my shoulder as he picked up the newspaper, his brows drawing together in a glare.

242

"Go back inside. I'll..."

"Do what?" My voice shook as I spoke. "We can't do anything. Whoever left that is long gone."

"This is a threat." He shook his head, staring down at the red circle.

The other word circled on the page was my name.

My stomach twisted as nausea crept up. Fear stiffened every muscle in my body, my heart still racing. Whoever had left this here clearly wanted to scare me, and they had succeeded.

I heard the back door slam and looked up to see Alice rushing to us with a frown. "What happened?" she asked. Sammy handed her the newspaper and her eyes widened. "What the fuck? We should probably call someone."

"I don't think they can do anything with that," I said. "It's not like Bud is going to be able to find David with a newspaper."

"Do you think it was David?" Alice asked with a frown. She looked over the paper once more and then handed it back to Sammy. "We would have spotted him... right? I mean all of us are on high alert. I look out the window every five minutes. It would be really ballsy of him to show up in broad daylight."

She had a point. "I can't think of who else it might be," I said.

The entire situation exasperated me. Where was David? Was he lurking around every corner, waiting for me to be alone? Or was it someone else? The woman who stopped us at the theater?

"I'm so tired," I whispered. "I just want things to be normal. Is that too much to ask?"

"Until we catch him, it might be," Alice said. "But it's going to be okay. Could it have been that lady?"

"Maybe?" I looked at the paper again, scouring for any other clues.

"This is an old paper," Sammy said. "Printed last year. Whoever put this here has kept this article for a while."

"It could have been someone random too," I said. "Some people still blame me for what happened."

Sammy and Alice shook their heads. "It pisses me off," Alice muttered. "You didn't know."

"I didn't. But not everyone believes me."

In fact, a lot of people still blamed me. Even though I was a victim in that situation, many felt like I was some sort of harlot who had tempted Thomas into being a serial killer. Because of course that's how serial killing worked.

It was insane and made no sense, but that was part of why everything had been so hard for us. It wasn't just David who hated me—there were people I'd known my whole life who now thought twice before talking to me. It was the strain of knowing that my boys had been impacted so deeply by all of this, to the point that I worried about them going to school and being bullied.

Alice pressed her lips into a line, looking over my car. She crossed her arms, her gaze darting to me.

"I don't know what you're about to say, but I already don't like it," I muttered.

She snorted. "We're getting to know each other too well. Take the day off. Go home, reset."

I immediately shook my head. "I can't. We're about to have the dinner rush."

"I'll pay you. I rather you be safe, Sarah."

"I can't take advantage of you like that. You already do so much for me."

Her gaze softened. "Sarah, I care about you. And I know how hard of a worker you are, and I appreciate that, but beyond you working for me—I want you to be safe. *This* is scary."

"I just want to work," I said. "I want to forget about it. I need to stay busy. If I go home right now, I'll fall apart. I can't do it. Please."

Sammy gently rubbed my shoulders, not interfering. Alice gave him a pleading look, but he shook his head. "Whatever you decide. I go where she goes."

"Okay." Alice rubbed her temples. "Okay, fine. Stay for the rest of the shift. Not a single minute over. And if anything else happens or anything feels off, you'd better tell me. Okay?"

I nodded. "Thank you."

She grimaced and glanced back at the newspaper. "This is some scary shit. I wasn't here last year when everything happened to your sister, but I just... I hate the idea of someone coming around like this. It's dangerous."

"I know," I said. "I'm sorry—"

She held up her hand. "Don't do that."

I made a face. Alice offered me a patient smile as I tried to find words that weren't completely apologetic. "I need the normalcy of working. This could have been nothing. Maybe just an angry local."

"It's too much of a coincidence," Sammy said. "I'm starting to wonder if that woman is related to the Thomas Connor situation."

"Maybe he had a secret family," Alice said.

"Maybe?" I echoed.

I hadn't thought about that. But at this point, anything was a possibility.

There were a lot of unknowns when it came to Thomas.

Sammy gave my shoulder a gentle squeeze. "I still have to tell everyone about this."

I sighed. "Can it wait until I finish working?"

"No," he said. "Colt would kill me. Your sister would kill me. Everyone would kill me."

Alice stepped toward the door. "If you don't tell them, I will."

I fought a groan. "Fine. I'm going back inside."

Sammy chuckled. "Right behind you, angel."

CHAPTER TWENTY-EIGHT

CAM CLASPED my shoulder before sitting down next to me on a barstool in his kitchen. "Sarah is okay," he said. "Everyone has checked in on her. She'll be getting off work in a bit."

The pictures of the newspaper came through right as our meeting with the contractor started. I'd spent the last few hours slowly losing my mind, trying to focus on our work while wondering if Sarah and Sammy were okay. Sammy had assured me several times that Sarah was fine, but I still worried.

"Hal is bringing the boys over for the night," Cam said. "And Emma is joining us too. Take a deep breath."

I did as he said and breathed out, my shoulders sinking, releasing some of the tension. "I'm sorry I was distracted in the meeting. I kept worrying David would show up at the cafe and something would happen."

Cam gave me a quizzical look. "Don't apologize for that. We're all worried."

I slumped over and rested my head on the cool counter. The meeting had gone well, at least. We were one step closer to getting our dream set up for the future of Citrus Cove Wine & Ciders. We were also bouncing around new names for it that would be eye-catching on shelves.

I pulled my phone out and checked my messages, scrolling through my conversation with Sammy. A photo came through of him sitting in the booth, golden light clinging to him. I let out a low whistle.

"What?" Cam asked.

"Your brother is hot," I said.

Cam wrinkled his nose. "Keep it in your pants, sir."

I grinned, sending Sammy back a kneeling emoji before looking back at my friend. "I wish we had the license plate for the car David was driving. It would be easier to get info. I just want to find the son of a bitch."

"I know. Hunter has been trying to get more information. About Sammy's apartment too. He's convinced it's all related somehow."

"It could be," I agreed. "I'll do some more digging. We're gonna find him, one way or another."

"We will. He won't hurt Sarah or the boys again." Cam let out a slow breath and propped his chin up with a hand, studying me with the nosiness of someone who'd known me forever. "So..."

"Yesss?" I drew out dramatically.

"Aside from everything going on, how's it going?"

"Fishing for information, are we?"

"Maybe."

"For you or Haley?"

"Both?"

I snorted and sat up, thinking about Sarah and Sammy. "I don't know where to begin. The guitar really meant a lot to Sammy. Thank you for pitching in. Both you and Hunter."

"We were happy to help. The picture of you two made me

smile. I think it's been a while since I've seen either of you this happy."

I rubbed my chest, thinking about Sammy's expression when he picked up the blue guitar. "Getting to know him this way has been... invigorating? Exciting? I mean, I've known him my entire life, but I'm learning new things about him."

Cam smirked. "You should have seen Hal's face when I told her I walked in on y'all."

I snorted. "I'm sure she was amused. And then things with Sarah are amazing too. I'm scared I'll fuck it all up."

His brows knit together. "You can't worry about that. You deserve to be happy, Colt. You deserve to be loved. It makes me happy the three of you have found each other."

"Me too."

"What about being a dad? I mean, we've talked about kids a few times and it always seems like you didn't want them."

I swallowed hard. "Honestly, I've always said that because I didn't want to carry on my dad's name. Like I'd somehow turn into him and fuck them up."

"No. That could never happen—"

"I know," I said. "But it's still a fear of mine. But with Davy and Jake, it feels natural. I'm still getting to know them. Sarah said she talked to them about polyamory, and about the three of us dating."

"Did she say how they responded?"

"Good? It sounded like it went well. But I don't want to rush anything, given how David treated the boys. I don't want them to feel like they have to like me."

Cam's expression turned lethal. "Fucking hate David."

"You and me both. Some of the things he said to Sarah that I know about now, especially with intimacy... It infuriates me, Cam. If I would have known—"

"You can't do that to yourself," he interrupted. "You can't

think about what you would have done. I've been there. I tortured myself for ages about how I treated Haley in high school. But you can't change the past. You can only focus on the future."

"I've been given a second chance," I said. "And I just want to show Sarah and Sammy that I'm worthy of it."

"You are. I can't think of anyone else more deserving."

The front door swung open and we looked up as Davy and Jake piled into the foyer, followed by Haley, Emma, and Donnie.

"Shoes in the cubby!" Haley reminded them.

Jake groaned, but kicked off his shoes next to Davy's. I grinned as they immediately beelined it to us.

"Hey," I said, offering a high-five.

"Hi, Colt." Jake met my palm with a full force slap. Davy snorted and leaned against the bar, eyeing me suspiciously.

Cam leaned over and ruffled his head. "How was school?"

"It was fine," Davy said. "We have homework."

Jake groaned. "Why did you tell them that?!"

"Have Colt help," Emma said. "He's good at math."

"Am I?" I echoed. Davy and Jake's gazes turned to me. "I'm pretty good at it. I'll help, then we can watch a movie."

"I brought sheet masks," Emma announced as she sat her dog purse on the floor, opening it up so Donnie could hop out. He was wearing a polka dot sweater and boots today. "And unicorn headbands."

She held up a pink fuzzy headband with a spiraled rainbow horn.

"I want one," I said immediately.

"A unicorn headband?" Davy questioned.

"Yep," I said. "Back me up, Cam."

"I fear that I, too, need a unicorn headband," Cam said.

Emma tossed me one and I grinned as I pulled it over my head and pushed it back into my hair.

"You look like that orange muppet," Cam snickered.

I struck a pose, earning a few giggles. "Orange muppet, at your service."

Davy and Jake both grinned, which was a win.

Haley laughed as she opened the fridge. "I'll make some snacks, Emma will order pizza, and you two help them with homework. What movie are we watching?"

"Avengers!" Jake exclaimed. He bounced on the balls of his feet with the type of energy I distinctly recalled having at that age. "Or something superhero."

"Jake, you picked last time," Hal said. "It's Davy's turn."

Davy wrinkled his nose as he pulled his backpack off and set it down. "I don't know. I can't think of any movies off the top of my head."

"Just think about it," Emma said lightly. "It can be whatever your heart desires, so long as it's age appropriate."

"Jake can pick," Davy said.

I wondered if he didn't like being put on the spot. "How about we narrow it down to five and you choose which one we watch?" I asked. "Would that help?"

His eyes brightened. "Yes."

"We'll do that, then." I let out a soft hum and slid closer, looking at the papers he pulled out. My eyes widened. "This is the math they're teaching these days?"

"Yeah, man," Cam said. "Their homework is ridiculous. I thought we had it bad."

"Are you staying the night?" Jake asked.

I hadn't planned on it, but... "Sure," I said. "If that's okay."

"You're always welcome," Haley said, setting out a flight of sparkling waters. "Though you might have to sleep on the couch."

"I think my old bones can handle it." I leaned down to scoop Donnie up, holding him to me and ruffling the patch of hair on top of his head. He leaned into me, his tail wagging. "Do we match?"

Jake giggled, and Emma barked out a laugh. "You do," she said.

"Wonderful." I sat Donnie down and pulled my barstool closer to Davy. He climbed up on the one next to me and spread out the worksheets.

"Jake, pull yours out too," Cam said.

Jake sighed dramatically, but fished them out of his backpack.

"Do you do a lot of math?" Davy asked. "Our teacher says we have to know this for the real world."

I wasn't going to be the one to tell them that most people didn't need to know the difference between a parallelogram and a rhombus in the real world. "It depends on what you end up doing," I said. "I use quite a bit of math at my job."

"What *do* you do?" Jake asked.

"Colt is the mastermind behind our ciders," Cam said, smiling at me. "He's very smart, even though he's goofy."

"Aw, shucks," I teased.

"I can see why Mom likes you," Davy said.

"Yeah," Jake chimed. "You're not like dad."

"*David*." Davy muttered his correction under his breath.

Damn. The room tensed, although each of us did our best not to show it. I blew out a breath and offered him a smile.

"Is it okay that we like each other?" I asked him.

He held my gaze for a moment and then nodded. "Yep. She told us earlier."

"She talked about polyfamory?"

"Polyamory," I chuckled. "Although, I like that word too."

I glanced up at Emma and Haley, who were watching us

with expressions I couldn't read. Emma gave her a sly smile and then gave me a subtle thumbs up.

"Alright," I said. "Homework, snacks, a movie, pizza. What are we missing?"

"We need a pillow fort," Jake said.

"We're too old for that," Davy said.

"You're never too old for a pillow fort," I said. "We'll build the best one the world has ever seen!"

Jake laughed, but Davy winced as my voice raised. My heart caught in my throat as I focused on him for a moment. Jake was already laughing into a story about recess today for Haley and Emma to listen to.

"I'm sorry I raised my voice," I said softly to Davy. "I was being a little dramatic, wasn't I?"

"It's okay," he said.

"You know, I don't talk to my dad either. And he used to yell at me a lot. It wasn't fun."

Davy looked up at me, his eyes widening. "Really?"

I nodded. "Really."

"Do you miss him?"

Fuck. That was a hard question. "I miss what could have been," I said honestly.

Davy weighed my words for a moment, but then his shoulders relaxed. "I understand."

"But you know what? I found the right people."

"People who love you a lot," Cam interjected, offering us a smile. "Colt is like a brother to me. I love him as much as I love Haley, just in a different way."

Haley looked up at us. "I heard my name."

We chuckled. Cam leaned over and snaked an arm around her waist, tugging her close to him. She planted a kiss on his cheek.

"Alright, enough romance and bromance," Emma said. "I'm

ordering pizza. Homework had better be done by the time it arrives, or I'm eating every single piece."

"Noooo," Jake protested.

Davy snorted. "There's no way you could eat every piece."

"Never underestimate a lady's appetite," she said. "I could absolutely eat every bite, and still have room for something chocolate."

"It's true," Haley said. "Between the two of us, we used to eat all the pizza in college. And drink all the beer."

Emma nodded. "Back in the day."

"We're getting old," Haley sighed.

Emma feigned being offended, holding her hand over her heart. "Ma'am, we are not that old. You take it back."

I grinned as I reached for the pencil on Davy's paper. "Alright, gentlemen. Time to do math."

CHAPTER TWENTY-NINE

STARS GLITTERED in the sky above, the moon shining high. Sarah's front porch light was on, but the rest of the house was dark.

I opened the car door for her and she got out. She wore worry like a tattered coat, her brows drawn together into a scowl. More than anything, I wished I could take her somewhere she could relax without the weight of everything happening on her shoulders.

After the article had been found, I sent a picture to our group chat to let everyone know. The rest of Sarah's shift, almost everyone stopped by at some point for a meal or a cup of coffee. Haley came for an early dinner just to be present. Hunter and Honey showed up around the same time and ended up sitting at a booth together, which was admittedly fun to eavesdrop on. Apparently, they had a running bet about who would win the Super Bowl.

Even Emma dropped by with the boys before heading back to Cam and Hal's.

Which meant I had Sarah alone in the house again.

Colt checked in on us every hour. He and Cam were stuck in a long meeting earlier and I'd assured him Sarah was safe.

"Emma said she's bunking at Haley and Cam's with the boys," Sarah said sheepishly. She held up her phone, showing me a picture Cam had snapped.

I snorted and leaned in. "Is that our boyfriend?"

Her laughter made me grin. "Yep."

All of them wore sheet masks and someone had convinced Colt and Cam to put on unicorn headbands. Actually, knowing Colt, he'd probably volunteered.

"Please send that picture to me," I chuckled. "I need it for blackmail against Colt and Cam."

Her grin never left as she texted me the pic.

It was something else to see my brother like this, but it made me happy. He and Haley were so in love that it almost hurt to see. It brought me a lot of joy to see Colt had joined them too.

"If they end up having kids, Cam will be a great dad," Sarah said. "Davy and Jake feel safe with him and Haley. I really don't know what I would do without them."

"I know he likes being an uncle," I said. "Any time he talks about the boys, he's proud."

Sarah nodded and then looked down at the ground, clearly thinking about something. "Do you want to come in? Should we text Colt?"

"We can," I said. "Even though he's clearly in sheet-mask-and-unicorn-headband mode."

She giggled as I pulled out my phone and texted him.

Me: I have Sarah alone at the house. Saw you're over at Cam's. Are you staying there or do you want to join us?

Colt: Staying here, I ended up joining in on movie night. I think we're all bunking at Cam and Hal's since they have plenty of room. If you have dinner, bring me the leftovers ;) Otherwise, enjoy a date together.

Colt: P.S. Tell Sarah the boys are happy and not to worry about them

Colt: P.P.S. I did math homework with them and I'm glad I went to school when I did.

Colt: P.P.P.S. take care of our girl :P

He texted a picture of him, Davy, and Jake. Even Davy was wearing a sheet mask. I showed it to Sarah and her face softened.

"I love him," she whispered, and then her eyes widened.

I grinned even wider. "You *love* him."

Her cheeks bloomed pink and she covered her mouth. "Is that weird to say to you?"

"No," I said. "Although maybe you should tell him."

When she blew out a breath, a cloud hung in the air. I'd forgotten how cold it was.

"Let's get inside and get you warmed up," I said.

We walked up the stairs, wood creaking underfoot as she pulled out her keys. I ran my hands up her side and she breathed out, unlocking the door quickly.

We stepped in and shucked off our jackets and her bag. I turned the lock and met her gaze in the dark.

"Sammy," she whispered. "I need you."

Her soft plea went straight to my cock. I picked her up with ease, throwing her over my shoulder. She squealed as I took her up the stairs and straight to her bedroom, tossing her on the bed. I flipped on a lamp, golden light splashing over her body. My heart pounded as the desire to worship her washed over me.

I knelt down at the edge of the bed and started with her feet. Her breath caught as I started to rub one of them, her head lifting.

"I thought we were going to have sex," she whispered.

"We are," I said. "We have all night and I'm a patient man. I'm going to make you feel good in every way possible, angel."

I took my time, massaging the soles of her feet and listening to her soft moans and sighs. I made my way up her ankles and then rose up, leaning over her to unbutton her jeans. I slid them down her gorgeous hips, tugging them free.

She sucked in a breath as I massaged her calves next, slowly making my way further up. Her eyes fluttered shut, her lips parting as she relaxed into my touch.

I reached for her shirt next. She sat up partially to help me pull it off. I tossed it to the floor, sighing contentedly as I took her in. I wanted to hold her soft rolls and breasts and hips while I pumped in and out of her. Fucking hell, she was gorgeous. How was I so lucky?

The bra was the last to go. I unclasped it and trailed my fingertips over her bare skin, drinking her in. My cock throbbed as her nipples hardened.

"Everything about you turns me on," I whispered. "I can't stop thinking about you. You're always on my mind, Sarah. *Always.*"

She whimpered as I brought my hand between her thighs, tracing her pussy through her panties.

"I'm so wet," she rasped.

"Show me, angel."

I looped my fingers in the band of her panties and peeled them down, breathing out in reverence. She was finally naked beneath me. I lowered down between her sweet thighs and nudged them apart, exposing her completely to me. I traced the shape of her pussy, her dark pink labia and her protruding, aroused clit. She glistened, wet and ready for me.

I wasn't in a rush. I wasn't even going to take my jeans off until I made her come twice. Not only was I patient, I was determined to give her the night she deserved.

I rested my palm on her mound and moved my thumb over her clit, circling her slowly. Her fingers gripped the blankets, her hips responding to my touch. *Fuck. I could do this for hours.* Her little gasps were music to my ears.

"Good girl," I whispered.

A soft whimper parted her lips. I withdrew my thumb and gently worked a finger inside of her.

My eyes widened. "Baby, you're soaked. Tell me what feels good."

"Everything," she rasped. "It all feels so good, Sammy."

I added a second finger, thrusting them in and out as I used my other hand to push back her hood, pressing the tip of my tongue against her clit.

Her sweet voice rang out as I set a steady pace, licking her as I thrust my fingers repeatedly until adding a third.

Could she take my entire hand? The thought grasped me and wouldn't let go. The very idea of fisting her nearly made me come in my pants.

I drew back breathlessly. "Do you have lube, angel?"

"Lube? Do we need it?"

"I would like to try to fist you, if you think you'd like it."

"Your whole hand?"

"Yes, but only if you want to."

She thought about it for a moment, and then nodded. "I want to try it... I've never done anything like that before. But being with you and Colt at the same time, feeling so full..." Her pink tongue darted over her lip and she offered a playful smile. Fuck, I was a goner for her. "The lube is in the drawer. The key is under the coaster."

I could feel her getting even wetter. My cock strained against my zipper, but ignored it as I pulled my fingers free and slid off the bed quickly. I picked up the coaster and found the key, then unlocked the table drawer.

When I pulled it open, I expected to find lube. I didn't expect to find several toys, all of which looked like a lot of fun.

I couldn't help but smirk. "Angel, which one is your favorite?" I asked, eyeing each one. She had a whole arsenal that I wanted to take full advantage of.

"Oh." She sat up slightly, cheeks flushed. "The rose..."

Perfect. I plucked the red silicone rose out along with the bottle of lube. The top had a hole in the center that would fit over her clit, the inside containing a vibrator with different speeds. I was familiar with this little devil, and pleased that she had one.

Her gaze swept down to my bulge. "You're so hard," she whispered.

"I can't help it. You're the sexiest woman I've ever seen and I'm about to fist you and use this rose on your pussy. It's a dream come true."

Her cheeks were almost as crimson as the toy I held. I spread out between her thighs again and uncapped the bottle of lube, squirting a generous amount on her. She gasped from the chill of it, but I used my fingers to warm it up, working some inside of her. I added more to the hand I intended to fist her with.

Pre-cum dripped from my cock, my hard-on pressed against the bed. I grunted as I grabbed the rose, fitting it over her clit.

I paused for a moment just to take in the sight of her. "We'll take it slow," I promised. "Okay?"

"Okay," she said.

I could hear the nerves wavering in her voice. "Promise me that you will tell me if I need to slow down or if it's too much."

"I promise I will."

Our gazes locked, and I smiled, feeling her relax a fraction.

I pressed the button on the rose and it started to buzz. She immediately arched, her moan drawn out.

Fuck. Fuck, this is hot. I'm going to end up coming just from watching her. "Stay still, angel," I rasped, keeping the rose in place even as she writhed.

"Fuck," she gritted out. "*Change it*—change it to the next one."

I pressed the button again, changing the rhythm to a thumping one. She nodded frantically, still moving her hips.

I used my weight to hold her legs in place as I slid two fingers inside of her.

"Oh fuck. *Fuck.*"

Witnessing Sarah unravel this way nearly sent me over the edge. I grit my teeth, holding on to control for dear life as I carefully slid a fourth finger inside of her. *So close.*

"You're doing so good, angel," I praised.

"Break," she gasped. "Break from the rose."

I drew the rose back, keeping my four fingers together inside her. She panted, her body relaxing around me.

"Fuck, Sammy, you have a big hand." She swiped her forehead, but then she smiled. "How much is that?"

"Four fingers. We have my thumb and then the hardest part —my knuckles and the back of my hand. You're taking me so well, angel."

"Thank you." Her head fell back on the pillow. "Try your thumb now."

I gently eased my fingers back and added my thumb. She nodded, encouraging me to continue. My gaze never left her as I slowly pushed my hand into her pussy, spreading her around me.

"Fuck," she moaned. "Don't stop."

I did as she said, pushing further until my entire fist was inside her.

God, I was gonna come in my pants. Blood roared in my ears, my breaths quick as I stared at my hand. I could feel her around me, clenching my fist, milking me.

"Sarah," I whispered, kissing her inner thigh. "Fuck, angel, I can feel you squeezing me so tight."

She nodded quickly, her breasts rising and falling with each pant. "The rose."

The rose.

I wanted to kiss whoever invented this little thing. I picked it up and held it against Sarah's clit, moving my entire hand inside her as I pressed the button. The rose came to life and Sarah cried out, her body reacting to the bolts of pleasure.

Fuck, I was going to come. *Not yet. Not yet, damn it.* I thrust my hips against the bed, groaning as I fought for control. I watched—thirsty, hungry, fucking *desperate*—as Sarah came for me.

I could *feel* her orgasm around my hand.

Fuck. Hot liquid squirted from her, soaking the toy and my arm. I tossed the rose to the side, replacing it with my mouth. Her fingers curled into my hair as she humped against my face, her movements desperate and raw and submissive to the pleasure created between us.

The taste of her stained my lips, my tongue, my soul.

I thrust my fist deeper as she trembled.

"Sammy," she gasped. "I want you inside me. *Please.*"

This was going to be harder for me than her. "Beg me."

"Fuck," she groaned. Her words were rapid and laced with such frenzied abandon. "Please. Please, please. I'm begging you. I want you to fuck me. *Please.*"

I carefully pulled my hand free and grabbed hold of my jeans, yanking them off with a sense of urgency. Within a few seconds, all my clothes hit the floor, my cock dripping for her.

I crawled up her body and pulled her legs around my waist,

rolling us together. She squeaked as I sat her on top of me, her palms planting against my chest.

"Ride me, angel. I want you to ride me until I fill your pussy up with every drop of my cum."

She reached back and grabbed hold of my cock, guiding it inside of her. The moment she sheathed me, I groaned, my eyes rolling back. I was so fucking hard I could barely think straight. She'd short-circuited my brain. Seeing her on top of me, breasts in my face, nipples there for me to suck—I fell further into mindless bliss.

Fuck. Fuck. Fuck.

I grabbed hold of her hips and drove up. She fell forward, her lips brushing mine as I fucked her mercilessly, driving in and out. Nails raked over my chest, the biting pain chasing the pleasure.

I nipped her bottom lip and felt her clench around me, taking me to the edge. I wrapped my arms around her, holding her in place as I gave a final pump, grunting as I came.

She collapsed against me. "Fuck," she panted. "That was... That was so good."

I moaned as my entire body relaxed into the blankets. I stroked her hair absentmindedly, floating on cloud nine.

"Stay the night," she whispered, raising her head to look up at me.

Going to sleep next to the woman of my dreams and waking up next to her? The only thing that could make it even better was if Colt were here with us too, but I would revel in my time with her.

"I'd love to." I kissed the top of her head, breathing out slowly. My cock still throbbed inside of her, filling her with my cum.

"Maybe you can wake me up a certain way..."

My brows shot up. "Oh really?"

She smiled against my chest. "Only if you're interested..."

"Angel, of course I am. Tell me what you want me to do."

She hummed, looking up at me. "Like..."

"Use your words."

Her lips parted and she hesitated before telling me. "I want to wake up with you inside me. Touching me. Kissing me."

"Yes," I whispered. I fought a groan and lost, tightening my grip on her hips. "What else do you want me to do?"

She sat up slightly and reached for my hand, bringing it around her neck. Her eyes searched mine as she tightened my fingers along the sides, holding me there.

The trust in her gaze was the greatest gift of all.

I tightened my fingers and she sucked in a startled breath, her eyes widening. She licked her lips, a smile forming.

"Alright, angel," I whispered. "I can do all of that."

I released her and she smiled, slowly moving off my cock. We'd made an absolute mess and it'd been damn worth it.

"I say we clean up, shower, get back in bed, go to sleep, and then I'll wake you up in the morning," I said.

"Sounds like the perfect plan."

CHAPTER THIRTY

THE ONLY GROCERY store in Citrus Cove was a tiny evergreen building on the corner of Main Street that had been here as long as I could remember. The paint on the asphalt was faded, barely marking the lines for parking spaces. They had at least changed out the lights recently, so even though it was gray and stormy and cold, the lights were bright enough to keep everything lit.

Last night was perfect. We all watched a silly movie, and enjoyed sheet masks, and I'd gotten to hang out with the boys more. Emma and Haley made cocktails while Cam and I enjoyed a beer. It was the perfect end to the day after the two of us were stuck in a seemingly never-ending meeting, and Sarah's scare at the café.

But knowing Sammy had been with her the whole time calmed me down. Knowing she was safe and loved made me feel better.

It was going to storm all day today, and I worried about snow over the weekend. Or even worse, ice. I was gonna stock up on groceries in case things got bad.

It looked like everyone else in Citrus Cove had the same damn idea. It was Saturday so that added to the crowds.

I pulled out my phone and shot Sammy and Sarah a text to our group chat.

Me: Morning, sugar and princess. How was your date?

Princess Sammy: I'm going to get you back for calling me princess.

I smirked.

Me: You can try

My phone dinged and a photo came through. I damn near dropped my phone, all my blood rushing to my cock.

It was a selfie of Sarah in bed with Sammy, his hand around her throat. Their hair was mussed, his lips tugged into a smirk and her eyes glazed over with lust.

Me: I'm about to walk into the grocery store and now I can't even remember my name

I could hear their giggles from here.

The One That Could Be Ours: Three-way date this Saturday?

Me: Yes, please. I'm picking up groceries in case Texas shuts down from the pending cold. Text me if y'all need anything

Princess Sammy: I placed an order I'm picking up later for us, but maybe grab necessities? TP, hot chocolate, firewood if there is any left

I grinned.

Me: Alright. Be good, see you in a bit

I slipped my phone in my pocket and got out of my truck. I beelined for the front doors and grabbed a basket, weaving around the people darting in and out. I headed straight for the firewood and found that it was disappearing into baskets as quickly as the stocker could put it out.

I grabbed a couple packs and headed for the hot chocolate

aisle. Sammy was kind of bougie with his taste, so I considered getting the powder in a glass bottle.

I frowned, trying to decide between that and the regular packets.

"Colton?"

Ice froze every muscle in my body, panic clawing at my chest.

"Colton? Is that you?"

Don't turn around. Fuck. Fuck, fuck, fuck, fuck—

I felt my father's gaze on me as he stepped closer. I finally looked up, my heart thumping wildly.

"What do you want?" I reached for the bottle of hot chocolate powder, holding onto it like it was some powerful stone or source of strength because, god, my knees felt fucking weak.

I couldn't remember the last time I'd seen my dad, but running into him in the grocery store was not how I pictured reconnecting.

His eyes filled with tears. "I just... I don't know if Hunter Harlow told you, but—"

"He told me. And I told him my father wants nothing to do with me."

"That's not true," he breathed out.

Fuck, he looked old.

"I've changed," he said. "I know what I did was wrong, and I'm sorry. I wasn't good to you. I'm so sorry, Colton."

My eyes pricked but I bit back the tears. "I'm not interested in what you have to say, John. I've lived my whole adult life without you. I don't know why you're trying now."

I started to push past him, but he grabbed hold of my arm. I yanked myself free, fighting the way my vision dotted. The cold, clawing panic made me feel like a child again.

"Don't ever fucking touch me again." I met his teary gaze. "Ever. Do you fucking understand?"

"Can we please talk?" he pleaded. "I just want to know you. I want to know my son. I've changed, Colt. I've changed."

"If I want to talk to you, I'll find you," I said.

He took a step back with a dejected nod. This man used to scare the shit out of me. He used to raise his hand and I'd flinch. He used to look at me and I'd feel every muscle in my entire body tense up.

Now he just looked old and frail.

"I'm sorry," he whispered.

"Your words mean nothing to me."

Before he could say anything else, I grabbed my basket and steered out of the aisle. I practically ran to the toilet paper, grabbed a big pack, and then fought my way to self checkout. Sweat rolled down my neck and every minute in line was a minute in hell. By the time I finally got out to my truck, I felt like I'd run a fucking marathon.

I slammed my door closed and every muscle collapsed. I leaned my forehead against the steering wheel, breathing in. Out. In. Out.

"Fuck." My vision blurred with tears. Seeing him had been so unexpected, which was stupid. It was a small town, I was just really good about avoiding him.

I needed to get to the house and check the pipes. Then I needed to check over Sarah's house, even though she didn't ask.

Autopilot kicked in. I blinked and was pulling up behind Sammy's car in Sarah's driveway. The front door flew open and I was met with Sarah.

Her smile melted into concern. "What happened, baby?"

My breath hitched. "I saw my dad," I whispered.

Sarah's eyes widened. She reached for my hand, tugging me into the foyer and shutting the door behind us. Then, she wrapped her arms around me in a tight hug.

"Cam took the boys to school and Emma is upstairs work-ing. Sammy is here too," she whispered against my chest.

I nodded, inhaling her sweet scent. It had become a warm, comforting blanket to me. I heard footsteps and glanced up as Sammy came around the corner.

Sarah looked up at him. "He saw his dad."

"Oh shit."

Sammy tugged us into his all-encompassing arms and I somehow ended up in the middle of the two of them. I blinked back tears, taking a shuddering breath.

"I just didn't expect it," I said. "He looked so fucking old."

"I'm sorry," Sammy murmured, kissing the top of my head.

I sniffled. "I feel better with both of you."

"Good," Sarah whispered. "I work a late shift again today. Come cuddle on the couch."

"I need to check your pipes."

She flashed me a teasing grin and I snorted.

"Sarah Bently. Not like *that*."

"Okay, but..."

I shook my head as the three of us took to the couch. I ended up in the middle again. I leaned against Sammy and Sarah leaned against me.

There was so much comfort in just being in their presence. I was finally coming down from the panic. "He said he was sorry and that he'd changed," I said.

Sammy let out a soft hum. "Do you believe him?"

"I don't know." I sighed. "I need to think about it."

"Well, whatever you decide, we support you," Sarah said.

"Thank you."

"What I don't support is you surprise-buying me new shoes," she said, poking my side.

I grinned. "Sugar, that's not negotiable. Sorry."

Sammy chuckled. "I agree with Colt. Not sorry."

"I can't take being spoiled this way."

"Tough." I kissed the top of her head and the three of us relaxed. "Tell me about your date."

"If I tell you, I'll want to go upstairs, and Emma is here," Sarah teased.

"Come on. Just whisper in my ear."

"I'll tell him," Sammy said, leaning down to whisper in my ear. "First I ate her out, then I used her rose toy while I fisted her."

My mouth fell open. I grabbed his hand and splayed out his fingers. "This big-ass hand?"

Sarah giggled, hiding her face as her cheeks turned pink.

"That has to be an Olympic record." The two of them laughed harder and I shook my head, simply amazed. "I'd like to see this happen some time. For personal reasons."

"I think we can do that." Sarah slid her hand into mine.

"We definitely can," Sammy agreed, flexing his hand. "When it warms up, the three of us should have a picnic at the Harlow tree."

I smiled. The Harlow tree was famous in Citrus Cove. It was a mysterious place that was whispered about amongst locals.

It was literally just an old oak tree. But it had names and hearts carved in the bark from all of those who'd fallen in love in the Harlow family, stretching all the way back to when the farm was started.

Last year, when Haley and Cam got married, they added their initials to the tree.

"Do you think the tree has room for three initials?" I teased.

"Sure it does. I already know the spot."

Sarah and I looked at him. "You already picked out a spot?" she asked.

His dimples flashed. "Yeah, angel. And there is enough space for the boys to add their initials too if they wanted one day."

Her eyes filled with tears and so did mine.

"Such a fucking romantic," I mumbled, breaking the tension. "When did you have time to pick out the spot?"

He hesitated. Now it was his turn for his cheeks to turn pink. "The night I picked up Sarah, I decided to swing by the farm. I didn't tell anyone, but I walked the vineyard up to the tree. And picked out a spot, telling myself it was stupid because both of you were off-limits."

"That was in the middle of the night," Sarah said.

"Yeah." He shrugged. "Couldn't sleep with two sexy, beautiful, amazing people on my mind. Ended up staying the night at my parents' because Pops found me. I think they've been waiting to know who I was interested in."

"Surely they know by now," I said.

He shrugged. "Maybe? If Hunter or someone else told them."

"Maybe we should tell them..." Sarah trailed off. "Unless you think it's too soon. Which is fine if—"

"I'll tell him," he said with a nod. "Does Honey know?"

"I think she does, but I'll talk to her too."

Sammy ran his fingers through my hair, rubbing my head. "Maybe you can come with me."

"You want me to?" I asked.

"My parents love you. I think they'd like to know."

"Okay." I was suddenly nervous again, but for completely different reasons.

"We don't need to do anything today," Sarah said, squeezing my knee.

"I think I just need to relax today," I said. "Seeing my dad fucked with me some. I've successfully avoided him for years,

271

so running into him wasn't expected. Also, I still need to check your pipes. It's going to get super cold."

"The cold may miss us," Sarah said. "But I won't argue with you about it. I need to start getting ready for work."

"Maybe we can both go with you today," Sammy said.

"You don't need to," Sarah sighed. "No one will attack me during the middle of a shift. Too many people."

Sammy and I immediately shook our heads. "Sorry, sugar. You're stuck with one of us until David is found. And Sammy, you still need to make some calls about your home insurance and apartment and all that..."

He sighed dramatically. "Yeah, I do."

"So I'll check the pipes, Sarah will get ready for work, and Sammy will do that."

Both of them groaned dramatically. I grinned and grabbed ahold of Sarah's face, planting a kiss on her lips. Then I turned and did the same to Sammy.

I'd take all the kisses and bits of normal routine with them I could get.

CHAPTER THIRTY-ONE

sarah

EVERY DAY over the next week was full of taking the boys to school, going to work, worrying about all of the things happening around me, and being coddled in the best way possible by two very hot men.

The cold had ended up skipping us, which meant our little town had raided the grocery store for nothing. But, it was good for business, and all of my shifts passed by quickly. The new shoes helped too.

I felt re-energized. Even though David was in town and that scared the hell out of me, I wasn't alone.

I leaned over the kitchen counter and read through the recipe I'd written out. It was based on one Honey had given me long ago, but I'd made some adjustments. I was off today and had decided I'd spend the morning baking and trying out something new before my date this evening.

Honey bullied me (with love) into taking another night away from Davy and Jake. It had been too long since she'd had her grandsons for a sleepover. Now that we'd worked through our feelings, I was relieved to have her more in my life again. She had yet to pry about Sammy and Colt, but the smirk on her face when they were mentioned told me she approved.

It was hard to accept help, but I was slowly learning to trust those around me when they offered to help. For ten years, my default was to handle everything on my own. It had felt like a weakness to ask for assistance, but I was coming to realize that it wasn't.

So, I'd bake something new, use my family as tastebud guinea pigs, and take my kids to Honey—and then see Sammy and Colt.

My date with Sammy earlier this week had just been us kissing in the car, so I was ready to spend more time with him.

Paws clicked on the hardwood. I looked up as Donnie came into the kitchen, his butt wiggling once he spotted me. I knelt down to pet him as Emma came in too, dressed in a suit and heels.

My brows shot up. "Okay, you look stunning. Who are you conquering today?"

She grinned ruthlessly. Her lips were painted bright red, the exact color of her heels. "I'm going on a date."

"A *date*?"

"Yep."

"With who?"

"This guy I met at the grocery store. Which is not exactly how I pictured picking up hot guys, but this is a small town, so I'll take what I can get."

I snorted. "I have a hard time believing it. What's his name?"

"Kyle," she said. "He's hot. We're having lunch."

I didn't know a Kyle. I crossed my arms as she poured a glass of water and downed it. I wasn't sure if I should pry more or not. Part of me really wanted to, but I didn't want her to think I was unsupportive.

But also—unless Kyle was Superman, I doubted a Citrus Cove man could handle the raw power pouring off her.

A knock echoed from the front door and she held up a hand before I could move past her.

"I got it. I can answer the door from here on out."

I sighed. "Emma, I can still answer the door."

She was already leaving the kitchen. I heard the door open and a terse voice, followed by a grumble, and Emma's snappy tone.

She came back into the kitchen with Hunter Harlow in tow, his eyes aflame. Seeing the two of them next to each other could have been the perfect picture of irony. He was wearing a backwards baseball cap, sweater, jeans, and boots that had been through the mud. Meanwhile, not a single hair was out of place on Emma's head.

"You look like you're about to take over the world," Hunter muttered. "Who are you going to stab with those heels?"

"You?" Emma said sweetly.

I snorted and glanced at Donnie. He didn't hate Hunter Harlow the same way Emma did. He sat, his tongue lolling out as he watched the three of us.

I pulled a bowl down as I spoke. "Hunter, what are you doing here?"

Emma crossed her arms. "He claims he's here to add more cameras around the house and to fix the one on the porch since it failed. I think we should maybe get a professional to do it instead of Mr. Handy Hillbilly."

Hunter's jaw stiffened. "I don't know how you live with her."

"I live well with her," I said defensively. "But Emma, Hunter is good with this stuff. He'll get everything secure."

She rolled her eyes. "Fine."

"See, maybe you can be nice to others," Hunter gritted out. "Instead of acting like a bratty only child."

My heart immediately skipped a beat. Emma's eyes darkened and her body language stiffened, but it was so subtle that Hunter didn't catch it. But, I sure as hell did. A flare of temper creeped up my spine.

"I'm off to my date," she said. "Good fucking luck."

"Emma," I said softly, but she was already out the front door.

Hunter crossed his arms and then relaxed. I shook my head at him and grabbed my wooden spoon, pointing it at him.

"That was mean," I said. "And I didn't think you could be like that."

His lips parted in surprise. "I was teasing her."

"No," I said firmly. "That wasn't teasing. You have no idea who Emma is and instead of making any effort, you're constantly a dick. Emma was not always an only child, but she is now."

His eyes widened. "Oh. Fuck."

I continued to wave the spoon at him like I had countless times when I'd scolded my own boys. "Emma is the only reason I've remained sane for the last year, so I'd appreciate it if you stopped being a complete asshole, especially in my house. I'm happy to have you make sure the cameras are working and that we're safe, but Emma is part of our family."

He swallowed hard, his cheeks turning red. "Dammit," he muttered. "I'm sorry, Sarah. I didn't know that about Emma."

"Don't apologize to me," I said.

He took a breath and held it for a moment before releasing, his shoulders deflating. "Something about her drives me insane. She gets under my skin so easily."

"I don't care," I said. "I like you a lot. And I like your

brother even more. But I will kick you out of my house next time you're an asshole to her."

"Yes, ma'am," he said, wincing. He leaned against the fridge as I started to get the ingredients I needed out of the cabinets. "Whatcha making?"

"Muffins. I'm trying out something new. I'll give you some if you can get it all working properly. Do you think someone could have tampered with the camera?"

"I think so," he said. "Otherwise, the one on the front porch should have worked fine. We have Emma's word that David showed up, but the fact that we don't have it on camera is frustrating. I'm sorry, Sarah. I know it's been a lot and it's scary. I've scoured the whole fucking town for him."

"It is scary," I sighed. "But Colt and Sammy have been keeping me company."

"Yeah. Makes me feel better, honestly."

"Has there been any more information on Sammy's apartment?" I asked. "Since you know everything."

He chuckled. "Maybe not everything. But as far as I can tell, that woman left town. There was a room checked out under a fake name at the Citrus Cove Motel and they left the day Sammy's apartment was broken into. Part of me wants to think it was a coincidence."

"And the other part of you?"

He pressed his lips together and rubbed his jaw. "I don't know. I have to wonder if David is somehow related to it all."

"David? Why would he break into Sammy's apartment?"

"Well, if he's obsessing over you..."

I hadn't thought about that. I crossed my arms and leaned against the counter, looking out the window above the breakfast table. The idea that Sammy and Colt could be in danger didn't sit well with me.

"I know what you're thinking," Hunter said. "But this isn't your fault, Sarah. He's not a good person."

"I worry that he might try to hurt Sammy or Colt."

"And we all worry he might try to do something to you and the boys. And Emma." He shrugged. "We're in this together. I know I missed some of what happened last year by being gone, but I'm here to help. And I'll do whatever I can for my brother and Colt, and for all of you too."

"Thank you," I whispered.

"I've got to say this, Sarah. I've never seen either one of them like this, especially Sammy. I mean, we've all known Colt has loved you for years. But Sammy has never been with anyone he cared about like this. Hell, the only reason my mom isn't already on your doorstep making wedding plans is because Cam keeps taunting her with grandchildren."

I grinned. "I need to go see her at some point. Are they okay with... the three of us?"

Hunter smiled gently. "I don't see why not. I'm too possessive to ever share the person I love with someone else, but the three of you seem to be making it work. If anyone can make it happen, you can. And I think you deserve all the love. Mom and Pops will see that."

My eyes prickled with tears. "This is the part of you I wish you'd let Emma know."

He shook his head. "She wants nothing to do with me and never will. Not after..."

Hunter trailed off and I narrowed my gaze on him like a hawk. "Not after *what*?"

His cheeks turned red. "Nothing. I'm going to get the cameras set up."

"Hunter Harlow," I said, picking up my spoon again.

He made a zip and lock motion with his hand and lips and glided past me. I shook my head. I was tempted to text Haley and ask what she knew about whatever the hell *that* was, but I also needed to get baking.

I decided to put a pin in it as the sound of power tools hummed through the house. I pulled out the rest of my ingredients and got started on making the batter. I was taking the pumpkin bread recipe I'd perfected and turning it into a muffin, but I wanted to add a crumble top.

Maybe it was stupid to entertain the idea of having my own bakery, but I found myself thinking about it again. Could I even find the time for that between raising two boys and dating two men?

The next couple of hours passed quickly as I baked. I got lost in the process, all of my stress melting. By the time Hunter was almost done with the cameras, a delicious pumpkin scent wafted through the warm kitchen.

As I pulled the trays out of the oven and placed them on the stove top, I glanced at the clock.

"Shoot," I mumbled.

It was time to get ready. I made sure everything was turned off and ran upstairs to change. I decided I wanted to dress a little sexier tonight, and would have opted to wear something underneath that was outside of my norm too, but I didn't own any lingerie.

But, it felt good to look sexy. I couldn't think of a time before dating Colt and Sammy where I'd had the chance to.

I slipped on a black bra, black panties, and a snug sweater dress. I dug knee-high boots out of the closet and pulled them on, studying myself in the mirror.

Well, it would have to do. The dress hugged me a little more than I would have liked, but I felt good.

I went back downstairs and stopped in the kitchen doorway.

Hunter was mid-bite into a muffin, making eye contact with me.

"These are really fucking good," he said, crumbs falling into the floor. "I'll pick those up."

I stifled a laugh. "Good enough to buy?"

"Hell yeah," he said. "I'd buy them."

I smirked. "Good to know. You can take a couple more, but the rest I'm taking to Sammy and Colt."

"Lucky bastards," he sighed.

A knock at the door made my stomach squeeze. Hunter was already moving as I opened the door.

The sheriff, Bud, stood there with a grimace, another officer by his side. "Hey, Sarah. Hunter. We need to talk to you if you have a moment."

"What happened?" I breathed out.

"Well. It seems that David Connor is missing."

Missing??

"Do you want me to call Colt and Sammy? Actually, nevermind, I'm already texting them," Hunter said behind me.

My pulse raced. How could David possibly be missing?

All I could do was nod and step aside to let them in. I sat down on the couch across from Bud and the other officer, who was named Tammy. Hunter stood behind the couch, his arms crossed.

"If we could talk to her alone..." Bud trailed off, giving Hunter a pleading look.

"Nope. Her boyfriends are on the way too, so better get going before you have a full house."

My cheeks turned bright red.

Tammy cleared her throat. "We need to know where you were Sunday."

"I was here at home," I said. "I worked an early shift and

got off around six o'clock. I came home, made dinner for Emma and the boys, then went to sleep."

"Can we talk to the boys and—"

"This is absurd," Hunter interjected.

Bud sighed. "We just have to check. Neither one of us thinks Sarah had anything to do with this. But with all the trouble recently, things are tense."

"You can ask Emma," I said. "But not my boys. They need to stay out of this. They've been affected enough by all that has happened. They need normalcy, Bud."

Tammy and Bud nodded. "Alright," Tammy said, making notes.

"Why do you think David is missing?" I asked.

"We found the car he's been driving. It turns out he exchanged his truck with a man named Ron, who owned a small gray Toyota. He's been staying in a motel south of Austin. He checked in Saturday night at a new place, but didn't check out when he was supposed to. He's just gone. We're trying to find him."

"Oh." My shoulders sank.

"I'm sorry to ask, Sarah, but did you make something with pumpkin?" Bud asked.

"What does that have to do with anything?" Hunter asked.

"Nothing. It just smells good..."

"Oh for Christ's sake."

"They can have a muffin, I guess," I said, looking up at Hunter.

"At least make them pay for it," he mumbled, heading for the kitchen.

Bud sighed. "I'm sorry to add more stress. After what happened to your sister, it would be understandable if..."

I raised a brow. "If *what?*"

Tammy and Bud looked at each other and I shook my head.

Was I understanding what they were insinuating? That I had *anything* to do with David's disappearance?

Fury came hard and fast. "You know what? No. No muffins for either one of you. You know where I was Sunday, so you can leave. If you're insinuating what I think you are, you need to get out."

"We have to cover our bases," Tammy said.

"I would never harm someone," I said, standing up. "That's not who I am or who I've ever been. Bud, you've known me since I was a damn teen. You know I would never hurt someone."

Bud winced and stood up too.

"I've got the muffins," Hunter said, coming back to the living room.

"No muffins for them."

"Oh. Perfect." Hunter bit into the top of one, mean-mugging them both as I ushered them to the door.

"If you have any real questions, just call me to the station," I said. "You have my number."

I opened the door right as Colt and Sammy came up the steps. Bud and Tammy stepped past them.

"We need to interview them too, Bud," Tammy sighed.

"Interview us for what?" Colt asked.

"David is missing," I said. "They insinuated I killed him."

"Now, Sarah," Bud protested. "We just have to check all our boxes. That's our job."

"Don't fucking '*Now, Sarah*' her," Sammy snapped, glowering. "Really, Bud? After all the shit that has happened? What night do you need to know about?"

"Sunday night," Tammy said tensely.

"I was fucking Colt that night," Sammy said.

Both of their mouths fell open and I stifled the giggle that bubbled up.

"Any more questions?" Colt asked sweetly.

"Nope. We'll let you know if we hear anything else."

I wasn't sure if I'd ever seen Bud move so fast. We watched them get into the cruiser and drive off. And of course, some of the neighbors were eyeing us from their houses.

"Is that Rachel Jackson using her vacuum on the lawn?" Hunter asked with a mouthful of muffin.

We all looked at the woman on her lawn three houses down watching us as discreetly as she could.

"For fuck's sake," I sighed. "One of you might as well kiss me."

Sammy grinned and grabbed me, planting a kiss on my lips. Then he handed me off to Colt, who did the same. I laughed as he released me and held up my middle finger as the two of them kissed.

"My god, Citrus Cove will explode," Hunter said. "Also, my poor eyes. I'm going back inside."

The three of us followed him and I sighed, plopping down on the couch.

David was missing.

Good riddance was my first reaction. The second was— *why?*

"How are you feeling?" Colt asked, sitting next to me.

Sammy winked at us and went to talk to Hunter in the kitchen. I leaned against Colt and stared at the wall.

"I don't know. If they found him dead, it would solve a lot of problems. But I don't want that, I just want him out of my life."

Colt nodded, running his fingers through my hair. He kissed the top of my head. "I'm sorry. My gut reaction was that I was glad, but..."

I nodded. "It's just concerning."

"I can swing by and try to get more information..."

"No, I think it would be better not to... I'd rather think about our date tonight. Honey has the boys."

"Oh, I know. I'm ready for our date too."

"Let's kick Hunter out, grab some muffins, and go to your house."

"Sounds like a plan, sugar."

CHAPTER THIRTY-TWO

sarah

I'D NEVER WANTED a margarita so damn bad.

And after the day I'd had, I deserved one.

Colt ran his fingers through my hair, massaging my head and giving me playful kisses as Sammy came to the living room with two margaritas and an unopened cider in the crook of his arm. His sleeves were pushed up to his elbows, his forearms muscled and perfect. The butterfly tattoo drew my attention in the ambient light Colt had set up for us.

Dinner, muffins, and now drinks—it was almost enough to make me forget that my ex-husband was missing and I'd been questioned about whether I was the one to kill him.

"Your strawberry margarita, madam," Sammy said, handing me a glass.

I took it with a grin. He'd even put a fresh strawberry on top.

"And a cider for our baby." Sammy handed the can to Colt and he took it. It popped as he opened it.

"Are you really more of a cider guy?" I teased him.

"I mean, I do make ciders for a living."

Sammy ran his tongue over the rim of his glass and winked at us. My skin flushed.

"I'll be glad when we have everything up and running again," Colt continued, narrowing his eyes on Sammy's tongue. "Sugar or salt?"

"Sugar," Sammy said. "How's it all going with the winery? Admittedly, I'm ready to be singing to crowds again."

My eyes widened. I sometimes forgot that Sammy could play the guitar and sing. I'd only had the chance to hear him a few times, but when I had, he was always wonderful.

Colt took a sip of his cider and hummed, still massaging my head. I felt like I was being petted, and honestly, I enjoyed it. "It's going. We have construction plans ready, but I hope we'll be up in the fall. We'll see."

Sammy settled on the sofa next to me. He was so much taller than both of us that it was almost comical watching him squeeze in. If we ever lived together, we'd need a huge couch. One that could fit three adults and two children and *why am I thinking about this?*

"How are you feeling, Sarah?" Sammy asked.

I took a sip of the margarita. "Better now." Being sandwiched between the two of them made it easy to forget all of my other worries. During dinner, the three of us had talked more about David. Eventually, we decided tonight was a date and wanted to focus on that.

I wanted to cherish every moment I could have with Colt and Sammy.

Colt reached over and plucked the strawberry from my drink. "Open up."

I held his gaze as I parted my lips. It didn't matter how many times I saw it, it turned me on when his nostrils flared and his eyes darkened with lust. I bit into the fresh strawberry, feeling like I was being roasted over hot coals.

"Mmm." Sammy raised a brow. "So maybe we should have a fresh fruit tray on our next date night."

"Agreed." Colt finished off the strawberry and chased it with his cider.

"I'd like that," I said.

My thoughts turned back to the first night the three of us were together. With everything that had been happening lately, I was glad to spend time with them again. Hopefully we could manage to make this a more frequent occurrence, but I worried my life was too complicated.

This was working for us. At least, it seemed to be working. In my spare moments, I'd started reading a book about polyamory and had already learned about attachment styles and communication. It felt good to set us up to have a healthy relationship, but it was also making me aware of just how bad my relationship with David was.

"Tonight, I have one goal," Colt announced.

"Oh yeah? What's that?" I asked.

He slid his hand over my thigh, giving me a gentle squeeze that went straight to my core. All my thoughts turned to sex and I squeezed my thighs together as I imagined riding them both.

"I want to make you forget about everything that has been happening lately," he said.

"I support this goal," Sammy chuckled. "I also have some evil plans for us."

"Oh really?" Colt asked.

"Yep. Sure do."

Heat crept up my spine and I took one more sip of my drink before setting it down on the coffee table. Maybe I'd try and take the reins for once? I rose up and surprised us all by straddling Colt.

"Fuck." He almost spilled his cider as one hand settled on my hip, squeezing me.

Sammy let out a dark hum as he sipped his drink, lips curling into a smirk. "Maybe I'll just watch and see where this goes."

"You're going to let me fend for myself?" Colt rasped.

I ran my hands up his shirt, tugging at the button near his collar. "Poor thing. What if I want to make you forget too, hmm?"

"Sugar, I can't even remember my name right now."

"Can you remember mine?" I teased. "Or Sammy's?"

"No amount of whiskey, sex, or drugs could make me forget either of your names."

I leaned in, our lips hovering over each other. I was one breath away from kissing him. He let out the softest moan and gripped my hair. Sammy plucked his drink out of his other hand before it spilled all over us.

"I'm so lucky I got a second chance," Colt whispered. "I never dreamed you'd let me try."

"I've always wanted you," I murmured. "Even after I was with David. I used to always wonder how things could have been different, but now, I wouldn't change anything. I have the boys. I have you. I have Sammy."

My gaze slid over to Sammy. His dark eyes assessed us, his brows drawn together. The outline of his erection pressed against his jeans, his muscles stiff.

Now what? I was straddling Colt. I could feel both of them looking at me with a hunger that turned me on. *Abort, abort, abort.* Maybe I didn't like being in control. I had no idea what to do next.

When I looked at Sammy, I realized he already knew that.

Sammy slowly licked the rim of the glass and then his lips. "Go on, angel. Take control."

I was going to combust. "I thought you might tell us what to do..." I trailed off.

He smiled and leaned forward, blue eyes flashing with need. "Do you want me to take over, angel?"

"Yes," I whispered. "Maybe I'm not cut out to be a Dom."

"What do you think, Colt?"

"She could be," he grunted. He ran his hands up my body, cupping my breasts. I gasped, rocking against him.

"If she wanted to submit, she'd ask us, right? Because she knows how to ask for what she wants."

"Damn you," I mumbled to Sammy. "Will you pretty please take over? Will you tell us what to do?"

Sammy leaned forward, sat his drink down on the table, and stood up. He stepped up behind us and cupped his hand around my throat, tipping my head back.

"I've been thinking about fucking the two of you together again all week. About all the things I could do. All the things I wanted to try..."

"This is hot," Colt mumbled. I felt his lips press against the base of my throat, his tongue tracing my pulse as Sammy kept me in place.

Yeah, this was where I wanted to be. Straddled between two devoted men that looked at me like they would kneel before me during the day and put me on my knees at night.

Sammy hovered over me, his lips nearly brushing mine. "Good girl. There's a gift for you in the bathroom from us. I'd like you to change into it."

"A gift?"

"We picked it out," Colt whispered, moving his hips beneath me. His cock throbbed against my core.

"Evil," I squeaked. "Both of you are diabolical."

I squeaked as Sammy lifted me off Colt and patted my ass. "Go. I have plans with our boyfriend I must take care of before you return."

My eyes widened as Sammy reached into a bag on the floor. He paused, glancing back at me.

"Go on."

Colt smirked at me. "Curious to see what he has in store?"

"Yes, I am." I was already turned on. "I'll be back."

Their gazes raked over me, hotter than coals as I took off to the bathroom. I shut the door behind me and curse under my breath.

Folded on a towel on the bathroom sink was the gift.

The lingerie set was emerald green velvet with black lace. I ran my fingertips over the set, coveting the texture of it. Tears prickled, my throat thickening. I'd never worn anything like this before.

"*You can't return it,*" Colt called.

Dammit. I picked it up and shook my head. They knew how to give gifts, that was for sure. It looked like it would fit me perfectly.

I heard a grunt from the living room. Whatever Sammy had in store for us, I wanted a part of.

Quickly, I undressed and shimmied into the lingerie set. Just like I'd suspected, it fit me like a sexy glove. The bra cupped my breasts, the panties rising up far enough over my stomach to be comfortable.

I felt sexy.

I *was* sexy.

A shiver passed through me as I traced some of the stretch marks I had, thinking about the way they'd worshiped me. The way they'd kissed me and loved me and...

Another grunt echoed from the living room. I opened the door, my eyes widening as I reentered the living room.

Colt was bound with black tape to a chair. Naked. Sammy's dimples showed as he held up the roll. "Bondage tape. Works like a charm."

"That looks..." I found it way hotter than I could have ever imagined. "That looks like fun."

"It is. Do you remember our safeword, angel?"

"I do." I swallowed hard, looking at Colt.

"Fucking hell," he rasped. "You tied me up and she looks so fucking gorgeous. What am I supposed to do?"

"Be a good boy and watch me eat her out." Sammy crooked a finger my way. "Come here, angel."

I met him halfway, winding my arms around him as he lifted me into a kiss. He stepped back and sat on the couch, pulling me over his lap. Colt groaned as we kissed. Heat skated across my skin from every fevered touch and stroke and grab. *Fuck.* I was so wet.

Being with him was as easy as breathing. I rocked my hips against him, feeling his erection in his jeans pressing against me.

I met Colt's tortured gaze past him. He moved his hips, his cock hard and pre-cum dripping from the tip. "Are you really going to make him watch the whole time?" I whispered.

"Mmm, just for a bit. Until he's begging to fuck you."

"I'm already begging," Colt moaned.

"Can you hear that? That doesn't sound like begging." Sammy nipped my bottom lip.

The pain sparked more lust. I gripped his shirt and pulled it off, tossing it to the floor. My fingertips grazed over his chest, feeling his muscles. He kissed my neck, collarbone, breasts...

"Fuck. I'm dying," Colt rasped.

"I'm going to take my sweet time," Sammy huffed. "Lie back and let me worship you, angel."

He moved me off his lap and laid me back on the couch

cushion, grabbing the back pillows and throwing them off so we had more room. He stood and stripped off the rest of his clothes, his cock springing free.

"Fuck." Colt shook his head, his muscles straining against the bondage tape that held him in place.

Sammy stroked his pierced cock and turned, rushing to the chair. He gripped Colt's hair, pulling his head back as he kept stroking himself.

Seeing him so dominant and Colt so submissive... My eyes widened and I spread my thighs, sliding my fingers against my pussy.

This was so hot. I'd read stories with scenes like this but never in a million years did I dream I'd end up in one. I'd seen how dominant Colt could be too, and that only made seeing him obey sexier.

"Please," Colt rasped. "I want to suck your cock while you eat her out. *Please.*"

"Not yet, baby."

I pushed the fabric swath to the side and pushed two fingers inside myself, moaning. Colt strained against the tape again, his breaths quickening as Sammy leaned over him, stroking his cock for a few seconds.

Then, he released him.

"You son of a bitch." Colt shook his head.

Sammy smiled ruefully as he came back to me, kneeling on the floor. He came to the edge of the sofa and leaned down, pressing his face against the velvet between my thighs. "So fucking gorgeous," he whispered against my pussy.

A raspy moan left me as he moved his mouth lower, breathing in my pussy. Need buzzed in my blood, my entire body responding to him like two magnets drawn together.

"Sammy," I whimpered.

I raised my head as he pushed my thighs apart, his gaze sweeping over me with deep appreciation.

"She looks so damn good," Sammy said. "Too bad you can't have her yet."

Colt shook his head and managed to rock the chair, scooting toward us. I stifled a laugh, covering my mouth as he shot me a razor sharp look. "Oh yes, keep laughing, sugar. Remember I'll happily have you begging for my cock soon."

Sammy chuckled as he raked the panties down and traced his tongue up my inner thigh until he came to my pussy. I cried out, fingers gripping the sofa as his tongue met my clit, sending shockwaves of pleasure through me.

He wrapped his arms around me and dragged my ass to the edge of the couch, pushing my legs back so he could drive his tongue inside me. I gasped, shaking as he drove me close to coming.

"Don't stop, don't stop." I was so close. I was so close and I needed this so badly—so, so badly—

Sammy kept going, his fingers circling my clit in a way that pushed me past the breaking point. I cried out, arching against him as an orgasm blinded me.

"Good girl," he huffed against my pussy before driving his tongue into me again, carrying me through the lasting waves that wrecked me.

I melted beneath him, panting hard. He leaned back and stood up, going to Colt and kissing him hard. His lips were still wet with my cum, and Colt seemed to love that, the two of them kissing deeper.

Sammy plucked a set of safety scissors off the coffee table and looked up at me. "Come help me free him, angel. Crawl to us."

Crawl? Could my knees even handle that?

Well, I was sure as hell going to find out.

I slid off the couch onto all fours. My body swayed as I crawled to them, stopping once I was kneeling between Colt's legs. Sammy had taped his arms, torso, and legs—but that meant his cock was exposed.

I slid my hand around his shaft and brought the tip to my lips, licking him tentatively.

He groaned, sweat beading his smooth tan skin. Sammy gave me an approving smile as used the scissors to cut open the tape around Colt's torso and arms.

Colt immediately shook them free and slid his fingers in my hair, pulling my mouth down on his cock. I moaned around him, sucking him eagerly.

I reached up and grabbed Sammy's cock too, stroking him as I sucked Colt.

They both cursed, moans following. More tape was cut away and soon, Colt was finally free of the bondage.

He took full advantage of it.

He pulled my lips off his cock and pulled me to stand, rising up from the chair. I gasped as I was pressed between the two of them, Colt kissing my neck and shoulders while Sammy kissed down my chest, nestling his face between my breasts.

"I want both our cocks in you, sugar." Colt reached down the backs of my thighs and lifted me. Sammy stepped forward, bringing them around his waist, the two of them holding me together.

Colt's hands slid around, playing with my nipples. My breasts were teased in his palms, the head of his cock rubbing against my ass.

"I've never been fucked there," I rasped.

"Never?" Sammy asked.

"Never."

"Lube," Colt said.

Sammy nodded. "I've got her. And bed."

I squeaked as Sammy carried me, Colt following after him down the hall to the bedroom.

"We don't have to if it's too much," I said quickly.

Sammy collapsed on the bed with me, rolling us so I was beneath him. "Do you want to try?"

"Yes," I said sheepishly. "I do."

"Then we'll give it a try."

CHAPTER THIRTY-THREE

WHEN YOU SPENT years pining over the woman you loved in high school, you did ridiculous things like buy new sex toys and leave them in a box unopened *just in case*. Well, the *just in case* moment had arrived, and I opened up a box with a new butt plug and washed it.

Being tied to a chair while Sammy went down on our girl had nearly sent me over the edge. Every muscle in my body buzzed with need. I needed to fuck her, I needed to fuck him, I needed to be fucked and *fuck*. I was a horny, desperate mess.

Lube. We needed lube and towels. I was glad now more than ever that Sammy and I had stopped by a clinic this week to get tested for STDs and STIs. We'd both tested negative, which meant I didn't need to worry about grabbing condoms.

I got the rest of the supplies and returned to my bedroom. Sammy was busy kissing Sarah, his hands roaming over her. Her dark hair sprawled out over the blankets, her moans sent a jolt of need straight to my cock.

I joined them on the bed.

Her eyes immediately darted to the black silicone toy. "You think that will fit?"

"It will." Sammy sounded confident.

"We'll take it slow," I said. "And if you don't like it, we'll stop. Okay?"

She nodded and made a noise somewhere between a whimper and a squeak.

God, I loved making her blush. It was becoming my new favorite thing. Maybe I had a corruption kink?

"Now what?" Sarah asked, batting those pretty dark lashes.

Sammy looked at me. "Do you want your cock sucked or do you want to fuck her ass with the toy?"

Excitement rolled through me. "Her ass," I whispered.

A smirk tugged his lips as he moved up the bed. "Thought so. Turn over. Ass out, angel."

She did as he commanded. The bed shifted between the three of us as we all changed positions. We spread out the towels in case she squirted.

Now, Sammy's back was against the headboard, his thighs spread and long legs caging her in. She was on all fours, her mouth hovering right over his cock. Her perfect ass faced me, round and soft and biteable.

My fucking god. My life was perfect.

"Hand me a pillow," I said to Sammy.

He tossed me one and I slid it under her stomach for extra support. I then slapped one of her ass cheeks playfully. "Comfortable?"

"Yes."

Sammy gathered up her dark hair and glanced over at the side table. He leaned over and took a hair tie from the top, using it to put her hair in a bun.

Her pussy shined, slick and wet. I traced her with the tip of my finger, pausing over her engorged clit. She gasped, her spine arching.

"*Colt.*"

Right, right. I was supposed to be playing with her ass for the first time. Still, I continued to circle her slowly, enjoying every soft cry and moan.

Sammy's blue eyes were fixed on me, fire in water.

He slowly guided her open mouth to the head of his cock. He blew out a breath between gritted teeth, his head falling back against the headboard with a grunt.

I pushed two fingers inside her cunt, feeling the patch of rough flesh inside her. She cried out around his cock, her hips moving as I leaned down, pushing my face between her ass cheeks and rimming her.

"Fuck," Sammy grunted. "*Fuck.*"

Both of them had been reduced to using a single word. I could barely think straight. My tongue traced her ass, my fingers buried inside of her. Her body rocked against me as her head bobbed up a down, Sammy gripping her hair as he fucked her throat methodically.

I wasn't sure I'd ever been this hard. My cock throbbed relentlessly, begging for her slick cunt to be clenched around me. The only reason I wasn't balls deep inside her right now was because I wanted to see if we could put the plug in first.

I drew back, pulling my fingers free too. She moaned in protest, but I grabbed hold of her ass, spreading her cheeks and looking at my prize. "Relax, sugar."

She made a *mmph* sound. I reached for the bottle of lube and uncapped it, dripping it onto her. Her muscles tensed and she started to pull off Sammy's cock, but he grabbed hold of her head with a gentle *tsk*.

"Keep going, angel."

The sucking sounds continued, my cock jerking in response. I closed my eyes for a moment, grasping for control.

There was the part of me that wanted to pump her full of my cum, and there was the part of me that wanted to take her over the edge so many times she lost count. That wanted to fuck every hole, to make her orgasm relentlessly.

And *then* to pump her full of my cum.

Control somewhat regained, I started to work the lube around her ass again, teasing her slowly. Sammy let her draw a breath and she pulled back, dragging in harsh breaths.

"How does this feel?" I asked.

"Good." She looked at me over her shoulder, eyes dark with lust. "You can keep going."

"Wonderful. You're so fucking hot, Sarah." I continued to play with her until I was able to gently ease a finger inside of her. "Fuck. And tight. Really really tight. We'll see about working the toy in."

She whimpered.

"Too much?" I asked.

"No," she whispered. "It's different."

"It is."

Knowing her virgin ass was ours only turned me on more.

"Once he gets that toy in you, I want to fuck him while he fucks you," Sammy said. He looked up at me for confirmation and I nodded.

"Please," I said.

Sarah moaned in agreement. I pushed my finger in and out before reaching for the plug. We'd give it a try to see if she could take it. I placed the tip against her and slowly eased it inside. She moaned louder, her muscles tensing before fully relaxing.

"Good girl," I purred. "You're taking it so well. Soon, you'll be taking my cock too."

Her nails scraped up Sammy's thighs and he thrust his hips up, his expression full of bliss. Sammy pulled her mouth off his cock, giving her a few moments.

"It's so much," she rasped. "Don't stop."

I pushed the plug further until it was all the way inside her. "There we are," I said. "You did it, sugar."

She breathed out, relaxing. "It feels good."

"I need to see." Sammy rolled out from beneath her and crawled over to me, taking a look. His cock glistened with a mix of pre-cum and her saliva. "Perfect," he whispered.

"She is," I agreed, my cock throbbing. "I need to fuck you or her or I'm gonna come."

"Fuck me, please," Sarah said. "I want to know what it's like to have the plug and your cock in me."

Sammy squeezed my ass. "And I'm going to fuck you while you fuck her."

I nodded eagerly. Sarah moved further up the bed, adjusting the pillow under her and giving us more room. She looked over her shoulder at us, skin flushed, body on full display.

Sammy ran his palms over my body as he knelt behind me. His lips grazed my neck, sending shivers through me. Every touch made me gasp.

He was smooth. One moment he was kissing me, the next he shoved me over Sarah and used lube to prep me for his cock. He was just as hard as I was.

Fuck. I wanted this so badly.

"Are you ready?" Sammy's voice was rich with lust. We both felt it. The need to be together, bound and tied and fucking.

"Yes," I said.

"Yes, please," Sarah rasped.

I shoved the head of my cock inside her right as Sammy

pushed into me. The three of us moaned together. *This* was heaven. Her slick cunt clenching around me, his cock filling me. My mind spiraled between the dual sensations, pleasure washing over me. I'd never been fucked like this with my cock in one hole and another inside me, but it was perfect.

"Oh god, I'm so full." She rocked her hips, her muscles squeezing the life out of me and nearly making me come.

"Hold on, hold on," I rasped. "Fuck. You're milking my cock, sugar. Stay still for a moment."

Sammy pushed further into me as Sarah went still, his fingers digging into my skin. He bit down on my shoulder, the pain only intensifying the enjoyment.

"God, you feel so fucking good."

I shuddered, every nerve in my body alive. Pleasure rippled through me as we started to move against each other. Sarah sank back, taking my cock deeper as Sammy grunted, thrusting into me hard.

"I can feel you fucking me through him," Sarah whispered.

"Fuck," we both said.

A frenzy overtook us and Sammy tightened his hold on me, pushed me forward, and started fucking me mercilessly. His balls slapped against me as my cock slid in and out of her cunt, her cries ethereal as she took me. I was already so damn close to coming that it was taking every ounce of control, every ounce of—fuck, I was praying, *praying* I wouldn't come yet because I wanted to make this pleasure last as long as possible.

"Harder," I grunted.

He wrapped his arms around me, his hand sliding over my throat as he took control. I was his sex toy and she was pure fucking bliss.

I knew she was about to come. I felt the shift in her body, the way she milked me, the way her cries and breaths changed.

"Come for us," Sammy growled. "I can hear it in your pretty little voice, angel. Come for us."

Her fingers dug into the blankets, her back arching as she came. I couldn't hold out any longer as she orgasmed. I cried out, finally giving into the release. With it came the relief of pleasure that reached down into my veins, my blood, my bones. I flooded her with my cum as Sammy kept fucking me, his breaths erratic.

I relaxed completely as he released me, my body melting against Sarah as he kept going. I grunted, basking in the waves that warmed my body, all while Sammy used me.

"I'm coming," he gasped.

He drove into me once more and paused, hips jerking as he came, heat shooting inside me.

He collapsed against me, his forehead against my back. The three of us were a mess, all covered in sweat. I breathed in the scent of sex, musky and sweet.

Sammy let out a soft groan as we melted against each other. A few minutes passed before anyone was capable of speaking.

He raised his head. "I think it's time for the aftercare loaf."

A soft giggle escaped Sarah and I snorted. "The what?"

"The aftercare loaf. I baked a fresh loaf of bread."

"You baked bread for aftercare?"

"Yep."

"What kind of bread?" Sarah asked.

"It's sourdough with brownie batter mixed into it."

"Oh hell fucking yeah," I said. "Bred and bread."

The two of them burst out laughing as I got out of bed.

I love you both. I almost said it. It was on the tip of my tongue, my whole body full of so much love that it was hard to contain.

Eventually I'd be brave enough to tell them.

CHAPTER THIRTY-FOUR

sarah

MY EYES slowly opened and I realized that I was snuggled up between Sammy and Colt. A soft moan left me as I lifted my head, looking at the clock.

Fuck, it was already five a.m. I needed to get up, run home, grab muffins, take them to the cafe for Alice, go back home to shower, then have breakfast with Honey and the boys.

I carefully slipped out from under the covers, but then Sammy's arm looped around me.

"Where do you think you're going?" he murmured sleepily.

Holy shit, Sammy's morning voice was hot.

"I have to go," I whispered. I turned over, kissing him fully. He moaned, his hand cupping my breast. Dammit. "We'll sneak in more time later."

"Okay, okay," he mumbled. "Are you sure we can't sneak something in now?"

I chuckled and kissed him again, melting against him. I drew back and pressed my forehead to his with a sigh. "I have to run a couple errands and then pick up the boys."

"Okay," he sighed. "Text us where you are and all that."

"I'll be fine," I said.

Colt snored as I got out of bed and gathered up my clothes.

Being with Colt and Sammy last night had been a religious experience. And it was worth being a little exhausted from lack of sleep.

I glanced at the two of them. Sammy had rolled into the middle of the bed and was now spooning Colt, the two of them intertwined.

I love them.

But being with them also scared me.

The way they looked at me, touched me, worshiped me... I wanted it, but I also worried I didn't deserve it.

I pushed those burdening thoughts out of my head and headed down the hall to the front door. I slipped on my shoes and grabbed my bag, sighing.

It was easy to envision this being forever for us—having a house, sharing a bed, giving the boys their own spaces, and even land for them to run around on.

In my ideal world, I was running my own bakery. Colt had his winery back, Sammy was happy and doing what he loved, and the boys weren't having issues at school.

It sounded perfect.

And impossible.

Even though it was what I wanted, it was just a dream—one I didn't know how to make come true. Sometimes I felt like I was going two steps forward and three steps back when it came to healing from everything that had happened.

Until David was found and there wasn't any more trouble, I wasn't really sure I could go after what made me happy.

I pulled on my jacket and stepped outside, heading for my little Honda. Home, muffins, cafe, back home, then breakfast, then work later. *Why would they want to be with me when I'm all over the place all the time?*

The nasty thoughts and self-doubts were raging this morning. I did my best to push them aside as I got into my car and pulled out of the driveway.

I took a sip of hot coffee as I pulled into the empty Citrus Cove cafe parking lot. The blue building sat alone, the sky the color of crushed grapes. If I didn't know any better, I'd think I was the only person in all of Citrus Cove.

Despite the flash of guilt at texting so early in the day, I sent Colt and Sammy a message. It wasn't even six a.m. yet, but they had been clear about wanting to know where I was, no matter the time. My location pin was turned on for the two of them and everyone else in our family in case something happened.

I hated that we had to think that way.

David was supposedly missing. A small part of me wondered if something terrible had happened, but all I could think was *good.* He'd done so much harm to me and the boys that I didn't feel bad about karma coming back around to him.

Though he could pop back up at any moment. Maybe he wasn't actually missing, but just hiding away.

Next time I saw him, I would be stronger. That was the promise I'd made to myself.

My Honda's engine whined as I put it in park, sitting still for a moment. It was freezing today. I rubbed my icy fingers together and opened the door. A breeze lifted, numbing my cheeks. I snatched my purse, my coffee cup, the box of muffins, and then headed for the back door to the cafe, thinking about Davy and Jake.

I worried about how all of this would affect them, especially at school. After all the trouble they'd already had in their classes, I wasn't sure what to do. I knew it wasn't healthy for Davy to constantly deal with other kids who were being mean because of his father. The fact that the police had shown up to our door meant everyone would be talking again. It didn't matter that the boys had been with Honey, kids would still talk because their parents would be.

It was probably time to bring Emma and Haley to the parent-teacher meetings. Having the extra backup would surely help me convince the principal that I needed this shit to stop.

Puffs of vapor escaped my lips as I held my coffee cup in one hand, balancing the box between my forearms and body, and dug in my purse for the key with the other. "Where are you?" I mumbled.

I felt the cool metal and fished it out of the dredges of my purse.

I looked up and froze, shock rattling me.

Whore. Slut. THIS IS YOUR FAULT.

Those words were written in red on the door. An article was taped there from a local newspaper with Thomas Connor's face on the front, along with the faces of all the women he'd killed.

I couldn't breathe. Nausea bloomed as I stumbled back. It was just like the article that had been left on my car, but so much worse. Every single woman's face was taped to the door, their names written in furious, jagged letters. The one in the middle—she looked familiar but I couldn't think straight.

You're next.

Just like Thomas had written for Haley.

My hands shook as I pulled out my phone, snapping a picture and sending it to the group text chat.

Colt immediately called me. "Sarah, where are you? Are you safe?"

"I'm at the cafe." My voice trembled, my heart pounding. I could feel my phone buzzing as Haley called me too. "Haley is calling—"

"Please don't hang up. I have Sammy calling her so she doesn't freak out. We're on our way, okay?"

"I'm sorry," I whispered. "I didn't mean to wake everyone up. I—"

I heard him yell Sammy's name as tears blurred my vision. I kept looking into the eyes of all the women Thomas had killed.

I should have been up there too, right?

"I'm here, Sarah," he said. "Talk to me. Stay on the line. We're on our way."

I heard the muffled slam of a door and Sammy's voice in the background. "Hunter is on his way too, angel. Are you safe?"

"Sarah," Colt growled. "Sugar, please answer us."

"I'll get in my car," I said.

"Do that."

I rushed back to the Honda. I yanked open the door and slid in, tossing the box of muffins onto the seat and putting my coffee in the cupholder. I threw my bag to the floorboard.

"Someone wrote on the building," I said. "They put an article about Thomas up and pictures of all the women. I don't understand why this is happening. If it's David, it's just so..."

It wasn't like David to do something like this. But then again, I'd never really known the man I was married to.

"We're on our way. Sammy is calling Hunter and Cam."

They were on their way. I forced myself to breathe. They were—

Movement out of the corner of my eye made me scream. The end of a crowbar hit the window and the glass shattered.

"*Oh god!*"

Colt's shouts echoed from the phone as I tried to shield myself as best as I could. Pain sliced my skin as a hand grabbed my hair through the broken window, twisting my head.

"Stupid bitch," a man's voice snarled. His voice sounded familiar, but I couldn't tell why. "You deserve to die."

I fought back, raking my nails over his hand and arm. He slammed my head against the steering wheel and I saw stars, blood dripping into my eyes.

Fight. I have to fight. I have to.

I grabbed the coffee cup in the holder next to me and threw it, splashing the scalding liquid over him. He yelped and released me, giving me the second I needed. I slid across the seat into the passenger side and opened the door, blood still rolling down my face as I stumbled out onto the ground.

Everything was spinning. I felt like throwing up but the need to get away kept me moving.

The hum of a truck and wheels peeling over pavement echoed around me as I crawled away from my car. My head spun as I made it to the sidewalk and heard a shout.

He wasn't David. That was all I could think. It wasn't only David who hated me and wanted me dead, there was someone else too,

"Sarah, oh god," Hunter's face appeared. He knelt down next to me and I grabbed his hands as he helped me sit up. "Fuck. Okay. It's okay. You're safe, okay? You're safe. Sammy and Colt are almost here."

"Can't you take me home?" I croaked.

"No," he said firmly. "Can you focus on me?"

I really couldn't, but I tried. Everything wavered, making my stomach flip. "I'm sorry," I gasped. "I'm going to throw up."

"That's okay. Let it out."

I couldn't stop it if I tried. I threw up dinner from last night, my throat burning. He rubbed my back gently, talking softly.

"We're going to find out who did this and they're never going to see the sky again. I'm so sorry this happened."

All I could do was nod. I finished throwing up, breathing hard. Before I could protest, he scooped me up and carried me to the sidewalk, sitting me down.

Colt's truck peeled into the parking lot, skidding to a halt.

"I threw my coffee on him. I fought back." *I didn't freeze. I didn't freeze, for once.*

"Of course you did. You're a fighter."

The tears started up. Voices echoed and I felt Colt next to me, his face coming into my vision, eyes full of panic.

Hunter barked an order. "Sammy, get my first aid kit out of the truck."

"Hi, sugar," Colt whispered, his eyes tearing up. "Who was it? Who did this?"

"I don't know," I said. "I didn't recognize his voice..." I closed my eyes, my head throbbing.

Their voices hummed around me and Sammy's hand was on my face.

"She definitely has a concussion," Hunter said. "Let's get her to the doctor."

"I don't want the boys to know," I whispered. "There's already too much going on."

"They're going to know something is wrong," Colt said softly. "You can't hide—"

"You aren't their dad and I don't want your opinion right now," I snapped. I felt the sting of my words and winced, opening my eyes to look at him.

"Sarah, we're taking you to the emergency room," Sammy said firmly.

"I can't afford that."

"I'll pay for it—"

"*I don't want you to.*"

"Too bad," Colt growled. "We're taking you to the hospital. You're bleeding and you have a concussion."

I was too dizzy to keep arguing, so all I did was flip him off. And yes, it was rude. But instead of hurting his feelings, all he did was smile.

"Good."

"Fuck you," I muttered.

"We'll save it for another time."

I scoffed but was manhandled before I could get another word in. Gently manhandled, but still manhandled. Sirens blared in the air as Sammy picked me up and I shook my head.

"Why would you call an ambulance?"

The amount of stress was enough to make me want to fall apart. I sniffled as the ambulance parked between Colt and Hunter's trucks, strangers getting out.

Fuck, my head hurt.

Everything hurt. Wherever the glass had gotten me, the slicing pain was becoming more intense. I laid my head on Sammy's shoulder, listening to the chatter around me.

"Sarah. Stay awake." I felt Colt's hand on my cheek. "Please, sugar. Honey just pulled in with the boys."

Fuck. My eyes immediately opened as I heard Jake's voice in the distance. I spotted her pale yellow truck and shook my head.

"Don't you dare let them see me like this," I said firmly, looking him in the eye. "Do you both understand me? I don't need you here with me, I need you with them. Please, please. Please listen to me."

Colt nodded as Sammy put me on a stretcher. I gave him a scathing look, but then I saw the way his hands shook.

He raked his fingers through his hair. "We've got the boys. We'll meet you at the hospital. We need to make sure you're okay, angel."

I breathed out, accepting my fate as the two of them were pushed out of the way.

As long as someone was after me, I was a danger to Sammy. I was a danger to Colt.

The moment I could see them heading to intercept the boys, I closed my eyes and slipped into the dark.

CHAPTER THIRTY-FIVE

ALL OF US were shell-shocked by the events of this morning. It was evening now, but the fear had yet to wear off. Never in my life had I felt so damn scared than when I had heard Sarah on the phone.

I never wanted to experience fear like that again. One moment, I'd been snuggled in bed next to Colt, the next we'd been racing to get to her. Colt drove his truck like a race car, tearing up dirt and gravel to make it to her in time.

Whoever attacked her—I wanted to make them pay. They'd gone after her in the parking lot, which meant they'd been following her. There was no way they would have known to go to the cafe so early unless they were stalking her.

I rubbed my eyes. Everything was falling apart. I felt the same way I did last year when Haley was in trouble, only it was so much worse because I was in love with Sarah.

Honey tapped her foot, her arms crossed, her eyes shooting daggers at me and Colt. Everyone was crowded in the waiting room and doing our best to keep it together for Jake and Davy. The boys had clung to us on the drive over and

I'd done my best to be there for them. Davy was furious that we'd kept him from seeing Sarah, but I was doing what she'd asked.

I understood why she didn't want them to see her being put in the ambulance. God knows, I never wanted to witness that ever again. It was something I would never forget, as long as I lived.

Haley got up from her chair and came over to us, giving Honey a pleading look. This was the sixth time she'd tried to intercept the Honey stare down Colt and I were receiving right now. She was angry and maybe blamed us for what happened. I wasn't really sure.

"You're being rude right now," Haley whispered to Honey. "Stop tapping your foot. You're making me anxious."

"They should have been there with her."

Haley started to protest, but Colt shook his head. His knee wouldn't stop bouncing. "No, she's right. We should have."

I swallowed hard and looked at Jake and Davy. They'd been through too much. How was I supposed to help? What could I possibly say or do to show them everything would be okay? All I knew was I never wanted to stand between them and their mom again.

Cam leaned forward, rubbing his jaw. All of us were exhausted and frightened, holding ourselves together for Davy and Jake. He gave Honey a hard look. "None of this was their fault," Cam said. "Whoever is after Sarah, it's all connected to Thomas."

That, we could all agree on.

"Is she going to be okay?" Jake asked.

"Yes," Emma said. Her arm was around him protectively, her eyes burning with rage. "Your mama is strong."

The nurse stepped into the room and her eyes widened. We made quite the group. Honey, Haley, Cam, Hunter, Jake,

Davy, Emma, Colt, and me. My parents would have been here too, but we'd sent them on the mission to get food for everyone.

The nurse cleared her throat. I swore she was the same one we'd seen multiple times last year, which made sense given how fucking small the hospital was. I was pretty sure the tiles on the floor had been here since the place was built. "Okay, Sarah is awake. She has a bad concussion and she sustained several lacerations from the glass, but those will heal. She's going to be just fine. She asked to see her kids and Haley, but no one else yet."

I breathed out, my shoulders sinking. I reached over, sliding my hand into Colt's. He squeezed my palm hard. My heart raced as anxiety took hold of me. I was desperate to see Sarah.

Haley gave us an apologetic look before focusing on Davy and Jake. She held out her hands for them. "Let's go see her."

Davy glanced over at us, his gaze sliding to our hands intertwined. Both him and Jake took Haley's hands, following her and the nurse out of the room.

The tension in the room shifted once the boys were out of ear shot. "Fuck," I sighed. "This is a fucking nightmare."

Colt gripped my hand tighter, but remained silent.

Emma gave me a sad look. "Sarah is okay. That's all that matters. She fought back. Whoever this son of a bitch is, we're gonna get them."

"Bud is looking," Hunter said. "They can't keep escaping us."

I nodded, but I couldn't feel a damn thing right now aside from guilt.

Cam got up and changed seats, sinking down next to me. He didn't say anything, though.

Last year when Haley was in the hospital, he'd been a zombie for days. I hadn't quite understood the depth of his despair until now, and we knew Sarah was going to be okay.

"So, are the two of you going to explain things to me?" Honey asked.

"Honey, they're both tired," Cam sighed. "They're literally covered in Sarah's blood. Seeing someone you love get hurt is hard."

Her face softened. "I meant about the three of them, Cameron Harlow. Not about them not being there. Sarah goes where she wants. If anyone knows that, it's me."

Colt stood up, releasing my hand. "I need some air. All I can say right now is I love her and I love him. That's it."

My heart launched to my throat. I stared in shock at him as he pushed past Honey and left the room. *He loves me? He just said he loves me?*

I leaned forward, his words settling over me. Now wasn't the right time to talk about that admission, but...

Colt loved me.

A shaky breath left me and I raked my fingers through my hair.

Honey's shoulders sank. "I'm being bitchy, aren't I?"

"Yep," Emma chimed.

She was the only one ballsy enough to say it.

"I think all of us are scared and stressed. This is like Haley 2.0. and there's nothing we can do. Hunter, did you see the man who attacked her?" Emma asked.

"No," Hunter said. He grimaced and leaned back in his chair, giving me a grim look. "Well, I got a glance at him. When I pulled up, I saw someone running, but I also saw Sarah crawling on the pavement. I had to go to her first. I gave them the description. The problem was that it happened so early, no one else was really awake."

"He has to be somewhere close by," Emma said.

"I agree. I just don't know where."

This was the longest conversation I'd ever seen the two of them have without being rude to each other.

"It wasn't David, though," Cam said. "Which is more concerning in some ways."

It was. With David, we could expect him to behave a certain way. But whoever was going after Sarah was angry and vengeful.

They wanted to hurt her.

Seeing *You're Next* written in red again terrified me. The pictures of all the women plastered on the door, their names scrawled in a way that spoke of rage and pain.

I couldn't lose Sarah.

"Sammy, I'm going to go after Colt," Cam said softly. "Unless you want to."

I wanted to more than anything else, but I needed to stay here. "I need you to," I said. "He and I can talk more later."

Cam nodded and clapped my shoulder gently, squeezing me. "He loves you."

"I love him too. He doesn't know that yet."

Cam nodded, fighting a smile. "Noted."

He left us. Emma and Hunter glanced at each other and then he stood too. "I'm going to check on Mom and Pops."

"I'm going to go see Sarah," Emma said. "They can't hold me back."

They probably couldn't.

That left me and Honey alone. She sat down next to me and held out her small, weathered hand. I took it gently.

"I'm sorry," she said. "Sometimes I get a certain way. I love Sarah so much. I know I'm her grandmother, but she's a daughter to me. We've had a hard time with each other the last few months, but she and I are finally really talking again. I had some idea about the three of you after David showed up, but I don't think I fully realized your relationship until today."

"It works for us," I said. "I love them both, Honey. I really do. And I love those boys too. They deserve to have a father or two who love them."

"You're young," she said. "Is being a father really what you want right now?"

"Yes." That came out with no any hesitation. "I want everything. I want the broken hearts and the sadness and the tears of joy. I want the ball games, the fights, the sitting on the porch with Sarah and Colt and watching the sun set. I want to build a house we can grow in. I want to have a family. I want *this* family. I want it all."

She sniffled. "You know, I remember the day Sarah got married to David. I never liked that bastard. Colt showed up that day and I really thought she would go with him. I thought she would see that David wasn't right for her."

"He's manipulative."

"He is. He took her and turned her into someone she wasn't and I've watched her fight for years. I've watched her fight to be a good mom. I've watched her fight to hold herself together. I've watched her fight to see the good in a bad situation. I always wanted her to be with someone who would fight that hard for her." She took a deep breath. "But now, I want two people who will fight for her."

Tears sprang to my eyes. I drew in a steady breath before looking over at her. I leaned over, kissing her cheek. "Thank you, Honey."

She smiled. "It's not like you needed my blessing."

"No, but it helps."

Haley appeared in the doorway with Emma and the boys. "We are heading to the Harlow farm for dinner. Honey, do you want to come?"

"Sure. I can talk to Lynn all day."

Haley smiled. "Perfect. Sarah is ready for you and Colt. I'll be back in a few minutes and will be taking her home. Everyone else has been kicked out. With love, of course."

"Your husband is with my future husband," I said.

Haley and Emma exchanged glances with wide, knowing grins. I wondered if they'd placed a bet of sorts.

"Alright, I'll retrieve him and send yours in."

Honey winked at me and then they left as a group. I stood up and looked down at myself, wincing. Maybe changing a shirt was a good idea.

Colt appeared in the doorway, his eyes red. He was looking rough. I'd do anything to take the fear out of his gaze. "Hey."

"Hey," I whispered. "Are you okay?"

"No. Are you?"

"Nope." I crossed the room to him and tugged him close, kissing him hard. He melted against me, his fingers knotting in my shirt. I drew back, kissing his forehead. "It's going to be okay," I whispered.

"I don't know," he whispered. "I just don't know."

"It will be. Let's go see Sarah."

"I've got a bad feeling."

I couldn't disagree. The two of us walked silently down the sterile hall to her room. I poked my head in, knocking on the frame.

Fuck. Seeing her like this killed me. I hadn't even had time to process how angry I was at the person who attacked her, and I needed to put that away for now.

She was already sitting up and redressed in the new set of clothes Haley had brought her from home. Wherever the glass had cut her, she was bandaged up. Her hair was pulled back into a messy bun, and dark circles shadowed her eyes.

"Hey, angel."

Sarah looked up at us, immediately tearing up. Her gaze flickered from me to Colt and back again. "Hi."

"How are you feeling?" Colt asked.

She let out a broken laugh, her shoulders sagging. "Like I've been hit by a truck." She swallowed hard and looked away, a couple tears rolling down her cheeks. She took a slow, deliberate breath. "I can't do this right now."

Colt went to her, kneeling next to her. "What? What can I help with?"

"No, Colt. That's not what I mean."

I could barely breathe. I couldn't move.

"We need to take a break from *this*. From whatever this is. I can't do it. I can't right now, I'm sorry."

Colt looked like he'd been shot. I leaned against the doorway, my knees like jelly. This was the very thing I'd feared the most. I'd known we'd moved too fast, that we were diving in head first, that I wasn't good enough. I wasn't what either of them needed. Pain froze me in place, every part of me folding into agony.

"Why?" Colt whispered.

"I can't do this right now. You both need to go. Haley should be coming back for me."

"Let us help you," I said. "Please, Sarah, I—"

"Please don't finish that sentence." Her words came out in the softest whisper. She looked at me, shaking her head. "Please. Please don't do that right now."

But I love you. I love you, I love you—

"Please go. I need to rest. I need to go home."

"Sarah, please don't do this," Colt whispered. "We care for you. We can take a step back, we can take it easy, but—"

"No. I just need my sister right now."

He bowed his head for a moment, his voice wavering. "Okay."

I felt a gentle hand on my arm and turned. Haley's brows knit with worry. "I'm here, Sarah."

"Perfect timing." Sarah grabbed a bag with her discharge papers and ruined clothes. She wobbled for a moment as she stood, but steadied herself before Colt could help her.

"Can we help you get to the car?" I asked. *Hold it together. Hold it together for Colt.*

"No," Sarah said. "We've got it. You can go."

I paused for a long moment. She wouldn't meet my gaze.

The misery on Colt's face killed me as much as the pain I saw in Sarah's stance. "Colt, come on," I said gently.

He gave her one last pained glance and then left, pushing past me. I looked at Sarah, using my last bit of strength to speak. "If you need anything at all, please call us. We're always here for you, no matter what happens."

I took off after Colt before she could say anything else. Tears blurred my vision as I stepped out into the cold, heading straight for his truck. I opened the passenger door and looked in the back. He was splayed out over the back seat crying.

"Baby," I whispered.

"She just broke up with us."

I wanted to tell him it would be okay. But I didn't really know. All I knew was that everything fucking hurt.

sarah

"IF YOU KEEP CRYING like this, I might need to take you back to the hospital. Because this can't be good for your concussion."

My entire body shook with a sob. I sprawled over my bed, my face buried in my pillow, and I couldn't stop crying. *I did the right thing. I did the right thing.*

I needed to get it all out before the boys got home, because right now, I didn't have the strength to pull myself together.

I was so tired.

So, so tired.

Haley stroked my back. "Sarah, what happened? What's wrong? I've never seen Sammy or Colt look like that."

I couldn't even speak.

The panic that had gripped me was unlike anything I'd ever experienced. Being attacked at the cafe and feeling like I wasn't being listened to had triggered something inside me I hadn't felt since I'd been married to David. That wasn't Colt or Sammy's fault.

I knew them taking me to the hospital was logically the right thing to do.

But could someone tell my heart that?

I'd put them in danger. The fear that this was too much for them had taken over and I'd spiraled. I was the reason all of this was happening. How could they want to be with me? They didn't deserve this. They didn't deserve to always be in danger, always wondering if I was going to get hurt.

It was a lot. Between the threats, David missing, this attack —I'd done the best thing for all of us. Ending our relationship was the only way to keep them safe.

But it hurt. Everything hurt. I couldn't stop thinking about the way Davy and Jake had looked at me.

I felt like the worst mom in the world. I'd married a psycho and we'd ended up in a situation where people hated me so much, they felt the need to attack me and the people I loved.

How was I supposed to keep everyone safe if I couldn't even protect myself?

It wasn't fair to Sammy or Colt to put them through all of this. They'd already gone through enough.

"I broke up with them," I hiccuped.

"Oh my god, Okay, Okay, alright." Haley continued to rub my back gently. "So, I need you to dry those tears, Sarah. Because this isn't good for your head. I'm going to go down and get you some water and by the time I get back, I want them dried."

"You sound like Honey."

"Yeah, well. You're better off with me than her."

I sniffled as she left the bedroom and forced myself to breathe out of my mouth. God, I was a mess. I rolled over onto my back, tears rolling down the sides of my face and dampening my hair. I stared at the ceiling as I wiped them away, thinking about David.

Marrying him had been my greatest mistake. I thought about all the years we were together, all of the times I'd done whatever he said. I'd constantly changed who I was to fit into the mold he wanted.

These last few months, I'd started to learn who I was again. But, I was drained. I was tired of fighting. Soul sucking exhaustion had wrapped its arms around me, and wouldn't let me go.

What was I supposed to do?

The stairs creaked as Haley returned with a glass of water and a straw. Her blonde curls were piled on top of her head, her brows pulled together as she sat on the side of the bed and offered me a sip.

"Everyone is too good to me," I croaked.

"Sarah. Everyone *loves* you."

I fought more tears as I took a few sips. She placed the water on the side table then carefully laid down in bed, pulling me into her arms.

She let out a full body sigh, resting her chin on top of my head. "Do you remember when Mom died?" she whispered.

My eyes widened. It was something we never spoke about. Hell, I couldn't remember the last time her name had come up. "Yes."

"Do you remember how we swore we'd be there for each other?"

I swallowed hard. "Yes."

"I really failed you."

"No," I rasped. "No, you didn't. Haley, we've talked about this."

"That doesn't mean the feeling has suddenly gone away. My brain knows there were reasons for me being gone. But my heart still hurts when I think about how much I've missed. And it hurts even more when I think about how much you've had to do alone. David was never there for you. You've been a single mom since the day you gave birth to Jake and Davy. Why can't you see how strong you are?"

"Because I don't feel strong. I didn't do anything because I was strong, I did it because I had to." My voice broke and I fought the tears again, holding my breath. Emotional pain hit me full force again, like everything around me was shattering and I was being cut over and over. "Everyone treats me like I'm fragile. Everyone treats me like I'm broken."

"Sarah, you're so used to doing things on your own that you've forgotten that part of being loved is being cared for. No one does anything for you because they think you're fragile or broken. They do it because that's what we do for each other. If you were in my shoes, wouldn't you have done what I've done?"

I winced as I turned to the side, laying my head on her chest. "I've been a burden for months. Not knowing about Thomas really fucked me up. How could I not have known, Haley? How could I have missed that he was a completely different person?"

"None of us knew," Haley said.

"But should I have recognized something was wrong? I jeopardized everyone I love. I felt like that again today, more than ever before."

"But you didn't do this. Unless you're secretly an evil mastermind."

I shook my head. "No."

She gently stroked my hair. "So then why do you keep punishing yourself like you are one?"

"Because I should have known."

"No one knew David had a brother. The information that has come out about that family has been beyond anything we could have imagined, Sarah. You didn't do this. You didn't kill those women. You didn't try to kill me."

"I'm sorry."

She blew out a frustrated sigh. "I don't accept your apology."

"But—"

"No. I don't. I don't accept this. Tell me why you broke up with Sammy and Colt. I thought you loved them."

"I do." I couldn't fight the tears and let them roll, trying to keep breathing. "I love them so damn much, Haley. But after being attacked today, I realized I'm a danger to them. I'm too much trouble."

"I need you to look at me when I ask you this."

I looked up at her and my eyes widened.

Haley was *mad.*

"Did Sammy Harlow or Colton Hayes say you were too much trouble? Did they say anything like that? Or is that David talking?"

My eyes widened.

"Because I'm either about to go kneecap a couple of cowboys or tell you that you're still letting David control you."

I stared at her for a moment and laughed, then winced because laughing hurt. "You are something fierce."

But she had a point.

"You might be right," I sighed, looking away. "But I still need some time to work through some of this. I don't think either one of them will want anything to do with me now."

"I wouldn't be so sure," she said. "You should have seen them in the waiting room. You should have seen them with Jake and Davy. Hell, you should have seen Jake and Davy with the two of them."

I nodded slowly. "I didn't want the boys to see me being loaded up into the ambulance. And god, now there will be more bills, and..."

Haley made a face.

I narrowed my eyes. "What's that look for?"

She fought a small smile. "I don't think you'll have any bills to worry about."

"*Haley.*"

"It wasn't me."

"*Haley!*"

She made a zipping motion with her lips. "Not a damn word."

"You traitor," I sighed, but I was smiling now. "You're on their side, aren't you?"

"Maybe a little. I never expected you to end up with two people in your life who loved you, and who you loved back. I think it's beautiful. I think it's clear they love each other too. And I think all three of you are good people. Obviously, you have to decide for yourself if this is what you want."

She was right. "I just need some space to think."

"There were a lot of big emotions today," she said. "You made the decision to break up with them out of fear. I think taking some space would be good while you heal. You need to get some sleep. Today was hell, but you're safe now. I'm going to go downstairs and call Cam to check on the boys."

"Okay. Thank you."

I squeezed her hand and she kissed my forehead before rolling out of bed. I pulled the blankets up to my shoulders and tried to ignore the ache in my heart.

Earlier, I'd been so sure I was doing the right thing.

There was a part of me that believed maybe it *was* the right thing. There was also a part of me that was still scarred from not being loved in return for so long. The years with David had left me shriveled and starved, and Sammy and Colt had come into my life and began to heal me.

I was a mess.

I was a mom. I was always busy. I was constantly on the go,

constantly trying to heal from the past. Didn't I owe it to them —and myself—to trust that if they wanted to be with me, they would be?

I loved them. I was more sure of that than anything else.

Sammy and Colt had changed my life in so many ways. Fear was holding me back now, and maybe Haley was right. Maybe I still felt like David controlled me.

My eyes started to close and as I drifted off to sleep, all I could think about was how I'd made a mistake by breaking up with Colt and Sammy.

I was so tired of fighting and being afraid. Wasn't it time for me to let myself be happy?

It meant letting myself love again.

It also meant letting myself be loved.

CHAPTER THIRTY-SEVEN

"FUCK... FUCK."

It was six in the fucking morning. My eyes flew open and I stared at the ceiling as my head cleared.

Whimpers and grunts echoed from the living room. I scowled, wondering what the fuck Sammy was doing. I knew it was Sammy. I knew what he sounded like when he said fuck.

I raised my head, staring at the door.

I'd gotten into the habit of leaving it open since Sammy had temporarily moved in. I was kind of hoping he'd stay permanently.

It had been four days since Sarah had broken things off with us. I'd mostly been in bed, completely miserable and only leaving when necessary or when Sammy made me get up to eat. Everything was so damn upside down now, I didn't know what to do.

The other night we'd all been together, I'd been so damn sure that everything was going to be perfect. I loved her. I loved him. I loved being together. I wanted to build a life together.

"Goddamn."

"What the fuck," I mumbled. Was he jacking off on my couch?

I got out of bed quietly and snuck down the hall. The moans grew louder.

"*Fuuuuuck,*" Sammy grunted.

I rounded the corner quietly and paused.

Sammy's ass faced me in tight silver gym shorts, a workout shirt clinging to his back muscles as he moved his thigh out over a foam roller. He moved it back and forth over the floor, his skin covered in a sheen of sweat.

I hadn't been in the mood for sex. We'd cuddled and kissed and had watched movies, but we'd yet to have sex again.

But at the moment, that was all I could think about. Fuck, he looked good when he was sweaty and moaning like that...

The view went straight to my cock.

I crossed my arms and cleared my throat.

He rolled over onto his ass in surprise, looking up at me. His eyes then drifted to the outline of my erection in my boxers.

"Did I wake you?" he rasped.

"You did," I said. "What the hell are you doing rolling your thighs this early?"

"I went for a run." He licked his lips and got to his knees. His hair was slicked back with sweat and he was *dirty*. Somehow, that only turned me on more. "I want you."

"I want you too," I whispered. "I'm sorry I've been..."

"No, don't be sorry. We're both brokenhearted, Colt. I miss her just as much as you do and it feels weird trying to stay out of her way. Not that I've done a good job."

I hadn't either. We'd both been texting Cam, trying to sneak updates and check in on Sarah without crowding her. I'd texted her once to let her know I was thinking about her and was left on read.

The thing was, we'd been stalking her. Well-meaning stalking, of course. There hadn't been a day where one of us hadn't sat across the street from the cafe, keeping an eye on everything while she worked. Neither one of us wanted something bad to happen to her again.

Bud and everyone in the police department had been trying to hunt down the man that had attacked her. David was still missing, though, which made me nervous.

My thoughts kept spinning in circles. Sarah, the pain and destruction Thomas had caused, the danger, the fact that I'd fucked up and lost her again.

"Colt." Sammy's voice was a soft, pleading whisper breaking through the panic. "Come here, baby."

His voice was so gentle and sweet and I *needed* him right now.

"Fuck," I mumbled, crossing the living room to him. I couldn't stop the tears that threatened to fall and he reached up, pulling me down into a kiss as he thumbed them away. "What are we going to do?"

"We're going to be there for each other. Because I'm not leaving you, Colt. And I don't think we've really lost her either."

I wasn't sure. I tried to grasp the moment through, forcing a smile. "Not used to you getting on your knees."

Sammy snorted and reached for my hips, yanking me close. I grunted as he peeled my boxers down, my cock springing free. Even with the despair I knew we both felt, I was so fucking hard. Knowing he wasn't jacking off was kind of funny now, but regardless—hearing him huff and moan turned me on.

He wrapped his long fingers around the base of my cock, stroking me slowly. "Sorry to wake you from your slumber, princess."

"You're the princess—*fuck.*"

He took my cock in his mouth and damn near sucked my soul out of my body. I gripped his head, bucking my hips as pleasure shot through me. His stormy blue eyes held mine as he took me deeper, never leaving me.

I thrust harder, hitting the back of his throat. He grunted, his hands sliding to my hips, fingertips indenting my ass.

"Damn, Sammy."

All I could think about was taking his mouth, the way he bobbed his head, and the way every part of me needed him right now.

I tipped my head back, squeezing my eyes shut as he kept dragging me toward the edge. His mouth was hot and silky, his tongue working my shaft between sucks. He cupped my balls and a long moan left me as he played with them, teasing me.

Right as I was about to come, he pulled back. Everything stopped and I looked down at him, eyes wide.

"Fuck me," he whispered. "I want you to come inside me."

He didn't need to ask twice. I held out my hand and pulled him to standing, the two of us kissing madly as we backed our way down the hall to my bed.

In a rare show of dominance toward him, I shoved him onto the blankets. He rolled over onto all fours as I grabbed the lube, kneeling behind him and quickly prepping us both.

We needed reconnection. That need hit me hard as I kissed down his back, savoring the salty taste of his skin—

"Fuck me," he growled. "Fuck me raw, Colt. I need you."

Okay, maybe we'd savor each other later.

I pressed the head of my cock against him and was shocked as he pushed his hips back, taking me. Fuck, he was tight. I gripped his hips, a grunt leaving me as I forced him to be still.

"Fucking hold still," I rasped. "Hold on, Sammy."

He stretched his arms out, his back muscles rippling as he

buried his face into a pillow, stifling the sounds he made. I closed my eyes as he adjusted around me.

Something primal and needy rose up, clawing its way to the surface. I raked my nails over his back as he groaned. My hips had a mind of their own. I thrust hard, filling him with the rest of my cock.

A muffled curse left him, but I wanted to know what he was saying. I wanted to hear every moan and growl crystal clear. I worked my fingers into his short dark hair and yanked his head up, dragging my hips back before pumping into him again.

Fuck. The rhythm was rough and frenzied. I squeezed my eyes shut, my cock sliding in and out of him. He was taking every inch, pleasure mounting with each thrust.

I realized I wanted to look into his eyes as I came inside him. I pulled out, rolling him onto his back and pushing his thighs back. His cock was so fucking hard, his hand immediately closing around his shaft and stroking as I thrust back into him.

"Fuck, baby," he moaned.

I leaned down, kissing him hard, my tongue tangling with his. I couldn't get enough of him. He cupped my face gently, his touch a drastic contradiction to the way I was breeding his hot hole.

"I'm going to come," he rasped.

Hot jets of cum shot from his cock onto our stomachs. Watching him orgasm sent me over the edge, and I filled him as our voices echoing through the bedroom.

I panted as I leaned against him. I pressed my forehead to his chest, feeling his breaths. He ran his hands up my sides, stroking me gently.

"I love you," he whispered.

My gaze snapped up. I met his stormy blue eyes, getting lost at sea within them. "I love you," I whispered back.

He stroked my face, his hand holding my cheek. I closed my eyes, the intimacy and connection grounding me.

Both of our hearts hurt right now, but we had each other.

"I still believe she'll come back," Sammy whispered. "We love her. And I feel like she loves us. But she's been through so much that I think it's hard for her to accept that love."

"I want her to be with us," I said. "But if she doesn't change her mind, I want us to be together. I want you with me. I don't want you to move back out of the house."

"Are you sure?"

"More than," I said. "Although... I'd thought that maybe if Sarah was with us, we'd build a house. I own the land here, I bought it from Cam a long time ago. There's enough space... I'm just being stupid now."

"No you're not," he snorted. He stole another kiss. "I like this idea. I wonder how expensive it is to build a house."

"Expensive. But we'd have it forever."

His face softened. "We would."

A mischievous smile spread across my lips. "Maybe I should start a cooking channel, huh?"

"I mean, or you could help me make more content. You've got good hands."

"Oh do I?"

"Mmhmm. Maybe I could try them out in the shower first."

I raised a brow. "How do you want to test them out?"

"Well, I think it would only be wise to know what they feel like touching me."

"Right? God forbid I stroke a cucumber wrong. You have to make sure I do it right."

The two of us burst out laughing. I slowly eased out of him and we rolled out of bed, heading straight for the shower.

My heart was a little bit lighter now.

CHAPTER THIRTY-EIGHT

sarah

MY ROUTINE WAS BACK to normal, but I still didn't feel right.

The concussion had left me with a few headaches, but overall, I was fine. I'd taken a few days off, which meant I'd been in bed torturing myself over the decision I'd made to break up with Colt and Sammy.

Most of the cuts from the broken windshield were healing, but the cuts on my heart weren't.

Haley's words about David haunted me. I'd ended up calling Brenda to talk to her about it all and she'd been able to help me sort through some of my feelings.

I'd let fear get in the way of my happiness. After talking to Brenda, I was starting to realize just how much I was sabotaging myself. I ended up devouring a few books on polyamory, relationships, and being a parent because I also felt like I was failing in that area too.

Apparently all of that was normal. I wasn't broken, or helpless, or useless. I was healing from the past while fighting for a future I deserved.

I wanted to talk to Sammy and Colt again.

The other thing I'd realized this week was how much I loved them both.

I wasn't sure who I realized I loved first.

Maybe it was the day Colt crashed my wedding.

Maybe it was the night Sammy took me to the drive-through.

Maybe it was when the two of them held me tight and showed me that I was beautiful and deserving of romance.

Either way, somewhere in the last few weeks, I'd fallen in love with them so hard that it scared me.

Now that I'd given myself the time to think and the time to process what I wanted and needed in my life, I was able to take that soul-rattling fear and turn it into something else.

Hope.

I had hope for the future. Hope that everything would turn out okay. I still didn't know who had attacked me in the parking lot or who was after me. I didn't know where my ex-husband was or if he was even alive. But I had hope that I would make it through the storm and onto the other side. I just knew I had a happy ending waiting for me.

One that was happy for *all* of us.

I wasn't sure they'd take me back, though. I had no idea what the outcome would be or if they could forgive me for breaking up with them. They'd been scared too, and I'd withdrawn instead of being there for them.

Chatter echoed through the cafe and I blinked, coming to the present. Autopilot was fully on right now while I worked. I exchanged pleasantries with folks, carefully navigating the occasional nosy question, and took food to tables—all while thinking about my life.

What did I want in the future?

It was easy to dream. It was harder to make those dreams reality, but I wanted to put in the work to try.

"How are you feeling, Sarah?"

One of the tables I was serving was a booth of three old men. One of them was Mr. Johnson, who saw Honey regularly. He made her happy and was funny and sweet. I rarely saw him, but when I did, I always found myself smiling.

"I'm better," I said. "Everything has been a little wild."

"I've been trying to find that son of a bitch," one of the older men grumbled. "Keeping an eye out."

Everyone in Citrus Cove had heard about me being attacked. I hated the attention and longed for the day that I didn't have to deal with the chaos. I still gave him a grateful smile.

"I appreciate it. Y'all let me know if you need anything, okay? Mr. Johnson, if you happen to be going by Honey's today, let me know. I'll send some goods with you."

He grinned. "You know how to help a man out. I think I'll swing by after this."

"Perfect." I headed to the back of the cafe and spotted Alice walking in the back door.

She glanced up at me and smiled. "How's it going?"

"Good today," I said. "I think it's busier with the cold weather coming in this weekend."

Everyone was a little anxious about it. If the weather predictions were right, we could end up with ice and snow for a few days, which was apocalyptic with our infrastructure. Emma had already stocked the house with battery lamps, heaters, and food we could eat if the power went out. I'd also noticed that Cam had dropped off firewood and other supplies. I suspected it was actually from Colt and Sammy, but I hadn't argued with him about it.

"Yeah, yeah," Alice sighed, shaking her head. "You know,

when I lived in New York, this was never an issue. We could get several feet of snow and no one would bat an eye. Down here, it's the end of the world."

"True," I said. "We're built for heat, not the cold."

She chuckled. "Oh, before you run off. I meant to tell you that Colt got the muffins to me and they were fantastic. You can sell them here. Just let me know what you want to do."

My eyes widened. I stared at her for a moment, freezing in place. "You really mean it?"

"Yep. I think they would do great. If there's anything I can do to support you, Sarah, I'm here."

Tears filled my eyes and I stepped closer, giving her a hug. "You're too kind to me."

She squeezed me tight and then released me. "I honestly hope one day you stop working for me so we can actually be friends. I still have to be your boss right now and that sucks."

I laughed. "I hope so. I mean, I love this place. I don't want you to think I don't—"

"Believe me, I'm aware," she snorted. Her eyes darted past me and she raised a brow. "About damn time. I was wondering where they've been."

I turned around and sucked in a breath. Nothing could have prepared me for the way I felt when I saw Sammy's car pull into the cafe parking lot. I stared out the window, my heart pounding as he got out. He wore a bulky jacket over dark jeans and boots, his dark hair damp.

Now, all I could think about was Sammy in the shower. Colt in the shower. *Me in the shower with both of them.*

My cheeks turned red. The door opened, a cool blast freezing the air as he stepped inside.

He had his laptop bag with him, I realized.

Alice crossed her arms. "Why do you look like you're seeing a ghost?"

"We... It's complicated."

"Mmhmm. Okay then. Well, let me know if you need anything."

"Thanks, Alice."

Trey rang the bell from the kitchen and I sighed, shifting back into work mode. I loaded the plates onto a tray and dropped them at one of the tables while actively avoiding Sammy's searing gaze as he took one of the booths.

My phone started to ring in my pocket, but I ignored the buzz.

"How does everything look?" I asked the table. I received nods and sounds of approval. "Perfect. Enjoy your meal."

Don't look at him, don't look at him, don't look at him. My feet had a mind of their own. I approached his booth, finally meeting his eyes.

My phone started to ring again. I ignored it, tension creeping up my spine.

"What are you doing here?" I whispered.

"Getting food," Sammy said. He swallowed hard, his eyes softening. "Sarah, I—"

"You're a chef," I said, raising a brow. "You couldn't cook for yourself?"

He snorted, offering me a lopsided smile. "Rather eat here and keep an eye on you."

My heart skipped a beat. I'd missed seeing him in this booth. I'd missed *seeing* him, period. "Are you sure you want to? I don't want to waste your time."

"We've literally been sitting across the street keeping an eye on the cafe every day this week. I decided to finally come inside."

My mouth fell open. "Really?"

"Really."

"You've been stalking me, then," I said, unable to keep the tease out of my voice.

He raised a brow. "Is it stalking or protecting?"

The phone started to buzz in my pocket again and I sighed, pulling it out. The school's phone number flashed across the screen and I winced, answering it.

"Hello, this is Sarah," I said.

"Hi Sarah, this is Agatha."

Great. Just fucking great.

"I'm at work. What's going on?" I asked.

Sammy scowled. "Who is it?"

School, I mouthed.

"The boys got into a fight. We need you to pick them up."

I closed my eyes, trying to find a shred of patience, will power, resolve—*something.* "I can't pick them up right now."

"Can someone pick them up? They're being suspended."

"*Suspended?*"

"I can pick them up," Sammy said immediately.

"I don't want to burden you," I said quickly, but he was already standing up.

"Sorry, Sarah. We need someone to pick them up and if it can be you, we can try and straighten things out with David and Jake—"

"His name is Davy. How many times have I told you, Agatha?"

Sammy made a face. "I've got them, Sarah. I'll go pick them up and I can take them to Honey's."

I pinched the bridge of my nose. "Okay. I have Sammy Harlow coming to pick the boys up. We'll have to schedule a meeting next week. I can't do this right now."

"Alright, sweetie. I'll send you an email."

"Okay. Bye." I hung up rather abruptly, shaking my head. "I don't know why they would suspend Davy and Jake unless it was really bad. And that doesn't sound like them. I know there's been a lot happening, but they're good boys."

"Cam and I got into some pretty gnarly fights when we were younger," Sammy said.

"Well, I hope they didn't fight each other. I raised them not to... Would you mind taking them to my house? I'll be off in a couple hours."

"No problem. I'll stay with them until you get home."

I swallowed hard, studying him. My cheeks heated under his gaze. "Are you sure? I can call—"

"I'm sure. I'll text you when we get there."

"Thank you."

I wanted to kiss him right now so damn bad. Instead, I watched him leave.

CHAPTER THIRTY-NINE

I WALKED into the school and headed straight to the principal's office. I couldn't say it was the first time I'd ever been there. The building had hardly been updated since I walked these halls years ago.

I wrinkled my nose as I neared the doorway. It still made me feel anxious, even knowing I wasn't the one in trouble.

I'd jumped at the opportunity to help out Sarah. I'd do whatever I could for her. It had been a hard week and I was trying to keep myself together for Colt, but it was wearing on me.

Just have to remain hopeful.

Davy sat in a gray chair, his arms crossed and eyes on the floor. Jake sat next to him, refusing to look at his brother. Both of them looked grumpy and it was hard not to smile, because that certainly wouldn't help anything. But I knew a brotherly fight when I saw one, and it was clear they were pissed.

Whatever they were pissed about would eventually pass.

Jake looked up at me, his eyes widening. "Where's Mom?" he asked.

"She sent me, bud," I said. "Is that okay?"

"Yeah." He crossed his arms, shooting his brother a dirty look. "It's fine. I know she's working, anyway."

Yep, I recognized that look. Couldn't say how many times I'd given it to Cam or Hunter, but it'd been countless.

An older lady sat behind a desk and I recognized her.

"Miss Agatha," I said, flashing her a grin.

She'd been behind that desk for decades now. Her perfume was ingrained into the walls, the popcorn ceiling, the outdated carpet. She used to scare the hell out of me when I was younger.

Her penciled brows raised. "Sammy Harlow. Never thought I'd see you again."

"Oh, come on. I see you all the time at the grocery store."

She smiled and tapped her pen on the desktop. "Are you here to pick up the Connor kids? Sarah said she was sending you."

Connor kids. I tensed. I was certain the boys hated that and when I looked over at them, I saw how they'd both stiffened at the phrase. "Yeah," I said. "She sent me to pick them up."

Agatha leaned forward. "I thought Sarah was dating Colton Hayes."

"She is," I said. "She's also dating me. And I'm dating him." Well, part of that was a lie. Technically, Sarah broke up with me and Colt. But I wasn't going to tell Agatha that, especially after seeing how pale her cheeks turned and how wide her eyes got.

Disapproval radiated off her. It wasn't very often that I was reminded I lived in a small town, but I felt it at this moment. "All three of you are together?"

"Yes," I said. "And?"

"That's not very..."

"Very what?"

"Well, it's interesting, I'll say that. Just surprised you're dating her, given her *history*."

What the actual fuck? Am I gonna lose it on this old hag?

"Sarah is a goddess amongst us all and you're lucky there are children present, Agatha, because otherwise I'd have a lot more to say about that unkind comment," I said lightly. I slid my gaze over to Davy and Jake. They were both listening intensely and Jake looked smug. "Can we head out?"

Her expression was sour. "I just need you to sign this log for David and Jake."

"Davy," I said immediately.

She cocked her head. "Excuse me?"

"Davy," I said again. "He goes by Davy. I thought everyone knew that."

"We've told them but they don't listen," Jake piped up.

Agatha scoffed, clearly flustered. "I mean. His name *is* David."

I was about to throw hands with a woman damn near three times my age.

"Miss Agatha." I kept my tone pleasant as I leaned in, lowering my voice so the boys wouldn't hear me. "I have a million, and I do mean a million, Instagram followers who would love to call a school out on social media for not calling a child by his preferred name. It's not hard. It shouldn't be difficult to do this. Change his name in the fucking system, make sure the teachers get it right, or we will have a problem. Okay? And I'd like to add, I have no problem having my Mom get involved."

Using *the* Lynn Harlow as a threat was really all I needed. Mom ruled the boomers of Citrus Cove.

Her mouth fell open. "Sammy Harlow. How dare you speak to me that way—"

"Hand me the form," I interrupted, still remaining calm

and sweet. "If I hear about this again, I will make sure there is never another quiet moment here again. Understood?"

She shook her head at me as I snatched the clipboard, signed my name, and then straightened.

"Come on, boys," I said. "We're out of here."

"They are still suspended," she blurted out. "Sarah will need to have another meeting."

"That's fine," I said. "We'll see you there."

Her mouth fell open again. I was already thinking about how to convince Sarah to let me come to the meeting, because this was bullshit. Even though we weren't *technically* dating now...

My heart ached, but I nodded at the boys. "Let's get out of here."

They stood up, eyeing Agatha as we went for the door.

"Have a *blessed* day," I said.

The three of us left before she could make any snide remark. The back of my neck prickled with heat. I took a steadying breath as I led the boys outside.

"Your aura is plus one thousand," Jake said.

I had absolutely no fucking clue what that meant.

"Thanks. We're in my car," I said. "It's the one over there. Do you want to call your mom?"

"No," Davy said. "She's at work."

"Yeah, it's okay," Jake mumbled. "She'll be upset. This whole thing was stupid, anyways."

I raised a brow. That was a good sign they'd make up soon right? "Well... Do either of you want something to eat?"

"I just want to go home and never speak to Davy again," Jake muttered.

Well, never mind.

I winced as I opened the back door for them to slide in. I got in the driver's seat and turned on the car, blasting the heat.

What the hell was I supposed to do? "You know, I have two brothers," I said. *This sounds so stupid.* "We used to fight a lot."

Davy glanced at Jake, his arms still crossed. "I didn't do anything wrong. All I said to Rachel in our class is that Jake thought she was pretty because he's been saying it *all* year."

Oh god. It was a girl problem.

"You can... You can go to *hell*," Jake snapped.

Davy gasped. "How dare you say that? I'm telling Mom."

"No, don't tell her. But I still mean it."

I bit my lip, fighting to hold onto a poker face because otherwise I'd start laughing. "Well, that *could* be a little embarrassing, don't you think?" I asked.

Davy met my gaze in the rearview and glared. *Don't laugh, don't laugh.* "So you're on *his* side?"

I turned around in my seat. "I mean, all I'm saying is maybe Jake wanted to tell her that himself. Is that what made the two of you fist fight?"

Jake sighed, looking out the window. "I pushed Davy because I told him not to tell her and he did. Then he pushed me back. And I got mad."

"Yeah, and I got mad back because you were being stupid."

"Well, you shouldn't have told her. Rachel thinks I'm weird now."

"But you're not weird. *She's* the weird one."

"You think all girls are weird."

"Because they *are*."

"Alright, alright," I snorted. "How about we take the scenic route back to the house? And then I can make some hot chocolate."

"Can you make more lunch for us? Because it was all good and Mom can't cook like that and I'm tired of sandwiches," Davy said.

So the way to Davy's heart was food. I could work with

that. I fought a smile as I glanced around and pulled out of the parking spot. "Yeah, I can do that."

A familiar truck was idling at the stop sign across the street, and made my heart skip a beat. It was definitely David's old truck, but the windshield was dark enough that I couldn't see the person in it. The truck pulled out behind us as I rolled onto the quiet street.

It was probably nothing. We knew David wasn't driving that truck anymore. Right?

I focused my attention on the road as I turned left onto a narrow neighborhood road. The school was on the other side of Citrus Cove, on the opposite edge from where Sarah and the boys lived. It was a small town though, and it wouldn't take long to get them back to the house. I decided to take the long way to give them more time to talk through their grievances.

The boys continued to squabble, but they were at least speaking to each other. It wouldn't be long before they would be best friends again. I knew that cycle all too well. I couldn't tell how many times Cam and I had gotten into it. Even Hunter and I. Although by the time I was at the age where I liked to fight, Hunter was a little too old to really get into it with me. But, if I'd had a twin? The two of us would've been at each other's throats all the time.

I checked the rearview and frowned. That damn truck was still behind us.

My anxiety spiked. I didn't like that. I mean, it was a small town so maybe they were just going in the same direction as us... but it felt off.

I turned right and pulled onto the country road that would loop around Citrus Cove and connect to the small neighborhood Sarah lived in.

They turned right too.

I sped up, my knuckles whitening as I gripped the steering

wheel. The road curved and dipped, hugging the hills our small town was nestled in.

The truck wouldn't let up.

"What the fuck?" I muttered.

"You said the f-word," Jake said. "Why can't I say hell?"

"Did your Mom tell you not to say that?"

"Yeah."

"Then that's why. She makes the rules for us all."

The truck sped up, riding the tail of my car. My heart pounded as I moved to the lane over, but they followed right behind.

"What's wrong?" Davy asked, his voice pitching with worry.

"This guy is being an asshole," I said.

Both of them turned their heads to look out the back window.

"Is that David?" Davy whispered.

"No, I don't think so," I said.

"But that's his truck," Jake said.

The fear in their voices killed me.

"If it is him, it doesn't matter, because we're not stopping."

My stomach twisted as we came up on a curve. The bastard rammed into the back of my car, bumping us. The boys screamed as I gripped the steering wheel.

It hit us harder this time, metal crunching and the car lurching. I fought to maintain control.

They were trying to kill us.

The aggression terrified me. My knuckles turned white, my mind racing.

"We're going too fast," Jake cried.

"It's going to be okay," I said. "We'll pull over at the next stop and call the police, okay?"

I floored it, whipping around the curve. The tires squealed, but as we came out of the turn, I was able to put distance between us and the truck.

Breathe, breathe, breathe. Keep your kids safe.

I'd been raised on these roads, but taking a curve this fast scared the shit out of me, especially with them in the car.

I needed to get us somewhere safe. There was a gas station not too far up ahead, but this road was notoriously absent of anything else.

Why did I do that? I didn't have time to beat myself up.

The truck was gaining traction again. I had a little bit of distance between us, enough that I might be able to...

"I'm going to keep both of you safe but what I'm about to do is dangerous, okay? So tighten your seatbelts and hold on."

I glanced back as they tightened their seatbelts and held onto each other. Davy met my gaze and I realized he was mad. Hell, I was mad too.

"*Hold on.*"

I slammed my foot on the brakes the same moment I started to turn, putting my faith in all the donuts I stupidly used to do in the grocery store parking lot in high school. The car whipped around just in time to get out of the way of the truck barreling by. I caught a glimpse of the driver and my blood turned to ice.

The woman.

The one from the theater. The one from the cafe.

I floored the gas and took off down the road going back the way we came, using the momentum to get ahead. We took the curve a little safer this time and then it was a straight shot back into neighborhoods. Clouds were gathering quickly, the temperature dropping outside. It seemed the cold front was coming in sooner than expected.

"We're going to my parents' house, okay? We're okay."

Jake was crying. Davy was holding onto him, his eyes wide. I twisted in my seat, holding my hand out.

"I'm so sorry. That was scary and I'm so sorry."

They held my hand. And I didn't let go until I was pulling down the Harlow family drive and up to Mom and Pop's.

I threw open the door and pulled Jake and Davy out of the truck. The perk of being tall was that I could easily carry two eleven year olds to the front porch. Benny started barking as I rushed inside and put them down. I sank to the floor in the foyer, my heart still thrashing in my chest.

My mom's shout echoed through the house, and she emerged from the kitchen quickly, her eyes wide. "Oh my god. What on earth happened?"

Thankfully Jake was a talker, because he launched into the story faster than I'd driven.

"There was a truck that was trying to kill us! We thought it was dad but I don't think it was and it tried to run us off the road and Sammy drove really, really fast and then we almost died but—"

Davy threw his arms around my neck and I hugged him. I blinked back tears, glancing up at Mom. She sucked in a breath and I could see her going into parent mode, which was certainly not something I'd mastered yet. She'd had years of practice.

She put her hand on Jake's shoulders. "I'm so glad the three of you are safe. I think after that scare, y'all deserve some hot chocolate, don't you? We're going to make some calls and get our family together to help find who tried to hurt you all."

I heard Pops coming downstairs. He scowled with concern and Mom gave him *the look*. "We're making hot chocolate," she announced.

"I need something stronger than that," I muttered.

"Pops is already on it, sweet pea. Davy, are you okay?"

He squeezed me harder before letting me go. "I thought it

was him, but it wasn't. I saw her. It was that lady from the theater."

"Yeah," I whispered. "We'll find out who she is and get her out of our lives, okay?"

"Okay." He crossed his arms. "You kept us safe."

"I tried."

"Your driving is bad, though."

I couldn't help but laugh. "Yeah, it is. But we're alive."

He nodded and followed Jake and my mom to the kitchen. Pops pulled a bottle of whiskey out of a hidden cabinet as I shakily got to my feet.

I needed to call Sarah. And Colt. And Cam and Haley and Hunter and Emma and—

"Son, you need to sit down for a second."

I didn't have it in me to argue. I sat down on the couch, burying my face in my hands. I was still shaking. There'd been a moment there where I wasn't sure it was going to work. But a quick one-eighty was the only option to prevent getting hit.

She was nuts. We needed to get her name immediately and figure out how the fuck she was connected to all of this.

Going after children was insane.

Nevermind that she knew what car I drove...

It meant she'd been stalking us. It meant she could have been the one who destroyed my apartment.

Pops shoved a shot glass in my hands and I tipped it back, the burn down my throat centering me.

"Mom is already making calls. The troops will be blowing in soon. I'll call Bud."

"It was David's old truck, but he wasn't driving. It was the lady who harassed us at the movie theater."

He raised a brow. "So that's why you were at the tree that night, huh?"

"Not just for her. For Colt too. For them both. I love them."

He paused for a moment, and then a smug grin spread across his face. "I fucking knew it." He handed me another shot. "You know, I wasn't born yesterday. Mom owes me fifty bucks now."

My mouth dropped. "You made a bet on me?"

"Yeah, and I won. The day your apartment was broken into, I knew something was going on. You should have seen the way you looked at them, like no one else in the world mattered." He handed me a third shot. "You know, your mom and I remember Woodstock '69. This kind of thing ain't new."

"Like you were there?!"

"No. But—"

"Okay, no," I snorted. "I don't even want to know. Don't even finish this story."

He chuckled, but then his face softened. "Call Sarah and Colt, we'll handle everyone else."

I took it from him and exhaled. The shaking was starting to subside. More than ever, I was thankful for my family.

CHAPTER FORTY

sarah

"GO, GO, GO." I wasn't sure I'd ever driven so fast.

Rain pelted the windshield as I sped down the Harlow's driveway with Colt's truck on my tail.

The call from Sammy had sent me into a panic. I'd immediately left the cafe, but the drive over had made me anxious knowing what had happened.

Colt and I pulled our cars to a halt and I threw open my door.

"*Sarah!*" He called my name as he got out, the same fear in his eyes that I felt.

Freezing rain drenched us, but I could barely feel it. I grabbed his hand and the two of us rushed to the house, busting through the front door.

"Mom!"

Jake and Davy got up and I pulled them both into a hug. My knees were jelly, but I kept standing while holding them tight.

"Sammy drives like a race car driver and we almost died

but then he did this crazy turn thing and we're fine now," Jake said.

"It's called a *U-turn*," Davy quipped.

Don't cry, don't cry, don't cry. "I have no words," I whispered. "Are you both okay?"

"We're okay, Mom," Davy answered.

I hugged them again as tight as I could, looking at Colt and Sammy over the tops of their heads. Colt pulled Sammy into a hard kiss. Sammy's parents—Bob and Lynn—looked at each other with raised brows and then she sighed.

"Yeah, yeah."

Sammy rolled his eyes as he drew back from Colt. "They made a bet on us."

On us? I stared at him and Colt. I could only think about two things at the moment and that was one, thank god the boys were safe and two, *us*.

Lynn stood up and smiled. "I'm going to get started on dinner. Everyone else is arriving shortly."

"Thank you," I whispered.

"Mom, I think you're squeezing us to death."

I kissed the top of Jake's head and then Davy's too. Reluctantly, I released them as the door opened and everyone else piled into the living room. Honey came in first followed by Hunter, Cam and Haley, and Emma. I let go of the boys, releasing them to everyone else.

Cam and Hunter beelined for their brother and dragged Sammy into a hug. Haley pulled me into one too and I leaned against her.

"I need to talk to Sammy and Colt," I whispered.

"Yep. We've got the boys."

I squeezed her tight. Emma approached us as Honey and the boys started rambling. The horrific event was now a superhero story, and Jake certainly told it with flair. I leaned into Emma, shaking my head.

"When Sammy called me, everything stopped," I said. I glanced up at him and Colt again. Unsurprisingly, they still had their heads down and were talking with Hunter and Cam.

"They look like they're plotting," Emma said.

Haley and I nodded in agreement. My sister looked at me, her lips pressing together. "Sammy said he recognized the woman as the one that y'all ran into?"

"Yeah."

We needed to find out who she and her husband were. And how she was connected to all of this. We were all on the same page now.

Hunter cleared his throat. "I'm going to call the police and let them know what happened."

Sammy nodded. "That would be good. I haven't done that yet."

The man who attacked me at the cafe had to be her husband, right? But why?

I'd have to think about that later. Right now, more than anything else, I needed to speak to Sammy and Colt alone.

The hum of everyone talking over each other filled the house, but now that I knew Jake and Davy were safe, I crossed the living room to them and tapped on Colt's shoulder, interrupting their group.

"Hey," he whispered. I felt the weight of his gaze on me, Sammy's too.

"Hey," I said. Fuck, I was nervous.

Hunter looped his thumbs in his jeans, offering me a worried smile. "How's your head?"

"I'm okay," I said. "I'm thankful everyone else is too. I need to steal Sammy and Colt away from the two of you."

Cam nodded. "Go right ahead." His gaze darted to Haley

and his expression softened. "I'm going to go help my beautiful wife."

I glanced back and my eyes widened as Hal tried to reach a bottle on top of a cabinet. Cam was fast and already behind her, his hand on her lower back as he pulled it down for her.

"We can talk in one of the spare rooms," Sammy said.

Colt's expression was grim. We followed Sammy down a short hall and into a small bedroom that smelled like clean linen. He shut the door quietly.

I turned to face the two of them. Now that I was really looking at them, it hit me how tired they looked. I don't think I'd ever seen dark circles under Colt's eyes before.

Deep breath. I hated confrontation, but I had to do this.

"I am so sorry to both of you," I started. "I fucked up. I panicked and instead of talking to either of you, I shut down." My heart was beating so damn fast. "I am still healing. I am still picking up the pieces of who I am and learning how to be okay again. I am still figuring out how to accept being loved. For years, I was stuck in a cycle with someone who wore me down every day, bit by tiny bit. When I was attacked outside the cafe, all I could think was that I was putting you both in danger and I wasn't worth it, but that was David talking."

"Sarah—"

"Let me finish," I whispered. "I need to say this, please."

They nodded, listening intently.

"Colt, I've known you since I came to Citrus Cove. I never thought we'd have a chance together again, but we got one. And Sammy, you have changed everything in my life for the better. Because of the two of you, I'm realizing I deserve to be loved and cared for. I'm not the burden my mind has made me believe I am. I'm not perfect. I'm a mom. I'm a mess. My schedule is hard because I'm always at the cafe and when I'm not there, I'm trying to keep up with my boys. All of that is to say, I love both of you. I don't expect either of you to forgive me, but thank you for keeping my boys safe. Thank you for helping me with everything over the last few weeks. I understand if you want nothing to do with me anymore and will respect whatever you decide, but I want you. I want both of you in my life if you'll have me."

Colt breathed out and bent over, planting his hands on his knees.

"Colt? What's wrong?" I rushed forward as Sammy pulled him back to standing again.

He grabbed hold of my face, tears streaming down his cheeks. "How on earth could you possibly think we don't want anything to do with you?"

Suddenly, Sammy was pulling me between the two of them. I sucked in a breath as he leaned in, whispering in my ear. "Do you really think we'd walk away from you just because you're busy? We knew what we were signing up for when we fell in love with you."

My mouth fell open. "You... You love..."

"Sugar, we *love* you," Colt whispered. "I've never stopped loving you."

"I love you both," Sammy said, kissing the top of my head. "We'll get through this. But please don't ever doubt us wanting to be with you again, Sarah."

"I'll try not to." I wiped my eyes and leaned up to kiss Colt and then Sammy, melting between them. "I was planning on talking to you tomorrow, but then this happened today, and I just... I needed to say it."

"I'm glad you did, angel," Sammy said. "I think I scared the boys with my driving. Hell, I scared myself."

Colt blew out a shaky breath. "Sammy, getting the call about you scared the shit out of me. I need both of you to be wrapped in bubble wrap and safely away from these psychos. My cowboy heart can't take it."

"We need to find out who those people are," I said. "I don't know why they're doing this. And to attack the boys and you, I just..."

"She was driving David's old truck," Sammy said, shaking his head. "It was a total mindfuck. Pops fed me three whiskey shots because I was shaking so badly."

I grabbed his face and kissed him hard. "Thank you. I can't imagine what would have happened."

Colt and I wrapped our arms around him, a tangle of bodies and wild heartbeats.

"I don't want to change subjects too drastically, but the weather is getting bad," Colt said.

"Do the two of you want to stay with us?" I asked. "You can sleep in my bed..."

"Yes," they both said immediately.

"Hopefully we'll fit," I chuckled.

"We'll make us fit."

CHAPTER FORTY-ONE

I LOCKED the front door and kicked off my boots, propping them next to Sarah's shoes. The boys giggled from the couch as Sammy attempted to kindle logs in the fireplace. Sarah was snuggled up next to them in pajamas searching for a movie to watch.

We'd all had a quick dinner at the Harlow house before splitting up. Cam and Hal headed home, Hunter decided to stay with his parents, and Emma had offered to go back with Honey. After some time, I learned that both Emma and Honey liked watching the *Golden Girls* and shared an affinity for gossip—I suspected that me, Sammy, and Sarah were the topic. At least that's what Emma implied when she sent the rest of us to Sarah's house.

For the first time, it was Sarah, the boys, Sammy, and me. I felt at home.

The temperature had dropped dramatically and the rain was definitely going to turn to ice.

"Do you think there will be snow?" Davy asked.

"Maybe," Sammy said. "Hopefully it all melts, otherwise we'll be trapped in the snow until the end of time."

Jake gasped dramatically. "But I want it to snow forever."

Sarah snorted, ruffling his hair. "Forever trapped drinking hot chocolate."

"And eating s'mores," I said.

"That sounds fine," Davy said.

Fire started to spread in the hearth, finally catching on the logs. Sammy sat back triumphantly. "Got it. I am a god."

The boys laughed and I grinned, grabbing my laptop out of the bag I'd stopped to pack on the way here. Our plan was to put on a movie, but I was going to do some research while it was on.

But first...

"I think we should make a giant bed on the floor," I said.

Sarah started to get up. "No, no, stay put," I said to Sarah. "We got this."

"Yep, we do," Sammy said.

Jake ran upstairs with me, and we dug out blankets and pillows, hauling them back downstairs to create a cozy nest in front of the sofa. Sammy was already shoving the coffee table out of the way to make room, the fire flickering in the hearth and warming the house. Sarah turned on the TV, flipping through movies as we got everything set up.

Soon, the five of us were spread out on the floor, watching *The Nightmare Before Christmas*. I leaned my back against the couch as I opened my laptop next to Sammy. Sarah was between him and the boys.

I angled my laptop away from them as I pulled up my notes from the last few weeks.

I started with David's truck. Something was up with that. Somehow this all connected to him, and by proxy, Thomas— which meant maybe...

Could that couple be related to someone who was killed?

My stomach twisted as I pulled up a list of the names of women killed by Thomas. It made me feel sick.

Sammy glanced up at me with a frown. "What's wrong?"

Was my body language really that obvious? "Just researching some stuff."

He sat up slightly, taking a peek. "Ah." He raised a brow.

"I'm trying to connect some dots," I said quietly.

He nodded and settled back down next to Sarah, looping his arm over her waist. I looked at them for a moment and smiled. It was hard to remember that earlier today, our entire world was damn near torn apart again.

All I wanted to do was find the people doing this and get them out of our lives, so we could focus on what really mattered.

I slipped my phone out of my pocket and emailed myself the photos taken at the cafe from when Sarah was attacked.

The door had been covered in articles, all about the Citrus Cove Killer and the destruction left in his wake. The house on the outskirts of the town had been his hiding place. God, he'd ruined so many lives. Every day, I was thankful that Haley had made it out, and that Sarah hadn't been one of the victims.

Although, in many ways, she had been.

I visually combed over the photos, looking for anything that could be a clue. *Something.* We needed some sort of thread to connect things together.

What is it? Why would someone go after Sammy and the boys? Why would they attack Sarah? And where the fuck was David Connor?

In the article that had been taped to the cafe door, one of the photos of the women was circled in red. A chill rolled up my spine. Seeing *You're Next* circled was still terrifying.

If the couple was somehow related to someone who had

been killed by Thomas, maybe they were trying to deliver some sort of twisted justice on Sarah. It didn't make any sense to me —inflicting pain on an innocent person certainly didn't solve anything. But grief could push someone over the edge, and whoever was behind the events of today—they were certainly already unhinged.

I zoomed in on the woman's face on the door, squinting. *Jane Bell.*

A soft snore drew my attention. Sarah had passed out, and it looked like the boys were on their way to falling asleep too. I ran my palm over Sammy's shoulder gently, the connection warming me.

We were going to be okay, I reminded myself. All of us were going to be just fine.

I Googled *Jane Bell* and grimaced.

She'd gone missing about five years ago. Lived in a small town outside of Dallas. She'd only been twenty-three.

I held my breath, blinking back tears. It was devastating. I opened up Instagram and searched her name, scrolling through profiles until I found the one that used to belong to her. I clicked on one of the photos, my stomach twisting. It was just a picture of a sunset, but knowing it was the last post before she died added an eeriness to it. I frowned as I looked at the list of accounts who had liked the photo. The profile picture was a red dot. I clicked on it.

The words 'Never forget' were in their bio. Wasn't this the account Sammy had mentioned? The one who'd left countless comments on his videos?

"What the fuck," I mumbled to myself. I searched his profile and picked a random video, scrolling until I found a comment from the same account.

So this definitely had something to do with Jane Bell.

I switched back to her old Instagram page and scrolled

through accounts that followed her, freezing when I spotted a familiar face.

That damn woman from the cafe. The one who'd been stalking Sammy. *Elizabeth Bell.* Her Instagram was full of photos of Citrus Cove and articles about Thomas Connor. My palms turned sweaty as I continued to scroll. There was a Facebook page linked to her account. When I clicked on it, my stomach dropped.

"Sammy," I whispered. I looked over at him, but his eyes were shut.

"Mmm."

"*Sammy.*"

He pried them open, rolling over to look at me. "I am cozy and sleepy and you should stop working and enjoy the movie."

"No, look." I showed him my screen. He frowned, clearly not getting it. I clicked on the 'about' section, showing him the names.

His eyes widened.

Elizabeth Bell was Jane's *sister.*

She was also happily married to Ron Bell. *Ron.*

I hovered over her photo, recognizing her pinched features and while she had a blonde bob here instead of copper-brown hair, it was definitely her.

I nodded my head toward the kitchen and rolled to my feet. Sammy got up, the two of us glancing at Sarah and the boys. The living room was warm and cozy with the movie playing in the background, and they were sound asleep.

Sammy followed me to the kitchen. "I'm making us some hot chocolate," he said. "I'll need something if I'm going to be looking at this."

"Can you put whiskey in mine?"

"Yep, if I can find some." He rummaged through the cabinets.

I kept my voice low as I spoke. "Should I call the station and give their names? Maybe it would help?"

"I think that's a good idea, but with the ice storm hitting, you know they won't do shit until next week."

Sadly, he had a point.

I scrolled through Elizabeth's profile and shook my head. "What the fuck?" Every post was either about the Citrus Cove Killer, David being released on bail, or Sammy's videos.

Why was she so obsessed with Sammy? Was it because he had a large platform? On one of his videos she reposted, she'd added a caption '*He's dating a killer!*' More and more posts had the same unhinged messages. It all started around the time the three of us started dating. Any posts before that were entirely about Citrus Cove and the Connors.

I breathed out slowly as I came to the post about her sister's death. The caption rattled me.

My sister has been missing for years. They did nothing to help find her. They failed her and now she's dead. She was killed by a man who should have been caught. OUR SYSTEM IS BROKEN. HOW COULD THIS HAVE HAPPENED? JANE, you will be missed. I love you.

"Fuck." I put the laptop down on the kitchen table, sliding into the seat.

Tears pricked my eyes. I hated this woman for what she'd done to us, but I also hated that she'd been hurt too.

"This is sad," I said, rubbing my chest.

A comment from Ron Bell on his wife's post caught my attention. *Justice will be served. We'll get them, Lizzie.*

Was he the one who attacked Sarah? It would make sense.

I stared at his picture, anger bubbling up.

Sammy slid a steaming mug in front of me. "Whiskey and hot chocolate." He leaned over, looking at my screen. "He's the husband?"

"Yeah. Ron. He looks like the guy we saw at the cafe, right?"

"He does..." Sammy pressed his lips together. "Isn't Ron the name of the man who has David's truck? Since we have their names, can we find where they live?"

My jaws stiffened. I took a long sip of the hot chocolate, thankful he'd made it strong because I needed something for my rattled nerves.

"I think the profile that was harassing you belonged to them," I said. "Let me call Hunter and see if he knows how to find their address."

Sammy held out his phone, already ringing Hunter's number. I snorted and picked it up as he answered.

"Everything okay?" Hunter grunted.

"Hey, it's Colt. Sammy is here too. We were doing some research and I think I found something. Are you able to find someone's address if you have a name?"

"Yep," he said.

"Just like that, huh?" I teased. "You sure you're not a spy?"

Hunter sighed dramatically. "No, I just know how to google things. What's the name?"

"Elizabeth and Ron Bell," I said.

Sammy raised a brow and took a sip of his drink, watching my expression. I heard Hunter moving in the background and fought the urge to call him an old man. He wasn't, but he sometimes grunted like one.

"Well," Hunter said. "Give me a few minutes and I'll text you their address."

"Thanks." I hung up and leaned back in my chair, frowning. "I don't like this," I said.

"Me neither," Sammy agreed.

We sat in silence until Hunter's text came through. I clicked on the address.

"No fucking way," Sammy said.

"That can't be right," I whispered.

But if it was, then they'd moved into a house.

In Citrus Cove.

In this neighborhood. Right down the street.

My chair scratched as I stood up abruptly. "I'm going to go check it out."

"No, you're not," Sammy said, shaking his head. "Absolutely not. We need to sit tight, weather the storm, and then—"

The lights went out, dipping us in darkness.

"Goddammit," I sighed. I leaned over, peeking out the kitchen window. "It's just us."

"Maybe a breaker flipped," Sammy said. "I'll go take a look."

"No, it's okay, I'll do it. I need to stretch my legs anyway." I needed to do *something*, because what the fuck?

"And maybe walk off the desire to do something stupid?"

"Yeah, that too," I sighed.

I slipped on my jacket and boots before stepping out onto the porch. Carefully maneuvering down the icy steps, I walked around the side of the house. The grass crunched underfoot, the blades coated in ice.

Every other house in the neighborhood had lights on, so that was good news. My breaths puffed out into the still air as I shone my flashlight.

The metal door to the electric box was hanging open.

"What the fuck?" I muttered.

I leaned in and flipped the breaker, looking up at one of the windows. The lights flickered back on.

"Shouldn't have come out alone."

I jumped and spun around right as a fist hit me square in the face. I fell back against the house, recovering quickly enough to move out of the way as the man swung again.

He wore a black jacket with the hood up, but I still saw the angry burn marks from the coffee that Sarah had splashed on his cheeks. I saw his face, the same one I'd been looking at on my computer screen only minutes ago.

My phone hit the ground as I threw my body at him, knocking him back.

"You chose the wrong fucker to fight, *Ron*," I snarled.

"You're just getting in the way of the inevitable," he said. "My wife won't stop until they're dead too."

He moved surprisingly fast, drawing out a black pistol. *Fuck*. I dove to the side as he pulled the trigger, but the bullet hit my thigh.

Pain erupted like a lightning bolt and I cried out, hitting the ground. The scent of gasoline and smoke filled the air and I jerked my head back, my eyes widening.

Fear gripped me.

They'd set Sarah's house on fire.

CHAPTER FORTY-TWO

sarah

I SAT UP IMMEDIATELY, turning my head both ways, confusion settling over me. It was dark, the TV off. The only light came from the fireplace. Shadows danced along the walls, and my heart was pounding.

What the hell was that noise? Had I just heard a gunshot?

"Sammy? Colt?" I called.

Sammy rushed into the living room, his body tense. He opened his mouth to speak, but then fell silent as we both breathed in deep.

A burning scent filled the room, but it wasn't coming from the hearth. I breathed out. "Do I smell smoke?"

He inhaled and his eyes widened. "Wake up the kids. Now."

"Where is Colt?" I asked.

"Outside. Get them up." Sammy was already pulling on his boots. "Hurry."

He jumped up and yanked open the door. But then, his body went rigid. I stared in horror as he held up his hands, a breathless whisper rushing out.

"Sarah, get them out. Go out the back."

Fuck. What the fuck is happening? I shook the boys, getting to my feet quickly and pulling them up. I heard a voice outside, but I couldn't think about that right now.

"What's happening?" Davy asked.

Sammy slowly took a step back, revealing the woman from the cafe. She was holding a gun to his chest, her eyes burning with hate.

Fuck. "Run! Go to the neighbors' and get help," I growled, shoving Davy and Jake toward the back. I couldn't leave Sammy alone.

"Mom! There's fire in the dining room—"

I shoved them both down the hall, pushing them toward the back door. I pulled it open, my eyes widening as flames crawled over the porch. There was still enough room for them to get out.

"Go!" I yelled.

"But—"

"*Go!*" They took off running, dashing out into the back yard.

I turned back around. I couldn't leave Sammy alone. I rushed back to the living room, growling as I stepped closer to Sammy and the woman. "Let him go. I don't know why you're doing this, but we haven't done anything wrong."

She kept the gun on Sammy, her gaze pinned on me. "You're the reason my sister is dead. You had to know, you had to!"

"I didn't," I said, my voice trembling. "I swear I didn't. He tried to kill my own sister too."

"But he didn't. He killed mine. She was missing for years, and for *years* I hoped I would see her again—that we would find her. But he was caught and we found out the truth. Then they let your husband *out. On bail.*"

Sammy slowly took a step back. "So, you tried to kill an innocent woman and her children, Elizabeth?"

She sneered at him. "She's. Not. *Innocent!*"

The moment she moved her hand, Sammy grabbed her wrist and twisted. The gun fired off, the bullet flying past me and hitting the wall. More smoke filled the living room as Sammy knocked the gun from her hand, shoving her back out the door.

I barreled after him. His arms wrapped around me, stopping me right as she screamed, her feet slipping on the ice that spread over the porch. It happened so slow—everything around me turning to molasses as she fell back, her body hitting the stairs at an angle that wasn't natural—

Crack.

Sammy pulled my face against his chest, holding me tight. We both went still, breathing hard as an unsettling silence followed.

Thump, thump, thump—his heartbeat thrashed in his chest. My breaths came faster.

Be strong. You have to be strong.

"Sarah," he whispered, his voice trembling. "I need you to call 911. We need to find Colt. Grab your shoes and get out of the house."

The sound of crackling wood followed the scent of rubber and chemicals burning, growing stronger as the fire roared hotter. Our house was on fire. We'd lose everything, we'd—

He released me. I darted back through the doorway and pulled on my tennis shoes and pocketed my phone. Sammy carefully made his way down the steps and out into the yard.

"Colt's been shot!"

No, no, no, no. My hands trembled as I called 911.

The operator answered. "*9-1-1*, what is the address of your emergency?"

I rattled off my address as I stepped outside, my ears ringing.

"What is your name?"

"This is Sarah Bently. We need help. The house is on fire and my boyfriend has been shot. We were attacked and there's a dead woman, too."

Lights across the street flickered on and I breathed out in relief as I spotted Davy and Jake. A few neighbors were coming out. My mind was moving so fast, panic setting in along with the cold blanket of adrenaline. I had to keep moving, had to keep helping.

Colt. Get to Colt and Sammy.

I stepped around the woman on the stairs, refusing to look too closely. Blood pooled across the sidewalk, her body unmoving.

"Don't look," I whispered to myself. "Don't look, don't look."

I rushed around the house, heart hammering. My lungs sucked in cold air, a gasp leaving me as I saw the flames that stretched over the back of the house.

"Is the patient conscious?"

Sammy was kneeling over Colt. There was another body in the grass, too, but they weren't moving.

"Tell me how to stop the bleeding," I rasped, falling to the ground next to Colt. He was breathing hard, blood gushing from a wound on his thigh.

"Is the patient—"

"He's awake, the wound is in his upper thigh."

Sammy yanked his belt off and pulled it around Colt's leg, yanking it tight.

"Tell us, you're on speaker phone," I pressed the button and set it on the ground.

"*You're going to want to apply pressure to the wound, try to slow as much blood loss as possible. They're four minutes out.*"

Colt cried out, gritting his teeth. "Where are the boys?" he rasped.

"They're safe," I whispered.

He reached for me and I wrapped my arms around his chest, letting him lean back on me. Sammy ripped off his coat, using it to apply pressure.

"Fucker got me in the thigh." His voice was shaking, barely louder than a whisper. "I managed to knock him out. He still has a gun."

Sirens wailed into the ice storm, flames burning brighter. I turned my head, looking over at the man on the ground. He started to stir.

The operator continued to talk as I released Colt, crawling fast for the gun that gleamed in the flaming glow emanating from behind us. He lifted his head and reached for it, but I snatched the weapon before he could, sliding it further away.

"You bitch," he snarled.

A police cruiser pulled up first, skidding to halt and bumping into a curb. I rolled back as he tried to grab me, kicking at his hands. Two of the officers rushed toward us, pulling him back. I recognized Tammy and exhaled sharply with relief.

A fire truck and ambulance arrived next and the yard was flooded with people. I got to my feet and ran back to Sammy and Colt.

"Hi, sugar," Colt rasped, his breathing slowing.

Sammy shook his head. "They just got here, Colt, you're doing great. It's going to be okay, I promise." His voice broke but he looked up at me and then at the paramedics rushing toward us.

Shouts echoed around us as they took over. Sammy pulled

me to my feet, holding me tight as they lifted Colt, swarming around him. Tears blurred my vision as Jake and Davy broke through the line of people, throwing their arms around us.

"Is he going to be okay?" Jake sobbed.

Sammy pulled the boys into our hug. They trembled from the cold and I tightened my arms around them, using our body heat to huddle in the frigid air.

I looked down and winced. Sammy read my mind, lifting both of them up so their bare feet weren't on the grass.

"Let's go with them," I whispered.

We followed the paramedics to the ambulance and Sammy glanced back at the house, his eyes widening. "Fuck."

I couldn't look. All I could do was watch as Colt was loaded into the ambulance.

Bud approached us warily, lines of exhaustion etched into his face. "Let's get everyone to the hospital and we'll sort all this out."

"Their house needs to be checked," Sammy said. "Right before this happened, Colt and I realized that they bought a house down the street."

He nodded. "We'll go. Let's get you warm and safe."

CHAPTER FORTY-THREE

sarah

EVERYTHING WAS A WHIRLWIND. Between talking to officers and having the boys checked out by a nurse for smoke inhalation, and filling in our family on the phone—I didn't have a moment alone. Through it all, I couldn't stop worrying about Colt.

Because of the ice, we'd made everyone stay at home. It was too dangerous on the roads right now, and we'd promised to keep them updated, which meant either Sammy or I were on the phone constantly.

Sammy sat next to me in the waiting room. I leaned against him as I listened to Cam talk on the line. Jake and Davy were passed out in the chairs next to us, blankets wrapped around them. Sammy's hand gripped mine and I held onto him just as tight.

"Any more news yet?" Cam asked.

"Not yet," I said.

"I hate this fucking weather. The only reason I'm not there right now is because ice is sticking to the road."

This was the fifth time Cam had said that.

"It'll be okay," Haley said in the background.

"Is Emma okay?" I asked. "I haven't talked to her yet but the house is..."

"She's okay." Hal clearly snatched the phone from Cam, her voice clearer. "Don't worry about the house right now. How are the boys doing?"

I glanced over at them. "They're exhausted and traumatized. I can't even think about how we're going to work through this."

Sammy squeezed my hand. "We'll handle it, angel."

My eyes teared up, but I was well past crying. I leaned harder into Sammy.

"It'll be okay," Haley said. "This sounds awful, but... David is gone now. We can put all of this behind us."

"I hope so," I whispered. "We need a fresh start. One where no one is getting hurt and everything is normal."

"You'll get it. You've got Sammy and Colt... Did you talk to them?"

"Yes," I said. God, that felt like ages ago. "Before we came home earlier."

"I figured. I'll be more nosy later."

"I'm sure you will be. Well, pour a glass of whiskey and sit tight," I sighed. "That's what we're doing."

"Well, no whiskey for me, but—"

"What do you mean no whiskey for you?" I asked, both my brows shooting up. Sammy immediately turned his head, his expression mirroring mine.

BABY? he mouthed.

"I'm not in the mood for whiskey, that's all."

"Hmm." I narrowed my eyes at the wall. *That* was suspicious, but I'd circle back around when we were together. *Am I going to be an aunt?* "Are you—"

Bud appeared in the doorway. "Have a moment?"

"Bud just got here," I said. "I'll call y'all back in a bit, okay?"

"Okay," Haley said. "I love you both. Talk to you soon."

I hung up and slipped my phone into my pocket. Sammy stood up, running his hands over his jeans. Both of us were still covered in blood and dirt and smelled like smoke. I followed him to the hallway, the two of us stepping out of earshot of the boys even though they were asleep.

Bud blew out a breath, his shoulders sinking. "David is dead, Sarah. They found him in the house the couple bought. It looks like they were really unwell people and when they found out his bail was posted, they decided to take justice into their own hands."

Unwell was quite the understatement.

Sammy wrapped his arms around me. I leaned into him as the shock settled in.

David was dead.

"How did he die?" I whispered.

"They shot him."

I let out a shaky breath. I didn't have any more tears left to cry, and certainly wasn't going to shed them over David.

But it was strange knowing he was gone.

"The Bell woman is dead. When she slipped on your porch, it cracked her head. The man is still alive and in custody and will be charged with multiple murder attempts. He admitted to attacking you in the parking lot. He also admitted to tampering with your car."

"Is the house..." Sammy trailed off.

"They put the fires out. It looks like it was the back part of the house and kitchen. They started the fire on that side. The other half of the house is still standing, but with the weather, it's severely damaged. I'm so sorry, Sarah. This has been absolute hell for you and your family."

"But it's over," I whispered. "It's finally over."

Bud offered a gentle, sad smile. "It is. Any updates on Colton?"

"He's alive," Sammy said tightly. "That's all we know right now."

"Alright. Call if you need anything. After this storm passes, we'll figure everything out. We've got your statements and as for the house..."

"We'll worry about it later," Sammy said. "We're all alive. That's all that matters. Is there any way you could do us a favor?"

"Sure. What do you need?"

"Could we get some t-shirts to change into? And a couple for the boys, along with some socks."

"Yes. Let me see what I can do. Might be hospital socks."

"That's fine," I said. "Thank you, Bud."

Bud clapped Sammy's shoulder and left us. I turned toward Sammy and looked up at him, shaking my head.

"He's dead," I whispered.

Sammy sighed. "I can't say I'm sad, but I'm sorry."

"I mean I can't say I am either. He's really out of our lives for good." It was hard to believe. "I don't know what to do with myself. I can't even think straight right now."

"All we can do now is wait, angel," he murmured. "Wait to hear about Colt. And then we go from there. The storm will pass and we have our family to lean on."

He was right. He settled his hands on my shoulders, rubbing them gently. A soft moan left me and I closed my eyes, leaning into him. Relief rolled through my body.

"Hmm. Note to self, give you massages more often."

"Yes, please."

He leaned down, kissing my neck gently. I turned around,

hugging him hard. He held me tighter, pressing his cheek against the top of my head.

"When all of this is over, we're going to build the perfect house on Colt's land. And it's going to have all the room we need to grow. A good kitchen so you can start your business up, a place for me to film things, maybe even a secret sex room."

I gasped, stifling a giggle. "A secret sex room?"

"Yeah. I mean, we have to hide the butt plugs and paddles somewhere. I want a sex couch too."

"Oh god," I whispered. I looked up at him with a grin. "We'll have to soundproof it."

"Oh we will. No one will hear a damn thing."

A rustle drew our attention. "Where is he? Where is my son?"

We both looked down the hall. Sammy let out a *hmm* as an older man speed-walked toward us with wide eyes. A nurse trailed behind him, trying to slow him down.

I wasn't really sure if I'd ever seen Colton's father up close, but I knew it was him. There were physical similarities, and it was interesting seeing a glimpse of what one of the loves of my life would look like in thirty years.

Admittedly, damn good looking.

Sammy reached out to slow him down before he could push past us. "We're still waiting on Colt, and I hate to be the one to say this to you, but I don't think you're who he wants to see," Sammy said.

The man slowed, his eyes full of sadness. "I just want to know if he's okay. They called me to let me know and I got scared that I wouldn't be able to make things right."

"He's alive," I said quickly. "He's in surgery right now getting the bullet taken out of his leg. We don't know anything else."

"You can stay until we know how it goes," Sammy said.

"But then you should go if you're able to drive through this weather. We can let Colt know you stopped by, but until he's open to mending bridges, I don't think this is the right way to see him."

"Thank you," he said. He leaned against the wall, his shoulders sagging.

The nurse gave us an apologetic look before heading back to the front desk. Sammy rested his chin on the top of my head as we studied the man that had seriously hurt Colt.

He eyed the two of us. "Can I ask..." he trailed off.

Sammy sighed and released me, holding out his hand. The man shook it slowly. "I'm Sammy Harlow, this is Sarah. Colt is our... boyfriend doesn't sound serious enough."

"We love him," I said simply.

"My name is John," he said.

"Yeah, we've heard about you." Sammy did not keep the bitterness out of his voice.

He was not pulling punches right now, but I couldn't blame him. We were both stretched thin and beyond frazzled. I wasn't sure either one of us had the capability to be polite right now.

John rubbed the back of his neck. "I have a lot of regrets. Kicking him out is one of them."

I scowled. "It damn well should be. I have two sons, they're eleven. I cannot imagine kicking them out as a teen for coming out. Part of being a parent is being there for your child and you weren't there for him."

"I shouldn't have kicked him out," he said. "I didn't know that for years, though. It took some time before I started to unlearn what I was raised to believe. I don't expect him to ever forgive me, but I just... I just need to know he's okay. Everyone's posting online about what happened tonight, and all I could think driving over here was if I lost him, I..."

"Your fear is understandable," Sammy said. "But Sarah and

I have been through absolute hell tonight. So maybe grab a cup of coffee, take a seat, say a prayer or whatever, and keep your pity party to yourself."

John took a deep breath. "I think I'll do that."

"There's some coffee next to the front desk," I said. He gave us a nod before wandering off. I raised a brow at Sammy. "Maybe a little harsh?"

"He's lucky I didn't break his nose. I'm feeling generous tonight."

I snorted. "Alright, princess."

A wide grin broke out and he relaxed, leaning against the wall. "I can't believe out of all nicknames I could have, the two of you went with princess."

"I mean you are bossy."

He barked out a laugh and tugged me close, tipping my chin up. "I'll remember this when we're back home and you're in my bed."

"Do you think we'll have to play nurse with Colt?"

His eyes lit up. "You are full of surprises."

"Well, it's either flirting with you or having a breakdown," I said. "Think I'll choose the first option."

Bud returned to the hallway with a stack of clothes and socks.

"Thank you," Sammy said, taking them from him.

"Happy to help. Call me if you need anything else. I'm going to get back to the station."

I waved at him as he left before going through the stack of clothes in Sammy's hands, pulling out two fresh shirts and socks for the boys.

"Go change first," Sammy said. "Before you go back into Mom mode. We've both got blood on us, angel."

I looked down at myself and sighed, because he was right. I grabbed a t-shirt off the top. "I'll be back."

I went down the hall to the bathroom and changed quickly, throwing my shirt in the trash. I leaned over the sink, washing my hands, arms, face, and neck. I splashed water over my hair too, smoothing down the flyaways.

When I looked at myself in the mirror, I no longer saw the broken girl from twelve years ago. I was stronger and happier and though I was standing on the other side of yet another tragedy—I had hope.

Broken hearts mended stronger. I knew that to be true now more than ever.

Refreshed, I returned to Sammy, but he wasn't in the hall. I went to the doorway of the waiting room and leaned against the frame, watching as he knelt down and replaced Davy and Jake's socks without waking them up.

I love him. I love him so much.

I heard footsteps behind me and turned slightly as a nurse approached. "Hi. I have an update on Colton Hayes."

Sammy was immediately behind me. "How's he doing?"

"He's doing well. He lost a lot of blood but the surgery was successful and he's in recovery. The bullet didn't break any bones and didn't hit anything vital. He's going to be okay."

I leaned against Sammy, breathing out. "Thank you."

"Can we see him?" Sammy asked.

"As soon as he's in a room, yes. He'll probably still be asleep."

"Okay. I'm going to go let his dad know." Sammy slipped past me and headed toward the front desk.

The nurse shook her head with a sly smile. "You are one lucky woman."

I snorted and watched as Sammy talked to John. He was empathetic while still being firm, that much was clear. John rubbed his eyes and nodded, then shook Sammy's hand again before leaving.

"Is Colton single or..."

"Nope," I said. "He's taken. By the both of us."

"Oh. Okay, so you're *the* luckiest woman ever."

"Yeah," I said with a smile. "I am."

CHAPTER FORTY-FOUR

Three Days Later

I STEPPED into the hospital room carrying three cups of coffee. I handed one to Colt, another to Sarah, and settled in one of the chairs with mine.

"Thank fucking god," Colt said, immediately draining half of the styrofoam cup. "This tastes like ass. But it's caffeine."

Sarah laughed as she sipped hers, wrinkling her nose. "It's... it is definitely caffeine."

"I will make you both the best damn cup of coffee tomorrow morning when we're home," I promised.

The last few days had been the most frightening and exhausting of my life. But, we'd made it.

Colt was already healing. After they'd gotten the bullet out, everything else had gone smoothly.

Fun fact about Colton, he was a horny unhinged fucker when he was on drugs. When he woke up the first time, he'd asked Sarah if she wanted to 'take a ride with a cowboy', which had sent the two of us into a fit of hysteric giggles.

The weather had taken a miraculous swing, which meant we'd been able to see our family. The moment the ice melted enough on the roads, everyone had come by the hospital. Now, the boys were safe at my Mom and Pops with Cam, Haley, Emma, Hunter, and Honey. It was a full house, and exactly what we all needed right now.

David Connor was dead. The Bells killed him after they decided to take revenge due to the murder of the wife's sister.

I couldn't say I was sorry about that. Maybe it was kind of fucked up, maybe it wasn't, but all of us felt a sense of relief when we'd found out David was gone. Telling the boys had been hard, but I was glad that I could be there to support them when Sarah broke the news.

"I'm ready to be in my own bed. With both of you," Colt said.

"You won't be able to do anything," Sarah laughed. "You literally just got shot."

"You underestimate me," Colt protested. "My tongue is working fine."

I snorted. "You're an insatiable little slut."

Colt smirked as he downed the rest of his coffee. "I sure as fuck am."

I took a sip of coffee and nearly spat it back out. "Oh god. This is awful."

"Maybe I can bribe Emma into stopping by with real coffee," Sarah said.

I nodded. "Please."

Sarah was already texting her. I relaxed in my chair, basking in the sunlight pouring through the window. It was still cold as hell outside, but the ice had melted and central Texas had returned back to normal.

The house was destroyed. That was one problem we still had to figure out, although we had a rough plan. It sounded like Emma was temporarily moving in with Honey and taking over Haley's old bedroom.

We were all going to be moving into Colt's house. I'd already been shopping for a larger bed for his room so Sarah, Colt, and I could fit. The second bedroom would be the boys' while we started construction on a new house. It would be tight quarters for a while, but it would be worth it.

Hunter, being Hunter, was already pulling strings for us to get a builder moving fast. Sometimes it felt like there wasn't a single problem in the world my older brother couldn't handle. He always knew someone, always knew what to do. Unless Emma was in the room—then he looked like he was taking a flailing skydive.

"So, tomorrow we'll get you home. And fed real food. And..."

"And we'll be together," Colt said. "We'll finally just get to be together."

Sarah smiled and the way the happiness reached her eyes— I could watch her smile that way forever.

I get to make her smile that way forever.

sarah

Spring, One Year Later

THE HARLOW OAK tree twisted up toward the denim blue sky, not a cloud in sight above the dark green leaves. The vineyard bloomed in the distance, promising a full harvest this fall.

A warm breeze rolled across the grass, ruffling the hem of my wedding dress. I smoothed back my hair with a smile and turned to look at our family.

It was a small gathering of loved ones. Haley, Cam, Hunter, Emma, the guy Emma was currently dating, Sammy's parents, Alice, Honey, Mr. Johnson, and my boys. Even Colt's father was here, which had surprised Sammy and I. But Colt had done some emotional reparations with him over the last few months, and I smiled as I passed by him.

Sammy and Colt stood beneath the tree, both as handsome as ever. Colt wore a brown cowboy hat with a rose boutonnière, an ivory shirt with a tie, and brown pants and boots. His blonde hair was slightly mussed, his blue eyes shining with tears.

I shook my head at him. "Don't you dare cry, Colton."

"No promises, sugar."

Sammy grinned at him. He wore a jacket with the same boutonnière, a plaid shirt, and matching pants and boots. His dark hair was combed back, eyes on me as I walked up the hill toward them.

The dress was perfect. Our wedding bands were perfect. I knew beyond a shadow of a doubt that today was the first day of the rest of my life loving two men who cherished me.

I had a plan. I knew what I wanted and needed now, so different from the girl who'd once thought she was marrying the love of her life.

I stopped right in front of them. Colt wiped his eyes, which earned a few chuckles.

"Angel, you're beautiful," Sammy whispered.

"So are you," I said.

Colt grinned as he offered me his arm. I took it, looping my other through Sammy's as we faced the oak tree.

Our wedding was a little different than most, given that there were three of us, but every bit as special. While we didn't have someone officiating it, and legally there were complications—today we were exchanging rings and carving our initials into the Harlow oak tree.

"I love you," Sammy said.

"I love you too," Colt said.

"I love you both."

Sammy slid a ring onto my finger, the diamond glistening in the dappled sunlight. I grinned as I slid a band onto Colt's finger, and then he did the same to Sammy.

Everyone clapped as Sammy whittled a heart and our initials into the bark.

S + S + C

I leaned up and kissed Colt, wrapping my arms around his neck. He released me, pulling Sammy close as I kissed him next. I laid my head against his shoulder as he kissed Colt.

This was the wedding I'd always dreamed of.

I stretched out in the grass, laying my head in Colt's lap as the sky turned pink and orange. It'd been a few hours since the ceremony. Afterwards, we had lunch at the new winery. It had taken months of building, but the brand new wine barn was finished and we'd have a grand opening in a couple weeks.

Between the construction of our new house, my small business growing rapidly, and Cowboy Ciders—the new name for their business—we had a lot on our plates. But, with these two by my side, I had no doubt we would flourish.

To end the perfect day, we wanted to watch the sun set. Sammy stretched his legs out next to us, smiling dreamily as he plucked his guitar strings. His eyes were a lot less stormy these days, just like Colt was a lot less sad.

A melody floated around us, one I didn't recognize. I let out a soft, dreamy hum.

"What is that?" Colt asked. "I haven't heard you play that one."

"Your song," Sammy murmured. "I could never write a love song before the two of you. The first version was a little different than this one, but I think it's finally right."

God, I was a lucky woman. I beamed at him. "Are you going to sing it for us?" I asked. "Pretty please?"

He sucked in a breath, his cheeks turning red.

"I want to hear it," Colt urged. "Sing for us."

Sammy cleared his throat. "Well... Here goes...

...Sun-washed porch
Three rocking chairs
Every morning
We sat there
And watched
Our babies growing up
A life we built
With hands weathered by love

Over the years,
We've had our battles
We've earned our scars
But every moment together
Was a dream kissed by wishing stars
I burn for your fires
I feel our souls dance
I'm forever grateful
We stole our chance

Moon-touched flowers
Three pairs of boots
Every night
We strengthened our roots
We paved the way
And marked the path
To find our happy ever after
One that will forever last

Over the years,
We've had our battles
We've earned our scars

But every moment together
Was a dream kissed by wishing stars
I burn for your fires
I feel our souls dance
I'm forever grateful
We stole our chance..."

As he finished, Colt and I held on to each other, tears streaming down our cheeks. I had no words.

Sammy offered us both a shy smile as he traced the butterfly inlays on his guitar. "Was it that bad?"

"It was fucking beautiful," Colt whispered. "Fuck."

"Sammy, I had no idea you could write like that," I hiccuped. "Thank you."

"Well, I have the perfect inspiration. I wrote about my husband and wife."

Colt thumbed away his tears, and then mine. He leaned down and kissed me. "Thank you for the second chance."

"Mmm, thank you for being jealous of Sammy and asking me out."

"Hey, now. That worked out."

"It did," I giggled. "And thank you to my old Honda for not working that day."

Sammy snorted and put his guitar aside, grabbed my hand, and kissed my knuckles. "Thank you for being the beautiful, strong, loving person who shared her life with us."

"Oh." My cheeks turned pink and I took a breath. "Okay, you can't say things like that. My makeup will run."

"I mean, maybe that's the goal," Colt teased. "I do like it when your makeup runs."

"*Colton Harlow,*" I scolded.

His eyes widened. "*Sarah Harlow.*"

Sammy hummed appreciatively, his face smug. "You both sound damn good saying our last name like that."

Colt smirked, his eyes roving down my body. He ran his hand over my stomach and then cupped one of my breasts. "Hmm. How keen are you about keeping this dress on?"

I raised a brow. "We're out in the open."

Colt glanced around. "They can't see us out here."

Sammy trailed his fingers up my inner thighs, sending a bolt of heat through me. "He's right, they can't," he agreed. I shot him a dirty look and he raised his hands with a faux innocent smile. "I'm just saying, angel."

I grabbed hold of Colt's tie and sat up, pushing them both back into the grass playfully. The three of us laughed and then I ended up in the middle, the two of them propping up to look down at me.

Looking up at the two of them, I thought about how scared I'd been that I wasn't worthy of their love. That I didn't deserve happiness. I'd been scared we were making a mistake, one that could hurt us all.

But knowing how it all would end, and the way our future was beginning—I was so thankful we'd stolen the chance.

I smiled. "The dress can come off."

also by clio evans

Contemporary/Small Town Romance:

CITRUS COVE SERIES

Broken Beginnings (Citrus Cove 1)

Stolen Chances (Citrus Cove 2)

Hidden Roots (Citrus Cove 3)

STANDALONES

The Perfect Gift (Christmas Cuckold Novella)

Monster Romance:

CREATURE CAFE SERIES

Little Slice of Hell

Little Sip of Sin

Little Lick of Lust

Little Shock of Hate

Little Piece of Sass

Little Song of Pain

Little Taste of Need

Little Risk of Fall

Little Wings of Fate

Little Souls of Fire

Little Kiss of Snow: A Creature Cafe Christmas Anthology

Little Drop of Blood

Little Heart of Stone

Little Spark of Flame

about clio evans

Hello Creatures!

Clio Evans is the author of the Citrus Cove Series, Creature Cafe Series, Warts & Claws Series, and more. A lover of myths, legends, BDSM, and queer joy in media–Clio enjoys writing the perfect kinky happy endings for her characters.

They're from Austin, Texas, and living their best life eating chocolate and drinking coffee.

Join them on Instagram, Facebook, TikTok, or their newsletter for new releases, updates, and more!

www.clioevansauthor.com

www.ingramcontent.com/pod-product-compliance
Lightning Source LLC
Chambersburg PA
CBHW030338120726
47901CB00007B/1831